Y-City Station

Eric C. Stricker

PUBLISH
AMERICA

PublishAmerica
Baltimore

First printing

This story focuses on what was formerly a realistic location in Arkansas, and it includes references to certain factual businesses and products, historical radio and sports personalities, and a number of other actual places. Nevertheless, this novel is purely a work of fiction. The characters, names, organizations, activities, events, and incidents expressed in this work are creations of the author's imagination, and they are presented solely for fictitious purposes. Any other resemblance to actual organizations, events, incidents, names, characters, or persons living or dead, is unintended and entirely coincidental.

ISBN: 1-4137-7452-0
PUBLISHED BY PUBLISHAMERICA, LLLP
www.publishamerica.com
Baltimore

Printed in the United States of America

Book One

One

About halfway between Gentry and Decatur up State Highway 59, a dusty little fork splits off quietly from the main road and runs west. Hardly anyone in the whole world knows it's there, and, unless someone were confused or had any particular business that would cause him to turn left at that fork, he would invariably keep on going straight and just pass it right by. If his car were to run out of gasoline right then and there, or if all of a sudden he was overcome by the powerful need to quench his thirst with an icy cold Royal Crown cola or a Grapette soda pop, then he'd probably be inclined to stop at our old Billups gas station located in that little triangle of land that separates the main state highway from that unpaved county road that bears off slightly to the west. Back then, the county road had no name or designation, and for as long as I can remember, no one ever referred to the intersection as a *fork*; we all simply called it the "Y."

Once removed from the junction, the "Y" stubbornly follows its own course after turning at an angle almost due west over the two railroad tracks that run mostly parallel to Highway 59. Over the years, the slight ascent that leads up to those tracks followed by the abrupt curve that bends sharply around to the left have deceived a significant number of unfamiliar drivers, both local and out-of-state. In the worst cases, the next-of-kin usually blamed our "Y" for laying their unsuspecting deceased into premature graves, for contributing to the unfortunate loneliness and sadness of a few mothers and girlfriends now left behind, and for unexpectedly increasing the wealth of the Perkin's Funeral Home in Gentry or the Waxmann's Funeral Parlor and Chapel in Siloam Springs. There are warning signs at those tracks, but no lights or safety gates. Our house, and several others, were about a mile out toward the northwest on that little side road, and all the folks who lived up there–probably no more than eight or ten families–were basically just like us, dirt poor and trying to get along the best way we could.

We all knew the dangers of turning at that fork and making that crossing; after all, it was our road, and we drove it or walked along it every day. However, I confess that, in all the days that I lived there, I never traveled out to the extreme west end of that road. I had no idea where it led or ended, although my daddy said that if someone were to follow it out far enough, it would wind through a whole lot of farmland and forests and eventually lead over to Cherokee City and then further out yonder to Oklahoma. I had never been to Oklahoma.

Every now and then, a passing motorist might become distracted and somehow lose control right there at our junction, resulting in the unexpected change of his location and the redirection of our attention and energy toward that which now was a serious accident. Regardless of the circumstances, the outcome was always the same, and whenever it happened, it always left us wondering why. From the corner of his eye, the northbound driver might catch no more than a transitory glimpse of the split in the road and become instantly curious about it.

Why, I wonder what's up that way? he might think.

Without giving it any thought whatsoever, the driver would swerve rashly to the left and across the pavement directly into the path of another oncoming vehicle. Why? What caused such behavior? In those days, the road was less congested, and some of the more fortunate drivers who attempted this thoughtless maneuver got away with it, but through the years, the special floral arrangements and homemade crosses that cropped up along the roadside south of our station served as grim warnings to all who passed by. In particular, I remember witnessing one driver, who raced narrowly across the path of an approaching southbound, tractor-trailer and then barely clearing the little rise just at the railroad tracks. In that very moment, he must have felt like the luckiest survivor in the world. Without knowing it, however, he had already committed himself to make the crossover by extending the front of his car directly over the tracks, but at first glance, he looked down the track to the left–in the wrong direction–and, upon seeing nothing, he gunned his engine forward without a second look, only to push his car and his short-lived luck across the second track–directly into the path of an unstoppable Kansas City Southern freight train. Tragically, the locomotive struck the automobile at breakneck speed, shoving it through a blistering inferno at least five hundred yards down the rails where it finally disintegrated. I have never forgotten the sight of that burning car; it was eternally engraved on my mind. Over the years, surely thousands of people have passed through our "Y" every day, but I don't believe anyone ever really knew how many human lives were changed so radically–even forever–by the little decisions they made right there in our insignificant little intersection. And no one will ever know why.

We lived there for as long as I could remember. After being wounded in the war, my daddy came home and rested up for a while. A little later, he and my mama got married and moved in with my grandparents. They owned a big, old house on several acres of land with lots of good shade trees, some fruit trees, and plenty of space for a large vegetable garden. Just behind their house, they had a slowly deteriorating barn, and three broken-down chicken houses, one of which we still used. Behind our chicken houses, a heavy forest crept into our property from way out yonder. In those days, I was just learning about life, and I remember the exquisite contentment I experienced after coming back in from playing under the cover of those trees until sundown. Everyone in our family would be drinking cold, homemade lemonade and resting there on the back porch after a long, hot day. Exhausted, I would come in, and Mama would hand me a glass of lemonade; I would gulp it down at once.

"My, goodness, child! Why, you must've been awful thirsty," she would say.

"Yes, ma'am," I would reply. "Can I have another one?"

"Yes, but you drink it slower this time."

Mama would get me another glass, and I would gulp it down again. Then I would go back out and lay down flat on my back in the thick grass and stare up at all the stars emerging in the blackening sky. The lightning bugs would appear, and I would try to count them, but Mama would send out my little sister, Tawna Rae, and she would run down and jump onto my chest and then roll off into the grass.

"Tawna Rae!" I would say. "You made me lose count of them fireflies!"

I knew that Tawna Rae idolized me. Whenever she giggled, something in my heart stirred, and for some reason, I felt like I was her special protector. She was a delicate little girl, and she was always soft and gentle with me. Her little face was pleasant and so transparent that some of the veins just beneath her skin were visible. Tawna Rae's hair was short-cropped, shiny, brown, and naturally curly, and in our whole family she was the only one who had brown eyes. Her arms and legs seemed awkward and gangly, and she had a fragile neck. Her hands were slender, her fingers thin and feminine, and her wrists seemed so tiny. Mama usually dressed Tawna Rae in soft, cotton dresses or in denim overalls, and even though she was dainty, she was always getting her clothes muddy or dirty, and it seemed that Mama always fussed over her for it. Once again, Tawna Rae would giggle, and we would roll around in the grass together until we both got all itchy, and then the mosquitoes would start biting, after which we would flee again to the cover of our screened-in back porch.

If the St. Louis Cardinals happened to be playing a game that night and if our weather was good, then our radio would surely be tuned in to KMOX, and Granddaddy, Daddy, and I would be listening intently. When Harry Carey announced that Stan Musial was coming up to the plate, I would secretly pray:

"Oh, Lord, please…please…please, let him…no, help him…aw, shucks, Lord–why, Lord, you're God! Just *make* him hit a home run!"

For me, there simply was no other baseball team in the whole world like the St. Louis Cardinals, and, of course, Musial was my all-time favorite player because he and I were both left-handed, and we both played first base–not to mention the fact that he was a real gentleman. Of course, Wally Moon was also one of our favorite Cardinal players; that season, he was a rookie, and we especially liked him because he was from Arkansas.

Whatever the outcome, after the game was over, we would all sit there on that back porch until everything around us became silent except the locusts, the crickets, and the frogs down at the pond. Somehow, when things got quiet, we could smell the hay and count a million stars, and way off in the distance, we could hear the muted horn and the outlying strains of another freight train coming ever closer down the line. Of course, with a Cardinal victory, the hay smelled a little sweeter, the stars shone much brighter, and the horn of the train sounded a whole lot more spirited.

"Well, what a way to end a great day," someone would say.

"You betcha."

"Well, indeed. We can be thankful for God's true blessings," Mama would say.

And after a few more moments of silence and personal wonder, each one of us would slowly and individually make our way to bed, except for Mama. She was always the last person to go to bed. She would make sure that the day came to its proper ending. She would stay up and wash the glasses, dry them, and put them away so they were ready again for the next day. In those days, people stayed together and helped each other out, and my grandparents were delighted that we were there. We were a close family.

Two

Shortly after the war was over, Daddy decided to continue serving our country each month as a member of the Arkansas National Guard, but his job didn't pay enough to support Mama and him. One day, as it happened, he stopped to buy some gasoline down at the gas station by the "Y," where he noticed a sign in the big window. The sign simply stated, "Help Wanted."

"Sir," Daddy said to the manager. "I'm looking for work."

Daddy told the man that he was a hard-working, reliable, decorated veteran just home from the war and that he needed a job. Subsequently, the owner hired him, and he worked at the station for about six months or so before I was born. Daddy worked there routinely for several more years, and then the station owner decided to put the old place up for sale. The owner complained that fewer and fewer customers were stopping for gas and oil, and even the number of regulars was diminishing. The man said that running the station had become too much work for him to keep up with, and he really couldn't make it work anymore so he put the business up for sale. For a long time, there were no takers, and then he offered it to my daddy "for a good price." Of course, my daddy believed that with lots of hard work, he could make money in the oil business. He saw this as his opportunity to become his own boss, so he borrowed some money, bought the station, and tried his hand at running a family business until eventually there were still more mouths to feed than our lonely gas station could support.

It was not easy. Nothing ever was. The station itself was already old and in serious need of repair; it needed to be cleaned up and painted, and the roof needed some new tiles. The Billups sign was old, and its paint was peeling off. The driveway was cracked all over and stained with oil and grease; the pumps were slow, too. The station had one indoor garage bay for oil changes, wash jobs, and small car repairs, but the garage door sometimes got stuck halfway up the track, and it had a couple of broken glass panes that needed replacing. Out back, there were six or seven broken down cars, unsightly piles of old tires, and discarded batteries, worn-out car parts, oil drums, little heaps of trash, and all kinds of other rubbish that needed to be hauled away. Initially, Daddy repaired the garage door and replaced the broken glass. He put new bulbs in the glass globes on top of the pumps, repainted the sign, and rewired its lights so the station could be seen from a distance at night. During the weeks that followed, Daddy tried to load as much of the backyard trash as he could into the bed of his old pick-up truck and to haul it away to a dumping ground, but for some reason, it seemed that the more he hauled off, the more junk we accumulated. Daddy never actually found enough time to get to it all. He would wake up early and open the place by five o'clock in the morning. If a customer stopped, the bell would ring, and Daddy would run out to the car on the driveway.

"I'd like four dollars worth of regular, please," the man behind the wheel might say.

"Yes, sir," Daddy would reply. "And a good morning to you, too."

Daddy was proud of his Billups shirt and hat; they made him look handsome. First, he would fill up the tank with gasoline; sometimes it took him almost ten minutes. Then he would wash and dry all the car windows, check the engine oil, the water in the radiator, and the battery, and finally, he would check the air in the tires, too.

"Sir, that'll be four dollars, sir," Daddy would remind the customer.

The customer would pay, and then he would drive off. Generally, however, the gas business was slow, and sometimes it seemed like there were many long and quiet waiting spells between our customers.

"I'll tell you what your problem is," my old Granddaddy said one time.

"I've analyzed this situation, Clayton, and I can tell you…part of your problem is your location. You're not far enough away from either Siloam Springs or Sulphur Springs, and you're too close to Decatur and Gentry. They don't need gas when they're driving by here, so they don't stop. Nobody wants to stop here; this is the middle of nowhere. They all fill up their tanks before they leave Gentry or Gravette or Joplin, and when they get to Siloam Springs or Springdale or Ft. Smith, they fill up again before they leave. Yessir…that's just exactly what they do."

"Well, what should I do, Paw?" Daddy would ask. "What can I do? I cain't *make* 'em stop here."

"Well, you need to *create* a need for them to stop here," said Granddaddy. "You need to make 'em think they need to stop here an' make 'em feel like they want to stop here. Put in an icebox with some ice-cold pop in it. Offer them some coffee, or sell 'em some ham sandwiches and so forth. Put up another sign."

"Aw, shucks, Paw. I don't know 'bout that…" Daddy said. "I think that's a good ideal, Paw, but I don't know as we can afford it."

Daddy thought about it for a while, and then he and Mama discussed it for a while, too. In fact, they talked about it for a long time. Then, after a month or so, Daddy asked Grandma to watch my brother and sister at home, and he asked Granddaddy to sit in the station and watch me.

"Paw, if we get a customer, you just let Jefferson Davis pump his gas," Daddy said. "He knows what to do."

Daddy and Mama took his pick-up truck and drove off to the south down Highway 59. We had no idea what they were up to, but we learned later that they drove down to Siloam Springs to visit Sloan's Lumber Yard. As I recall, it was the first time they ever went anywhere without us. Later that evening, after a slow day, Granddaddy and I couldn't believe our eyes upon their return. It wasn't difficult to recognize our pick-up truck, but from a distance and in the twilight, we had no way of knowing who the two individuals were who climbed out of it. Their faces were all smeared black and their clothes were covered in yellow paint; they were laughing loudly and dancing all around–grabbing and pushing at each other–and acting almost as if they were drunk. The shorter one had a red bandana tied around his head.

"Boy, what is all that ruckus goin' on out there?" Granddaddy asked me.

He got up from his chair and went behind the counter where Daddy kept a shotgun.

"I don't know, Granddaddy. It sure looks like our pick-em-up truck, but those folks don't act like Daddy or Mama," I said.

Cautiously, we both stepped outside, and as they drew closer—still laughing and carrying on—we recognized them as Daddy and Mama.

"What in tarnation are y'all doin' out here?" Granddaddy asked. He was holding the shotgun, and he pointed it away toward the ground. "And what are y'all doin' in that get-up? Y'all look like ya both got tacked on to the back end of a school bus gettin' painted!"

"Daddy? Mama...is it you? I ain't ever seen y'all like this before!" I said.

"Well, we're sorry, Paw. We're sorry, boy. We never meant to frighten ya," Daddy said.

"Yeah, we was out jist havin' a little fun together, that's all," Mama said.

There were two big sheets of plywood and a load of other supplies and small equipment items in the back of our pick-up truck. The plywood sheets had been painted black, and in big, hand-styled, yellow letters, Daddy and Mama had painted two signs that said "*Y-City Station*" at the very top. On one of the signs, they ran out of room for the letter "n," which was added on the next line down directly below the "o." They also painted "*flats fixed*" and "*hot coffee*" and "*fresh ham sandwiches inside*" on the next few lines. It turns out that, while they were painting, they got a little sloppy with the colors, and then they got carried away with the whole mess and started throwing paint at each other—"all in good fun"—they said.

These signs simply delighted my granddaddy, for he had a great interest in all this—the signs being his idea in the first place. "Yessir..." he said. "That's the way it ought to be. You'll be gettin' customers left and right now—more'n you can handle. And, what's this here? *Y-City*? *Y-City Station*? What's that mean? Where'd you come up with that...why, that's a catchy ideal, all right! I can tell you that in no time we'll be in the big time with that!"

Daddy said that he and Mama had discussed giving our station a name, and since it was a station that was located right in the middle of the "Y," it ought to be called "the station at the Y." But Mama said that would be too hard for people to remember, let alone to say. Then she went on to explain that no one would ever say that we lived near "the city at the Y."

15

"There ain't any city at the Y," Daddy said.

"Well, of course, I know that," Mama said. "But them houses up there are just like a little city to me. Why, you could say that they're *our* little city, as a matter of fact," Mama said. "It's our little city at the Y."

"But they ain't at the Y!" Daddy insisted. "And besides, it ain't a city!"

"I know they ain't at the Y. They don't need to be *at* the Y to be a part of it. The Y is down the road from the city—and who knows? Maybe one day, our little city will grow way down past the Y. So, the way I reckon it, if the Y is down the road from our little city, which is actually a ways up the road from the Y, we'll just call it *'Y-City,'* and then we'll call the station *'Y-City Station!'* Ever'one will agree to that."

"Well, I reckon…yeah…well, it sounds mighty good to me," said Daddy, who was confused by her logic but knew that, at this point, agreeing was better than fussing about it any longer.

"I like it," Granddaddy said. "Y-City Station. It's super."

While Daddy and Mama were busy trying to do all that explaining to Granddaddy, who thought the whole idea was absolutely perfect and didn't need any explaining, a customer stopped outside and came directly into the station. Because of all the commotion, no one heard the bell ring, but, at that hour, no one was even expecting the possibility that any more customers might come in. Everyone was thinking about the new name and the new sign, which was resting alongside the pick-up truck.

"Good evening, sir," said Daddy. "What can I do fer you? Can I fill her up?"

"Well, actually, no. I just saw that sign out there, and I thought I'd stop in for a moment. I don't actually need any gas, but I would like to have a Co-Cola and one of them ham sandwiches, please."

That evening, we all worked hard to place the signs where they belonged. We made some wooden props for the backs of the signs, and we set them up on the shoulder of Highway 59—one about a hundred yards south of the station—and the other about the same distance to the north of it. From that day on, our place became known all around those parts as *"Y-City Station."*

Three

Eventually, Daddy concluded that putting up signs to notify passers-by that we fixed flats and sold coffee and ham sandwiches didn't actually accomplish much over the long term. After we put up the signs, our business seemed to pick up somewhat, but then after a few months, sales seemed to flatten out again. Daddy did all he could to clean up our station and make it more attractive. He tried to enhance the business by offering special prices to friends and neighbors, giving discounts to local farmers, and opening credit accounts for the more regular customers. He asked all our customers to tell their friends about our station, and sometimes they did. One day, someone in a beautiful, black Lincoln–I think it was a 1953 model–stopped at our station. The car had white sidewall tires and was as shiny as a brand new silver dollar.

"Fill it up with Hi-Test, please," the driver said.

"Yes, sir," Daddy said.

While Daddy was pumping the gas, the driver got out of the car and walked back to talk.

"You know Harlan Cooley?" the driver asked Daddy.

"Yessir. He's a member of our church and buys gas from me now and then. Mr. Cooley owns the IGA there in Gentry."

"Me and him go way back…been friends a long time. He told me this'd be a good place to fill up."

"Yessir," Daddy replied. "I appreciate you stoppin'. Would ya have a cup o' coffee?"

"Why, sure. That'd be mighty fine," the Lincoln driver replied.

While Daddy checked the Lincoln's oil, the water, and the air, he summoned me to bring out a cup of coffee for the gentleman. I brought out the coffee, and the man said, "Well, thank you, son. You're a fine boy!"

"Thank you, sir," I said. The man reached into his pocket and pulled out a quarter, which he gave to me.

"Oh, I couldn't take it, sir," I said. "I'm pleased to serve you, sir."

"That's all right, boy. I want you to have it for being so polite. Here. You go ahead and take it."

I looked at Daddy, and he nodded.

"Thank you, sir. I 'preciate it."

I went back inside the station, and he and Daddy talked for a few minutes while he drank his coffee. After paying for his gas, he got back into the Lincoln and drove off.

"He was an awful nice man, Daddy," I said.

"Yeah, I guess he was. An old friend of Mr. Cooley…said his name was Vance Yoakum…a lawyer, from Little Rock. I'll have to thank Mr. Cooley fer sending him our way."

We usually sold more gas on the weekends than on weekdays, and business always seemed to be better in the warmer months, too. Offering coffee and ham sandwiches for sale helped our business initially, and after a time, Daddy found an old ice box for pop and cold drinks, a small freezer for popsicles and ice cream, and an outside pay telephone. All of these were great conveniences, but they didn't really bring in the customers.

Whenever school was out, I would get to help Daddy at the station. Tawna Rae, who was the baby and thus the darling of our family, and my brother, James, usually had to stay home with Mama. James was his name, but we always called him J-Earl for short. As long as they didn't fight each other, they could play together out in our backyard, but whenever one of them began to squawk and provoke the other, Mama was right there to pull them both by their ears back into her kitchen. She would put one of them on a chair facing one corner of the room and the other one on a chair in the corner directly opposite. I can relate, from my own personal experience, that there is almost no greater punishment than sitting and staring uselessly into the corner where two kitchen walls come together. Worst of all, she'd make me sit there–for an hour or more–without saying a word. Mama was in no hurry. And the instant she let me off that chair–I don't dare to think even for a moment that I'm going back out in the yard to play–absolutely not! In Mama's mind, my part in all that squabbling resulted in the total forfeiture of my freedom for the whole rest of the day, and from that moment on, I became Mama's property. Now it was my privilege to help Mama take care of the house and then help her dust the furniture. After that, I got to clean the floors and wash the windows, and then it was time to fold the clothes and work in her garden. And when all that was done, I got to wash the dishes, scrub the bathtub, and then help Mama prepare supper by setting the table and slicing the bread and carrying out the slop for the hogs in the pen out behind the barn. Mama's discipline was designed to make life as fully miserable as possible, and she had a thousand ways of keeping me away from the fun of fishing, swimming, or playing ball, so every day I looked forward to the opportunity to help Daddy down at our gas station.

After our vegetable garden came into production, Mama put up a table under the shade tree just to the north of our station, and she would try to help the business by selling lettuce, tomatoes, squash, bell peppers, okra, and whatever else she could. During the summer months, people seemed to stop a little more frequently for the vegetables or the cold pop than for the gasoline, although it seemed to me that all the different items helped to sell each other. I guessed that most of the local people who didn't have gardens of their own figured that they could get our vegetables and gas and save by not having to make extra stops down in Gentry or Siloam Springs.

We knew about seven or eight of the families who lived on our road past the Y. Most of the neighboring places near us were only a few acres apart, but as one drove farther west on our road, the spaces between the places grew larger and the houses got much further apart. Of course, there were families and farms clear out to Cherokee City, and even more who lived past Flint Creek, but the only people we knew out that way were those who came to our church on Sundays. We were members of the West Bethel Baptist

Church. It was called the West Bethel Baptist Church because the missionaries who started it came out from the Bethel Baptist Church that was down in Gentry. As yet, our church didn't have any land or a building of its own, so we met temporarily in the Grange House, which was about a mile or so west of our house on our road.

Except for Sunday mornings, we seldom ever went out toward the Grange House. Basically, we were all humble folk–just plain, rural people. We were all independent of one another in the various ways that we thought and worked, and yet, we were all thankful, even proud, to take part in the opportunities that were ours. We were all deeply respectful toward each other about that spirit of independence, but we were also mindful of our community responsibilities and duties as neighbors. Everyone who lived out there made some attempt at farming or ranching. Practically every household had some sort of a tractor and a barn, a large garden, a great stand of trees, a dog or two, and usually some chickens and a few goats. Many of our neighbors raised more than a few cows, and a few of them kept hogs. Most people had a small pond where they could swim when the days got hot or where their boys could fish for bluegill, largemouth bass, and an occasional catfish or two.

On this side of the Grange House, nobody could claim to be real farmers, except maybe the Blantons or the Riggins. The Blantons raised a fine herd of Dutch Belted cattle and actually did plant various crops on their place. The Riggins, who professed to be farmers, were actually more like ranchers. They rented one of the larger spreads out our way and never really planted anything, but they did attempt to work three chicken houses. They might have produced a good crop of broilers and fryers every eight to ten weeks or so, but they were not hard workers, and their operation wasn't particularly sanitary. Indeed, they had a reputation among our neighbors for being downright lazy. When others were cashing in their chickens, the Riggins were all sleeping in. On two or three occasions when the time came to market the chickens and clean out their houses, Mr. Dudley Riggins went off missing for a few days–creating a wild searching frenzy among all the folks who knew him. Mrs. Riggins, and the others who knew him really well, initially suspected–and with good reason–that her husband had probably disappeared over into eastern Oklahoma under pretense that he was merely visiting Willie Ninefeathers, his old army buddy who had been wounded in the war.

However, the most trustworthy sources, namely, the law, maintained that the real reason why Mr. Riggins went off missing had almost nothing to do with the visit itself and practically everything to do with the location of the visit. In Oklahoma, Mr. Riggins could obtain something a whole lot stronger to drink than was available here in Benton County, which was dry. When everyone was just about ready to give him up for dead, Mr. Riggins would suddenly appear again–red-faced, disheveled, and dirty–smelling of alcohol and other disgusting odors.

Usually, Deputy Sheriff Jimmy Lee Watkins represented the law that brought Mr. Riggins home in an official police vehicle.

"We found him," Deputy Watkins said. "Here he is…"

"Why, Dudley, where have you been?" Mrs. Riggins asked in a high-pitched voice. "Don't you know that we had chickens to market?"

"He saved my life," Mr. Riggins would later explain. "During the war, we was in combat together in France, and old Willie Ninefeathers–he's a full-blooded Kickapoo Indian, you know–he saved my life. He took the one that was meant for me, and ever' now and then, I need to head over there to pay my respects. Yessir, Willie saved my life. Besides, them chickens'll survive another week or so."

Whenever Mr. Riggins could control his little secret and prevent any corporate financial loss, it often seemed that their chicken business suffered on account of some other reason such as a spreading disease or an infection that would attack and kill off most of their birds. Of course, this always brought out the county inspector, who would decree their place "quarantined" and shut them down for at least eight to ten weeks. The inspector would cite them and admonish Mr. Riggins to get the place cleaned up or he would shut them down for good. To be sure, under the quarantine, they couldn't raise any chickens, so they'd have to let the place "rest a spell," and while the chicken houses were "restin'," the Riggins were "restin'," too. And if it wasn't some problem like that, then it had to be "the foxes are gettin' into our houses at night," or "maybe it was wolves," or perhaps it was "the thieves what came in and stole all our birds while we was in church." And if none of this was logical or correct, it was "clearly the work of the devil." With the Riggins, a loss was always the fault of someone or something else.

Most of the folks in our community believed that the whole Riggins family was a strange group. Mr. Riggins, who walked with a limp, had stained yellowish-brown teeth that had been filed-down. He always talked out of one side of his mouth which caused him to sound like he was trying to speak while he was chewing a whole mouthful of Wheaties. No one ever understood him right off; he would always have to say something two or three times to make himself understood. On top of that, he was a teller of tall tales, so his thoughts and ideas didn't carry a lot of value in our community, nor did his reputation. Personally, it seemed to me that he constantly smelled of something either sour or rancid, and he always wore the same pair of greasy overalls. On the right side of his belt, Mr. Riggins always wore a huge key ring that had over a hundred keys on it and must have weighed ten pounds. Since none of us around those parts ever locked our houses, we all wondered why in the world he needed all those keys.

"He claims to be a trained locksmith," one gentleman said.

"Why, I'd bet that he's got the key to every door in Benton County," another fellow said.

"Well, as a matter of fact," said another, "he does. And I've heard that he sneaks up around folks' houses after they have left their homes to go to town, and he locks up their front doors behind 'em, just so he can come around later and offer to try one of them keys on the door and let 'em back in again."

"Yeah, and sometimes he charges 'em, too," the first man responded.

"Well, I certainly haven't heard of anyone needin' his services," a fourth man said. "Did you ever need him to open your door, Henry?"

"I cain't say that I did…and if I did, I didn't recollect that I did," Henry replied.

"Well, I'm a tellin' y'all…I've heard about it, and y'all'll be hearin' about it directly, as well–I'll garonntee y'all that, and I'll put it in writin,' too" said another, who was trying to mimic Mr. Riggins' odd speech.

"Aw, what do you know about it, anyway?" the third man asked.

"Nuthin,'" said the last, and they all had a great laugh together about old Mr. Riggins.

Locally, Mr. Riggins' greatest claim to fame actually related to his wife.

All over town, he let it be known that, back in the summer of 1948, he and Mrs. Riggins had gone up to visit relatives in Springfield, and they all went out to attend the Ozark Empire Fair. At the fair, Mr. Riggins and all his cousins convinced Mrs. Riggins to stand up in the annual beauty contest.

"Well, I'm a tellin' y'all, she was the most beautiful girl in that whole fairgrounds; she stood up right there and turned around and walked straight away with title of Queen of the Ozarks," Mr. Riggins would often report to everyone. "And I'm here to tell ya that she won that contest hands-down…yessir, she won that contest fair and square. There wasn't another girl at that fair as pretty as my missus, and she's still as beautiful today as she was then."

Regardless, none of us ever found anything in that woman that we would call attractive, nor did we ever see any kind of official ribbon, trophy, or yearbook–neither a plaque nor a certificate–to verify that Olah Mae Riggins was, in fact, the bona fide Queen of the Ozarks. We all knew that, when someone wins something at the fair, the winner gets some type of official recognition for winning in that category. Without the Riggins ever producing any actual proof for such a claim, most folks in our area simply went on about their business and really didn't care much if she had ever won anything or not. Of course, people might think differently if Mrs. Riggins would have only produced some visible evidence that could satisfy every curiosity and eliminate all the doubt, but she refused. Besides, local logic had it that, if she really was that beautiful (which she wasn't), and if she truly did win that prize (which she didn't), then why didn't they put up a sign in her honor right under that other sign on Highway 59 that says, "Entering Benton County"? We all knew that, if Mr. Riggins' claim was true, they surely would have put up a secondary sign that said, "Home of Mrs. Olah Mae Riggins–1948 Queen of the Ozarks." No county in the Ozarks–leastwise none in Northwest Arkansas–would ever allow such an honor to remain private or hidden away from the public community. The people of Benton County generally believed that, if everyone had the responsibility to brag about something, then everyone was entitled to his share in it–if only it were true.

The Riggins also had two children, a boy and a girl. Both of them were just a little older than most of us, and for some reason, we also thought they were a little strange as well. The boy's given name was Scott, but his parents–

and everyone else—had always referred to him as Sky. My first memories of Sky Riggins placed him somewhere about fifteen years old. Big and bulky for his age, Sky was just about as lazy as his daddy, and he wasn't very smart. All his life, he grew up hearing the strange way that Mr. Riggins talked, and I reckon he probably thought it was the normal way that everyone talked, so that became his excuse for having a speech impediment. Sky Riggins skipped out of school most of his life and spent the greater part of his waking hours either fishing or sleeping in a hammock that he had rigged up on the Riggins' back porch. The lesser part of his working hours usually found him tinkering around with the old family tractor. Sky would putter around with it for a while, and when he got tired, he'd go lie down in the hammock for a little nap, after which he would return with a much clearer head to continue his work on the tractor. Now and then, he'd get the old thing running, and then he'd drive it wildly around their fields until it went dead again. When that happened, he became disgusted with it; kicking the tractor, he would go into a rage, shout curses at it, and jump up and down for a minute or two. If there were any lying around, Sky would pick up rocks and hurl them at the machine until he became exhausted and threw himself down in the dirt. Finally, he would get up and leave the tractor right where it died and walk back to the porch for another nap.

Sky's sister, Flora, was eighteen months younger than he was. Flora was named by her mother, who had learned somewhere in her distant past that the word *Flora* meant flower.

"Wuuu-weee!" Mrs. Riggins exclaimed upon that discovery. "I like how that sounds! And blame me if someday I don't swear right now on my confederate Daddy's grave to name my first little girl Flora! Flora…my sweet little flower! It just rolls right off the tongue, slides off the lips, and sounds so lovely!"

Mrs. Riggins was just a little disappointed, not to mention unprepared, when her firstborn child turned out to be a boy.

"Well, goodness!" she exclaimed. "Why this ain't gonna work. I hadn't reckoned on having a boy!"

"Why, what're we gonna call him? We gonna call him Flora?" Mr. Riggins asked.

"We cain't call a boy *Flora*!" she shouted. "What are we gonna call him?"

In his strange way of speaking, Mr. Riggins said, "Well, I've got jist the name fer him." Mr. Riggins said something like, "Nnskahht," and he repeated it several times.

"What? What did you say? You sound like you're a sneezin'! What is that you're a sayin'?"

"Nnskahht!" he said. "Nnskahht!"

"Is that a name? What kind of name is that? What is it? Who ever heard of it?" she badgered. After he said it a few more times, Mrs. Riggins became frustrated with him and said, "Why don't you just try to write it down for me so as maybe I could read it?"

Mr. Riggins ran out and found a pencil and a sheet of paper on which he wrote the word "Scott," and then he came back in and showed it to her.

"Oh! Now I understand," Mrs. Riggins replied. "Scott! Why, yes, of course, that's a good name…yes, great…uh,…great, Scott! Why, I never thought of that! Yeah," she was thinking out loud. "Scott 'n' Flora…yes, that goes real well. And then we can call him little Scottie Riggins! Why, that'll go real well with Flora!"

The second time around, Mrs. Riggins made good on her historic promise. As far as we could tell, Flora was probably the most regular person in the Riggins family. In fact, she was probably just a bit advanced–what some people might refer to as charmingly mature for her age. Her face was not particularly attractive, and like her brother, she was not intelligent by any means. Already at thirteen years of age, Flora was almost as well endowed physically as any woman in the entire county, but she was most unladylike in both her carriage and her appearance. Moreover, she was totally ignorant of her loose behavior, and she was quite unaware of the intensity of her seductive powers over most of the young men who came into her presence. Worse still, she was entirely naïve regarding any of the real reasons why some of the older boys and young men from various parts of Northwest Arkansas began to frequent the Riggins' farm. Of course, their strategy was to appear to engage either her father or her brother in some sort of practical business, but neither the father nor the son were intelligent enough to guess what was really going on.

One older boy by the name of Johnny B. Harper, whom everyone feared just a little on account of his size, had been out visiting Sky at the Riggins place one afternoon. Johnny B. was from a place called Black Oak over somewhere south of Fayetteville. Nobody knew what the "B" in his name meant, and no one ever asked. He was a certifiable troublemaker, and he was fond of receiving much attention and being known as *Big* Johnny B. He and Sky had gone outside to work on the old family tractor. While they were out back trifling with the engine, Flora came outside and sat down, presumably to sun herself a little in the backyard. Wearing the shortest and tightest denim shorts she could find and a loose-fitting blouse, she was anywhere near from being dressed properly. Her hair was long, very curly, and shiny blond; it caught the sunlight just right and reflected it brightly. Flora's feet were shoeless, her white legs were bare, and with her knees apart, she sat there stirring up the mud continually with her toes. Within minutes, she had mud crawling up past her ankles, and it was obvious by her mud-slapping sounds that she was trying to catch Big Johnny B's attentions. A moment later, Big Johnny B looked up and saw her for the first time ever.

"What is…uh, who is that?" he asked. "Where did she come from?"

"Oh," said Sky. "That's my sister. Her name is…Flora."

"Well, Sky! Why didn't you tell me you had a sister…especially one like that?" Big Johnny B asked, and then to Flora, he said, "Hey there, you little slice of fishbait! How are you?"

"What did you call me? My name is Flora!" she said. "How did you come up with that? What do you mean by that?"

"What?"

"Fishbait?"

"Aw, I dunno." Big Johnny B said. "I guess I was just a teasin' you, that's all."

"Well, you ought not to be teasin' people ya don't rightly know," Flora said.

Then Sky shouted over to his younger sister, "Well, ya ain't worth nuthin' but fish bait, anyway!"

"You keep outta this, Sky Riggins!" said Flora. "It ain't none of your bidness!"

From that day on, Big Johnny B fell under Flora's spell, and "Fishbait" became Flora Riggins' new nickname, but neither Sky Riggins nor his father ever understood why.

Four

The next winter was a hard one, and it seemed to have a heavy impact on our business at the gas station. Daddy tried to remain as optimistic about it as he could, and we all tried to encourage him, but we all sensed that this wasn't exactly what people meant when they said that someone they knew had struck it rich in the oil business. That spring, in an effort to help Daddy really succeed, we all decided to pitch in and make his business our family's business and see it work. With the weather getting warmer and the days longer, we were all looking forward to the end of the school year and to the beginning of summer vacation. Mr. McLemore had been pouring on the homework, and I was getting tired of it; I was ready for school to end, and I began to count the days. Even though I knew I'd be working at the station, I suspected that there would be plenty of time to go fishing, to go swimming, and to play baseball to my heart's content. For some reason, we were all excited by our commitment to the station, and we truly believed that something great was going to come from our part in it.

School finally ended, and I got to help out in the station everyday. Early during that summer of 1957, Sky Riggins turned sixteen, and a whole other family of Riggins–his cousins–came down for a short visit from Ginger Blue, Missouri. They stopped in at our station to ask for directions, and Daddy pointed up our road where the Riggins' farm was.

"It ain't far up that way," Daddy commented. "Would you like me to fill yer tank up for you?"

"Yes sir, I'd be much obliged if you would," said Uncle Riggins. "I'd appreciate that a lot. As we'll be around fer awhile...my name is Gilmore...Gilmore Riggins. I'm Dudley Dan's older brother."

"Well, pleased to meet y'all," my daddy said. "I'm Clayton Stafford. Welcome to Stafford's Billups...uh...I mean...welcome to Y-City Station."

"It's my pleasure, Stafford. And that's my wife, Beulah, and my three boys in the back seat...Tex, Lloyd, and Milton." They all said hello while Daddy pumped gas.

This clan of Riggins sure seemed different from that other one. Mr. Gilmore Riggins acted like he was trying to impress my daddy with his flashy brown suit and tie, his western hat, and his alligator cowboy boots. For a hat, Mrs. Beulah Riggins looked like she was wearing part of a peach tree in bloom with a black fishing net that covered over the top of her face which she kept high up in the sky. Somehow, I sensed that trouble was sitting back there beside those big hillbilly boys in the back seat of that old Buick. Milton was about my age, I guessed, but Tex and Lloyd were older and bigger; they acted like they were ready to pick a fight with anyone who came along and who might look at them cockeyed.

"That's a mighty fine Buick you got there," Daddy said.

"Well, thank you, sir. Glad you like it. She drives real good, and we like it."

"Say, Mr. Riggins, y'all gonna be around awhile?"

"Yes sir. Be here 'bout a week to ten days or so, I reckon. It's a visit to our kinfolk. Then we're all a headin' back up home and probably take young Sky up with us. For the last two years, Tex has gone out hay-balin' in Kansas, and this year, we thought we'd send Lloyd with him and invite cousin Sky to go, too. It'd be good for all of them to go together this summer. They go from farm to farm and bale till there ain't no more hay. Puttin' up hay's hard work, but they can earn themselves some money doin' it, and I'm of the opinion that it does boys good to get out there and see the world and learn a little about life–know what I mean?"

"Absolutely," Daddy said. "Yes sir, I agree."

Daddy checked the water and the oil under the hood of that Buick and the air in its tires. He complimented Mr. Riggins about his car again, and then he said, "Well sir, that'll be four dollars and a quarter." Mr. Riggins paid my daddy, and out of the corner of his eye, he spotted me sitting over on the bench between the garage and the door, and then he reached into his pocket and flipped me a dime. I caught his dime and put it in my pocket. Before the Riggins left the station to drive up our road, I stood up instinctively and said, "Thank you, sir."

My parents were raising me to become a southern gentleman. The only thing more important in this world than being a southern gentleman, they said, was being a Christian, and my daddy and mama said that they had always intended to kill those two birds with one stone by raising their kids to be both Christians and gentlemen at the same time. In their minds and hearts, which quietly testified to being a little more autonomous than most of our average Southern Baptist brothers and sisters, a true gentleman was synonymous with being a Christian first, and a Southern Baptist second.

"Son," which my daddy frequently called me, "you need to understand that being a Baptist don't make you a Christian. Somehow there are a lot of Baptists who get their names on the church rolls, but they ain't on God's rolls up yonder."

"Yes, sir," I said.

"You want to grow up to be a complete southern gentleman. When the roll is called up yonder," he went on, "you'll be there for sure as long as you are a Christian first and a Baptist second. And when a man brings up his boy to follow after that pattern, he gets three things for the price of one–a Christian, a Baptist, and a southern gentleman. Now, son, that's what it means to be complete, and it's a deal that's hard to beat. A Christian is always a southern gentleman, and a Baptist Christian is almost always a southern gentleman, but a so-called gentleman may not always be either a Christian or a Baptist. Now I believe that there are some Christians sittin' in the Presbyterian Church and maybe a few of 'em are hidin' around in the Methodist Church. But they simply ain't complete. You will always find that a complete southern gentleman is a born-again Christian who was raised up in the Baptist Church."

"Yes, sir," I responded.

29

After I reflected on that awhile, I asked, "Well, Daddy, what about Tawna Rae?"

"Well, in that case," he said, "you can bet that me and your Mama'll bring her up to be a complete lady that'll be both a Christian and a southern Baptist."

"Yes, sir," I said.

It was hot that day, and Mr. Riggins' dime got the better of me. A dime was just enough for me to get an icy cold Nehi orange pop and a Dreamsicle bar out of the little freezer box inside. But, for some strange reason, I didn't feel much like an honorable gentleman about taking his dime, partly because I hadn't worked for it, and the other part because I sensed that there was something suspicious–maybe even evil–about Mr. Gilmore Riggins' intentions.

Five

We lived farther out from the Y on our road than the Riggins, so we could observe them and their cousins as we came down to the station each morning. In the early morning, when Daddy and I passed by their place, everything was dark at their house except for a solitary light bulb left on in the kitchen. The light was bright enough to illuminate some of the back yard. With the help of that light, I could see Gilmore Riggins' Buick parked right up in front of the barn door. Dudley Riggins had a very old but reliable Ford that was parked in the mud beside the barn. He also had his own small junkyard that consisted of old, broken-down cars, car and tractor parts, wash tubs, engines, and rusting machinery. Everything was dead quiet. The Riggins had several dogs–all friendly and of mixed variety– and all lazy. They only barked when they got hungry, or when Sky would beat them in a malicious fit of frustration or lost temper, which he was prone to do every now and then.

The Riggins' house was a two-story wooden clapboard construction with large, white-trimmed windows all around. Some of the windows had two shutters; a few had one, and a couple of windows had none. Not all of the shutters were fixed firmly to the building, so in a wind or rainstorm, it wasn't uncommon for them to flip and flap around, but the Riggins were all oblivious to any noise the shutters made. The clapboard siding on the house was a grayish, faded-blue, and the trim around the exterior windows and doors was also pale and peeling away. There were three wooden steps up to the portico, which faced off to the south. Even in the darkness, we could see where the Queen had decorated it with two, strange-looking plants that were growing out of the bowls of two old toilets sitting about six feet apart. On the other end, there was a large swing that hung down from the ceiling. On the stairway, one of the steps was raw, unpainted wood, an indicator that Mr. Riggins must have recently replaced it. The faded white railing around the edge of the porch had grown uneven over time, and a few of its supporting posts were missing. Seeing that, I recalled from one of our unusual stops out there the peculiar remark that Mr. Riggins made about it:

"Why, lookie there! Someone must have needed them slats for somethin'. I reckon he jist he'ped hisself to 'em!"

Curious as to what that meant, Daddy asked, "Why, who would have done that, and where do you suppose they've gone to?"

"Well," said Mr. Riggins, "beat's me! I never noticed it before today. Maybe young Sky needed 'em to whup them ole dawgs with."

In the front of the Riggins house, there was a large, tangle-branched elm tree on the western side of the front lawn, but it was dead now–nothing more than a colossal skeleton completely devoid of any leaves whatsoever. The old tree cast a hideous shadow on that whole side of the house. To its east, just across the walkway but still west of the driveway, there were two big oak trees–one much older and taller than the other–but both in full green leaf. In the dark, the house looked majestic and stately, but when the sun came up, the light revealed the truth: the Riggins' house was crumbling apart.

The Riggins' house was certainly large enough for two families. However, we learned later that morning that the Queen had required Sky, Tex, Lloyd, and Milton to sleep out in the barn. About ten-thirty that morning, the whole Riggins tribe came through our gas station, and they all stopped for one of those useless but necessary, introductory visits to inform people in the community officially that they were receiving kinfolk.

"Mama said that all the boys should sleep in the barn so they could get ready for hay-balin' season," Flora announced.

"Truth is," said Lloyd, "she didn't want you comin' near and corruptin' any of us boys."

"No, Lloyd. You got it backwards. Aunt Olah Mae don't want me gettin' anywhere near little Missie Sun Flower," Tex said.

"Why is that?" asked Lloyd, but no one was listening to him.

"Well, I don't bite," said Flora. "And besides, Mama don't want y'all to be rasslin' around in her parlor room. Mama's got a lot o' nice things set up in there, and she don't want 'em destroyed. Y'all are just a bunch of big ole hillbilly galoots, and she knows that y'all would wreck the whole room. And if y'all want the real truth, according to Mama…she says…y'all stink." Flora leaned over toward the boys and whispered those last two words.

"That's enough, Flora!" Mrs. Riggins admonished, and then she glared at her daughter.

After a brief season of this kind of chatter, while the adults drank coffee and Daddy served a customer or two, the Riggins got up to leave.

"We're goin' down to Gentry today," Gilmore Riggins exclaimed. "And tomorrow," he said, "we gotta go into Siloam Springs for a while. And I've heard that early on Thursday evenings they hold a big auction up there at Maysville. We want to get in on that."

When he said all this, I decided to excuse myself quickly from their presence so as not to be around in case he wanted to wink at me and throw me another dime. His wink and dime made me feel like he was placing me under some kind of spell or curse by which he could control me and make me do things for him. I didn't want any part of that, and besides, it was gentlemanly to dismiss myself quietly and go out to the back of the station. Probably thirty minutes after they were all gone, my daddy came out back and caught me moving some junk from one spot to another.

"Why there you are boy! What you been doin'?"

"I been tryin' to clean up out here a little bit. I like he'pin' you here. And besides, I'd rather work out here than sittin' around listenin' to all them noisy Riggins."

"Well, my goodness!" Daddy said. "We need to put you on the payroll here!"

"Yes, sir," I said.

"Aw, them Riggins are all right, son," said Daddy. "Long as they buy our gas and coffee and such. They'll be all right, but I admit that they do tend to get on yer nerves after awhile."

"Yes, sir," I replied.

We saw them five or six times that week but not everyday. After they had been there for about a week, they all headed back down to our station. We could see them coming down the road, but this time they had to wait awhile for a black, Kansas City Southern diesel pulling a long, heavy load of freight cars coming up the tracks from the south. After the train passed, the Riggins slipped across the tracks and pulled into our quiet station. The Gilmore Riggins family was leaving, and they wanted a full tank of gas to drive home on, and the Dudley Dan Riggins family wanted to see them off. Sky Riggins was in the back seat with the other three boys, and, except for Milton, they were all bound for Kansas to bale hay.

"We'll be on our own for almost three months," said Tex. Apparently, Tex was looking forward to leaving home and getting away from his parents as a celebration of his newfound freedom.

Sky smiled brightly, and he tried to say something, but because no one paid much attention to him, no one understood what he was trying to say. No one really cared anyway.

But just then, for some absurd reason, Milton started to make fun of Sky and mimic his speech handicap. He did this for a moment or two. After he saw that no one was paying attention to him either, he began to romp up and down on the car seat until Lloyd jabbed him in his stomach.

"That's enough, Milton," Lloyd said. "What's wrong with you? Leave him alone. He cain't he'p it."

"Well, as far as I'm concerned," Flora stated, "I've had more than enough of y'all. Why don't y'all jist stay up there forever? And keep Sky up there, too!"

Tex said, "Why, little Missie Fishbait, ain't you just a tad sharp in your tongue! You'd soon be a missin' us and wantin' to come up there lookin' all around for us before too long. By the way, your nickname suits you, don't it?"

"You shut up, Texaco," she said. "It ain't none of your bidness! Y'all just get on up that road...stinkin' bunch of hillbillies! Instead of goin' up north to bale hay, why don't y'all go down south an' pick cotton? That's where y'all belong!"

Flora, who fancied herself somewhat of a princess by virtue of her relationship to the Queen of the Ozarks, never quite understood that she was as much a child of the hills as they all were.

Surprised at her outburst, Dudley Dan looked over at his daughter and said, "Now Flora, Honey, is that any way we talk to our kinfolk? Less try and do better, Honey. Less let 'em be on their way in peace, now."

"Well, they started it!" Flora said.

Daddy filled up the tank of their Buick, and he checked the water, the oil, and the air. Gilmore Riggins paid the bill, and then they all said their good-byes again. I had already had enough of their hugs, kisses, sobs, and tears, so I had retreated earlier to my self-appointed post out behind our station. I didn't spend all my time out there working, but as good fortune would have it, Daddy came out after they were gone and found me moving junk again. I wasn't doing it so much for him or for the station as I was for me; I just didn't like all that unsightly mess out there.

"You workin' out here again, boy?"

"Yes, sir," I answered.

"Well, here. Let me give you a little wage for your help." He reached in his pocket and pulled out some change, from which he gave me a shiny new dime. I did not feel guilty about working for my daddy or taking his dime. I continued to work out in the junkyard most of that afternoon. For some inexplicable reason, I kept thinking all afternoon about Sky Riggins leaving his family and going so far away to work for the summer, and I wondered why. It seemed like a silly and unnecessary decision to me when there was plenty of work for him here in Northwest Arkansas, especially at his father's place. When I looked around, I suddenly realized that the whole sky had darkened as if a cloudburst would follow, and I decided that I needed to get back inside the station as quickly as possible.

Six

The next week, after Sky was gone, Daddy announced to us what we all suspected–that times were getting harder, and, as we all feared, he had concluded that he could no longer support us by running the station as our only source of income. Even after they added tires, batteries, minor car repairs, car washes, and even small grocery items, nothing seemed to help; the more options we added, the fewer customers we attracted. No matter what we tried, the station simply couldn't meet the needs of our family. As time passed, things only got worse, and we all believed that Granddaddy was right–the real problem was our location. When things seemed absolutely hopeless, my grandparents offered to help out.

"Aw, Paw, it ain't the lack of help. We got plenty of help. It's customers we ain't got! That's our problem. I just cain't keep it goin' without the people to bring us in the money."

"Well, what are y'all gonna do?" my grandma asked.

"I dunno."

"We could sell out, and try our hand at somethin' else."

"We ain't sellin' out, and we ain't tryin' somethin' else," Granddaddy shouted. "Besides, who would buy the place when it ain't really makin' any money?"

After much discussion and lots of praying around the table after supper at our devotional time, the adults all decided to keep the station. Daddy would go over to Springdale, up to Joplin, or down to Ft. Smith and look for work as a truck driver, and we would pray that his new boss might arrange for him to be home on weekends, at the very least on those weekends when he had to work at the Armory. My grandma would watch J-Earl and Tawna Rae while Granddaddy, Mama, and I would run the gas station and attempt to keep it open, even for the slightest income.

Daddy first checked with Arkansas Transport Lines in Springdale, but they weren't hiring any new truckers, and neither was their competition, Mid-States Truck Lines. Central Freight Haulers had a small terminal there, but they had no trucks and they weren't hiring either.

"I'll tell you what, partner," the office manager at Central told Daddy. "If you can get yerself up there to Joplin and go by and see a man by the name of Preston Waldrup at Interstate 66 Express, you jist might be in bidness. I heard they was hirin' a whole bunch of new, young, bob-catters like yerself, and they're pushin' some brand new equipment all across America's Main Street–U.S. Highway 66."

"Thanks for the tip," Daddy said. "I'm much obliged to you, sir."

"Well, you tell ole Preston that I sent you to him," the office manager said. "My name is Dixon...Merle Dixon."

"I will, Mr. Dixon. Thank you so much."

The next day, Daddy drove his pick-up truck up to Joplin. Later that afternoon, he came back all smiles, and when he brought us some Hershey's chocolate bars and some Wrigley's chewing gum, we all knew that he had found work.

"Y'all wouldn't believe it!" he said.

"Well, tell us all about it!" Mama said.

"They got a whole fleet of spankin' new trucks–mostly GMCs and some Internationals–and a big terminal up there. They were a hirin,' and I talked to the big boss, and after a while, they took me out to check me over and see if I could drive one of them trucks and trailers. I did just fine, and the man brought me back inside and says, 'We need a man to run that rig up and down–from Joplin to St. Louis–straight up 66 and back again,' he says, and then, 'and that's four to five full runs a week with every other Saturday, Sunday, or Monday off, depending on the schedule. And every now and then, you'll get a run or two between Tulsa and Chicago, too.'"

"I told him that we was livin' at Y-City Station, and that I'm also servin' in the Guard and needin' a full weekend a month, and he says to me, 'Where in the daylights is Y-City Station?' and then he says to me, 'Now, don't you be worryin' about bein' a Guardsman, son. We'll see to it that you get a drivin' schedule that allows you to be at all those Guard meetin's,' he says. 'We're proud to work with all our boys that served our country,' and then he says, 'I salute you, son!' Think of that! And he saluted me! Can you believe it? I felt like some kind of big shot. I told him where Y-City Station is, and he said he had never heard of it before, and he said it didn't matter to him anyways. And then he says, 'Well, son, you want the job or not?'"

"So I told him, 'Yes sir, I do, sir,' and he told me, 'Good. You start next Monday, so be up here bright and early.'"

"Well, what was his name, Clayton?" asked Mama.

"His name was Waldrup–Mr. Preston Waldrup–and he seemed like such a nice man," said Daddy.

"Well, I think we ought to bake him some bread or a cake or somethin' fer you to take up to him when you go up there again, and tell him thanks fer he'pin' us out in our time of need," said Grandma.

"Yes, that'd be a great idea," said Daddy.

We were all very excited that Daddy had found work as a trucker, and it appeared that his job would pay much more than what the station was bringing in. We would keep the station open and running as long as people would stop and buy gasoline. If nothing else, the few regular customers and the folks who dropped in to drink coffee and sit around for a while would be happy. My imagination was running wild with Daddy driving up and down U.S. Highway 66. I kept thinking of all the places he'd see, and how he'd end up in St. Louis or maybe even Chicago once in a while. Why, he could stop and see the Cardinals actually play in St. Louis, and if everything worked out all right, he might even see the Cardinals play against the Cubs in Chicago! What an event that would be! The next thing I was thinking was that, surely, he would take me with him, and then I would see all those things with him for myself. He and I would have a wonderful time together traveling up and down that road. Why, he could teach me how to drive that truck, and we could be truckers together! This whole idea set me to daydreaming, until the station bell rang and brought me back to reality.

"Hello! Anybody here?"

"Yessir, we're in here. Sorry. How can we he'p you sir?" Mama asked. She was thinking that she better get used to the idea of serving the customers and pumping gas.

Seven

On Sunday morning, we all got up and had a big breakfast of scrambled eggs together with smoked ham, grits, and homemade biscuits and gravy. After eating breakfast, we all got ready for church. We always went to Sunday school classes first and then to the worship meeting afterward. That morning, my Sunday school teacher, Brother Dwindle Pickett, was teaching us the Scripture where Jesus was teaching that if your right hand leads you into temptation, you should cut if off. I couldn't imagine how my right hand could lead me anywhere, and, after hearing Brother Pickett's teaching on it, I was trying to figure out what Jesus might have meant by that. I was thinking that I am sure glad I was born left-handed. In the next moment, Brother Pickett said that Jesus also taught something about your right eye carrying you away into temptation, too, which really perplexed me. I kept giving serious inner thought to what Jesus was saying, but it was useless for me to concentrate that day because Daddy would be leaving that afternoon for his new job in Joplin.

"Son, are you a listenin' to me? First you couldn't say yer memory verse, and now you ain't payin' a lick o' attention! Do I need to tell your father about this?" Brother Pickett asked.

"No, sir. No. Please, Brother Pickett; please don't tell my daddy. I won't do it again, sir," I said.

So Brother Pickett went on with his lesson, and in spite of all my thoughts about Daddy leaving for Joplin that afternoon, I tried my best to listen. Before the hour was past, somehow in typical, every-Sunday-morning fashion, Brother Pickett managed to shift his topic from that morning's Bible lesson about the right hand and the right eye to all ten of the Baptist sins against drinking liquor, womanizing, card-playing, and movie-going, not to mention smoking, dancing, cursing, and fishing or swimming on Sunday afternoons. He made it very clear to us that no church-going, Baptist Christian could ever hope to be saved from any of these activities, and all who participate therein could fully expect to burn in the fires of hell for doing so.

"Boys, do y'all understand me?" he would ask.

"Yes, sir," we would all say in unison, but no one in the class ever dared to challenge him to explain what the other two missing sins actually were (although Brother Sherwin Loomis, our Sunday school superintendent, had already explained to us that fishing and swimming on Sunday only counted for half a sin each).

Now, in our culture, when parents raise their children to attend Sunday school and church on a weekly basis, the children learn to trust the preacher and the Sunday school teacher almost as unconditionally as they trust their parents. After all, the family preacher and a child's Sunday school teacher represent the kind of character–equal to parents or very close friends–in whom children actually place their greatest trust and confidence. With the blessing of their parents, young children naturally recognize these people almost as family members who qualify to address those exceedingly personal issues that relate ultimately to the salvation of their eternal souls. To be sure, truly responsible parents who really love their children, as mine do, never fully release to such individuals their own accountability before God to teach their children to think for themselves. Nevertheless, society views the family preacher and the Sunday school teacher, ideally, as people who claim to place the best interests of their flock over their own and who desire to communicate openly and truthfully with their sheep and the little lambs. For that reason, I never expected any deceptions from Brother Pickett, intentional or otherwise. In our Sunday school class, for example, Brother Pickett explained how Jesus taught us so much about the hypocrites, but it seemed to me that, the more our teacher sought to enlighten us on this matter, the clearer it became to us that Brother Pickett himself was just about as big a hypocrite as anyone could ever be, ancient or modern. This was my own informed opinion, of course. Perhaps I was not as much aware of it before, but on a certain day in my life early that summer, I arrived at the heartbreaking conclusion that people cannot always trust the Sunday school teacher, the deacon, or perhaps even the pastor–to tell the truth or to minister first to the needs of their flock before providing for their own–regardless of what they say or how close to the family they seem to be.

One Sunday morning in the middle of June, Brother Pickett concluded our Sunday school lesson a good while before the church worship meeting began. Of course, we were delighted to gain an early release from our class. Minding our own business, Donnie Joe Shavers and I were out running around on the Grange House lawn, and, as it turned out, we happened to run completely around the house and down into the backyard. We weren't meaning any harm or trouble by it, but as we chased each other around, we ended up out behind the church outhouses where we happened to bump into three or four of those sanctified church leaders–one of them in particular being Brother Pickett. And there they were–all standing around and smoking their cigarettes between services–and hiding it all from the pastor. Donnie Joe and I were filled with astonishment, and the men were as embarrassed as a troop of sneaky little boy scouts whose den mothers just caught them cheating on their merit badge work in front of the whole jamboree. We caught them red-handed and with all the evidence, and they were totally red-faced with guilt. They knew it, too–first, because they tried to hide it the very moment we appeared–and second, because they tried to turn the tables around on us and make us out to be greater sinners than they were.

"Hey! What are you boys doin'? Why are y'all runnin' around desecratin' this little plot of holy ground? You boys ain't supposed to be chasin' each other all over this churchyard!" said Deacon Ellis, who tried to speak with some kind of clerical authority. However, in our minds, all the weight of his official influence simply disappeared like the cigarette smoke that faded into the wind just as it came out of his mouth.

"Yeah! You boys get on out of here! Y'all are supposed to be up there gatherin' together in the church house for the worship meetin'; now get on back there," Brother Pickett said. While he was talking, he was also blowing smoke all over the place, waving his arms all around to get rid of it, and, simultaneously, trying to destroy the evidence by stomping his cigarette into the grass. He looked ridiculous–like a dancing clown with two broken legs trying to perform a jumping jig. Suddenly, at that point in my life, Brother Pickett's word and personal example became as useless to me as they were disheartening.

"And y'all better not say anything to anyone about what y'all saw back here–not a word!" Brother Simpson said.

"And especially not to the reverend!" the deacon said.

Donnie Joe and I flew off like two scared sparrows. During the worship service, we didn't look at Brother Pickett, and he didn't look at us; I cannot even remember what Pastor Sutherland's message was about. The next week, just before our Sunday school class began, Brother Pickett–that rotten hypocrite–drew me privately aside from the rest of the class to confess what a sorry example of a Sunday school teacher he was.

"Now boy, I'm a scoundrel, and I know it," he said. "But you need to keep absolutely quiet about what you saw last Sunday morning out behind them outhouses. Nobody needs to know what we done, and you don't need to rattle your mouth about it. I know it ain't good that I smoke, and I know that it's gonna kill me. Somehow, I just got started with it. I made a bad choice by goin' down that road, and now I got to live with my troubles. Somewhere along the line, it's got the better of me, and I just cain't quit it now. It's a nasty, expensive habit, and it's bad for yer teeth and yer health. You don't ever want to start it, boy. You see to it that you don't you follow after me, you hear me boy? You don't do what I do; you jist do what I say," Brother Pickett said.

"Yes, sir," I said. And then he started to get all over me about Donnie Joe.

"Besides," he answered. "Why are you–of all people–runnin' around with the likes of that Shaver boy? What kind of choice is that? He ain't no good for you, son. He'll lead you down the crooked road, and you're too good a boy for him. Why don't you just stay away from him? His whole family ain't nothin' but a bunch of thievin' connivers."

"Yes, sir," I said.

All during his lesson that morning, Brother Pickett seemed to smell so much like smoke that I just wanted to get away from him. It was peculiar to me that I had never noticed it before then. I knew he felt guilty about smoking and then preaching at us not to do it. I wondered how he could justify telling others not to do what he did all the time. That sure seemed hypocritical to me. And I kept thinking about all those times in his Sunday school class when he would tell us, "Now boys, Jesus can wash away ever' one of yer evil practices, and He can cure all yer sicknesses. All you have to do is obey Him." Even I could tell that Brother Pickett's preaching and his behavior didn't seem to square up right. I also knew that, if there was any way he could, he would somehow blackmail me before my daddy, for not cooperating with him. And it astounded me to think that he so strongly disliked my friend, Donnie Joe. I sensed primarily that Brother Pickett and those other men were coming down hard on us simply because they were adults who had been embarrassed by a couple of young boys like us. Of course, they were all adults, deacons, and Sunday school teachers–men we were supposed to trust and admire. They were sorry Christians and not very good gentlemen, but they were good Baptists.

Eight

After church, we returned home for our Sunday dinner, which was always a weekly highlight and a special time that our family enjoyed together. On Sundays, Mama and Grandma always worked hard to prepare a dinner of fried chicken, roast pork, or roast beef. And what would Sunday dinner be without mashed potatoes and gravy? Usually, they would serve two or three different vegetables–corn, fried okra, green beans, or black-eyed peas as well as mixed greens and salad with lettuce, tomatoes, cucumbers, peppers, and carrots. I looked forward to Mama's hot biscuits with butter and honey dripping all over them. For dessert, we could count on having an apple pie or a cherry pie, although sometimes we had peach pie, which was my all-time favorite.

Our Sunday dinner that afternoon was supposed to be a very special event, for my parents and grandparents had invited the most extraordinary guests–the reverend and Mrs. J. D. Sutherland–the esteemed pastor of our church and his wife. Mama and my grandparents wanted our preacher to be on hand to offer a special blessing and to pray over Daddy before he departed later that evening for Joplin.

For whatever reason, everyone at the West Bethel Baptist Church considered it a great collective privilege to sit under the teachings and ministry of Reverend Sutherland. After hearing Brother Sutherland's first sermon, the worshippers of West Bethel carefully reminded him that God never made any mistakes in directing His shepherds to the right pulpits. Concerning his candidacy for the position, they offered but a singular, immediate conclusion: he was heaven-sent, and they could prove it. In the minds and hearts of the church members, Dr. Sutherland belonged to West Bethel Baptist Church simply because God had sovereignly decreed it. Brother Sutherland, however, did not initially share these same convictions with our congregation, and his first reaction to their offer was to turn it down. Upon hearing this, the members of the church falsely interpreted his rejection of their offer as a form of genuine, spiritual humility, which only elevated their level of admiration for him.

Brother Sutherland insisted that, when God first called him to preach, he had surrendered completely and without delay. As a result of his instant, positive response, he was certain that God had promised him a great ministry which he falsely interpreted to mean that God intended to elevate him to national prominence as a preacher. But when the home office originally sent him out as a candidate for ministry in our church, he concluded that, somewhere along the line, the leaders of the denomination had gotten their signals crossed up, and, for whatever reason, the Sutherlands ended up with us in Nowhere, Northwest-Arkansas. Somehow, serving at West Bethel Baptist Church simply did not correlate with Brother Sutherland's concept of God's sovereign will for his preaching ministry. With little true humility, Brother Sutherland presented himself to us as a preacher who was equal in stature to those pastors whom God had already firmly entrenched in places like First Baptist Church of Tulsa, or Little Rock, and even Dallas.

Nevertheless, to prove their case to the Sutherlands, the deacons and church members simply cited the Bible. They pointed out that, in the Scriptures, God had sovereignly directed both Moses and Elijah, but He never called either of them to dwell in the court of the great Pharaoh or in the palace of the mighty King. If anything, God led them both to forsake those locations of royalty and temptation; God called these two great leaders to ministries of sacrifice, service, and humility among those who worked the land and dwelt in simplicity out in the dry desert. This is how they knew that they were right–Reverend Sutherland was their Moses and their Elijah. No one at West Bethel would ever disagree or complain, and no one in Tulsa,

Little Rock, or Dallas would ever know the difference–or care about it–for they could claim as many spiritual giants as they wished; we claimed none but Dr. Sutherland alone. Eventually, the Sutherlands became flattered by this sort of logic, and they began to warm up to their call to West Bethel. After Reverend Sutherland had time to think it over, he expressed his call like this:

"I know that, in His sovereign wisdom, God has merely delayed opening to His servant the great doors to a much grander ministry of destiny in the future, therefore, I now have no alternative but to accept this modest office and make every human effort in the months ahead to increase the size of West Bethel Baptist Church to rival that of each of her sister congregations in the surrounding region."

With no further regard for any reality behind this transaction, the Sutherlands thenceforth belonged to us by whatever decree–divine or otherwise–by which, they became attached to us, and we became obligated to demonstrate our sincere gratitude to God as well as our unquestioned obedience, support, and loyalty to His servants.

With the passing of time, the Sutherlands acquired a sincere interest in the members of their congregation, and they learned to appreciate the ministry God had given them. In the same way, many folks in the church eventually realized that Reverend Sutherland and his wife were two very eccentric individuals, although they never criticized the pastor or his wife. With all their quirks, the Sutherlands also possessed the true Christian capacity to minister compassionately and to serve the spiritual needs of the sheep in their flock, nevertheless, they were selective in their utilization and application of it. Instead, they followed a more distant and self-serving path in everyday life– taking full advantage of whatever benefits and opportunities the faithful were willing to accord them. Both Sutherlands thrived on the slightest bit of attention that might come their way; at times, they even competed for it.

We thought it strange that Reverend Sutherland never called his wife by her name, Darla, but he constantly addressed her as "Mommy," even in public. Stranger still, his wife never called him by name or referred to him in any way other than *Reverend* Sutherland. Practically everyone in our community who knew him addressed him as *Brother* Sutherland, *Pastor* Sutherland, *Reverend* Sutherland, *Dr.* Sutherland, or *Mr.* Sutherland. His closest friends simply called him "*J.D.*" But perhaps the strangest thing of all was that nobody knew what the letters "J.D." actually meant.

Upon introduction to him, people making conversation might frequently ask him, "Well brother, what does 'J.D.' stand for?"

"I'll tell you, sir, there isn't a person on all of God's green earth that knows the answer to that question!" Brother Sutherland would reply. "I don't know what it means, and surely, my mama, who gave me that name, never told me what it means! So, if I don't know, and she don't know, then you don't *need* to know!" he would say.

Every Sunday, the Sutherlands, who lived on a back road off state Highway 68, perhaps seven or eight miles to the east of Highway 59, would drive all that way up to the Grange House to lead our church services. It was amazing to me that the Sutherlands would actually drive so far away from home two or three times each week just to minister at our church, especially when there were so many bigger and better churches in and around Siloam Springs and Gentry. It didn't make much sense to me to come way out here for church, but at least they traveled up to the Grange House in style; Pastor Sutherland drove the newest, shiniest, blackest, and biggest Packard Patrician that anyone in Northwest Arkansas had ever seen, and every year he turned that one in for next year's model.

"Mommy can't stand ridin' in one o' those other cars," Brother Sutherland would say.

As embarrassing as it was, our little church was poor and unable to provide full compensation befitting the Sutherlands. The church paid them in cash and in sundry items; every week, Mrs. Robinson brought them a few loaves of home-baked bread; the Perkins family would give them several sacks of fresh vegetables; the Sheltons might bring them some cream and a gallon or two of raw milk; and the Morgans always provided a bag or two of whatever fruit was in season. The Sutherlands were never ungrateful; they always expressed their sincere thanks for these items to everyone in the church, but they also knew how to get along quite well without the church's help. They were well-established, and, over the years, they had inherited or obtained a wide variety of socially beneficial positions and financially lucrative opportunities long before they ever became associated with West Bethel, although this was not broadly known among the members of our church. In addition to preaching, Reverend Sutherland also served now and then as a part-time professor at the University in Fayetteville. Actually, he and his wife were shrewd business people. Mrs. Sutherland had inherited a fine jewelry store in downtown Ft. Smith, and they both held joint interests in land development, real estate, and several restaurants in the Tulsa area.

Brother Sutherland was a tall man–strikingly handsome–with ice blue eyes and silver gray hair. He possessed a winsome but imposing personality and maintained many diverse interests and talents. He had led a most interesting life, and his Christian testimony reflected that a remarkable transformation had occurred somewhere in his background. A divinity graduate from one of our denomination's theological seminaries, Reverend Sutherland later received an honorary doctoral degree from a small Baptist college somewhere. By our standards, he was unusually well-educated, and he spoke with great authority and knowledge about practically every topic. He could communicate effectively on anyone's level, although he preferred to use the common and local vernacular because he believed it endeared him to all the folks in the church and in the community. One thing was certain: whenever he talked, no one ever dared to interrupt him.

Pastor Sutherland usually wore a custom-made, western-style suit with a vest and a fancy bow tie that he always hand-tied for himself. His suits, which he purchased exclusively on his occasional trips to Dallas or Kansas City, were decorated with the most unusual but fashionable embroidery, and the left-breast pocket inside all his jackets was especially fitted to conceal a .32-caliber Smith and Wesson revolver, which accompanied him everywhere he went. A wound received in the war caused the reverend to walk with a slight limp, but he always kept a wooden cane at his side for assistance. He wore the most expensive rattlesnake or alligator boots and a white, ten-gallon Stetson. Generally, he was pretty adept at concealing his tattoo, but every now and then, Brother Sutherland's right forearm somehow got unintentionally exposed to display a faded-blue, angled anchor with the words *U.S. Navy* above and *U.S.S. Thrasherfish* below it. Whenever that happened, he would say something like:

"Now, y'all know that, before I got saved, I was a mean, cussin' and brawlin,' drunk of a sailor in the navy during the war. And that's where I got me this old disgraceful piece of artwork on my arm. But now it don't matter, for that was before the Lord got a hold of me and–yessir!–He saved me!"

said the reverend, strongly emphasizing the word *saved*. "Yessir! But don't y'all go out there and get yourselves all tattooed up, now. No, sir! Don't y'all be a doin' what I done, for I can tell y'all, it ain't right. I am a sure proud of my service to my country, and I am double-proud that the Lord got hold of me and turned me around, but I am truly ashamed of these arm marks, which I do not sanction today."

Every now and then, the reverend would preach a hell-fire sermon that could frighten and convict even the most murderous and slanderous demon, and, when he did, he would begin his message by standing to the right of his pulpit, holding his Bible in his left hand, and his wooden cane in his right. Further to the right of his pulpit, Reverend Sutherland kept a heavy oak rocking chair, into which he would sit about halfway through his sermon. He could preach either way, standing at the pulpit or rocking in that chair, and whenever he wanted to emphasize his point, he would thump his cane so loud on the pulpit or the hardwood floor that no individual in the church–man, woman, or child, sitting anywhere from front to back–could possibly sleep.

Reverend Sutherland was motivated by the dead-serious opinion that his congregation totally lacked the ability to live the Christian life apart from his leadership. In his mind, he was clearly on a higher spiritual plane than they, and they were devoid of even the slightest aptitude to grasp it. And rightfully so, after all, wasn't a pastor supposed to be the spiritual leader? Therefore, as God's chosen and trained servant, he–and he alone–maintained the God-inspired mission to correct their weekly spiritual deficiencies, and, simultaneously, to rejoice with deep pride in his own ability to impart all the great, divine blessings as only Reverend Sutherland could provide them. In the reverend's mind, God simply wouldn't have it any other way.

"Now, you brothers and sisters," he would say every so often from his pulpit, "I just want to remind y'all today how grateful I am that the Lord has brought us all together here at West Bethel Baptist Church. You know, we're a blessed people…yes sir…a truly blessed people, and I understand how wonderful…what a truly great privilege it must be for y'all to sit like little sheep under my guiding hand. And I'm a truly blessed man to be here tonight to share my wisdom with y'all from that exceedingly vast treasure trove of great spiritual insight that God has so mercifully, albeit abundantly, poured out on me. Yessir, why…the Lord could have placed me anywhere else…yessir, indeed! And maybe He should have…but for your sakes and by His grace, here I stand–truly, and I'm proud to be His anointed but 'umble preacher to whom He has given this most dauntin' of tasks–and that'd be the savin' of y'alls souls in this here community of desolation."

"Amen, Brother!" someone would shout out.

"Yessir, preach it, Brother," another would say.

"Well, thank y'all fer that. And I just want to remind y'all to keep on a prayin' fer me and a thankin' the Lord fer me because I'm a doin' my best to pray fer y'all."

"Amen!" and "Amen!" would ring out all over the room.

But Brother Sutherland also had a sensitive side, too. He could play the guitar, the banjo, the accordion, the piano, the organ, the trombone, the harmonica–and he could direct the music of the church, too–though, not all at the same time, of course. Moreover, both he and his wife could sing; every Christmas, he would lead the church choir, and every Easter, he would direct the semiannual church drama. During those occasions, the Sutherlands never failed generously to provide holiday turkeys and hams for every family in the church. Outside of our church, the Sutherlands had traveled extensively around the world, and, in spite of their eccentricities, they were well-known and generally well-liked by people all over Arkansas. It was even rumored widely that the Sutherlands had many friends who were active in state politics all the way up to the governor's mansion.

Apart from her husband, however, Mrs. Sutherland was something of a social and spiritual enigma within our church body, if not in all Northwest Arkansas. Also egocentric, she was a big, round woman who always demonstrated unquestionable support for her husband, loyalty toward his office, and respect for his ministry, and she demanded these in return from each church member as well. She would tolerate no negative thoughts, words, questions, or deeds levied against the pastor; in her mind, these were considered abominations worthy of instant excommunication from the church, and she was always prepared to administer this justice–single-handedly, if necessary–to anyone who ever crossed her and on a moment's notice. Even the deacon board was careful around her.

Nevertheless, Mrs. Sutherland was both grand and grateful, but neither gracious nor graceful; she always wore a huge, multicolored hat with long feathers and a netted face veil, under which she wore her hair all puffed up and brushed all over the place. Mrs. Sutherland had dark brown eyes and deep furrows in her face, and she painted on more make-up than anyone I had ever seen, except perhaps her teenaged daughter, Starla, who also caked it heavily all over her face. Although Mrs. Sutherland never failed to greet all the church people, she stood at arm's length and seldom ever conversed with anyone in the church. Despite her frequent displays of genuine goodness and generosity toward many in the church, the pastor's wife impressed everyone as a cold, arrogant, indifferent woman who simply came to church, played the role of pastor's wife during the service, and then after the closing hymn, retreated back into the solitude of her Packard–sometimes waiting there as much as an hour or more for her ministering husband.

Nine

Now Granddaddy, Daddy, and Brother Sutherland were all sitting in the parlor while Grandma and Mama were in the kitchen making dinner; Mrs. Sutherland was sitting out on the front porch, and Starla was in the bedroom with Tawna Rae.

"Well, Brother Sutherland," Daddy said, "I sure appreciated your sermon this mornin'." I wondered if he really did, or if he was just making small talk with the preacher.

"Well, good!" Brother Sutherland replied. "Good! I'm glad ya did!"

"Yessir, Reverend," Granddaddy spoke up. "That was indeed a mighty good sermon."

"Well, Arliss, I'm so glad that it spoke to yer heart. And I hope this here Sunday dinner'll be as good as my message was."

I couldn't understand it all very well, but something in my young mind cautioned me to exercise a sensible form of skepticism before accepting the advances of any strange people or ideas. Personally, my instincts told me that even the good, well-educated, well-traveled Reverend and Mrs. Sutherland might actually be two different individuals from those they appeared to be. Even at my age, I was able to sense that they were more motivated by what they got out of their people than how they could serve and minister to them. I could have been completely wrong, but I believed that most of their attempts at graciousness were simply overboard performances designed for no other reason than to play people like fiddles–stringing them politely along and exchanging their cheap, Sunday-afternoon attention for whatever free chicken dinners they might receive. I reckon what struck me the most was that my parents and grandparents seemed to go along with all this nonsense– or else they covered over their true feelings pretty well. I decided that it was too soon to make a conclusive judgment, but, for the moment, I chose to believe that either the adults were all hoodwinked, and that it was simply easier or more judicious for them to play along, or I was too young to perceive accurately what was going on. In the meantime, with the hypocrisy of Brother Pickett fresh on my mind, I also determined that it certainly could do me no harm to practice some discretionary suspicion in the presence of both the reverend and his wife.

J-Earl and I went outside on the front lawn to throw the ball around a little, but I quickly became bored with that. Little brothers–and even little sisters, at times–were pretty good to have around when they were needed; usually, they would join in readily with the game, but they weren't much on talent yet, so I couldn't count on them for too long. Apparently, one of God's purposes for younger brothers and sisters was to help their older brothers–although without their knowledge or intention–to develop in patience. After a few minutes, J-Earl got tired of missing the ball and having to chase it, so he went inside, and I decided to sit up on the top step of the front porch. I looked up the road, and, off in the distance, I could see Donnie Joe riding his bike back and forth up by his place. He was stirring up a lot of dust.

I sat there on the step for a few minutes, and then Mrs. Sutherland asked me, "young man, do you go to school?"

"Yes, ma'am," I responded.

"Do you like school?"

"Yes ma'am," I said, stretching the truth just a little.

"What grade are you in?"

"Sixth grade, ma'am."

"Who is your teacher?"

I felt a little like she was putting me on somebody's witness stand to cross-examine me, and her questions were beginning to annoy me.

"Mr. McLemore," I replied.

"I see," she said. "And I expect you'll be makin' every effort to attend our Vacation Bible School at West Bethel this summer, won't you, young man?"

"Well…I…I dunno…"

Just then, thankfully, my grandma interrupted our brief discussion when she came out to announce that dinner was now ready. Being a gentleman, I held the front door open for Mrs. Sutherland.

"Why, young man, that's mighty sweet of you to open that door fer me!" Mrs. Sutherland's voice vibrated as she spoke.

"Yes, ma'am," I replied. Privately, I kept thinking that Mrs. Sutherland would drive me crazy if I had to stand there much longer and answer many more of her questions. She was going so overboard with that "mighty sweet of you" performance, that I thought I'd get sick for sure.

We went in, and we all stood at our places. Daddy asked the reverend if he would pray over the food. Brother Sutherland offered up his standard prayer of grace, which I had heard him pray so many times before a potluck dinner event on the grounds over at the church. I knew that he had memorized most of his prayers from his little black prayer book, because on special Sundays, when the season called for some different or unusual prayer, he would always pull out his prayer book. On those Sundays, he would insist that the members of the congregation bow their heads.

"Every head bowed, and every eye closed," he would say.

When the reverend was sure that most eyes were fully closed, he would read from his prayer book. I knew this because I would sneak a peek to see if he had his head bowed and his eyes closed, and, when I did that, I discovered that not only was he praying with his eyes open, but also that he was reading the prayer out of his little book. Every now and then, while he was reading such a prayer, he would stumble over a word he hadn't pronounced for a while, or he would sputter through part of the prayer because the print on the pages was too small or unclear. This I also didn't understand. It seemed to me that if you really wanted to pray to God from the heart–all you really had to do was talk to Him–you didn't need to read it out of some ancient guidebook. The problem with a prayer book is that it might not really be your prayer, and if it wasn't your prayer, how could God really answer it? To me, it was like copying someone else's book report, and, in our class, Mr. McLemore would never let us get away with that. Almost everyday, he would say:

"Now class, you will be graded on what you submit, so make sure that you do your own work."

After Brother Sutherland ended his prayer, we all sat down to enjoy the tastiest fried chicken this world has ever known. My goodness, Mama and Grandma could really cook! They served chicken, mashed potatoes, delicious creamy gravy, all kinds of vegetables, and biscuits with butter and honey. For dessert, they had baked a couple of peach pies. You could compliment both of them, but they would each say something like, "Well, I had lots of he'p."

Around the table, the adults talked about the weather, local politics, and the church. After awhile, they asked the reverend some questions about his travels overseas. We were not allowed to talk or interrupt while the adults were talking at the table, and, for the most part, we were not interested in what they talked about anyway. Mama would not allow us to leave the table until the last person was finished eating, and we always had to ask Daddy to excuse us. If there was a dessert, which there was that day, we would have to sit through almost another half hour of adult chatter until we could leave the table. That day, it wasn't easy to get out of there, but the longer I sat there, the deeper my spirits began to sink because the reality of Daddy's departure was setting in quickly.

It was almost four o'clock when Brother Sutherland said, "Well, Arliss; Clayton; we got to be goin' soon."

"Reverend, before you go," Mama said, "we wondered if you'd offer up a prayer of safekeepin' and blessin' over Clayton? Y'all know that he's found truck drivin' work with a hauler up there in Joplin."

"Why, yes ma'am, I knew that, and of course I would. An' by the way, let me just first of all tell you how much I enjoyed yer dinner. It was just dee-licious, and I believe it was like near on par with that spiritual breakfast I served up to y'all this mornin' in the Grange House, don't y'all think?" bragged Brother Sutherland.

"Well…yes sir…perhaps that could be, Reverend," Mama said timidly.

"Well, we'll just be leavin' directly, so less all gather 'round here in the parlor before we go, and I'll just bless Brother Clayton…"

We all gathered around hand in hand in a big circle in the center of our parlor. Daddy was holding Mama's left hand and to Daddy's left came Tawna Rae and then I was next. J-Earl stood to my left, and to his left was the reverend, followed by Mrs. Sutherland, and then Grandma and Granddaddy stood in their places immediately to my mama's right.

"Why, Mommy?" the reverend asked. "Where's our little Starla?"

Mrs. Sutherland broke away from the circle, wiped off her left hand, and disappeared; a moment later, she returned with her daughter. For some strange reason, Starla walked in the opposite direction all the way around the backside of the circle to me, broke my grip on Tawna Rae's little hand, and stood between my little sister and me. She moved into the gap and grasped our hands, and then Mrs. Sutherland rejoined and completed the circle right where she stood before.

Then, with a solemn, almost funerary voice, the reverend said, "Less all bow our heads in prayer." I figured that he hadn't prayed too many prayers of safekeeping and blessing over others, so this would probably be a struggle for him.

"Dear Lord, we 'umbly come before Thee today, and we...uh...yes...and Lord...we beseech Thy eternal presence today...on behalf of our own dear Brother Clayton and his family today..."

It was a long, strenuous prayer–indeed, one I hadn't heard before–and as it wasn't one from the prayer book, I sensed somehow that it came a little more from his heart. At the end of the prayer, there were several "amens," and then the circle broke loose. Again, Brother Sutherland thanked my grandma and my mama for the dinner and the hospitality and turned to shake hands with Granddaddy and Daddy. Mrs. Sutherland shook hands with Grandma and Mama.

"Ladies, I had the most wonderful time here this afternoon. Now y'all remember that the Vacation Bible School needs lots of cookies and cold drinks–don't ferget, no Co-Cola–mind you, but Kool-Aid or some such kid's drink as that."

In a minute, they were in their Packard, and after tooting their horn, they drove away and were gone. The weather was hot, the road was dusty, and they stirred up a lot of dust.

Everything about them is flamboyant, I thought to myself.

Ten

Later that afternoon, after the Sutherlands were gone, we all helped Daddy pack an old, borrowed suitcase for his trip to Joplin. Now, with no outsiders present, the reality of Daddy's forthcoming absence began to set in for all of us, and we became strangely and unnaturally quiet. Earlier, we had engaged in noisy discussions and debated a whole set of animated plans, but now we were advancing toward that moment when all the clamor would elapse into silence. Heretofore, everything true about all our previous experiences with the man who served as our father, our husband, and our son—not to mention our teacher, guide, shield, provider, protector, and all the other individuals he represented—would change instantly when that bus departed from our station.

In another moment, we were all moving about, trying to help Daddy get ready.

"Daddy," said Tawna Rae, "you'll need these here socks fer yer trip," and she would run over to him and tease him with the socks—acting like she would give them to him, and then when he'd reach for them, she'd draw them back to herself again. Only six years old, she was tender of heart. Her legs and arms were so petite, her hands were slender, and her fingers were long and graceful. Her head sat up high on her long, thin neck, and her face was always bright with a cheery smile. She was wearing a yellow tee shirt under her overalls, and she was our sunny little girl.

Daddy finally got a hold of the socks, and then he grabbed her, too, and held her close and tight to his chest. His voice broke, and he could barely speak.

"Oh, Tawna Rae…oh, Sweetheart…I'm gonna miss you so much," Daddy said. "You're Daddy's precious little baby."

J-Earl saw the attention Tawna Rae got, and he wanted some, too, so he tried to tease Daddy like that with his belt and his Billups hat, but it didn't quite come off like it did with Tawna Rae. With his blond hair and blue eyes and his thin, elongated arms and legs, he was almost as cute as his older sister, but he was a bit clumsier. He dropped the hat, and he tripped on the belt, and then he got so embarrassed and hurt that he began to cry. It was the hurt and embarrassment of failure–the most painful, heartfelt sorrow of a little boy after he realized that his performance could not possibly match his deep desire to please.

"Oh, no, J-Earl," Daddy said. "Come here, boy…come here to Daddy. It's okay; it's gonna be all right. You don't need to cry anymore." Daddy reached down to pick him up, and now, for the first time, J-Earl realized that Daddy would be gone much more than he would be here.

"Okay, J-Earl…now give Daddy a big hug, a handshake, and a kiss."

J-Earl continued to sob while he hugged Daddy and kissed him on the cheek. In the next moment, our whole family came undone, and we were all crying. There was no stopping it; all our hearts were breaking, all eyes were awash in tears, and there were no dry faces in the house. Struggling with his own sobs as tears ran down his face, Daddy turned around and looked straight at me, and he said, "Now son.…" His voice broke, and then, "You know I'll be back just about ever' weekend…" He sobbed again, and then he said, "But you look after things 'round here while I'm gone. Next to Granddaddy, you're gonna have to be the man of the house, and that's a big responsibility. You be a good example before yer sister and brother; obey yer Mama, and you keep things a runnin' round here at the house an' he'p yer Mama and Granddaddy down at the station, okay?"

"Yes, sir," I replied. As I recall, it was the first time I had ever seen him cry.

"Daddy," I said, and I looked at him straight in his eyes. "I won't let you down."

"Thank you, boy. I know you'll do me proud."

After a while, we all regained our composure, but time had run out.

"Clayton," Mama said.

"Yeah?"

"I made you a little lunch for yer trip," she said. "It's in this here sack. You take it along, and when you get hungry on that bus, just take it out an' eat it. An' while yer eatin' yer lunch, just be thinkin' about me, okay?"

"I will."

"And there's some cookies and cakes in there, too,—fer Mr. Waldrup."

We put the suitcase in the back of the pick-up truck, and then Daddy hugged and kissed Mama and Grandma. He hugged and kissed the rest of us, and then he said, "it's time to go." He said his last good-byes, and then he walked toward the back door.

"Daddy?" I asked. "Can I ride down with you and Granddaddy?

"Yeah," he said. "I'd like that."

Granddaddy, Daddy, and I all climbed into our pick-up truck. I sat in the middle. It wasn't fully dark yet, but everything was quiet all around. The Joplin bus usually came by our station about eight thirty-five or so. The bus stopped only if the driver could see any passengers waiting in a visible location on our station grounds. Granddaddy started the pick-up truck; shifting the lever around my legs, he backed it up, and then he pulled it around, and the next moment, we were driving east on our little road. The road was deserted now because it was Sunday evening. There were also no trains at that time either. Granddaddy drove us up over the tracks, and then he pulled the truck around and into our Billups station on the right side of the pumps so when the bus arrived, the driver could see us waiting there. We waited there for a good while. I noticed that both roads were deserted. In the truck, we were all silent. It was not a time to talk, and as my life was about to change so dramatically, I tried to think it all through and evaluate it in my mind.

Our station was dark inside, and everything appeared quiet and secure. We never operated the station on Sundays because we believed that God would bless us if we honored His day. Inside the front window, just to the right of the station door, there was a sign painted decoratively in large black letters on a white background; it simply said, "Closed." The sign's left side was tilted somewhat upward and backward so that whatever light might reflect on the window glass in front of the sign actually concealed the first three letters of the word from view. Tonight, because of its skewed position in the window, our "Closed" sign was simply ineffective in the performance of it duties. Anyone who passed by could tell that the station was closed without any help from the sign. It was just another piece of extraneous junk and therefore, useless.

That the station should be closed seemed somehow incongruous to me, for the whole idea of a station was first conceived earlier in someone's mind and then constructed by another's hands with the specific objective of providing service to others and making a living. To accomplish those purposes fully, logic required that it remain open for business. And yet, on this Sunday evening, here it was: our station was closed. While we waited there, I quietly wondered how passing travelers would interpret "Closed." Would they merely interpret the station from a distance?

"Why, look up there–up ahead! Why, there's a gas station! But shucks! It's all dark and shut up; must be closed for the weekend. Well, we'll just have to keep on drivin' and keep on lookin' till we find another one that's still open tonight. Why, they'll be open for business again tomorrow morning."

Or would they need the sign? Of course, if they got their information from the sign, they'd almost have to be right up next to it to read it: "Closed."

"Why, that sign says, 'Closed.' Hmm. Wonder what that means? 'Closed.' Closed for tonight? Closed for vacation? Closed forever? Wonder why they closed?"

Without saying anything, Daddy and Granddaddy just sat there waiting– in our little truck at the little station–waiting away quietly for the bus. The decision that determined our present wait had already been made awhile back, and, of course, the bus was nothing more than an impartial element in this overall grand plan. We would ordinarily have little or nothing to do with a bus, but in my mind it now represented an evil monstrosity of progress coming up the road to initiate a whole series of additional choices creating even more events that would ultimately change our lives forever. No one knew why; it was just the result of a decision–a consequence. Starting tonight, it would swallow up my daddy, take him away from us, and eventually put us out of business. The monster that would defeat us was now on its way, and we could do nothing about it other than wait passively for it. But worst of all, its point of attack was right here at Y-City Station–the center of our lives and of Daddy's original hopes and dreams for his family. Presently, from his perspective, it seemed that his quiet submission to this iniquity was the only way to keep those hopes and dreams alive, although in his absence, I would not go down without a fight–regardless of the consequences. I was determined to do all I could to keep that station open, and that was my decision. But I also knew intuitively that there was little that any of us could do to make the operation profitable. Once you were out on that road, you had to follow it to its end. Like Daddy said, "I cain't make the people buy their gas from us."

The bus was unusually late. As the darkness fell, my heart continued to ache, but I resolved at least passively to support the plan rather than outwardly fight it. We waited quietly in our pick-up truck there in Y-City Station. Adjacent to the two vacant railroad tracks and situated in that hapless triangle between our road and State Highway 59–there we were–waiting between two roads; going nowhere, and wondering why. It was dark and closed but not abandoned. In another moment, Granddaddy whispered:

"Here she comes."

Crawling up Arkansas Highway 59, its headlights glaring ahead like the eyes of some hideous night animal stalking through the darkness–first to the right, then a little to the left, and now straight toward us–the bus made its way slowly and ever closer. There was a lighted panel at the top of the windshield, and it said, "Kansas City." In the next minute, it prowled slowly across the dark state highway into Y-City Station. Its engine growled two or three times, its brakes hissed, and it finally halted directly in front of us. The powerful engine continued its muffled rumble and murmured breathing. Shining directly in our faces, the headlights of the bus froze us momentarily, exposing everything inside our truck cab and lighting up our whole station area. The bus driver opened the door.

"This is it," Daddy said. "Y'all take care of everything here, now, okay? I gotta go now." His voice was cracking.

"Okay," said Granddaddy. "We'll keep it all covered. We'll be prayin' fer you, too, Clayton."

"Bye, Daddy!" I said, choking out the words. I was fighting them as hard as I could, but the tears poured forth and rolled down my face. "I...I promised you...that...that I wouldn't let you down. See you soon!" I know that he wanted to tell me that he loved me as much as I wanted to tell him that I loved him. But we just let it be; we weren't much on sharing our strongest feelings too openly, because I reckon that was the way we communicated our love. We didn't have to say it; we just knew it.

Daddy never looked back. He climbed aboard the bus, but it was too dark for us to see anything. Within a few seconds, the silver-streaked creature with the brown-painted words "Jefferson Lines" on its side panel was now heading on its way up the road to its destination.

Book Two

Eleven

After Daddy was gone, Mama and Granddaddy ran the station, and I helped throughout the rest of that summer. Back at the house, Grandma kept Tawna Rae and J-Earl, and this arrangement seemed to work out well. We had always been used to tough times and living on short money, but together with Mama's garden and our station, we managed to do somewhat better after Daddy went on the road. It was everyone's hope that Daddy's truck driving would be a temporary solution to our financial problems, but one afternoon, I overheard Mama and Granddaddy agree that the station would probably never be able to support us completely.

"Ever'thing is a changin' so fast," Mama said. "Time was, when you could run the family bidness, and make it work fer you perty well, but these days it's too much against you…prices goin' up…people don't pay their accounts…and goodness! I know you got to collect yer receivables before you can pay yer own bills."

"Well, Norma Jean, that's all true, but I'm convinced what's hurtin' us first of all is our location. The state is buildin' new roads out yonder, and they're all goin' ever' which way around us, and none of 'em are comin' to where we are," Granddaddy said. "Why, shucks! If we had the same gas station over on Highway 71, we'd be makin' so much money—we'd have two or three gas stations. We just don't get the traffic they get over there."

"Well, I reckon yer right, Granddaddy. But to me, it just don't seem fair. The moment you buy a little bidness–why, then they invent another three to put you out of bidness."

"Come on, now," Granddaddy said. "We ain't outta bidness, Honey. Don't you go worryin' yer perty little head over all this. Just remember that the Lord is lookin' after us all."

"I know," said Mama.

Except for those times when Daddy had to attend National Guard meetings down at the armory in Siloam Springs, he was back with us most weekends. His boss allowed him to drive his truck down from Joplin as long as he kept it parked and locked up all weekend while he was home. Daddy said that the work was good, and that he liked driving trucks over the road. He liked pulling a long trailer. He drove up U.S. Highway 66 from Joplin to St. Louis two or three times each week–sometimes even more–and once or twice he made the short run from Joplin to Tulsa. He said that he hadn't gone to Chicago yet.

"When you were in St. Louis, Daddy, did you drive by Sportsman's Park? Did you go see the Cardinals play?" I asked.

"No, I didn't. Not yet, son," he replied. "I don't get over in that part of the city. It's a pretty big place. But I'll tell you what–if I get the chance, I'll try to go there, and you know what? One of these days…maybe I'll take you and J-Earl along with me on a run up there. What you think of that, boy?"

"Really? Wow!"

Daddy said that he had lots of time to think when he was driving out on the highway. He said that he always thought about Mama, and us kids, and Grandma and Granddaddy, and of course, our station. He said that he always wondered what we were doing, and how things were going without him there. He said that he could imagine Mama baking bread and peeling potatoes and cooking dinner together with Grandma. He said that, somehow in his mind, he could see us sometimes–working at the station–wiping windshields and pumping gas. He would dream about Tawna Rae running in the backyard, J-Earl chasing her around, and both of them playing on the swing that he put up out there. He would think about Granddaddy sitting in the station and talking with some of our regulars who would come in and sit a spell. Daddy said that there was a lot to see out on that road.

"Every day's a new day up there, and around every turn there is somethin' new to see," Daddy said. "I seen some perty nice cars and trucks, and I seen some awful bad car wrecks out yonder on that road, too. In some places, that Highway 66 is bumpy and hilly and real curvy–I mean to tell you–it's a killer in some places, and you got to watch out. But I'll tell you what; things out yonder sure get dull when you have to drive the same old routes day in and day out."

When Daddy was gone during the week, Granddaddy and I would go down about six o'clock every morning to open the station, and Mama would come down later in the day after she finished some of her house work. As soon as we got there, Granddaddy would always make the coffee while I would go to the back room and turn on the lights and the gasoline pumps, raise up the main bay garage door, turn on the fans to get the cool air circulating through the station, and then make sure the rest rooms were clean. Our family believed in cleanliness, but keeping a gas station clean was practically impossible. People would come in and make a mess of everything and just leave it for someone else to clean up–especially in the rest rooms. I couldn't understand how people could come in and use our facilities and leave them like there were no facilities to use at all. People might come in and clog up the toilets or throw the paper all over the floor. And for the life of me, I don't know why some of them ever wanted to use a toilet because they couldn't hit it anyway. Then there were others who would mark up the restroom walls and spread grease and oil all over the sinks. They would steal our soap, our rags, and our towels. Keeping the rest rooms clean and sanitary was almost a full time job. After I would complete all my regular station chores, I would go back in, sit down, and drink coffee with Granddaddy.

One day, Granddaddy was sitting there sipping his coffee and reading the *Tulsa World* newspaper. The sun was up and already bright; there wasn't much wind, and I knew that it was going to be a hot day. Whenever Granddaddy finished reading the paper and there wasn't much other work to do, he would start in with his regular routine of teasing me.

"Hey, boy! How long you gonna wear them overalls?" he asked.

"I dunno," I said. "How long you gonna be wearin' yours?"

Whenever he teased me, I knew he liked me to make a game out of it, so I would usually try to tease him back.

"Mine are fresh and clean this here mornin,'" he said. "But I'm gonna tell you what, boy; you stink like you been up yonder cleanin' out one of ol' Riggins' chicken coops."

"Stink? I don't stink! I ain't been up there in a long time."

"Tell me, boy. What's yer girlfriend's name? Is it Flora? You been chasin' little ol' Flora Fishbait around?"

"Ain't got no girlfriends, Granddaddy."

"Come on, now. I know better than that. I saw how that little Starla Sutherland come jist a wigglin' right up next to you up at the house a few weeks back."

"I ain't had much time to thank about girls, Granddaddy."

"Well, wuhhhhh-weeeeee…and a pig soooeeee, boy! You surely will someday soon, I can tell you that with a good-as-gold garonntee," said Granddaddy. "Tow-headed boy like you! You'll have a whole string of girls hangin' on your arms before too long. And hey there, boy…who you gonna play fer…huh? You gonna play fer them Hawgs, ain't you boy?"

I loved the Razorbacks almost as much–well, just as much–as the Cardinals, in fact. Whenever he brought up the Hawgs or the Cardinals, I knew the teasing had just about come to an end for both of us; now our talk started to get serious–almost sacred. There were two national colors of Northwest Arkansas, and they were both red, and every Granddaddy, Daddy, and loyal son of the Ozarks dreamt–if nothing else–that at least one individual somewhere in their family line might somehow make an active contribution to that proud, ancient tradition that raised those colors high. Perhaps we were nothing more than dreamers. But after all; this was the land of opportunity and diamonds–however much in the rough–and all the successes of every native son began to develop with an infinite dream that germinated somewhere down in the infinitesimal recesses of the Arkansas heart. And when any one of us succeeded, we felt as if we all did.

"Why, yessir. You betcha, Granddaddy. I'm gonna play Hawg baseball fer sure."

"I ain't talkin' about baseball, boy! I mean Hawg football."

I could imagine myself playing baseball rather than football, but I wasn't going to argue against either football or baseball. I knew that my shared interest in being a Razorback was enough to make Granddaddy happy, and I knew that if he started all this with a hog-call that I'd better finish with one, too.

"Well, Granddaddy...wuhhhhh weeeeee...pig soooeeee! Go Hawgs!"

We laughed for awhile, and then a car pulled into the station driveway and brought our levity to an end. The station bell rang just as the car stopped next to the pumps. I went outside to fill up the car's tank with gas at the same time the driver got out of the car. It was Mr. Buford Crawford.

"Mornin' Mr. Crawford," I said. "How're you doin' today?"

"I'm a doin' fine, son," he responded. "Your Granddaddy inside?"

"Yessir. You want me to fill her up?"

"Yeah, that'd be fine; fill her up."

From his mouth, Mr. Crawford spewed a big wad of tobacco juice onto the station driveway just about every day. He chewed Red Man, and he kept his pouch in the right front pocket of his overalls. He also had a sack of Daytime Donuts and brought them inside the station. I filled his gas tank with Billups regular and checked his water, oil, and air. After I told Granddaddy the gas price, Mr. Crawford would request that Granddaddy put the amount on his account, so Granddaddy wrote it down in the accounts book that Mama kept on the shelf behind our cash register. There were just two old wooden chairs inside the station, and Mr. Crawford had already taken the one I vacated when he pulled into the station, so I sat down on the inside front window ledge. Mr. Crawford was one of our regulars because he stopped in just about every day to sit and visit, drink coffee, and eat donuts for an hour or so before driving on. Of course, before he could eat any donuts, he'd have to clear all the chaw out of his mouth. He usually did that somewhere out back of our station in the high grass out under the gasoline and oil tanks. Mr. Crawford would always leave a few donuts in the sack, and he would tell us to sell the rest, although we usually would just give them to anyone who requested them. It was a rare day when–by the end of the day–we had any left over. As one of our regulars, Mr. Crawford would usually buy his gas from us about once a week or so–always charging it up to his account.

"Hey boy," he said. "Want a jelly donut?"

"Yessir," I said.

He motioned for me to come back and pick out a donut.

Mr. Crawford lived in one of the places out our way, and he worked down in the truss plant in Gentry. His wife, Mrs. Lurleen Crawford, worked as a cook down at the college cafeteria in Siloam Springs. They had three children. Their oldest boy, Jack, was a junior at the high school in Gentry, and he played football. He probably would have been an outstanding quarterback—the position he most wanted to play—except that he had a hair lip which prevented him from pronouncing his words just right, and Coach Humphries was always afraid the other players wouldn't exactly understand the signals he called, especially under the pressures of a close game.

When Coach Humphries first saw Jack play in his freshman year, he noticed that Jack really threw the ball well, but somehow the players in the backfield were missing all his calls. The coach took him aside for a moment.

"Now, Jack, what high school do you wanna play fer?" Coach Humphries asked.

"Why, of courths, Coaths," Jack said. "Fer Yentry High Ckool."

"Jack, I think we' gonna make a minor change here and play you as a halfback instead of quarterbackin' because you can run and you can catch that ball perty good," Coach Humphries told him. "Leastwise better than you can call signals."

"Well, Coaths, I don't mind...that'll be fine."

From that point on, Jack played in the backfield, and ever increasingly well—in fact, he played so well—that the University of Arkansas granted him a football scholarship after his senior year. The local aristocracy of Gentry so associated Jack's habitual mispronunciation of the town name with his popularity and his celebrity to such an extent that it soon became fashionable for them to call the town "Yentry" as well. For a long time afterward, anyone who pronounced the name "Gentry" was considered either an outsider or grossly lacking in the local culture.

Jack Crawford had two younger sisters, Carol Ann, who was my age and in my class at school, and Lynnette, who was in kindergarten. All the Crawfords had dark brown hair and brown eyes except Mr. Crawford. Predictably, the Crawfords always drove a Dodge, and they were all lifelong Democrats—an oddity for natives of Benton County.

Legend had it that Mr. Crawford met Mrs. Crawford at one of the local

Ozark auctions, where they fell in love while competing against each other in the bidding for an old railway station clock.

"Now y'all, this here antique clock is a gen-u-wine Alpha Eternity model…it was especially handcrafted for the MKT Railroad at the Alpha Clock and Timepiece Works in Upper Devil's Falls, Massatu…Massatussa…Masschusess," the announcer said. He had a little trouble with Massachusetts. "That's somewhere up there in New England," he said.

"Folks, fer the last thirty-five years, this here clock graced the walls of the waitin' room in the M-K-T railroad station over at Big Cabin, Oklahoma. Now y'all know that there are hunderds o' thousands o' pairs of eyes that watched this here clock–some of 'em famous and some not so famous–and who knows a how many folks caught and missed their trains by this old clock. Rumor has it that Bonnie sat under that clock fer a couple o' hours while she was a waitin' fer Clyde to come by and pick 'er up. Yessir…she's a beauty…look at that polished mahogany…and we gonna start off our biddin' at a hunderd dollars…are you ready, Grady?"

"What? You betcha…I say…what am I…yassir…what am I bid…if not a nee-baw-naw…yassir, now, a come on…yes, a come on up and a what-am-I-bid?…Then a baw-naw-nee…and a baw-nee-naw-naw…my-bid…my-bid…my-biddee diddee dee…and a baw-naw-nee-naw-bid-me-now-of-ten-dollah-forty…up again now-to-a-baw-naw-nee…hundert dollah twenty up a nee-naw-nee-ninny-nanny-goat-billy…then a nippy-bidding-dippy on the bid-nippy-naw…" the auctioneer chirped away, faster, louder, and ever faster. He spoke so fast that the words became incomprehensible except for a "one-fifteen in the middle" and a "one-twenty-five" somewhere in the muddle.

"One-thirty-five!" shouted Mr. Crawford.

The future Mrs. Crawford took the bid still higher, and it went back and forth among five or six bidders for fifteen or twenty minutes or so until all but the future bride and groom dropped out. In the end, he out-bid her and got the clock, but he apparently felt so badly about taking it away from her that, in the next moment, one thing led to another, and he offered to give her the clock outright.

"Oh, my goodness, no! You are so unselfish and so generous, but I could never accept that clock, sir!" she exclaimed.

"Why, yes," he said. "Of course...please take it; I want you to have it."

"Oh, no," she said.

"Oh, yes," he replied. They went on and continued arguing like this, and then Mr. Crawford said, "well, you see...here we are a biddin' again over that blame clock!"

"Why, you're right! We are!" she agreed. "Do you suppose it is fate?"

Evidently, old Crawford sealed it when he said, "Well, I don't know what it is, but I think both of us should keep the clock."

"And how do you propose that we do that?" she asked.

"I think we were made fer each other...I say we get hitched, and then we can both have that clock."

"Well, I do declare!"

The future Mrs. Crawford liked that idea until she found out that Buford was a Baptist.

"Well, Buford, I cain't marry no Baptist!" Lurleen cried.

"Why, what are you?" Buford asked.

"What do you think I am? I'm a Methodist. Been one all my life and dyed in the wool, as they say. I'm...well, practically a daughter of Susannah Wesley herself!"

"Well then, you can marry me, Lurleen. Methodists and Baptists can marry...it ain't like one of us was Catholic or Hebrew or African. Why, they do it all the time–Methodists and Baptists."

Buford and Lurleen courted–and argued–for the next twelve months. It was a total year of pre-matrimonial bidding extremes. Which church would perform the wedding? What would be their wedding date? What church would they attend after the marriage? And so forth...and so on, all of which simply preceded a whole lifetime of confrontation and conciliation. Indeed, they truly loved each other.

They married in the Baptist church, because they decided to attend the Methodist church. Buford swore that he would never–ever, no never–renounce his Baptist baptism, nor would he ever–never, not ever–be re-baptized as a Methodist.

"You don't need to," Lurleen said. "We Methodists accept any old kind of baptism."

All the Crawfords, even Buford, were the most reliable of Methodists who never missed a Sunday morning service at the Shining Light Methodist Church in…where else?…Yentry, Arkansas. And they were big donors, too. Exactly one year after Buford and Lurleen were married, their Alpha Eternity, highly polished mahogany railway-waiting-room clock stopped dead on the day, and after much discussion, they decided to donate it to the West Bethel Baptist Church.

Twelve

That summer, for all the children of the church, Pastor and Mrs. Sutherland scheduled the church's annual Vacation Bible School during the first week of July. During the week before, the church sponsored a special contest for all the children in the church. The purpose of the campaign was to encourage the West Bethel children to go out and invite all the children—as many as possible—from the surrounding area to attend the West Bethel Vacation Bible School classes.

"We want to hold the biggest Vacation Bible School in all of Northwest Arkansas," Brother Sutherland said. We're gonna be bigger than Bethel in Gentry; bigger than Harvard Avenue in Siloam Springs; and we're even gonna try to be bigger than First Baptist over in Springdale."

When Brother Sutherland explained all that, the whole congregation sighed with premature exhaustion. In my own heart and mind, I wondered, "Bigger than Harvard Avenue in Siloam…or First Baptist in Springdale?" I knew nothing about those churches other than that they were really big. "Why those are the Goliaths of the church world! Where they gonna put all them kids out at our little Grange House?"

According to Reverend Sutherland's idea, each day the children of the church were expected to invite as many of their friends and neighbors as they could, and then everyday, the Sutherlands would count all the guests.

Whoever brought in the most outsiders to Vacation Bible School would win a free trip down to McCaulley's Dairyette in Siloam Springs. At the end of the week, the child who had brought in the most visitors for the week would win two free tickets to visit the Old Spanish Treasure Cave up just north of Gravette.

Word about the contest spread quickly among the West Bethel children, and the hope of winning the contest excited everyone in the church. The kids in the Sunday School began to think about all the friends and relatives they might invite. Mrs. Sutherland had arranged for all the church mothers to provide cookies and Kool-Aid for the snacks, and the Hillcrest Dairy was going to supply all the paper cups and ice cream bars necessary for the whole week. The Sutherlands had asked all the folk around to put up signs and to make the Bible school known among everyone. Back in early June, Pastor Sutherland had already asked Mama if we would put up a sign at the station, and, of course, we did. With my daddy gone, I now observed that the Sutherlands always seemed to approach my mama–rather than Granddaddy–with regard to their requests and their plans. This struck me as somewhat odd, and I wondered about it for awhile. It seemed to me that, to show respect, they should have talked to Granddaddy about it first. For whatever reason, this unusual strategy somehow reminded me of that day when we caught those two deacons and my Sunday school teacher in an inconsistency, and for the first time in my life, I began to question the veracity of Reverend Sutherland's faith and testimony. I decided I'd talk to Granddaddy about it all.

Granddaddy impressed me as someone who wasn't completely satisfied with the nature of the events unfolding around us. Although Granddaddy was indeed a Christian, a Baptist, and a gentleman, nevertheless, he studied these present activities with an almost scholarly interest and just a little suspicion. I believed that he may have sensed something deceptive, and I wondered if we were thinking similar thoughts. By his character and personal testimony, I knew that he never questioned the nature of his salvation. I was aware that, in his heart, he certainly had his reservations about the broader motivations of our denomination, but these circumstances were basically out of his control, and as long as he had any say in the local church affairs, he could keep respectfully quiet about what went on elsewhere. No one in Northwest

Arkansas was a more exemplary gentleman than my granddaddy. I believed in the Vacation Bible School because I had gotten saved there a couple of years back; it was a legitimate ministry, and I could lay up a solid testimony to that fact. Still, I felt there was something strange going on, and I was sure that Granddaddy probably saw it, too.

"Granddaddy," I began, "I have an important question."

"What is it, son?" he asked. He could tell that I was in a serious mood.

"Well, I noticed that the Reverend Sutherland asked Mama if he could put up some Bible school signs out in front of our station."

"Yeah. He did the right thing by askin'. We don't put signs up on other people's property without first askin'," he stated.

"Don't you think he should have asked you first?"

"Why, son, I'm amazed at your perceptivity! Maybe all our trainin's startin' to pay off now!"

"What do you mean, Granddaddy? I'm not followin' you."

"Well, here's what I mean, boy. We been tryin' to train you up to become a gentleman, and here you are–almost thirteen years old–and you're startin' to learn it! That's what I mean. Almost thirteen and you've a caught onto somethin' that the good old Reverend-Doctor may have missed his-self."

"Well, what do you mean by that, Granddaddy?"

"Well son, when a real gentleman has a request or wants somethin' from someone–especially when it's a lady–he doesn't just go first to the mistress of the house when there's a older man present, and well, normally that'd be her husband. The reverend has pulled what some folks call the old 'Mother Mary' trick, and it plays on the soft hearts of tender women–it intentionally takes advantage of their emotions. You see, son, a woman doesn't reason quite like a man does, and sometimes she makes up her mind with her heart instead o' her brain. That don't mean she's always wrong; it's jist the way God made her, that's all."

"Well, Granddaddy…I don't understand…who is Mother Mary, and how does she come into it?"

"Well, o' course Mary is the mother of our Lord Jesus Christ. And some people, when they pray and they want God to do somethin' fer them or give 'em somethin,' but they're afraid to come right out and ask Him fer it 'cause they think, 'Why, He's gonna reject me and my request and maybe strike me down dead.' They're already convinced that He flat out ain't gonna give 'em what they want. So they figure, 'Well, since God ain't really disposed to gimme what I'm a wantin,' maybe if I ask the blessèd virgin, that is, Mother Mary, and ask her fer it, she might could cry up a few tears and smooth it all down fer me with the Almighty, and He'll be more inclined to change His mind fer me because He ain't never turned down any request that the sweet and holy Mother Mary ever made.' That's what some folk actually believes.

"Now, son," Granddaddy continued, "that ain't the way a real man–especially if he's a gentleman–does his bidness. You see...a real gentleman initially takes up his case by meetin' firsthand with the other gentleman of the house–normally it's the woman's husband, but it could also be her Daddy or even her son–and he says somethin' like, 'Sir, I'd like to propose a small request, if I may, and I wonder if you'd be so kind as to enquire of the lady of the house if...,' and then he states his matter. He don't go straight to the woman 'cause it ain't proper; it shows disrespect to do it like that. A real gentleman respects the weaknesses of a lady, and don't try to take advantage of her."

"Granddaddy, do some people actually believe all that...that stuff about the Mother Mary?" I asked.

"Yessir! There's a whole bunch o' folk that believes in it," Granddaddy said.

After I thought about it for a few minutes, I asked him, "Granddaddy, do you suppose that Brother Sutherland was tryin' to take advantage of Mama by skirtin' around you 'bout them signs? You think he was tryin' to charm her to get what he wanted out of her?" Just that thought alone–in the absence of my daddy–that another man might attempt to take advantage of my poor, defenseless Mama, and on top of that, he being a *Reverend!* It began to make me angry.

"Well, boy, I'm gonna let you in on a little secret. Fer a long time, I felt like Brother Sutherland was a good man, upright, and a gentleman, too, and he ain't never given me a reason to believe otherwise. But in these last few years, I don't know what's got into him; it sure seems like he's changed. I'd have given him as much permission to put them signs up, just the same as yer Mama, but it puzzles me that he'd go around me, especially since yer Daddy's gone; he ought to know better than that. I cain't say that he was a charmin' yer Mama, but he sure figured out quick how to get what he wanted by askin' her first."

Granddaddy and I sat there together and thought about it for awhile. And then he also said, "It's of great interest to me that the reverend is having a contest to bring in lots of kids to the Bible school. That reminds me a little of what they do in the business world to get their sales up. Looks to me just a little like he's a usin' them kids to do his recruitin,' sort of. It'll be interestin' to see which kids get them prizes. You gonna recruit some kids fer that Bible school, son?"

"I dunno, Granddaddy. I sure thought about it."

"Now, boy, you seem a little discouraged after our talk. Are you all right?"

"Yessir. I'll be all right. I'm just a little tired, that's all." I could tell that the wheels of his mind were turning because he suspected a lot more than he was revealing. Granddaddy was like that. He would hold his cards until it was time to play them, and he knew exactly when. He knew how to bluff, and he knew how to call–and when. I wanted so much to tell him about that incident with Brother Pickett, Brother Simpson, and Deacon Ellis. But then I started thinking about it, and I was certain that, if I revealed it, somehow, Deacon Ellis would turn it all around and find a way to make it look like we were in the wrong. And then the possibility dawned on me that Brother Pickett might have intentionally let us out of Sunday School classes early so that it would look like we were playing hooky from Sunday school class so he could meet all his friends out back for a smoke. Then I wondered if they were meeting out there for some other reasons, too? My mind raced with all kinds of thoughts and questions regarding their true motives for meeting out behind the church, but I was too tired to think it all through carefully. I decided, like Granddaddy, to hold my cards. I'd play them when the time was right. The trouble was–at my age–I wasn't exactly sure that I'd know when the time was right.

Thirteen

Vacation Bible School would start on Monday, July first. I didn't know a whole lot of people to invite, so I thought I would just ask kids whose parents stopped in for gas at our station. In one car there were some kids from down around Cincinnati, Arkansas, but they were just passing through, so I couldn't invite them. The next day some kids from Anderson, Missouri, came through, too. None of them were relatives of anyone I knew, and they weren't staying in Y-City Station any longer than it took their parents to buy gas or them to use our rest room, so recruiting those kids for the Bible school was just a plain waste of time. Some of the local kids came through with their parents, but most of those kids went to our church, and they were already recruiting other kids, too. On Saturday, Carol Ann and her sister, Lynnette, came through with Mr. Crawford.

Surely, I thought to myself, *it would do no harm to ask her. The worst thing that could happen is that she would say 'no.'*

"Hi, Carol Ann. How're you doin'?"

"I'm doin' fine. How're you doin?"

"I'm fine, too," I said. "Carol Ann, would you like…uh…I mean…how would you like to…what I mean is…would you like to go with me to our Vacation Bible School next week?"

"What? What did you say?"

"Well, I'm just a wonderin'…our church is holdin' its Vacation Bible School next week, and I thought you might like to go…if we bring a lot of newcomers, we might could win a visit to McCaulley's down in Siloam."

"Do you mean…is this…like a date or somethin'?"

Now I was really embarrassed because she had totally misunderstood me. All I wanted was to try to recruit a whole bunch of kids for Bible school and win that trip to McCaulley's, and here I had Carol Ann thinking I was asking her out on a date of all things. I never had a date in my life and had no intention of having one now, and here I was–already in hot water about it– and with Carol Ann Crawford of all people! I had to think fast about it; what would a gentleman say to make it right?

"No, Carol Ann…it ain't a date…and I 'pologize fer that."

"It ain't a date?" she interrupted. "Well, if it ain't a date, then what is it?"

"Well, I was tryin' to tell you…and, my goodness! I beg pardon fer misleadin' you because I never meant to." I hoped that might clear me. I went on…

"I'm just a recruitin' other kids to come along with me to the Bible school, that's all. It'll be a fun time; they have a lot of super things planned fer that week."

"Where's it at?"

"Out at West Bethel…at the Grange House."

"Why, that's a Baptist church! I cain't go there!"

Carol Ann, that don't matter. Anyone can come…especially you Methodists."

"No, thanks. I don't want to. Besides, at Shining Light, we done had our Vacation Bible School."

"Yeah? How was it?"

"It was lots of fun. Ever' day we had special treats. They had a puppet show, and we went field trippin' out yonder to a poultry farm past Gravette; they had baby chicks out there, and them chicks was so cute! They had baby chicks, baby ducks, and, I tell you, their little baby pigs was jist darlin'. Why, we had a great time."

"They had baby pigs?" I asked.

"Yes, and they was as cute as could be."

"Well, after your Bible school, I don't wonder that you'd pass on ours."

I was embarrassed to ask Carol Ann, but then I really felt foolish when she said she didn't want to go. *If this was the best I could do at recruitin,'* I thought, *then I'll never win any prizes.*

A little later, Sue Linda Culpepper came through the station with her Mama, but after my experience with Carol Ann, I decided to let someone else try to recruit Sue Linda. And then after awhile, Donnie Joe's parents stopped in to buy some gas, and Donnie Joe was sitting in the back seat of their car.

"Hey Donnie Joe, how're y'all doin' today?"

"We're fine. You wanna go with me and be my guest at the Bible school?" he asked me.

"Donnie Joe!" I said. "You cain't recruit somebody that already goes to West Bethel!"

"Why not?" he asked. "It ain't against the rules!"

"Why, it sure is!"

"It ain't either! Who says it's against the rules?"

"O' course it is. You just don't do that!" And then, for the briefest of moments, Donnie Joe's expression hit me dead on. I stopped and wondered about it: rules? What rules? Surely the Bible school had rules about recruiting. But who made them, and where did you go to find them? Here I was defending the rules, and now it occurred to me that I had never heard them or seen them. I couldn't recall Brother Sutherland talking about any rules; he only said there would be a contest. I knew Donnie Joe, and I knew that he was not concerned about keeping those rules any more than he was about breaking them. Donnie Joe was simply a brute, and everything he did–he did brutishly–and that's not your everyday ladies' gossip thrown around down at the hairdresser's across from the five and dime on Main Street–that's just how he was.

For example, in baseball, the only rule Donnie Joe ever recognized was an umpire, and he would never argue with an umpire. With respect to authority, he always appeared to be a gentleman on the field, although he would actually do whatever he thought he could get away with. If the coach told him to step up to the plate and smash that ball right out of the park, Donnie Joe would attempt to carry out that act, as well as every successive one, to its extreme. If he hit the ball out of the park, it didn't matter to him where the ball fell with respect to the foul lines; he would simply interpret his action as a home run, play his hit for all it was worth, and run clear around the diamond into home plate–unless the umpire shouted "foul ball!" In running around the bases, Donnie Joe made every effort to knock out a few infielders and take the catcher out at home plate, but he never intended anything malicious by doing it. If you were on his opposing team, you simply tried to stay out of his way.

Donnie Joe's mind ran quickly from one subject to the other, and at this point, he was already focused on some other issue. He didn't think much. I can't really say why it was so, but for some peculiar reason, Donnie Joe the human being simply reminded me of an old boxer dog named Caesar that used to belong to Mr. Cecil B. Whittaker, who lived way out past our house. By no means one of our regular customers, Mr. Whittaker might drive his pick-up truck in and stop now and then at our station for one reason or another. Now, Mr. Whittaker was neither a very good driver nor was he inclined to keep his vehicle even the slightest bit clean. Caesar always rode around in the back bed of that pick-up truck, and he usually sat with his head and face straight up into the wind. One day, when they were coming down our road, Mr. Whittaker was taking the curves and the hills pretty fast, and one of the oil cans in the back broke open and leaked oil all over the bed of the pick-up truck. Back in that pick-up bed, Caesar–already slipping and sliding around from Mr. Whittaker's poor driving–suddenly came into contact with that oil, and he really began to lose his balance. Mr. Whittaker never slowed down for a curve or a bump, and after Caesar was thoroughly soaked with a can of Pennzoil 10W-30, Mr. Whittaker almost lost his dog overboard on the highway several times. But Caesar had no idea what was happening to him; he just slid and bounced around as if that's how life normally was for a dog that rode around in the back of a pick-up truck.

When they pulled into our station, Caesar jumped out of the truck bed, and he ran way off into the field across the east side of Highway 59. He was gone for a couple of hours.

"Don't you pay that dawg no mind now," Mr. Whittaker said. "He be back shortly, and he recover. He likes to ride around like that."

Mr. Whittaker sat there and talked on and on and spat tobacco in a can for about two hours. I was thankful that he used a can. Then Caesar came back. He still had oil and grime and dust all over his belly, his flank, and his hindquarters. It was obvious that he had been running; his heart was pounding, his muscular chest heaving and panting, his tongue sticking out and his mouth foaming all over the place, and his little stump of a tail wagging like the whole dog had just been charged up by a single stroke of lightning. He didn't really bark, but he just growled deeply. I took him over to the hose and filled up an old bucket with water into which he stuck his whole face–nose and all–and sloshed and slurped the water until he had enough. Then Caesar proudly strutted over to the right rear tire of Mr. Whittaker's truck, sniffed around for a few moments, positioned himself somewhat awkwardly before lifting his left hind leg, and then he released his floodgates all over the truck fender and the tire. When he finished, he raised his nose into the wind and pranced over to the front of the truck, where he crawled directly under the engine of Mr. Whittaker's truck and lay there panting until he fell asleep. When Mr. Whittaker was ready to leave, he simply said:

"Well, I got to go."

And the next thing we all heard was an awfully loud and terrible "THUNK!" Old Caesar had forgotten that he was sleeping under a truck engine, and the moment he heard his master's voice, he woke up from his sleep and immediately raised his rock-hard skull directly up into the oil pan and the frame of that truck. Dazed, Caesar merely pulled himself out and jumped right back into the bed of the pick-up just fast enough to avoid getting hit by Mr. Whittaker as he drove by. Now I don't know why, but Donnie Joe simply reminded me of that old dog Caesar.

"You know," Donnie Joe said, "we need to get out there and do some fishin' soon, or they'll all be gone."

"Yeah, I know. I been too busy here he'pin' at the station, Donnie Joe. Maybe we can go sometime like…well, maybe the week after Bible school."

Fourteen

On Sunday morning, Brother Pickett was acting suspicious during Sunday school again. Donnie Joe, Wayne Spillman, and I thought for sure that he was going to let us out early so he could meet out back for a smoke with his friends, but he didn't. We all went upstairs into the big room where the worship service was held, and I found my parents, who always required me to sit with them. It was a part of my training as a young Baptist gentleman. Donnie Joe and Wayne could sit just about wherever they wanted to, but when I raised that matter with my parents and grandparents, their response was simple:

"Those two boys ain't in trainin'–leastwise not by parents that require them to become young gentlemen."

Outside, the weather was clear and beautiful. The sun was bright and hot, and its rays beat down on the Grange House. Inside, the worship hall was hot and sticky. The windows were all raised up, but there was no breeze blowing through. The big room had four, black, Emerson ceiling fans, three of which were working, although they were rotating very slowly. The fans made a terribly monotonous, low-pitched humming sound, and if you began to give it any thought, that sound would stick with you in your head, and eventually it would cause you to go crazy. It was a form of church torture. The one in the area where we were sitting was broken, so no air was moving around us at all. The ushers had passed out little hand-fans, and people were fanning themselves as they sat in the pews and waited for services to begin.

In another moment, Miss Audrey Jane Bankston began to play the organ, and everyone in the hall became immediately quiet. Miss Audrey was the secret love of my life. She was about twenty-five years old, and from the time when I first saw her, I thought she was the most beautiful, elegant, and stylish person I had ever seen. She had the softest, most delicate hands and the longest, slenderest fingers, and they just seemed to move with grace over the keys as she played the organ. I never saw her talk to anyone; like an angel, she simply appeared when her presence was required, and she vanished when it was not. She was always well-dressed, and she had long, brown hair, the deepest blue eyes, and the sweetest face. For me, Miss Audrey was a type of everything that is beautiful. I knew that Miss Audrey was too old for me, but from that time on, she represented God's answer to my prayer about girls:

"Lord, I know this Miss Audrey's too old fer me, but when it's my time, please give me a girl who is as beautiful as she is. Give me a girl just like her." After Miss Audrey finished playing her first song, Brother Pickett and his group of Deacon friends stepped into the church. They were late, and I had a pretty good idea why.

Forest King, who sold used cars at Friendly Forest's Used Cars in Gentry, was our song leader. He was a flashy man all dressed up in the latest western wear. He had a heavy gold ring on his right ring finger, and he wore a sparkly big watch that rolled around on his left wrist. He was wearing the most beautiful gray, soft-leather cowboy boots I had ever seen. Mr. King liked to flirt with Miss Audrey from the pulpit; he would frequently wink at her, and I didn't like him very much on account of that.

Brother King started off the worship service that Sunday morning with a long-winded prayer and then he made everyone stand to sing the opening hymn–"Onward Christian Soldiers." Then he sat everyone down and greeted all the visitors before he made the announcements.

"Now, dear brothers and sisters," he said. "This is a special week for all of us because tomorrow morning, we're gonna kick off our annual Vacation Bible School. And don't forget our Fourth of July picnic dinner right here on the grounds this Thursday. We're gonna start our Bible school tomorrow mornin' promptly at eight-thirty right here in the Grange House. And there's gonna be a whole lot o' special events–I understand they got a contest goin' on for all the kids who bring in the most visitors and guests–and they're gonna have ice cream and puppets and maybe a field trip or two over to one of the poultry farms. So y'all plan to come now; bring out your neighbors and enjoy all the fun."

Somewhere, I thought I heard about a similar Vacation Bible school program taking place at another church, and I then wondered if Brother and Sister Sutherland were just copying our program from theirs. Furthermore, I really wondered sometimes about how these adults came up with their ideas about the so-called "fun" activities. For a kid growing up in Northwest Arkansas, how could a field trip to a poultry farm be considered fun? Why couldn't they take us all out to the lake and go on a boat ride or go fishing or visit a rattlesnake ranch somewhere? As I was going on thirteen, I convinced myself that I was probably getting too old for the Bible school program.

Brother King made a few more announcements, and then he led us in a few more songs. After that, he announced that the church was now going to take up its weekly offering, and they would be passing the plate directly.

"Would the gentlemen in the back of the church please come forward so we can receive our regular Sunday mornin' tithes and offerings?"

Four men came forward and stopped just in front of the communion table. Three of them were on the deacon Board, one of whom was Deacon Ellis. Each man was holding a shiny brass offering plate.

"Brother Ellis, would you mind sayin' the blessing over our offering today?" Brother King asked.

"Yessir." Brother Ellis cocked his head over at some strange angle to the right, and then he looked up to the ceiling. Then he said, "Church, let us pray." After that, he bowed his head down and began, "Dear Lord, thank you so much fer this wonderful opportunity to bring our 'umble tithes and offerin's to You today. Lord, we pray that You'd multiply these blesséd gifts from our hands today. Bless the hands that giveth and taketh, Lord; bless those who give, and bless those who receive; and bless us, we pray, that none of 'em may ever return void, Lord. Amen."

His prayer struck me as just a little odd, but I couldn't pinpoint exactly why. Now the four gentlemen turned around; two of them walked over to each of the respective, far ends of the pews, and the other two walked down through the middle aisle. They were all passing the brass offering plates back and forth through the hands of the worshipers sitting in the pews. People all over the church were pulling money and envelopes out of their purses and pockets and giving their tithes and offerings, and the brass plates began filling up. Deacon Ellis came to the end of our aisle to wait for the plate. Waiting for the plate to come back to him, he stood there for a moment, and then he looked all around the church. He looked up at Pastor Sutherland who had his head bowed and his eyes closed; either he was sleeping, or he was deep in prayer and meditation. Then Brother Ellis looked over at Brother King, who was staring at Miss Audrey, who was playing the offertory. While he waited impatiently for us to pass the plate to him, Deacon Ellis was squirming nervously back and forth, like someone who needed a cigarette. People in our aisle were fumbling around with both the plate and their money, and, as a result, the plate was moving very slowly through our aisle toward Deacon Ellis. Finally, the plate landed in his hand, and then, to my great disbelief, my eyes witnessed an act of the most heinous and blazing submission to the devil's temptation ever expressed in–of all places–the very heart of the church, not only right under everyone's nose, but also, as they say, "within the twinkling of an eye." It happened so fast that I was almost persuaded to believe that it really didn't happen–but it did. I tried to convince myself that my vision was blurred or perhaps my eyes were playing tricks on me–but they were not. I refused to believe it and wished I had never seen it, but all my refusals and my wishes simply ran contrary to broad-daylight reality. Just as Deacon Ellis received in his right hand the brass plate that was almost overflowing its contents of tithes and offerings, he grabbed a whole handful of cash and envelopes with his left hand and stuffed the entire bundle directly into his side coat pocket! The action of his hand was instantaneous–lightning fast–clearly that of a professional. The deacon certainly must have believed that no one saw him, but he was hopelessly wrong. In another moment, I became so nervous and frightened that I didn't know what to do.

Did he notice that I saw what he had done? What if he knows that I know? He might try to come after me.

But evidently no other person in the whole church witnessed a thing. This was even more shocking for me. How could no one see? Immediately, I grew terribly worried, and I squirmed and fidgeted throughout the whole rest of the church service. I heard not a single word of Brother Sutherland's message that morning, and I grew sick unto death. Because I felt like I was the only other person who knew about the theft, I began to feel as guilty as if I had stolen that money myself. Then, for a moment, I took some comfort in the fact that Daddy was here–he was home for the weekend. After church, I could tell him about it, and he would tell Reverend Sutherland, and then it would all be over. I just knew that Dr. Sutherland would march right over to that sorry Deacon Ellis, confront him face to face over his sin, and catch him red-handed with all that money stashed away in his coat pocket. I began to take confidence that the reverend would immediately strip the thief of his Deacon's title, excommunicate him out of the church right then and there, and commit him straight to hell. For some strange reason, it gave me great pleasure to think about that. But then, at that very moment, I looked over, and there was Deacon Ellis–sitting in the pew over there with a smirk on his face. I could see him; he was just sitting across the aisle on the other side of the church. He just sat there, sneering. I was certain that my facial expression wasn't very friendly. Suddenly, it was almost as if he must have felt me looking at him, and he began to turn his face over to look in my direction, but before his eyes met mine, I quickly looked down at the floor. The pressure of seeing him and knowing what he did was mounting. Furthermore, his presence in the worship hall was becoming oppressive to me.

How could he do that? I silently asked myself over and over again. *A deacon in the church–of all things–how could he do it?*

In my mind, my thoughts were racing as fast as my heart was pounding. I felt like I had to get out of that hall, but on that particular Sunday, Reverend Sutherland preached such a long and strong message that five people got convicted to come forward. The first three of them didn't come forward until the fourth verse of Just As I Am. In tears, they came forward, all claiming that they had "slid back into the ways of the world," and they needed the "cleansing power of re-dedication." Of course, Pastor Sutherland had to draw that part all out and ask each one of them to lay up some kind of confession before the whole church. After singing another whole round of the same song, two more people came forward to change their membership from some other church to ours. Brother Sutherland pointed out that they would accomplish this change "by letter," and then he asked the current church membership to approve their request, pending receipt of their letter, of course. I could understand stretching the service out that long for a salvation, but those re-dedications and membership changes surely could have waited one more week.

Fifteen

After the meeting was over, I quickly darted out of that church and tried to get as far away from Deacon Ellis as I could. I was so frightened that I expected to meet him around every corner and behind every tree. From a safe distance out on the Grange House grounds, I waited where I could see all the folks coming out of the church; I could just barely hear them greeting Brother Sutherland and shaking his hand there at the church door. My heart was still pounding, and I kept thinking that, somehow, the deacon was aware that I saw everything he did. I was so afraid that I thought he might sneak up on me from behind.

Maybe you didn't really see what you think you seen, my conscience told me. And then it said, *You did see it, and you know you seen it.* I felt tormented by my own heart.

In another moment, I saw Brother Pickett emerge from the church house, and he was shaking Brother Sutherland's hand.

"Why, you old hypocrite!" I whispered.

Then Brother Pickett came out, and Deacon Ellis was right on his heels. At that moment, it dawned on me that maybe both of them were in cahoots with each other; perhaps, they were both robbing the church. But why? Of course, I had no proof, but that's how my mind ran. After all, I figured that, since they were out smoking together behind the outhouse, maybe they were engaging in other wickedness together, too.

In another moment, Donnie Joe and Wayne were at my side.

"What are you doin' a way over here?"

"Yeah, who you spyin' on?"

"I ain't spyin'!" I said.

"Well, it don't look like that to me. What do you think, Wayne?"

"He's definitely a spyin' on someone…I believe he's a looking up there and studyin' that Becky Lou Hollister…"

"No, I ain't!" I said.

"Well, if you ain't spyin' on Becky Lou, you must be watchin' fer that new girl…what's her name?" Wayne asked.

"Her name's…uh…is it…Dawson?"

"Yeah, that's it. You're spyin' on that new Dawson girl!"

"I ain't either!" I said.

And then I was thinking to myself, *If these two are gettin' the impression that I'm a spyin,' maybe I'm just totally unable to conceal anything from anyone; it's probably all written in plain English straight across my face!* I felt embarrassed and tormented by it all.

Immediately, I took notice that Brother Pickett and Deacon Ellis were talking together and shaking hands, but then Mama called me.

"Boy, where'd you disappear to…and so fast?" she asked. "We got to get on home now."

We went home and had our Sunday dinner and our Sunday afternoon nap, although I had trouble sleeping. I wanted to tell Daddy what I had seen earlier at church, but I didn't quite know how to say it to him. And I was still afraid to talk about it, and then I thought, *Maybe it's best not to trouble him about it before he leaves fer Joplin again; if I tell him, he'll just worry over it up yonder while he's on the road.*

The next day, Vacation Bible School started. Mama said that Tawna Rae still wasn't ready to go that year, but she wanted J-Earl and me to go. I felt like I was getting too old for Vacation Bible School, and I was much more interested in the work down at the station, but Mama said that she and Tawna Rae would replace me while I was in Bible school, and I could come back to work in the afternoons after my class.

"Besides," Mama said. "I don't want J-Earl a ridin' his bike all alone up that far. You need to stay right there…ride up there with him, and keep an eye on him."

I wasn't very excited about it–especially the part about watching J-Earl– but I knew that Donnie Joe and Wayne would be going, and others my age would be there, too. And, to be honest, I had to confess that I was a little interested to see who would win the prizes for recruiting the most kids to Bible school, even though I knew it wouldn't be me.

Early that morning, as soon as J-Earl and I arrived at the Grange House, I knew immediately that the recruiting contest was all over. In fact, there really was no contest at all. Apparently, Starla Sutherland was getting the credit– and today's visit to McCaulley's Dairyette–for bringing an entire busload of kids up from Siloam Springs and all points south; she would be today's winner–hands down. It seems that, the good Dr. Sutherland had somehow managed to borrow an old church bus from somewhere down in Siloam Springs, and he and Starla stopped to recruit kids for Bible school everywhere along the way clear up to the Grange House. They even picked up Fishbait Riggins.

With renewed concern, I felt that Brother Sutherland's bus recruiting for Starla was another example of his unfairness and deception. I would almost say it was bordering on being hypocritical, too. It made me discouraged about attending the Bible school and even more discouraged about trying to recruit anyone.

"Donnie Joe," I said. "What do you think about that?"

"What?" he asked. "What's to think about?"

"About them recruitin' all them kids fer Starla?"

"I dunno," he said. "I guess he can do it if he wants to. I mean, he is the preacher, you know. He can do whatever he likes."

"Yeah," Wayne said. "He is the preacher…and preachers can do whatever they like."

"Well," I said. "Don't you think Starla ought to recruit fer herself?"

"Why?" asked Donnie Joe. "If your daddy was the preacher…wouldn't you get him to do all yer recruitin' fer you?"

"I sure would," said Wayne. "If I was the preacher, I'd do anything that

Starla asked me." He went on, "…and if I were Starla…I'd…"

"Well, you ain't either the preacher or Starla," I interrupted. "Y'all are downright stupid!" Sometimes I wondered how I ended up in the same class with those two individuals.

During the Bible school classes that morning, I had a great deal of trouble concentrating on the lessons, which I felt were somewhat childish to begin with. After all, here I was–right back at the Grange House the very next day after the theft–and I kept reviewing that awful event from yesterday. Furthermore, I fully expected to see Deacon Ellis jumping out at me from the baptistry, from the choir robe closet, or from behind the piano when he wasn't hiding in every other little nook and cranny of the hall. At the break time, Flora Riggins came over to say hello to me.

"Hey, J.D. You know what?" she said to me.

"Hi there, Fishbait. No. What?" By now, she had grown used to her nickname, and I understood that she had come to like it.

"My mama and daddy's gonna buy a café."

"What?"

"That's right. A restaurant. They're buyin' that old place called Sleepy's down there close to where fifty-nine and sixty-eight comes together. The deal is already in the works. And you know what else? I'm gonna wait on tables down there fer my folks, and it won't be long till I'm rich and outta here!"

"What do you mean, 'outta here!' Where ya goin? Well…that's somethin'! Are you folks givin' up the farm? I mean, are they goin' outta the chicken bidness?"

"No, Stafford! They ain't goin' outta no bidness. They're dy-versa-fyin'!"

"Dy-whats-a-fyin'? What's that mean?"

"They're expandin' all their bidnesses…gettin' bigger."

"How they gonna do that?"

"Well, when Sky gets back from out yonder in Kansas, he's gonna run our farm. We're gonna buy old Sleepy's Place and clean it all up…Daddy and Mama are gonna run our restaurant, and I get to wait on tables for tip money."

I couldn't imagine where the Riggins would come up with the money to buy a broken-down café, and I also knew that, within just one hatching and growing cycle, Sky would ruin whatever broiler business they had left. Moreover, I could not envision the Riggins family running any café or restaurant in which people would actually want to eat. This news was hard to believe, and I wondered if Fishbait was following in her daddy's footsteps at telling tall tales. On the other hand, she said the deal was already in the works, and it sounded like they were moving forward to acquire the property.

Sixteen

On Tuesday and Wednesday, the Bible school followed pretty much the same course and program that it had begun with on Monday. Pastor Sutherland brought up another large group of bus recruits, and Starla got all the credit and the prizes. I sensed that the Sutherlands would play out this game plan everyday for the rest of the week. It was especially discouraging for all those who really tried to recruit more kids, but by now, I had already decided that neither my interests nor my recruiting skills were strong enough to assist the Bible school in any valuable way. Thus, recognizing that the contest was basically fixed from the start, I figured that I would focus my efforts and my energies on more important matters.

Thursday was the Fourth of July, and after the morning Bible school classes, the whole church gathered together for our annual, West Bethel Fourth of July Picnic which was held right on the grounds at the Grange House. While all the kids were attending classes in the morning, some of the men of the church had arrived early to start fires for grilling, and by noon, the smell of hot dogs, hamburgers, roasted chicken, and barbecued ribs permeated the air all around the grounds. Mr. Harlan Cooley, who ran the local IGA grocery down in Gentry, provided two large tubs filled with ice and all kinds of soda pop. He also set up a big table upon which he donated hamburger and hot dog buns, sliced tomatoes, cheese, onions, pickles, mustard, and ketchup. He brought all these items down from his store, and with the help of Jimmy Skidmore, one of Mr. Cooley's workers, he set up a whole section of tables under the shade created by a large tent.

All the people of the church arrived within the hour after the Bible school was dismissed. The annual picnic was always a special time for everyone in the church. The women of the church provided all kinds of different salads, vegetables, casseroles, cooked foods, and home-baked desserts. Traditionally, the picnic was always a pot-luck affair–with everything set out together on several central tables–and everyone was free to take some of this or some of that. You could always count on the church folks to serve plenty of food for everyone.

Since it was the Fourth of July, Pastor Sutherland would bring out the American and the Christian flags from the Grange House, and then we would all form a big circle around the pastor. Together we would say the pledge of allegiance to each of the flags, just like we day everyday in the Bible school assembly. After that, Dr. Sutherland would present a short homily about the American freedoms that we share and enjoy. Then he would ask the venerable Judge William Cobb, who had retired several years ago from the county court over in Bentonville and moved somewhere out our way, to offer up a prayer for all the veterans and the soldiers who were currently serving our country. Judge Cobb was very old–well past ninety then, as I recall–and in spite of a gradual but advancing loss of hearing, he retained a sharp and witty mind. Everyone in the church loved and respected the old judge, and he was especially fond of the children.

"These little ones represent our direct touch with the future," Judge Cobb said. "Now y'all come an' gather round–quietly now–come on, while I pray."

The judge prayed over our country, our state, our community, and then over our church. He also prayed for the the veterans, and the soldiers, the mothers and fathers, and then he prayed for the children, and finally for our picnic. I noticed that the judge was able to carry on quite well in prayer without a prayer book; there was no question but what his prayers came from the heart.

After the judge finished, Reverend Sutherland said, "Now folks, less move on over toward those food tables and enjoy some o' that good picnic lunch."

The whole crowd moved up toward the tent where all the food was, and then Pastor Sutherland asked Brother Newton Odem, the head of our deacon board, to pray over the food. After the food had been blessed, two great lines of hungry church members formed around the buffet tables and slowly wound their way past some of Northwest Arkansas' finest summer cuisine.

Of course, Donnie Joe, Wayne, and I, together with Billy Stevens, Lester Henderson, Tommy Green, J.R. Thornton, and Bubby Dalton made every effort to crowd in at the front of the line–families notwithstanding–and put about three times as much food on those paper plates as they could hold. It seemed like everyone tried to out-eat the other on that day, but when it came to eating, no one could ever truly compete with the likes of Bubby Dalton. Bubby was one of the biggest and heaviest boys I'd ever seen, and he could eat a barrel of food. Wherever he went, he always had a pocket full of candy or a handy little sack full of cakes, cookies, or shelled pecans. He would say that he lived for shelled pecans. Bubby would eat all the time, and he claimed that, by eating, he was "in trainin' to become the biggest Razorback center that ever played the game."

"Why, I wanna take the place of three o' them linemen on that Razorback team. In fact, I'd like to replace the whole dang line!"

After eating as much lunch as we could hold–and then some–we would try to find a shady spot of grass and lie down for a little nap. It seemed like there were tables still full of food, but the afternoon was young, and the picnic would continue on until dark. We might lay there sleeping and dreaming away for an hour or so. Some of the men would walk off the appropriate distance, create two receiving pits, set up a couple of steel pins, and then play the game of horseshoes for the next few hours, while their wives would sit in the shade, watch their babies, and talk about their children, their gardens, their canning, their mending and sewing, and the quilts they would make for the women's missionary union of the church.

Suddenly, Buck Westerfield appeared out of nowhere–running across the entire Grange House lawn–and waking us up from our naps with the repetitious, personal announcement screaming from the top of his lungs that he had just now rounded up a whole bunch of Methodists, a couple of Presbyterians, and a few folks from the Haskell Avenue Church of Christ for a mid-afternoon, slow-pitch softball game that would commence here on the Grange House grounds in about forty-five minutes. Every year, the Methodists held their Fourth of July picnic in one section of the park in Gentry, and the Presbyterians held their picnic in another section of the same park. This year, the Presbyterians arrived at the park first, so they got the covered pavilion. The folks from Haskell Avenue Church of Christ had gotten a late start on annual picnics, but this year, which was their first attempt at an all-church picnic, they decided to hold theirs over at the far eastern end of Gentry Park.

The Methodist membership consisted of a large number of kids and teenagers, but hardly any of their adults ever wanted to play softball. Although the Presbyterians had a whole church full of old folks, they could field only a few qualified young players. Most of their people simply excused themselves by reason of "too many aches and pains in these bones to be playin' softball on this Fourth of July." As a result, all three of the other denominations joined together to create one team whose sole purpose was to challenge and defeat the West Bethel Baptists.

After the other team arrived, we practiced hitting and fielding for about ten or fifteen minutes, and then–within a short while–our game was underway. Any church member who wanted to play in the game could simply rotate in and out. Of course, we started the game with the utmost seriousness, but as time went on, it naturally got out of hand. At first base or in the batter's box, I was dead serious. I made a couple of good put-outs at first base, and I hit a single and a double. After I doubled, Lester hit one, too, and he brought me home. Bubby could hardly swing the bat, but that didn't matter. He got hit by a pitched ball and took first base, but he was so slow running to second base after the next hit that he was easily put out.

When it was my turn to rotate around and play left field and right field, or sit on the bench for a while, I began to grow bored very quickly–waiting for the seven year olds and the girls and everyone else–to hit the ball. We never let the little ones or the girls actually strike out or walk. They got the chance to wait as long as they liked for their pitch…and to swing all they liked until they hit that ball.

To accommodate all the players, we probably played a twenty-three- or twenty-four-inning game, the real score of which had been forgotten way back in the sixth or seventh inning. Eventually, many of the players–both theirs and ours–began rotating in and out of both teams to sneak in extra chances to hit the ball. I think I probably played about half the game before I decided it was time for me to rotate completely out of the game. Besides, by that time, I needed to pay a visit to the humble facilities out behind the Grange House.

I was in the outhouse no more than a minute or two, when I heard voices quickly approaching. At first, I thought that some folks were forming up a line outside and simply waiting on me to complete my business in there, but then, as the outsiders drew closer, I recognized the voices that now seemed to be all around me. Clearly, two of the voices belonged to none other than Deacon Ellis and Brother Pickett. However, I could not identify the third speaker. Suddenly, I became frightened. Overwhelming fear began to grip my heart, body, and soul, and I literally froze to the seat. In that moment, I sensed that, if I made the slightest sound, my presence would surely be discovered if it wasn't already known. In the next second, I fully expected the door to be wrenched wide open off its hinges–followed at last by someone either yanking me by my hair out of that little building or squeezing me down through the opening in the seat and into the filthy pit of eternal oblivion. With an uncanny grip, I seized the inside frame of the structure–and waited. The voices only got louder, and then I heard the rustling sound of cellophane and paper and the scratching of matches ripping against matchboxes. In another few seconds, I could smell the acrid odor and feel the warm, blue twists of tobacco smoke penetrating through the cracks and the tiny openings of the wooden framework. At that moment, I couldn't tell which was more repulsive–the smell of the smoke or that of the outhouse–but both was nauseating. The longer I sat there unnoticed, the more I resolved simply to sit there absolutely still–to wait and listen. I was most disturbed by what I heard.

"How much did you swag last Sunday?"

That was clearly the voice of Brother Pickett. Now I experienced an inner sense of relief, certain that my eyes had not misled me this past Sunday. Moreover, Brother Pickett had also just now confirmed my earlier suspicions–that he and the no-good, thieving deacon were in cahoots together–two rotten hypocrites both robbing the church. In secret, his own voice now incriminated him before me.

"I only got fifty-seven dollahs," the deacon said. "An' can ya believe it? One of the church members had the nerve to put an empty envelope in the plate; there wadn't even a dime in it! What a hypocrite who gives an empty envelope!"

"Anyone see ya do it?" said Brother Pickett.

"Nah!"

"Well, it ain't enough!" the third voice said.

Who was that? I quickly asked myself. I didn't recognize the voice of that person, and I wondered who it could be.

In the middle of all this, I just started to pray, *Now, please, Lord, please don't let them catch me in here! Oh, please, God! They'll kill me fer sure. Please don't let 'em find me in here.*

"We got to have more," the third voice said. "Way more than that!"

"Well, I'll tell ya what. Robbin' the church plates don't bring us nuthin'. We're just a wastin' our time takin' money outta them plates. All we're gittin' is nickels and dimes; it'll take us twenty years to get what we need this way."

"He's right. There ain't no big money in churches. We gotta go fer banks; that's where the money is."

"Well, it's a dern lot safer robbin' the church than it is tryin' to rob a bank. Does old Sutherland suspect anything?" the third voice asked again.

"He don't know nuthin'. He's too busy with his Bible school and recruitin' all them kids fer his sweet little Starla-pie–idn't she jist a little cutie-thing? Why…"

The third man interrupted abruptly, "Enough of that! You keep yer mind off that little tart, and ya focus on yer job. Less jist try to keep that old reverend completely in the dark…as much as possible."

"Well, I know…I know," the deacon said. "It's jist that you see a little sweetie cake like her, and…you know…yer mind begins to wander…"

"Hey, Deacon! I said enough of that now! We don't need fer our minds to be a wanderin'."

"We can keep this up fer a little while, but it don't bring much," said Brother Pickett. "I think we ought to hit that little bank down there in

Gentry…better still…how about hittin' the First State Bank of Arkansas up there in Decatur?"

"Well, I'm tellin' y'all this…it may be somewhat easier. I flat don't like all them eyes starin' at me up there in the church house. Sooner or later, someone's gonna see me!" said Deacon Ellis.

I didn't know how much longer I could stay quiet and undetected in that dreadful outhouse. I felt like I was starting to get sick, and I thought I might get all fidgety or maybe have to vomit if I didn't soon get some fresh air. Naturally, when I came in, I locked the outhouse door. But now I began thinking, *What if someone else comes down here and needs to use this facility, and they try to open that door?* And then I quickly added to my prayer list: *Oh, Lord…please don't let anyone have to use this outhouse until this is all past!*

Then the unknown partner in this crime trio said, "Well, less snuff out them smokes and get back up that hill. We're gonna take up the First State Bank of Arkansas in Decatur during our next meetin'."

Needless to say, I had already concluded my personal business in that outhouse sometime during the last eternity. Throughout the next minute or so, it seemed like I waited another eternity, after which I was finally able to unlock the door, thrust it open, and run out from there–gulping in all the fresh air I could. I ran as fast as I could up the hill to the Grange House, and I sat down in the shade next to the building. I was alone, and I felt it. This situation was getting worse–out of hand, even. I had to think it through, and yet I was frightened to death. My mind was churning thoughts all over the place. I wanted to keep a clear head about me and to avoid thinking thoughts that might be directed by fear. I just sat there for a long time trying to decide what to do.

Seventeen

For the present, I was satisfied that my current knowledge placed reliable and definite limitations on my initial suspicions. It was one thing to suspect Brother Pickett of evil-doing, but it was quite another to know that three men were involved. Moreover, the theft of fifty-seven dollars taken from the church offering plate also seemed to be on a different plane than the intent to rob a branch of the First State Bank of Arkansas, although my daddy always taught me–and I believed it to be true–that stealing is stealing, and sin is sin–regardless of the price tag. I was puzzled by the events and revelations of the past few days, and I wondered how and to whom I might best communicate this information in such a way that it might be received as truth rather than the fantasies of a young boy. Moreover, I wondered who that third, unknown individual might be. I couldn't say that I recognized his voice at all, and yet, I reasoned that it had to be someone who was a member of our church. Whoever it was, he was definitely present today at our church picnic–and that meant that he was somewhere on the grounds right now! Who was this person? I resolved to get up and go mix in with the church crowd to see if there was someone whose voice might reveal his face or establish his name.

I walked up to the front of the Grange House and bumped smack into my mama.

"Boy! Where you been a hidin'? We been a lookin' fer you fer the last hour!"

"I'm sorry, Mama! I been out back fer awhile…usin' the facilities."

"Fer an hour?"

"Yes, ma'am. I…I felt a little sick at my stomach, Mama. Maybe I ate a little too much." I tried to find an excuse that she could believe.

"That's all right, boy. We just didn't know where you was, and we been a little worried. Granddaddy, Grandma, and I are all gonna go on home directly, and we're gonna take Tawna Rae. We're all dawg tired, and we're gonna go set a spell on the back porch. You and J-Earl can stay fer the fireworks if you want to, but as soon as they're over, y'all get right on home then, you hear?"

"Yes, ma'am," I said.

I mingled around among the church crowd for awhile. I looked around at each face for a long time, but I just couldn't attach any face to that voice. I reasoned that, if I could locate Brother Pickett or Deacon Ellis, the stranger might be close by. I tried to listen for that voice again as long as I mingled around, but it never revealed itself. In the end, I could not locate either the face or the voice, although I saw a whole lot of people there at the picnic that I didn't really know.

Goodness! I thought to myself. *Do all these folk belong to our church?*

Some of the Methodists, the Presbyterians, and a few of the Haskell Avenue folks stayed after the game to partake of some good Christian fellowship with "their errant brothers and sisters of the Baptist persuasion," they said.

"Why, you Baptists sure know how to throw a good picnic," the Presbyterians said, trying to be complimentary.

"Yeah, it's 'cause we picnic jist like we baptize–we go whole hog–all out and all under, but ya' know, it's them Methodists what really knows how to party," someone from our church yelled out.

One of the Methodists said, "Now boys, let's not get personal or too rude here; after all, it is the Fourth of July. Besides, we all got to live together up there in heaven fer a long time–that is, of course–if y'all ever actually get there," to which there was a hearty round of laughter followed by a whole series of denominational jokes.

I wasn't in the mood for jokes, and I didn't find them particularly amusing. I sat around there for a good while listening for that certain voice, but I never heard it. A little later, I decided to go through the food line again. I took some apple pie and some cookies. I also had some cold watermelon, and there were still some cold bottles of Barq's Root Beer in the bottom of Mr. Cooley's soda-pop tub, but by now, most of the ice had melted to water.

After a little while, Lester, J.R., and Tommy came by.

"Howdy, y'all. Whatch-y'all been up to?"

"Nuthin'. We was thinkin' of goin' out fishin' tomorrow."

"Fishin'?"

"Yeah. Wanna come?"

"Where y'all goin'…and when? I mean, what time?"

"We thought we'd just play a little hooky from Bible class…"

"Are y'all goin' out there to old Slocumb's pond?"

"We might could…or maybe we could ride up there to the old Wilson place and fish at that pond. I mean, I don't care where it is, but I've had just about enough of Mrs. Sutherland's classes and Starla's prize-winnin's. Less get on out there and catch us a few largemouths."

"I was up at the Wilson place awhile back. That old place is all growed over with weeds, and the pond is filled with cottonmouths. Who runs that place now, anyway?"

"I dunno, but their hogs been out and runnin' wild all over the place…you cain't really fish out there anymore."

"Less go out to Slocumb's place. What do y'all think?"

In another moment, Donnie Joe and Wayne appeared, and they sat down. Then, right behind them, Bubby came over, too; he had a paper plate full of potato salad, a couple of thick slices of ham, some biscuits, sliced tomatoes and cucumbers, and the whole plate was topped off with almost half a cherry pie.

"Boys," I said. "Here's a riddle fer ya." I decided that it couldn't hurt to try to put my friends and classmates to a little test to see if they might reveal indirectly to me what I should do.

"A riddle?" asked J.R.

"Yeah. You know…kind of like a guessing game," Tommy said.

"Well, come on…what is it?" demanded Wayne. His curiosity was easily ignited.

"Well," I said. "Less just say that we found out that somebody…somebody like old…old Pastor Sutherland, for example…less just say we found out that instead of him bein' a reverend and all, that we found him out to be…well, less say, a murderer, so to speak."

"Well, so what?" Bubby replied. He had cherry pie all over his face and his shirt, and potato salad was dripping down off his plate onto his bare legs. In his appearance, Bubby was always a mess. "What difference does it make if he's a murderer or not?"

"Yeah, what are you gettin' at, Stafford?" Lester asked.

"Are you sayin' you know somethin' about him that none of us knows?" Tommy asked.

"No, I ain't really saying nuthin'…I'm a just thinkin'…what if…what if we only just learned somethin' new and completely different about someone we knew a long time, and until now, we thought he was all right, but now all of the sudden we learned he was some kind of a secret crook or a criminal that was sort of hidin' out–only hidin' out in plain view–right under our noses in front of us?"

"You mean like old Donnie Joe there? Why, he's a crook and been hidin' out in front of us all his life!" Bubby said. We all laughed for a moment, while Donnie Joe performed some strange kind of Indian dance. Then I continued.

"Yeah, sort of like that, only say it ain't Donnie Joe, but say it was Brother Sutherland instead, or somebody like…say…ol' Cooley up there." I said.

"Or Brother Pickett!" said J.R.

I didn't expect that, and the reminder of it caused me to shudder suddenly. I hoped it hadn't been visible, but I felt like it chilled me straight through to my bones on a hot July night.

"Yeah, maybe it was Brother Pickett or Deacon Ellis!"

This was too close to reality, so I tried to deflect their thinking.

"Ferget about them. It's got to be someone higher up–like the reverend." I stated.

"Yeah!" said Bubby. "You cain't have them to be some nobody who doesn't count. They got to be a big shot of some kind…at least a reverend…and maybe a coach or even a school principal."

"Okay, so let's say we find out that he's a swindler or a murderer. What do we do?" I asked.

Wayne said, "We don't do nuthin'. We cain't do a thing. Why, who would believe us, anyway?"

"Yeah," Donnie Joe added. "Who'd believe kids like us?"

"But don't we try to tell someone so he don't commit another swindle or murder?" I asked.

"Why, who swindled and murdered whom? Y'all let me in on y'alls little secret," said Starla, who suddenly appeared out of nowhere–joining our little circle and completely surprising all of us.

"Uh…uh…well, Starla…well, we been talkin' 'bout you and all those kids you been murderin' in that recruitin' contest," said Lester.

"Well, it ain't my fault if you big boys cain't keep up with little old me," she said, adding a magnetic little giggle. Now she had her audience, so she began to turn on her charm.

Wayne couldn't take his eyes off her, and Donnie Joe was equally captivated. The trouble with her was–she was cute–even with all her make-up. She had a pretty face and a trim figure with nice, attractive little curves. I figured that, in another year or two, she would probably create an awful lot of trouble for someone–and for her parents.

"We was just a riddlin'," Starla," said Bubby. His plate was just about empty, but it seemed that he was wearing almost as much food as he ate.

Before we had time to pursue the issue any further, Fishbait came over and sat down with us, and within a few minutes, we were a group of almost twenty young people, including two Methodists, one Presbyterian, and a completely worn-out, dirt-stained J-Earl Stafford who joined us, too. It was almost dark now, and folks were starting to gather together in small groups and families to wait for the fireworks which were about to begin.

Reverend Sutherland always paid for the fireworks, but Elroy Compton and Billy Blackwell arranged to set them off. Somehow, Elroy and Billy knew how to put on a show, and it was always quite professional and breathtaking for our little corner of the world, although this year's show seemed a lot shorter than last year's.

And so, the annual, West Bethel Baptist Church Fourth of July picnic came to its end, apparently with no one the wiser except me. "Oh, God?" I silently prayed. "In all your sovereignty and majesty and grace...why me?" After a very long day, J-Earl and I rode our bikes back down our road to our house. Mama was still up, waiting for us, as usual, and after we arrive home–as late as it was–she made us both take a bath.

After taking my bath, I decided to sit out on the back porch for a few minutes. I was tired, but I wanted to think things through a little bit, and the fresh night air was cooling off. Things were quiet; everyone had gone to bed. Off in the distance, I heard the sounds of a dog barking, but then it stopped. The crickets were chirping, as were some locusts. I sat there thinking for a long time.

Who was that third man? I wondered.

Way off in the distance, I heard the muffled sounds of a train, but it was too far away for me to know if it was coming or going.

Eighteen

On Friday, Mrs. Sutherland planned a field trip for the whole Bible school. As usual, J-Earl and I rode our bikes up to the Grange House, but after J-Earl went in to his class, I slipped out to the back where Donnie Joe, Billy, Lester, and J.R. were already waiting for me to go fishing with them.

"Come on, Stafford!" they whispered. "Less get goin'!"

"What took you so long?"

"I had to get J-Earl into the assembly first," I responded.

We waited out back until we heard all the kids start singing, and then we knew it was safe for us to get back to our bicycles and pedal quietly away. We had decided to go to Slocumb's pond which was out a way to the west and then north of the Grange House. Yesterday, I had arranged for Donnie Joe to bring an extra fishing pole so I wouldn't arouse any of J-Earl's suspicions about bringing a fishing pole to Bible school. Most of Donnie Joe's fishing gear wasn't all that good, but as long as you could throw out your line and pull it back again, that's all that mattered.

The Slocumbs were not generally open to other people fishing in their pond, let alone wandering around on their property. Of course, their opposition to these activities made their pond all the more appealing to us in the sense that a productive catch from Slocumb's pond represented more than mere fishing; it symbolized the challenge of pursuing a forbidden adventure, and if successfully accomplished, it corresponded with the consuming pleasure of having done so directly under Mr. Slocumb's nose. Slocumb's property was at the northwest corner of two intersecting roads, both unpaved, and to get to their pond, we had to continue going north along the road for about a quarter mile past their house, which faced the road that went west. Both roads were lined with a heavy growth of high grass, thick bushes, and tall trees. It was sunny, hot, and still. The only sounds that were audible were the crickets chirping and the soft fluttering of the big grasshoppers that were jumping in the high grass at the side of the road. The pond was set back away from both the house and the road, and as long as the Slocumbs were not out between the house and the pond, you could fish there to your heart's content. The pond was situated in a hollow around which several large trees provided shade and shelter. Although the pond was difficult to see from the north road, the road was quite visible from the pond– giving fishermen the advantage. To the west and the north of the pond, Slocumb maintained some beautiful pasture land, but there were lots of trees on the east and south sides.

When we arrived at the pond, no one was visible. The sky was clear, and obviously, it would have been better fishing had we started two or three hours ago. We left our bikes parked in the ditch, and, secretly, we all made our way over to the pond. Successful fishermen always fished by some adopted code. Long ago, we had established our own unwritten code of conduct for fishing, and the rules were variable, depending upon the fishing hole. The unwritten rules for fishing out at Slocumb's pond were simply "No talking," and "Don't get caught." We only fished with those who agreed to fish by that code.

When there were five people fishing in one location, it was important that we spread out around the pond. I liked to fish my way around the pond to find a good spot. At most of the area ponds that were familiar to me, I had a favorite spot, but I hadn't fished much out at Slocumb's, so I was still searching for that place. We were fishing with meal worms today, and our best approach was to cast a line in the water and wait to see if there were any nibbles. If the fish were biting around there, you might get a pretty good strike on the line, but you'd have to be patient and set the hook just right to pull the fish in. Sometimes the fish would play around with your meal worm, and you could feel a slight nudge on the line, but you'd just have to wait for that big tug, and if it never came, the best approach was to re-bait your hook and move a few yards to the left or right and then make your way, gradually, around the pond until you found that special place where the nibbles turned into outright strikes on your hook.

We were all quiet. Even back by the pond, you could stll hear the soft hum of crickets out by the road and the muffled calls of birds in the trees. Now and then, the grasshoppers would be jumping and swishing through the grass at the edge of the pond. Crickets and grasshoppers made great baits for pond fishing as well. Every so often, you'd hear a big slosh in the water as a fish might come to the surface and jump or flip–making a sudden popping sound across the water. At the edge of the pond, you could hear the muted croaks of frogs, and sometimes a big one would make a big splash into the water. Schools of tiny minnows and little bluegills would criss-cross in the shallow water, sometimes followed by a larger but certainly not a "keeper" bluegill, crappie, or striped bass. It wasn't unusual to see a good-sized snake slither down from a rock or across the top of a dead log into the water. Generally, snakes would scurry away from you, and they wouldn't bite unless they were provoked or stirred up for some crazy reason. We definitely knew better than to corner one. Pond fishing in Northwest Arkansas required vigilance.

I hadn't yet found my favorite spot at Slocumb's, although I made my way around more than half the pond. I had a series of nibbles at the little bend where the pond came up and created a mud hole just under the two trees that seemed to twist oddly toward the north. They were just nibbles; nothing more. I began to move on, but, for some reason, I turned and looked back toward the road only to see J-Earl just sliding off his bicycle down in the ditch and then picking his way through the broken-down, barbed-wire fence. He made his way carefully across the high grass of the pasture and through the smaller trees between the pond and the road.

"J-Earl! What in tarnation are you doin' here? You're supposed to be in the Bible class!" I whispered as strongly as I could.

"Well," he replied. "I noticed you and them other boys weren't in the meetin', and I looked and didn't see y'all anywhere. I told Mrs. Shelton, 'I got to go now to the outhouse,' and she nodded her head quickly. I ran out of there, and in that same minute, I saw y'all headin' up the road, and I figured, them boys is goin' out today playin' hooky from the Bible school,' and I begun thinkin' to myself, *Now J-Earl, do you wanna go to that field trip today?* and I said to myself, *No... I'd rather be a playin' hooky with them boys than go on that field trip with Starla and all them others.* I just followed y'all up the road, and here I am."

"Well, now that yer here, I reckon you need to know that here at Slocumb's pond there just ain't no talkin' cause if they hear us, they'll chase us outta here and no one knows if they'll call the law on us or not...no one's ever gotten caught here before to find out. So you got ta stay quiet, ya hear?" I said.

J-Earl nodded his head and didn't say anything.

"And, shucks, J-Earl! If I'd a known you was a comin', we could have brought our own poles to fish with instead of me havin' to use this old one of Donnie Joe's. But I don't suppose it really matters, anyhow, as none of us has caught anything yet. Yer gonna have to sit there and watch us, I reckon."

I didn't like J-Earl showing up because I knew the rest of my friends weren't very open to any little brothers tagging along behind. I also didn't like it at all that he played hooky from the Bible school, and I felt pretty guilty about it. Somehow, those words of Brother Pickett in the Sunday School–"Don't you be doin' what I do, now! You just be doin' what I say!"–rang out in my heart and ears now, and I felt like I was really leading J-Earl into some great hypocritical sin. What's more–I began to recall those convicting sermons that Reverend Sutherland preached about how believers who fall into sin suddenly start remembering what the Word of God says about their sins.

"When you fall back into sin, why, if you're really a true child of God, He's gonna bring you back! Yessir! He won't leave you alone out there in that pig pen. No-sir! I'm here to tell y'all that God's way to bring you back to the Father's house is to bring His Word back to yer heart and yer mind so as you'll remember His Words, 'cause He don't let them come back to you void."

And then I remembered this impressive sermon that Reverend Sutherland preached one time about the devil being the great accuser of our souls, and how he winds his way like a serpent into a believer's mind after that believer

113

has fallen back into sin, and he accuses that believer of all kinds of wrongdoing and being in cahoots with other evil men. Just then, I sensed that the devil was really trying to get at me. He was accusing me:

"You see there, boy! You ain't any better than that ol' Pickett! I got you just like I got him and that dirty ol' Deacon! Yeah! Those two scoundrels sold their souls to me years ago, and you know what, boy? I'm gonna get yours, too! You are that third man, boy! Yessir! My third man! And I'm gonna tell you what, boy; you are just about as rotten as that Deacon. And I'll have the lot o' ya. I got all o' ya by the scruff of your necks, and y'all belong to me now, yessir!"

I shuddered with the thought that the devil had me like he had Brother Pickett and that deacon. And when he called me his "third man," I almost thought I would faint. I became frightened that the devil might tempt me to rob some bank or even kill someone. And then, thankfully, I began to remember another sermon that Pastor Sutherland preached about overcoming temptation and praying against that old devil.

"If that devil's out there accusin' you," Dr. Sutherland said, "you just fall down on them knees and start you up a prayin' against that ol' Satan, because when he sees a believer prayin' down on his knees–the Apostle Paul tells us surely–there ain't nuthin' makes that old devil run away faster than seein' a believer down on his knees and prayin'."

I was feeling pretty low and scoundrel-like for leading J-Earl astray now, but I couldn't quite bring myself to fall down on my knees right out there in the mud at Slocumb's pond in front of all my friends. But I also recalled that Daddy said that God hears us regardless of how or when we pray, whether we are on our knees or just laying quietly in the bed.

"Son," he said, "I pray all the time when I'm drivin' in my truck or wherever. I just talk to the Lord normal like…I don't close my eyes, of course…but I know that He hears and answers my prayers."

I just stood there for a moment and tried to look like I was concentrating on my fishing. "Lord," I whispered, with my eyes wide open, "I'm a feelin' perty low-down and hypocritical right now about leadin' my little brother into playin' hooky. And Lord, what's really worse is that ole devil's tellin' me that he's got me like he's got Brother Pickett and that deacon! Oh God! Please don't let me be like them and rob churches and such!"

Standing there in front of Slocumb's pond, I was able to say at least that much of my prayer successfully before I was quickened back to reality by a great commotion of rustle and noise and human movement suddenly charging in my direction from my right-hand side. I had just enough time to turn to my right and see the blur of two or three of my fishing friends flying right past J-Earl and me in a flash. As Billy and J.R. ran by me, I heard Billy scream just above the level of a whisper, "It's old Slocumb with his dawgs!"

Now I felt this double sense of fear as well as guilt and urgency. The guilt of leading J-Earl into sin had been bad enough, but I was convinced that, not only did God hear my prayer, but also that He was answering it now with all the fury and the divine punishment that I deserved for skipping the Bible school, trespassing on Slocumb's property, and leading J-Earl into the same sins. I resolved to deal with these feelings later, but in that moment, our only recourse was to flee.

"J-Earl!" I screamed at the level above a whisper. "We gotta get outta here now!"

I grabbed J-Earl by the shirt and yanked on him, but he was quick and evasive, and he left me holding his breeze. J-Earl was off in the direction of the road, and because he was smaller, he made his way faster through the high grass and brush, and he was at his bicycle before any of the rest of us. I didn't like the sound of those dogs behind us at all. They sounded mean and monstrous, and I wondered if ole Slocumb kept big hounds or just wolves. I didn't know if these fears were worse than those which I experienced back behind the Grange House when I first became aware of the plan to rob the bank, but I also resolved to analyze that later. Initially, the sound of the dogs became louder and then, for some reason, it began to fade a little.

Fortunately, at the time of this alarm, J-Earl and I were on the north side of the pond which was a little closer and less exposed to the road. I was the last one to flee from that side, and I was thinking that Donnie Joe and Lester must have been fishing over on the south side of the pond. They would have to run farther around the pond and then over to the road, and, apparently, it seemed that Mr. Slocumb and his dogs took that route. That explained why the dog barks were fading away from us. So the chase party was well to the south of us, and we were able to make it through the fence and out to our bikes momentarily. In a flash, Billy, J.R., J-Earl, and I were up the road, out of sight, and gone.

Donnie Joe and Lester didn't fare so well. First of all, Lester made it to the fence, but he got all cut up by the barbed wire. The dogs got to Donnie Joe and pinned him down at the base of a tree just short of the fence. One of the dogs bit just into the leg of Donnie Joe's overalls and held him by his rapidly shredding pants, while the other dog just pushed his nose into Donnie Joe's face and forced him to lie back against the tree. They held him there but didn't really harm him. Evidently, Mr. Slocumb had trained his dogs not to draw blood unless their victim resisted or moved. With Donnie Joe pinned down by two dogs at the tree, Mr. Slocumb was free to pursue Lester, who, by now had squirmed successfully through the fence at a prominent cost of his own flesh. When he jumped on his bike, his hands and arms were pretty bloody. However, instead of riding to the north with the rest of us, to his good fortune and ours, Lester turned and rode south. On foot, Mr. Slocumb couldn't catch either party, so he turned back to deal with Donnie Joe.

Donnie Joe, however, was one not to get caught. We all believed that, one day in the future, he would make a great American army hero. With little regard for pain, Donnie Joe would rather die for any cause than become a traitor to the group. Even though he really was a thoughtless oaf, I really could admire his single-minded commitment even unto death for his ideal, however base it might be. Before Mr. Slocumb was able to get back to him, Donnie Joe, who understood animals very well, was able to relax enough to convince the dogs that he was no threat to them. As Donnie Joe settled ever more into a limp and wilted state, the dogs began to relax both their grip and their growl. Soon, he was petting both hounds, and in another minute, he fed them the bologna sandwich that he made for his lunch. In the following seconds, Donnie Joe was free of the two dogs, and he was up, gone, over the fence, and heading north on his bicycle before Mr. Slocumb could return back. Upon his arrival, Mr. Slocumb found his two dogs, face-to-face, alone, lying on the ground–tails wagging–and both of them licking an empty sheet of greasy and crumpled waxed paper.

Nineteen

J-Earl and I didn't bother waiting around for the Bible school classes to return from their field trip. Bible school field trips usually returned late. We rode our bicycles straight home, and we expected the worst. We figured that Mr. Slocumb had surely cornered someone–probably Lester and Donnie Joe–so we weren't surprised to see the law parked in front of our house when we arrived.

"J-Earl, I reckon we'd best tell the whole truth and nuthin' but the truth when we get inside," I told him as we walked up the stairs.

"Well, I reckon so," said J-Earl. "The whole truth and nuthin' but the truth."

Inside, Deputy Sheriff Watkins was talking to Mama, Granddaddy, and Grandma.

"You boys get outta Bible school early today?" Mama asked. "Was the field trip cancelled?"

"Well..." I started to answer, and then J-Earl interrupted me.

"We...we didn't actually...actually, we didn't..." J-Earl also tried to answer, but it seemed he could only stutter.

"Well, less talk more about the Bible school an' the field trip later," Mama said. "Right now, there's somethin' much more important that we have to talk about. Boys, y'all probably got off yonder to the Bible school too early this mornin' to learn what has happened, but Deputy Watkins is here because there's been a bank robbery down in Gentry, and somehow it might relate to us."

"A robbery?" I asked. I was dumbfounded to hear that it had already happened, and I hadn't yet had a moment to relate what I knew to anyone. It wasn't supposed to happen yet, and certainly not in Gentry; I was especially puzzled when Mama said it somehow might relate to us. What in the world could that mean? How could it relate to us? My heart started to pound within me again.

"A robbery?" J-Earl repeated. "Why, who done it?"

"When did it happen? How did it happen? How could it possibly relate to us?" I asked. My voice was breaking, and I was nervous.

"Well," said Deputy Watkins, "as best we can tell, we think it happened last night. There was this ol' nigger...uh,...pardon me, ma'am...an ole colored hobo man, who was evidently ridin' the freight cars goin' north; probably comin' up from Ft. Smith or from down further yonder maybe; somewhere down around Texarkana. Of course, the sheriff don't know it yet, but I personally have a hunch that this ol' hobo has been ridin' these freights over and over again–up and down the line–so he can survey out all the little towns and pick the one he wants. He's been watchin' us. Way we figure it, one of them trains come through Gentry late last night and slowed way down–which, of course, they're suppose to do, you know–and our hobo friend decides while the freight's a slowin' way down to slip off the train in Gentry while it's all dark and everyone's out watchin' the fireworks and what-not over yonder, or...maybe...I mean, of course, that it could have been after they've all gone to bed and already sleepin'. In any case, we're a workin' on the exact time. Yessir, way we figure it, this old nig...uh,...this colored boy's a smart one–he picks his town when it's empty, you see, and then he hit's the bank when no one's around. And then, as I see it, he lays low fer awhile until the next slow freight comes along through town, and he jumps on and rides up to y'alls Billups station where he jumps off and holes up fer the night–right where yer Granddaddy found him this very mornin'– sleepin' it off in one of them old junk cars out back of y'all's station."

"He was sleepin' in one of our old junk cars out back?" I asked. "Granddaddy, is that right? You catch him out there?"

"Well, son, I got down to the station early this mornin' to open it up, jist like we always do. As I was a makin' the coffee, I heard all this rustlin' and commotion and carryin' on out back, so I grabbed me that old shotgun we keep down there, and I lit out to see what's a goin' on out back. Lo and behold–if I didn't find this ol' colored tramp trippin' over bottles and a kickin' all them cans–and at the same time he was a tryin' to fight off a thousand hornets what built a big old nest in that beat up old Studebaker out there. I'd say that the ol' boy picked the wrong heap in which to sleep, he did."

"Well, how do y'all know that he's the one that done it?" I asked.

"Yeah," J-Earl echoed. "How do we know he done it?"

Mama detected just a hint of indignation in my tone, and a whole lot more mockery in J-Earl's.

"Now, you boys watch it. I don't like y'all's tone at all. It ain't gentlemanly, and I won't have it; hear me good now–do y'all hear me?"

"Yes, ma'am," we both said simultaneously.

"Mama, I don't mean no disrespect with my question, but I'm jist a wonderin' if they're dead certain about this colored hobo man. I mean–did they find the stolen bank money on him or somethin' like that?"

"Well, no, son, they didn't," said the deputy. "Of course, no robber's gonna confess that he hit some bank last night and then turn the loot right back over to the law when they catch him and question him the very next day. I've seen a hundert cases like this one at least a dozen times, and they're all alike. He's like all the rest of his sort and confesses only that he don't know nuthin' and that he never heard about any bank robbery. Claims he ain't guilty about it and claims he ain't never been to Gentry before. I mean to tell y'all that they never make my job easy fer me. Fer example, he says he was on a southbound freight and claims he jumped off somewheres south o' Decatur when it slowed way down up there, and then he says he walked clear down the rail line to y'all's station–believe it or not. It's a same ol' song, and I heard it a thousand times. Says he was tired, and he wanted to look fer a place to sleep out there by them old cars. I'll wager he don't know the difference between north and south or east and west. I'm surprised he didn't say he was on a west or east bound freight, fer that matter–know what I mean?"

"Well, did he have the money?" I asked. "How much did they…uh,…I mean, how much did he rob?"

"No! O' course he didn't have it–not even a brand new, shiny silver dime of that money! Not one red cent!" the deputy declared. "They always dump it somewhere, and then they tell a whole pack of lies 'cause they think they'll come back here later and get it, or else they work in cahoots with some other robber, and he holds their part of the swag until they get outta prison. No sir, I never expected to find any cash on that old boy. He's either stashed that cash, or posted it over to his cohorts till he can break outta jail and run off clear down to Florida to hide there in the swamps and the bulrushes. And when them niggers…I mean…when them colored thieves run the other way– way up north to Chicago and Minnesota and places like that, they take that money with 'em, and they spend it all at once. They dress up all fancy and get themselves a new Cadillac or a big ol' Buick and they try to put on a respectable life. And some of them never get caught. I tell y'all…that money's gone, and we ain't never gonna find it; yessir–I'm a tellin' you this cause I've seen a hundert cases of it at least a dozen times."

"Well, Jimmy," Mama said, "where is he now?"

"Why, Norma Jean, we've got our Mister Hobo down there in the Gentry jailhouse right now," the deputy said. "But I don't believe we can keep him there. We're gonna have to move him outta there before long, or the citizens of Gentry might get antsy over him…and…well…they might try to take the law into their own hands, if you know what I mean; it could get mighty ugly for that old boy. I don't believe the citizens of Gentry'll take very kindly to a colored man what stole their savings and is just sittin' around fer a spell in their jailhouse."

"How much did he get?" she asked.

"Oh, yes, ma'am. I'm sorry, but I forgot to say. We think he got about seven thousand dollars or so in cash. They're still a countin' their losses down there at the bank. I mean, that's a lot of money for the folks of Gentry to lose at one time. On the other hand, it don't compare to some of them professionals who might get twenty or thirty thousand. O' course, they don't keep a whole vault-load o' money in the bank in Gentry because it ain't a town full of moneybags like it is over there at Springdale. You know, they got some big-money folk over there. If them crooks're gonna hit any bank, then that First Ozark National in Springdale's the one you want. I mean, robbin' the Gentry bank is like stealin' a few nails from the twelve penny bin over at Grover's Main Street Hardware Store."

"Well, I agree," Granddaddy said.

"Well, I wonder what's a gonna happen now?" I said.

From what I heard last night while sitting in that outhouse, I was certain that this could not be the work of a colored hobo randomly passing through Northwest Arkansas on a night train, but rather it had to be that of those three hypocritical scoundrels–Brother Pickett, the deacon, and that unknown third man. And I was certain that they said the First State Bank of Arkansas in Decatur; thus, it came as a shock to me now to learn that they had pulled off a robbery in a Gentry bank instead. I thought they would plan and scheme a whole lot longer before they actually carried out their wickedness. Way down deep in my heart, I simply could not accept that this old black railroad tramp had anything at all to do with this awful crime other than to have stumbled innocently, inconveniently, and unintentionally into the very heart of a series of events that seemed to implicate him as the guilty party, though no more than circumstantially at this point. Of course, I could prove nothing, and besides, who would believe me anyway? Who was I? And, in comparison with a local Baptist church deacon and his Sunday-school teaching partner, both of whom were white and appeared to have fine, long-standing reputations in this local community, what were the chances that some unknown, colored, hobo passing through in the dead silence of a summer's night would not immediately be presumed guilty of *whatever* crime might happen? Nevertheless, what I previously sensed as an obligation to truth now became a responsibility to justice. I had to communicate what I knew as quickly and authoritatively as possible. But how? And to whom?

Twenty

It was already after noon by the time Deputy Watkins left our place. The deputy said that he and Sheriff Parker would come by the station the next day to determine if the hobo left any traces of evidence behind. Mama and Grandma made a late lunch for us, and we discussed all the day's events except our playing hooky from Bible school. Apparently, with all the excitement about the bank robbery, Mama had forgotten or overlooked her intention to return later to our discussion about the Bible school field trip, and since the deputy's visit did not relate to us trespassing on Mr. Slocumb's property and fishing in his pond, I was quite content to let that inquiry pass with the hope that all my friends were indeed equally able to slip away unidentified through Mr. Slocumb's hands–not to mention through the teeth of those dogs.

Just before we sat down for lunch, I cornered J-Earl, and I said, "If Mama don't raise the matter of that field trip, then you keep quiet about it, you hear?"

"I ain't sayin' nuthin' about it," he told me.

"Well, that's good, because you're as guilty in it as I am," I said. "We ain't gonna talk about it."

Then Mama called us for lunch, and we all sat down to eat.

"Granddaddy, you're like a real hero–capturin' that bank robber, today," said J-Earl.

"Well," said Granddaddy, "At the time, I didn't know he was a bank robber. I just heard a bunch of noise outside, and I just went out to investigate it and see what it was; that's all."

"Granddaddy," I said. "Do you believe he's the robber?"

"O' course he is," Mama interjected.

"Well, I certainly do!" said Grandma. "Ain't no doubt in my mind about it."

"I don't know," Granddaddy said. "He might be…only God knows, and that's fer sure. I reckon there's a whole lot of truth here that we don't yet know about," said Granddaddy. "You know, he could be the thief, but until I actually can say that I know a whole lot more about it, I'd prefer to withhold my judgment fer a while. Over the years, I've learned that we jist don't have all the facts, and it ain't always easy to collect them. You know, we humans been known to find a man guilty fer somethin,' hang him, and then bury him—only to find out a few years later–that we put the wrong one in the grave."

Grandma said, "Nope. Not this time. They got the right one, and I can feel it in my bones, Darlin'. I'm certain of it. I'm gonna tell you–the Lord arranged fer them hornets long ago to build that nest right in that old Studebaker out yonder. Yessir. He had His purpose in it. And He also arranged fer that colored man to tire out and jump off o' that train and climb into that car where all them hornets was jist a waitin' to fulfill God's purposes. No-sir! Not this time. He's the right one."

"Well, I think he done it, too," Mama said. "I believe he stole that money from the bank, and I think he stashed it somewheres–just like Jimmy Lee Watkins says–and he's got him a cohort somewhere that he's in cahoots with."

We talked it through over lunch until we completely wore out the subject. J-Earl thought the hobo was guilty, as did Mama, and Grandma. Granddaddy wasn't real sure about it yet, but I was convinced that the colored man didn't rob that bank. Of course, Tawna Rae had no earthly idea what we were talking about.

After lunch, Granddaddy and I went down to work at the station. We opened the place back up again, and that day, Y-City Station was all a-buzz. Mama came down to the station later in the afternoon. We had lots of customers, and it seemed that everyone who lived in Gentry stopped by to congratulate Granddaddy on the fine job he did to capture the criminal. Granddaddy insisted over and over again that he didn't really do anything heroic–in his mind, it was simply an ordinary and normal thing to do to protect your own property from an invasion.

"And, besides," Granddaddy said, many times; "the hobo was practically as old as I am; he was frightened to death of my shotgun–as anyone would be–and he put up absolutely no resistance at all."

With all the fanfare and the unusual number of customers, we tried to sell as much gas as we could. It was a busy day, and I recall pumping a lot of gas, cleaning a lot of windshields, and checking a lot of tires. And, for a change, I enjoyed the spotlight shining down on us that day. The mayor of Gentry stopped in and congratulated Granddaddy. The police chief came up as well, and the newspaper people from Gentry came up to interview Granddaddy.

"Boy, what ya think of your old Granddaddy, now?" they all asked me. "He's a hero, isn't he?"

"Yessir. I think he's just great!" I said.

"We ain't had any uproar in this area for a long time," the newspaper reporter said. "It's about time that we had a little more drama around here."

I was just thinking, *How can they wish fer that?* And then I thought, *Well, they can have all the drama they want–so long as it don't include me!* Besides, the way I figured it, the real drama around here might just be getting ready to begin.

Wait until y'all find out who really done it! I was thinking. *Y'all'll have yer fill of drama until yer sick of it!*

About four-thirty that afternoon, things at the station began to slow back down to a more normal pace. Granddaddy, Mama, and I were not used to this much business and commotion at our station, and after things settled down and got quiet, we all realized that we were extremely tired from the events and activities of that day. I wanted to talk to Granddaddy and tell him so badly what I knew, but the timing still wasn't quite right.

"Well, Granddaddy, what do you think?" I asked, attempting to make an effort.

"Right now, I believe that poor ol' colored man sittin' up there in that Gentry jailhouse's probably in the safest place there is fer him in all of Benton County. At least fer now. That deputy was right about one thing."

124

"What you mean, Granddaddy?" I asked.

"Well, son, they'll probably have to move that old boy over to the county jail in Bentonville. I reckon there's a whole lot of folk in and around Gentry's pretty mad at him right about now, and if enough of them got themselves together and charged that old jailhouse, the Gentry law'd have an awful hard time keepin' them outta there. I'm sure there's a whole bunch of folk would just as soon take him out and hang him from a tree in some deep hollow somewhere between here and Centerton and save the county all that money fer feedin' him in the jail and payin' fer his trial and what-not. And I cain't say fer sure, but I wouldn't doubt if that old Deputy Watkins wouldn't somehow leave his cell unlocked to tempt that hobo to up and run so's he could say, 'The boy jumped me, and I just had to shoot him.'"

Mama said, "Well, I expect they'd better move him fer his own sake, and they'd better do it in secret when folks aren't aware of it. I think he's guilty, but I ain't fer hangin' or shootin' him. He needs a fair trial, but it ain't real likely as he'll get it here in this county."

"Why do you think that, Mama?" I asked.

"Well, son, because there ain't no colored folks what live in Benton County, and that identifies him right on the spot as an outsider. All us insiders– them what lives here–why, we've all known and trusted each other at least long and well enough not to go robbin' our own banks because that'd be robbin' from ourselves, and we simply don't do that sort of thing around here. I know they do that sort of thing up there in places like New York and Detroit, but those folk ain't got no self-respect, and they cain't trust each other because they don't know each other. They're all outsiders up there. Why, just the other day, I seen in the *Tulsa World* where some ol' boy up there in Philadelphia or somewheres like that shot his daddy and his mama and his whole family fer a few dollars. So when you got somethin' like this what happens–a bank gets robbed and an outsider like this one suddenly appears and both on the exact same day–why, boy, that don't occur every day! It just don't happen! And when it happens like that, you know fer sure that he done it."

Granddaddy confirmed, "Yeah, I saw that in the *World,* too. Wadn't that awful? I just cain't understand them people! Whatever leads a soul to commit such a horrible crime?"

"Well Mama…Granddaddy, what if they got things all crossed up somehow, and they really are a holdin' the wrong man?" I asked. I began to grow a little concerned.

"Well, boy, like I said, it wouldn't be the first time. But I'll tell you this…yer Mama's right. It sure don't look good fer him. This old hobo boy, whether he done it or not, he's in a deep peck of trouble, he is, regardless of what time it is," said Granddaddy, who was now checking his pocket watch. "And speakin' of the time, it's time to go," We closed down the station for the night, and then we all went back home.

Book Three

Twenty-one

By the time we arrived back home after closing the station that afternoon, Grandma had supper all ready for us–to our great delight. I knew that Mama wouldn't feel much like cooking after a strenuous day like that. It had been a long, busy day, and I reckon that Grandma must have "felt it in her bones" that we would all be hungry and exhausted from the events of that day, not to mention the events of that entire week. We were glad that the week was over. We expected that Daddy would be arriving either late that evening or early the next morning for the weekend, and, needless to say, we were all anxious to see him.

"Do y'all know that we sold more gas and oil and more fruits and vegetables today than any other day since we been in bidness? Our total receipts was a hundert and seventy-three dollars and some change," Mama announced at the table.

"My goodness!" Grandma said. "Y'all were sure busy today!"

"That is definitely good news," Granddaddy said. "That'll make Clayton proud."

"Well, I tell y'all," I stated. "I sure pumped an awful lot of gas today!"

"It's sure good to have some money comin' in," Grandma said.

"Well, I'm a lookin' forward to seein' Clayton," Mama said. "Daddy'll be home either tonight or tomorrow, y'all. You miss your daddy, Sugar-Babe?"

"Yes, Mama," Tawna Rae said.

"I do, too," said J-Earl. "Mama, does he have to work at the Army this weekend?"

"No, not this weekend. But he will have to do two whole weeks of guard duty in another few weeks or so. I sure hope that Mr. Waldrup'll give him time off fer his Guard work."

Granddaddy said, "I believe he will."

"Well," I said, "we sure got a lot a things to tell Daddy when he gets here."

"I'll say."

After we all ate dinner, Granddaddy and I went out to sit for awhile on the back porch. We figured the Cardinals might be playing a little later on, so we thought we'd sit out there early and then tune in the radio just about when the game would begin. The weather was still hot and humid; my overalls were wet and sticky from sweating most of the day.

"Granddaddy?" I asked.

"Yes, my boy?"

"Can you tell me why we have colored people?"

"Colored people?"

"Yassir. Colored people. Where do they come from, and why do we have 'em?"

"Why, boy…what kind o' question is that? You got that colored hobo on your mind, don't ya?"

"Yes, sir. But, sir…I don't mean any disrespect with that question; I was just a wonderin' where they come from, and how they got colored, and what-not? I ain't seen many colored folk around here…why is that?"

"Well, son, my best ideal about it is that God made 'em the way He did fer His purposes, and of course, we cain't say we know what them purposes was or what they was for. We just know that, if God made 'em, then they're a part of His whole creation…just like He made red folks and white folks and yellow ones. He made black ones and brown ones, too, just like He made Egyptians and Israelites and Philistines, Greeks, and Hittites. Thing is, none of them–not a one of 'em–was perfect…they all got away from God. And God doesn't necessarily tell us how nor who strayed away the furthest. It just seems to me that He made a pattern, an' it called fer most o' the white folks to live and work in that part of the world we call Europe, and that's where most o' us come from, 'riginally. In that pattern, the black people lived mostly down in Africa...just like the yellow folks mostly come from around China and Japan and what-not. It's just God's plan and pattern, and it's the way it all works."

"Well, how come we don't have many of them around here? I mean...I don't believe I've hardly ever seen any colored folk 'round here," I said. Indeed, once in a great while, maybe a colored family might pull into our station and ask for some gas or oil or air, but they almost never got out o' the car. When I did see 'em, they was always quiet, well-mannered, and well-behaved, and they usually drove off and disappeared jist about as quickly as they had appeared.

"Well, we don't see many of 'em in these parts 'cause ain't none of 'em what lives around here," said Granddaddy.

"Why is that, Granddaddy?"

"Well, son...the reason is...well, actually, I believe there are several reasons. First of all, today, most of them lives further to the south of us–further down in the deep south–that is, where most of the cotton grows. Most of 'em come up from the heathen tribes down in Africa where they was bought and sold in the ol' slave trade. They brought 'em over here and made 'em slaves, mostly to chop cotton. Unfortunately, son, it's an ugly story that practically tore our whole country apart. Today, most of the colored folk still lives down close to where their daddies and mamas were slaves, although a lot of 'em moved away–up north–after the Civil War.

"Another reason why there ain't many colored folk here in the Ozarks is because most of the white folks who first settled into these parts were already poor people to begin with–some of them was even poorer than the slaves and they couldn't afford to feed their own–much less an extra slave or two. And another thing; there ain't a lot o' cotton that grows in these parts, so there was no need fer a whole 'nother group of poor folk to come here, too.

"An' another thing–it ain't exactly easy to get here from other places. Fer the most part, you got to have a specific reason to be comin' into the Ozarks, and the fact is, most of them slaves never hit on the right reason fer comin' here.

"Of course, I don't believe many colored folks actually want to live here in Benton County, partly because they ain't especially well-received in these parts. Whenever one or two of them does come around, people cain't help but notice 'em right away, and it ain't totally unusual fer 'em to be escorted quickly on their way, so to speak. That don't mean it's right to mistreat them. No-sir! No Christian gentleman ever mistreats another human being no matter what his color. God loves them colored folk just like He loves white folks. But that's jist how things are 'round here, and most people never give a second thought over it."

"Yes, sir," I responded methodically. "Well, I was jist sort o' wonderin' how that colored hobo is going to manage here in Northwest Arkansas then?"

"Well, son," said Granddaddy. "I don't know. But we cain't be worryin' about him too much. If he done it, God'll deal with him–it's that simple. If he ain't done it, why then we pray that God brings forward the man what done it, and that He releases the colored hobo back to his family."

"Family?" I asked, with fear. "Do you suppose he has a wife and kids somewhere?"

For me, the whole mess just kept getting heavier and stickier. The more I thought about this man, the worse things seemed to become for him. In my mind, I was thinking that, if an ordinary colored man could fall from one moment into some desperate, life-changing situation in the next moment simply by making a couple of bad choices, it seemed to me that it could happen to any man–white or colored. And not only that, but how would he know that he was making bad choices? And then I wondered, *What was the difference between an ordinary colored man and an ordinary white man?* And then I thought, *My goodness! This same thing could even happen to Daddy!* What if Daddy–out there in such an evil world–made just a couple of bad decisions and fell into some horrible circumstances that somehow would yank him right away from us? We might never know it! We could lose him forever, and we might never even know what happened. And worst of all, the whole thing could easily be someone else's fault–someone like those three hypocrites who could cleverly take advantage of another unknowing, unsuspecting, and innocent victim. The more I thought about this, the more I began to hate Brother Pickett, Deacon Ellis, and that third person for their thoughtless ignorance which ultimately led to their unintentional but real mistreatment of that colored hobo. The hobo probably had twelve or fourteen little colored mouths to feed and skinny bellies to fill. In my mind's eye, I could envision his little ones somewhere down in cotton country–with their big bright eyes and shiny white teeth–all sitting there on splintery, three-leggéd stools or a long, wooden bench around some homemade, uneven kitchen table and waiting on their Daddy to come home. In my mind's ear, I could hear them singing some tune about how "Daddy's comin' home tonight," and one of them says to another, "he's gonna bring us some catfish and cornbread." And across the room, their Mama is working away cleaning and cutting up poke greens, a turnip, and an onion or two, while she hums something about how her "Man be comin' home, by and by."

But he ain't comin' home, I thought. *And he won't be–thanks to those three scoundrels! And those little ones'll never know, and they'll never hear, and that whole family of little colored children are gonna grow up never knowing what happened to their Daddy on July the Fourth, 1957.*

"Hey there, boy!" Granddaddy's call startled me back to reality. "Why don't you turn on that radio and tune it in to KMOX?"

"All right. Yeah…that's a good ideal," I said.

There was, in fact, a game coming on the radio, but I didn't catch much of it that evening. I couldn't clear my mind of that colored hobo. About the only thing I recall from that game was the announcement that the All-Star game would be played next week from Sportsman's Park right there in St. Louis, and they were going to call that game live-and-play-by-play that day– July the ninth.

Twenty-two

When I awoke on Saturday morning, Daddy's truck was parked out to the side of our house, so I knew that he was home now. He probably got in very late, so he would sleep in for a few hours before getting up. Granddaddy and Grandma were already sitting at the kitchen table and sipping hot coffee. I poured myself a cup of hot black coffee and sat down next to Granddaddy.

"Mornin'," I said.

"Good mornin', boy," Granddaddy said.

"Mornin', son," said Grandma. "Did you sleep well?"

"Yes, ma'am."

We sat there at the table and drank coffee together for awhile. About a half hour later, Grandma got up and began to gather some things together for making breakfast.

Granddaddy said, "Less go set a spell out on the porch, boy."

We refilled our cups and removed ourselves to the back porch.

"After these many years, son, I've learnt when it's best to get out of the kitchen. When your Granny starts to makin' breakfast–especially when your Daddy just got home–it's time for us to back outta there."

"Yessir."

Sitting together with Granddaddy out on the back porch, I decided it was time to tell Granddaddy what I knew. I might have to confess a few things I didn't like–such as playing hooky–but I just couldn't stand the idea of withholding the truth that I knew inside of me, while an innocent man–colored or not–sat down there in the Gentry jailhouse.

"Granddaddy," I said, "I got somethin' very important I need to talk to you about."

"What's that, you say? Important? Well then, less talk about it, son."

"Granddaddy, this is so important, and it may sound so wild that you're gonna be tempted to think I ain't tellin' the truth. But, please…Granddaddy…I'm tellin' you the whole truth and nuthin' but the truth no matter how crazy it may sound to ya."

"Well, boy, I appreciate you wantin' to tell the truth. What is it, then?"

"Granddaddy, I know fer a solid fact that this colored hobo never robbed no bank in Gentry!"

"Well, son," said Granddaddy, "I'd like to believe that you do know that fer a fact, but the truth is, you wasn't there when it actually happened, and the case against that hobo is perty strong."

"I know it looks like that, Granddaddy, but in this case, I know the actual truth fer sure. The actual truth is out there hidin' behind the bushes, and it may be harder to find and believe than the so-called, temptational truth that's a ticklin' our noses."

"Well, son, less talk about it. Fer a moment, less jist say you're right on this. How you gonna prove your case then to the law? If, in your mind, the hobo never done it, then who did? Who robbed that bank then?"

"Well, Granddaddy, I'm a little afraid to tell you, because I know you ain't gonna like it and you might not believe it."

"No…why, no, son! I'm gonna believe you fer sure. I want you to tell it to me no matter how far-fetched it seems," Granddaddy said.

"Well, I hope indeed that you'll believe me, 'cause I'm a tellin' you the honest to goodness truth, Granddaddy. It was…it was three men that done it–three white men. It was…it was…Brother Pickett, Deacon Ellis, and a third, unidentified person that I ain't quite sure about yet!"

"Do you mean Brother Pickett and Deacon Ellis from out at our church?" Granddaddy was all startled and excited now.

"Well, yessir…that's exactly who I mean. I think they done it."

"Now son, thems some mighty strong charges to lay at the feet of a well-respected, church deacon and a Sunday school teacher! How can you say it? It sounds to me just a little like maybe the strange and wild ideals of a young boy. What makes you say it was these two gentlemen; and who is this unknown third fellow? Tell me, boy, how do you come up with all this?"

"Granddaddy, sir," I said, "I know it seems really far-fetched, as you say yerself, but I'm a tellin' you the honest truth. It's a long story. A month or so ago, Brother Pickett let us out of Sunday school class jist a little bit early. Brother Pickett told us to go up and sit on the front steps and wait up there until the rest o' the classes got out before the worship service began. Well, sir, we got a little bored settin' around up on them steps, and then the next thing I know–Donnie Joe took off a runnin'. I ran after him, and we both ran across the side lawn of the Grange House and around to the back o' the church. We didn't mean no harm by it, but a moment or two later, we run directly into Brother Pickett and Deacon Ellis. Both of 'em was standin' out behind the outhouse, and they was a smokin' their cigarettes; they was smokin' up such a storm that I b'lieve all the Cherokees out there in Oklahoma could read their signals."

"So they was out there and smokin' their cigarettes after the Sunday school and before the worship service you say?" asked Granddaddy.

"Yassir," I answered.

"Well, it certainly ain't a very good example before our young folk fer a Sunday school teacher and a church deacon to be doin' that sort o' thing."

"And they told us not to tell anyone what we saw. And later, Brother Pickett chewed me out fer bein' friends with Donnie Joe and said he was no good and would lead me down the wrong path. But then he apologized for bein' a smoker and said he couldn't control hisself, and he said, 'Boys, don't do what I do, but do what I say.' And the deacon told us that we'd better not let on to Pastor Sutherland that we saw them out there smokin' away."

"Well, boy," said Granddaddy, "I certainly appreciate you sharin' this with me, as it tells me a whole lot about them characters in our church. A deacon and a Sunday school teacher ought to be upright, Christian gentlemen that leads pure lives and don't bring our young folk into any temptations. Why, that's like havin' a football coach what challenges them boys to get out there Monday through Friday and works them all to death through their plays and their routines all week and then tells them, 'Now, boys, run yer laps and clear out yer lungs and eat yer vegetables and don't drink any alcohol or smoke any tobaccy as it ain't good fer yer careers,' and then that coach goes out hisself and smokes and drinks and carouses all weekend. It just ain't a good coach what does that. But son, I'm a little confused about how all that relates to the recent bank robbery."

"Well sir, it ain't done yet…there's more to it. You see, I been tryin' to walk a narrow path as far away as I could from that deacon and that Brother Pickett; I'm tryin' to stay outta their way. But last Sunday, durin' the worship service at the church, I don't know if you remember it or not, but Deacon Ellis helped to collect the morning tithes and offerings. He was servin' right down our aisle in the church, and when he come to our aisle…Granddaddy…" At this point, my voice cracked, and I began to sob just a little bit.

"Now, boy," Granddaddy said, "what's the matter with you? You don't need to be upset about all this."

"I'm sorry, Granddaddy," I said. "It's just that I know I heard Pastor Sutherland repeat at least a million times to keep our eyes closed during such worshipful events, and I know that now the devil is tryin' to convict my heart that if I jist hadn't peeked, I wouldn't be in all this trouble now. I keep on thinkin' that if I had never peeked, I wouldn't a seen what I shouldn't a seen!"

"Boy, you ain't in any trouble fer tellin' this to me. It's all right," he said.

"Well, sir, I peeked, and I saw that old hypocrite Deacon Ellis scoop outta the offerin' plate a whole handful of money, and he stuffed it all in his side coat pocket–just like it all belonged to him. Then I really started gettin' afraid."

"What's that? You say you saw Deacon Ellis takin' money right outta the plate?" Granddaddy acted surprised by this.

"Yassir, Granddaddy! It's true! I seen him take it, but Granddaddy, I just didn't know who to tell or how to talk about it with anyone! I mean, sir, who is gonna believe me when I say this? But I know he done it because I seen it. At first, I tried to tell myself, 'Now, boy! You didn't see nuthin',' but I cain't help it–I done seen it!"

Granddaddy began to laugh pretty hard, and at first I thought he was laughing at me, but then he said:

"Well, boy, I can see how you'd feel as a youngster that saw someone stealin' church money. Why, of course, then; who'd believe you?"

"But Granddaddy, it ain't over. There's still more. It ain't just the smokin' and the money stealin'. I know more still. You remember this week at the church picnic?"

"Well, yeah. Of course. It was the night of the bank robbery, and the next day, I corralled that colored hobo."

"Yassir. Well, that afternoon, we was all out there playin' softball with them Methodists and Presbyterians and what-nots. Ever'body was all over the Grange House grounds that day and enjoyin' the Fourth of July. I played a bunch of innings of softball, but I got tired of it because we wasn't really playin' it right. I mean they was givin' the girls all the pitches they wanted and not callin' strikes or balls on them. After awhile, I jist got tired of it, and I needed to go up to the outhouse fer a moment. I went in there and locked that ol' door and sat myself down no more than a minute when I heard these voices comin' toward the outhouse, and they was plannin' to do somethin' awful. First, I recognized Brother Pickett's voice, and the other one of them was Deacon Ellis, too. But there was three of them, and I got no ideal who that third person was. First they lit up their smokes; I could smell it. Then one of them asked Deacon Ellis how much he got outta the offering plate on Sunday, and he said, 'Fifty-seven dollars.' The other man said it ain't enough, and somethin' like it'll take them ferever to get what they need by robbin' the church. And I believe it was the third man what said they needed to rob the First State Bank of Arkansas at Decatur, but I cain't remember it all very well, as it all happened so fast. I thought I was a goner sittin' in that outhouse. Oh, Granddaddy, I thought they was gonna catch me fer sure and cut my throat or somethin' like that–I was so afraid. It was all I could do to keep from squirmin' and makin' any noise and what-not in that awful outhouse, but then, after another minute, they was done smokin', and they busted up their meetin'. I got outta that outhouse as quickly as I could, and actually, I went searchin' all over to find out who that third man was, but I never seen him."

"Boy, are you tellin' me the truth just how it all happened?" asked Granddaddy.

"Yassir. I ain't never lied to you, Granddaddy. Ain't ever had a reason to lie to you, and I ain't about to start. And, in fact, if all the truth be known, Granddaddy, then I'd also have to confess that I played hooky from the Bible school yesterday, too, but that had nuthin' to do with what I know about the bank robbery, other than I didn't really want to go out field trippin' at a time like this. I felt like I needed to get out somewhere and clear my mind a little, and think about somethin' other than them hypocrites."

"Well, my goodness, yes, son! I guess so! Anyone who'd been holdin' all that secret information inside would surely need to break away from it and clear his head of it fer a while," Granddaddy said.

"Yassir. Except when we got there–a bunch o' us boys went out there to Slocumb's place–and we all like near to got caught by Mr. Slocumb and his dawgs. The problem, of all things, was that J-Earl snuck away from the Bible school, too, and he followed us bigger boys up there."

"J-Earl? J-Earl come out there, too? On his own?"

"Yassir. And that's what I meant. I really got convicted by that, because I been angry at that hypocrite Brother Pickett and that scoundrel Deacon Ellis, and then, what did I do? By preachin' to J-Earl, 'You do what I say, and not what I do,' I done the same thing to him what they done to me!"

"Well son, it seems to me that you been through an awful lot this past week. Maybe you learnt some hard lessons, too. An' the thing of it is this– I do believe you're tellin' the truth, but we're gonna have a hard time provin' what you're sayin'. Fer example, it's one thing fer them to say they're gonna rob the bank in Decatur, but that ain't the bank what was robbed. Maybe they changed their plans that night and hit the bank in Gentry instead. And there ain't a lot that we can do without knowin' who that third person is."

It was good to have it out in the open. I felt that Granddaddy was a man I could trust and rely on, and I was certain that he really believed me. After hearing my story, Granddaddy assured me that he understood how I felt about the colored hobo being innocent, and he said that we would figure out a way to get all these issues straightened out with the law. Whatever it took, we would do the right thing. A few minutes later, Daddy came out on the back porch and sat down with us, and then Grandma appeared in the doorway. She offered us a little more coffee. Over her faded house-dress, printed with some pale, pink and yellow flowers, she wore her old white apron. The soft lines in Grandma's face disclosed the demanding struggles she had endured through the many years of her life, but her quiet, expressive features radiated the warmth and the deep affection of her selfless love for the three generations of her men now sitting there on the porch. Stubbornly, a few of the white hairs on her head resisted all her efforts to keep her hairstyle together and pulled back into a small, tight knot at the back of her head. As a result, she was constantly brushing the fly-away hair back to her temple and out of her deep blue eyes, which were still bright.

"I'm gonna be servin' breakfast in about ten minutes," Grandma said with a little grin on her face and a sparkle in her eyes.

"Well, we're all ready fer it," Granddaddy said.

"Good mornin,' Paw," Daddy said. "Good mornin,' boy. How's my boy been?"

"Mornin,' Clayton. How've you been doin'?" Granddaddy asked.

"Perty good. Had some good runs up and down Route 66 these past days; good weather, and no major accidents. Saw a couple of minor ones, but nothing of consequence, thank the Lord."

"I been doin' good, Daddy. We worked the station a lot, and we did our best bidness jist yesterday," I said. He put his strong hand on my shoulder and gave me a solid squeeze to remind me how much he loved me.

"Yeah, that's what your mama said. Paw, I understand we've had a lot o' excitement around here in the past several days."

"Yassir, and we need to bring you up to date on it all. We need to talk about it."

A few minutes later, we were all sitting around the table enjoying a great family breakfast. Granddaddy thought it was best that I communicate to everyone in the family what I had told him earlier that morning.

"My, goodness! What're we gonna do about all this then?" Mama asked.

Daddy said, "We're gonna think it through a while, and we'll pray about it. Then we'll know exactly what to do."

Twenty-three

After breakfast that Saturday, Granddaddy, Daddy, and I went down to open the station for the day. Things got off to a slow start that morning. Daddy wanted to look out back at the old Studebaker where Granddaddy caught the colored hobo. He and I went out there to look around. Sure enough, there was a big old hornet's nest between the cloth headliner and the roof of the car, and the hornets were buzzing all around. It looked like there was a sack of old trash papers and an opened can of what used to be Vienna Sausages. The car was rusting away, but the seat cushions inside were still soft and comfortable. There were still quite a few old cars out there and lots of automotive junk lying around. Although it never dawned on me before, anyone could easily see how a hobo might come wandering along after riding the freights and simply crawl up inside one of those old cars to hide, keep warm, and sleep for a night. After a while, we came back around to the front of the station just about the same moment that Deputy Watkins pulled into the driveway with his sheriff's car.

"Mornin' Jimmy Ray," said Daddy.

"Howdy, Clayton. Hadn't seen you around in awhile," the deputy said.

"Well, I been drivin' up and down Highway 66."

"Well, I guess you heard that your daddy captured that nigger bank robber."

"Yeah, Norma Jean told me all about it. Is he over at Benton County?"

"No, we got him down at Gentry, but we're fixin' to move him over to Bentonville before long. We expect that some of the Gentry folk may try to break down the jail and take him out and hang him, if we don't move him soon. There was a crowd down there last night on the street, but after a couple hours, they broke up and went home."

"What do we know about him?" Daddy asked.

"Well, he claims his name is Festus Williams, and he says he's from a place called Transylvania, Loosiana–which I ain't ever heard of."

"Goodness. Where in tarnation is that?"

"Well, I don't know. But I can assure you that we're checkin' it all out. The ol' boy says he's outta work, and was a headin' up north to Kansas City or Omaha or wherever to find some work."

"What makes y'all think he done it?" Daddy asked.

"Aw, Clayton; come on. He done it, all right. He denied it all at first, but after a couple hours of usin' our special methods o' enterrogation, so to speak, we got his full an' complete confession. He done it all right, and that boy's goin' to prison."

"What about the money from the bank? Did y'all recover it?"

"Well, see, that's what's funny about this case, and of course I'm here this mornin' to check out that old car that he slept in where Arliss found him yesterday. We hadn't located the money yet, but we believe he dumped it off with his cohort that was headin' south on the other KCS freight–he was southbound and goin' through Ft. Smith–I believe. We already called the railroad police and warned them and told them to check all the freight cars comin' into Ft. Smith from up this way."

"So y'all ain't so much as found a dime of that money, but y'all are sure this colored man's the one that done the job?"

"Look, Clayton, I cain't answer fer that money. I didn't steal it, and I don't know where it is. But you know as well as I do that when we catch some chance nigger slippin' up here through Northwest Arkansas like that– sneakin' through on the railroad lines on the very same night when the bank in Gentry gets robbed, we ain't naturally gonna delay too long puttin' the cuffs on 'im and puttin' this case to its final rest. Them people already knows their money's gone, and they ain't never gettin' it back unless, of course, ol' Joe shows us jist where he's put it. They jist want to see someone pay fer it. They don't want to wait too long to see justice served, and they don't give a Royal Crown whether he's white, black, purple, or green. Besides, what difference does it make when ol' Festus has already confessed to doin' it anyway?"

"Well, Jimmy Ray, just the same, I ain't sure he done it, fer what it's worth. If he done it, it seems like he'd a had the money on him, don't it? I believe someone else maybe done it…maybe someone from around here. And by the way, you don't need to get ugly about it."

"Now you watch it, Clayton. Just 'cause you don't happen to like the way we persecute the justice system around here don't give you any right to call us into questions about it. We're doin' a right thorough job of it–if I do say so myself, sir–and though we don't have the loot in our hands just yet, I believe we're gonna find it. But you, sir, can be dern sure we got us a confession, and that nigger's a goin' to prison, if he don't get hisself shot or hanged first! And on top of that, Clayton, you just remember that you ain't been seen around here fer sometime yerself, which means that you might could just as well be a suspect a settin' there in place of that nigger right now, if we didn't already have him and his confession. Now, if you don't mind, Clayton, I'd be grateful if you'd allow me to walk out yonder and look around at them cars and junk and all that what-not out there."

"Well, Jimmy Ray, I'm sorry to get you all upset. You just go right ahead and look out there all you like. And by the way, I can easily demonstrate without a doubt where I was at the time of that robbery from my log book and my receipts and such. I practically live up there on Highway 66, and there's people up there what could testify fer me, if need be."

The deputy spent a couple of hours looking and poking around out behind our station that day, but he found nothing. Of course, how could he? Clearly, there was nothing for him to find. Between customers, Daddy, Granddaddy, and I talked a lot that afternoon about what to do. Daddy said that he didn't much like how Deputy Watkins got so easily angry with him.

Granddaddy said, "Well, ever'one knows that from the time you married Norma Jean, there's been tension between you two. It's as simple as that, Clayton. You married the girl he wanted, and he's been sour about it ever since. Don't pay him no mind–jist give him a wide berth–and keep an eye on yer back."

"Well," said Daddy, "in spite of his prejudices and fer his own good, we got to figure out how to get around ol' Jimmy Ray in order to help him see that Brother Pickett and the deacon may have been the ones what robbed that bank. We may have to go directly to Sheriff Parker, Paw, and talk to him."

"I believe yer right. Well, I can probably talk with him tomorrow or Monday," Granddaddy said.

Twenty-four

The next day, of course, was Sunday, and now that my family knew all the details that I had been able to share with them, we were all going to be keeping watchful eyes on Brother Pickett, Deacon Ellis, and Brother Simpson. However, when I got to Sunday school that morning, I was surprised to learn that Brother Pickett was out sick and had arranged for a substitute teacher for our class. The substitute's name was Mr. Jack Martel, who had been a member of our church for just a little over a year. Mr. Martel had come up to Northwest Arkansas from somewhere around Valley View, Texas. In Texas, he had worked on cattle ranches and oil rigs, but now he was a foreman in a small poultry plant operated by Purina Farms. Many of the young people in the church liked and respected him because he was well-built like a fine football player, and he drove a fairly new, deep-green colored GMC pickup truck that was always clean and highly polished. With a perfectly trimmed, full moustache, Mr. Martel was handsome and always well-dressed in a western-style, dress jacket, and he wore the nicest cowboy boots any of us had ever seen, except perhaps those worn by the Reverend Sutherland. That Sunday morning, we examined Mr. Martel in our Sunday school class.

"Mr. Martel, do you smoke?" I asked him.

"Why, no, son, not at all. What's yer name?"

"His name is Jefferson Davis Stafford, Mr. Martel," Donnie Joe shouted, before I could answer, "But most folks just call him 'J.D.' Some people call him Stafford."

"Well, J.D., why do you ask?"

"Well, sir, it's only that our other Sunday school teacher's a heavy smoker, and he told us not to do it," I answered.

"Yeah, he coughs a lot…" reported Lester.

"And he smells like smoke…" Bubby added.

"And," said Tommy, "he's probably out there today dyin' from lung cancer."

There was a lot of giggling and laughing going on in the class, but we were all trying to get on the teacher's good side by pointing out all the faults of Brother Pickett.

"Well, I don't know yer regular teacher, but I'm happy to fill in fer him today, and we ain't gonna talk much about him or his bad habits. We cain't fix him, but we can sure work on you boys and he'p y'all keep on the straight and narrow pathway."

We asked Mr. Martel if he had a girl friend, and how he liked his pickup truck. He tried to answer all our questions, which made his teaching different from Brother Pickett's. Furthermore, Mr. Martel made all these personal applications about the Christian life from his own experiences; we were all amazed by his visit with us that day. He also told us how he was trying to be a good Christian–not just on Sunday mornings–but everyday and in every way.

"God wants us to be faithful everywhere and at all times," Mr. Martel said. "You don't have to hide it. You don't need to be ashamed about it. You boys can be proper Christians whether someone is watchin' y'all or not, and believe me, boys, it makes a whole whale of a difference."

None of us had ever heard that expression before, and when he said 'whole whale,' he looked right in Bubby's face and emphasized the word so forcefully that it seemed to hit us all–just like a whale–pinning each of us to the backs of our seats.

"Yassir, gentlemen," Mr. Martel continued. "I've got these folks that work fer me in the plant, and so many of them claims to be a Christian. But then I hear them behind my back a cussin' and a swearin' and a takin' the

Lord's name in vain all the time, and I can tell you, I ain't impressed, and I don't believe God is impressed either! But then they come around near to me, and everything is 'Yassir, Mr. Martel,' and 'The Lord bless you, Mr. Martel,' and it's as plain as day that they's a puttin' on what I call the 'Christian show.' Boys, why cain't they be honest? It's because they know I'm their boss, and they's simply puttin' on the show."

Brother Pickett never called us 'gentlemen,' and he never told us any stories like that from his real life. Mr. Martel taught us the lesson, and then He told us how he went through the plant everyday inspecting and making sure that only healthy chickens got through the eviscerating lines. He talked about how they have these new processes now to grow bigger chickens faster, and how they were developing plans for the beneficial use of all the feathers and heads and claws and all that other refuse from the bird that no one wants left over. We were so impressed by his teaching that Sunday school was practically over before we knew it.

After Sunday school was over, our complaints about Brother Pickett accompanied us as we made our way upstairs to the worship hall.

"Why cain't we have Mr. Martel as our regular teacher?" J.R. asked as we walked around to the front of the Grange House.

"Yeah, why do we have to have ol' skin-Pickett fer our teacher?" Donnie Joe asked.

"That's right," said Bubby. "and how about that 'whole whale' of a difference, boys? Brother Pickett's the whale that makes the whole difference–I can tell y'all that! And think about it! Can you imagine anythin' less than…a whole whale?"

Donnie Joe said, "why, anythin' less would be jist half a whale, and no one's ever seen jist half a whale!"

"Well, I ain't ever seen a whole whale!" Tommy Green said.

"Course you did!" said J.R.

"Yeah? When was that?" asked Bubby.

"When we all seen you, Bubby!" replied J.R.

Everyone–including Bubby–laughed heartily on the way up the stairs and into the worship hall. Before the worship service began, I kept looking around to see if Brother Pickett might emerge. He never showed up, but sure enough, Deacon Ellis and Brother Simpson came walking slowly up the stairs from around the side of the building and up where the outhouses were out behind the Grange House. They both reeked from stale cigarette smoke. Seeing Brother Simpson with the deacon, I suddenly thought, *I wonder if he is that third, unknown man whose voice I haven't been able to identify yet?* I thought I would strike up a conversation with him just to hear the sound of his voice.

"Good mornin', Brother Simpson!" I said.

"What are you up to, young Stafford, if only but fer no good?" he asked gruffly. "And what's good about it, anyway?"

"Well, sir," I said. "I jist wondered if you was a baseball fan?"

"What if I am?" he asked. "What's it to you?"

"Well, they're a playin' the All-Star game this week."

"Well, I ain't a fan, and I ain't got time fer it," he growled. "Less all move along, now, and get inside fer the services. You boys ought to be keepin' yer minds on the services—not on baseball! Sports is nuthin' but the temptations of the devil!"

"Yassir," I responded. However, his voice brought me no recollections; I just couldn't identify the sound of his voice as that of one of the conspirators from the bank robbery group.

We all sat together as a family. Of course, I was spellbound once again by Miss Audrey Jane; she sat there on the organ bench, and—as stunning as ever–she was looking like an Italian Madonna playing the organ. She moved gracefully as she played, and her long, slender fingers lovingly caressed the ivory keys up and down the scales producing the most enthralling, angelic choruses that must surely accompany the saints when they pass from this earth directly into the Father's presence in heaven. Her music combined with the radiant beauty of her face to create a Rembrandt-like sense of pure light that emerged out of the shadows in the dark corner where the organ stood.

Mr. King appeared at the front and called upon everyone to stand for the opening hymn. After the first song, Mr. King offered up the morning prayer, and then Pastor Sutherland stepped forward to make some announcements. He thumped his cane on the floor to get everyone's attention.

"I just want to inform y'all that we had our biggest and best Vacation Bible School ever this past week. Of course, my daughter Starla won all the daily contests of recruitin' the most outsiders, and that means that Starla is also the big winner of the free tickets to the Old Spanish Treasure Cave up north of Gravette. We had a total of a hundert and three new, visiting students, and durin' the Bible school there were forty-three professions of faith, and nineteen re-dedications to the Christian life. Now, folks, let's give little Starla and those professions and re-dedications a big round of applause."

Pastor Sutherland led all the hand-clapping, and when the noise died down, he continued: "Now, I also want to address that this year's church picnic on the grounds was a big success, too. All the day's activities and events were great, and we had a chance to minister in softball to our Methodist, Presbyterian, and Church of Christ brethren as well. However, most o' y'all know that the bank in Gentry got robbed on the night of the Fourth of July. I'm aware that many o' y'all had accounts in that bank, and of course, this is a terrible thing. I just want to challenge y'all, church, to rise up to the occasion to reach out to our poor brothers and sisters who are in need at this time. Less all commit to support and he'p each other in this very serious time when money is short and the bills continue to come in. Folks, we're gonna take up a special collection for the next four Sundays to share our blesséd wealth with our neighbors in need, and to get us started out on the right foot, I've got a brand, spankin' new hundert dollar bill right here that I'm gonna place in that plate fer this special collection." Pastor Sutherland stepped down off the stage and walked over to the offering plates that were sitting on the communion table, and he put his hundred dollar bill right in the top plate. Then he walked back up to the stage.

"Yassir, less all give till it hurts, folks. And one more thing. Y'all know they caught a colored man that confessed to the crime, but he ain't sayin' what he done with all that money. I just want to call y'all to a full constraint of yerselves and to be in prayer about this issue. Church, remember this: we've all been down that road before, and it ain't right just to take the law into yer own hands and go hang that poor soul. It just ain't the Christian thing to do. If you choose to go down that path, you'll pay the price fer it, too. Less all commit to turnin' this over to the Lord and remember what He said about revengence– 'revengence is mine sayeth the Lord!' In fact, I'm a gonna challenge y'all to pray over that lost colored boy! Remember that the Lord also said that we pour heaps of burnin' coals on our enemies when we're a prayin' over them, so I believe we need to be dumpin' out them hot coals by the bushel-full on that colored man's head–fer his own sake to confess, and fer our own sakes–so we all get our money back."

The whole place was literally resounding with men all over the auditorium shouting "Amen!" and "Yassir!" and "Preach it, Reverend!"

Mr. King led the church in a few more songs, and then they took up the regular tithes and offering. Our whole family had its eyes glued on that offering plate, but nothing unusual happened other than the fact that people all over the church responded to Pastor Sutherland's initial call to give a lot of money. After the collection, Mrs. Henderson sang the special music for the morning, and then Pastor Sutherland preached a very strong message followed by the typical, Just As I Am invitation, which resulted in numerous people stepping forward that morning to get saved, to rededicate themselves, or to join the church. Before Pastor Sutherland closed out the service with his final prayer, he said, "Church, this has been West Bethel Baptist Church's best Bible school week ever, and I just want y'all to know that we're a gonna start our new building program real soon!"

Before he had to leave town again, Daddy wanted personally to communicate to the pastor about what I had seen and what we all knew. Of course, at the door of the Grange House, there was a long line of people waiting to shake Brother Sutherland's hand. Daddy waited until the end of the line, and when he finally got to the door, the pastor said, "Clayton, it's always good to see you in our church services; how's the truckin' bidness treatin' you?"

"Just fine, Reverend; just fine," Daddy replied. "But I got to share somethin' sort of private with you Brother Sutherland, if I may, sir."

"Why, yassir, Clayton, of course. Less just step back inside and sit down together there in the last row."

They moved back inside the Grange House and sat down together on the last row of church benches.

"What you got on yer mind there, Clayton?" Reverend Sutherland asked.

"Well, Reverend," Daddy replied. "This is confidential, sir, but I believe it to be true, and I'm just concerned–if indeed it is true–that yer aware of it. It has to do with my oldest boy–Jefferson."

"I see," the reverend responded. "Wants to get baptized, does he?"

"No sir, it ain't that," Daddy said. "It's somethin' he seen goin' on in the church, and we believe maybe you ought to know about it, in case you might want to investigate it any further."

"I see. What's a goin' on then?"

"Well, sir. It sounds far-fetched, but it could be true. Last week, Jefferson saw one of the offering takers steal some of the money out of the offering plate, and he knows who done it. We ain't goin' to name any names yet, but you might want to keep yer eyes open and on the folks what takes up our collections, sir."

Reverend Sutherland appeared shocked and grieved by the idea that someone in the church might steal from his offering plate.

"Clayton, do you mind tellin' me who done it?"

"Well, Pastor, I prefer not to right now. Less maybe wait and see what happens for a couple of weeks or so. But, what's more…apparently, my boy also overheard some folks speakin' at the Fourth of July church picnic last week, and they was a talkin' about robbin' a bank up in Decatur."

"In Decatur? Well, that's it, then," said Reverend Sutherland, who looked somewhat more relieved when he heard this. "You see, that don't actually matter much then. We don't need to worry over that. It was the bank in Gentry–not Decatur–what was actually robbed, so in that case, it couldn't have been any of our people. Jefferson must have heard things all wrong–since they was talkin' about robbin' the bank in Decatur."

"Well, sir," Daddy said, "I know it's hard to believe, but it might could be true, and if it is, my boy knows who done it, and that colored hobo they's holdin' in the Gentry jailhouse is probably innocent. I'm a tellin' you this in confidence, of course, 'cause we cain't prove nuthin'. But God knows all about it, and the most important thing is that they might try it again, so maybe we need to keep our eyes open, Reverend."

"We got no way of knowin' if somebody stole money outta the offering plate, 'cause we don't know how much went into it before the funds were stolen out of it," Pastor Sutherland said.

"Yassir, I understand," Daddy said. "I just want to make you aware of what we know, Brother Sutherland, that's all. And Reverend, I'm sorry that I took up so much of yer time, but I consider it important fer you."

"Well, Brother Clayton, I am grateful fer what you shared with me; I appreciate it a lot. I'll keep an eye on them boys that collects our offerings in the weeks ahead. Thank you, Clayton."

"Yer welcome, Pastor."

After that, we all went home for our regular Sunday dinner and our naps afterward.

Twenty-five

About four o'clock the next morning–Monday–Daddy woke up, said good-bye to Mama, started up his truck, and left Y-City Station for Joplin. I was sound asleep and didn't hear him leave. Granddaddy and I woke up a few hours later, and we met for coffee out on the back porch.

"Well, boy," said Granddaddy, "now the reverend knows what you seen, and I expect that he'll do some thorough investigatin'. I'm gonna drive over to Bentonville later today and talk to Sheriff Parker. Boy, it's our Christian duty before God and our civic duty before our country to be honest and up front about the things we know. If we know somthin' to be true, we got a responsibility to tell the truth about it. We don't hide it."

"Yassir," I replied. "That's exactly what our Sunday school teacher told us yesterday."

"Who, Brother Pickett?"

"No, sir. Yesterday Brother Pickett was out sick, and we had a substitute whose name was Mr. Jack Martel."

"I don't know him real well; I seen him around the church a few times, though. He impresses me as a fine young man," Granddaddy said.

"Well, Granddaddy," I said, "I appreciated what he told us boys. In fact, I thought it was a lot better than what Bother Pickett normally talks about."

A little later, Grandma prepared us some hotcakes for breakfast, after which time Granddaddy and I went down to open the station. Mama said she would be down later, and when she got there, Granddaddy would drive over to Bentonville to talk with Sheriff Parker. Both of them agreed that I shouldn't try to run our station alone, although I felt like I could do it.

We got the station all opened up before seven thirty, but there was hardly any business that morning. Out behind our station, there was a long freight train of identical, empty coal cars sitting idle on the south-bound track. The cars were all marked, "Kansas City Southern." The train was divided in half right where our road connected up with State Highway 59 so any approaching traffic could cross over the tracks. Everything was peaceful that day. The sun was already hot, and the humidity was up. Birds were sitting up on the telephone wires that ran parallel to the tracks, and every now and then, a whole flock would fly off and out over the fields. They might be gone for three or four minutes, but then they would all re-appear and light back on the wires together.

About eight o'clock, Mr. Crawford pulled into the station. I ran out to ask him if he wanted me to fill his tank.

"Don't need no gas this mornin', boy," he said. He opened his car door, and he climbed out and spat a big, brownish-green juice-ball of tobacco slop all over the driveway. He grinned at me sarcastically, almost proudly as if to say, "How'd you like that wad o' t'baccy, boy?" I thought his tobacco habit was absolutely disgusting.

When he got out of the car, he grabbed a sack of doughnuts and that day's edition of the *Tulsa World*, and he slammed his car door shut. Then he opened up the bag and said, "Here–get you a jelly doughnut, boy. They're fresh hot ones, and I tell you, son, they are goo-ooo-ooo-uud."

I grabbed a warm jelly doughnut out of the sack and began to eat it. While I was eating the doughnut, I asked him it there was anything good in today's newspaper.

"What's that you're sayin' there, boy? He asked. "I cain't understand you! Your mouth's all full o' jelly doughnut!"

A few seconds after I swallowed down the doughnut–and spilled a spoonful of jelly on my clean shirt–I repeated: "I said, hey there Mr. Crawford…anything good in that paper today?"

"I dunno boy. Hadn't read it, yet. But I'll leave it here fer you so you can read it later when I'm done with it."

"Thanks," I said.

Mr. Crawford was definitely right about how good the doughnuts tasted–mine was tasty-good! He went inside to sit and chat with Granddaddy. In the garage, I had an old steel water pail that I would invert and use now and then for a seat. It was easy to move the pail around from place to place, especially into the shade as the sun moved over the station during the day. I went into the garage and found the pail, and I filled it with warm water. Then I went back outside and walked over to the spot where Mr. Crawford spat his tobacco juice, and I threw the water on that mess to clean it up so somebody wouldn't step in it later. Then I found a nice shady spot, I inverted the pail, and I sat down on it for awhile–waiting for anything interesting or something meaningful to happen.

I sat there for a long time, and nothing important happened at all. Hardly any cars passed by. I decided to examine a little more carefully the condition of our station. I noticed that there were a lot of tiles that were faded and broken up on the roof. No telling how many years of wind, hail, snow, ice, and rainstorms they had endured. Made of a reddish kind of natural clay, the tiles formed an unusual roof that simply wasn't used much in Northwest Arkansas. I wondered why. I knew they were expensive, but there was plenty of clay around, and it seemed to me that clay tiles made a strong, naturally attractive roof. I wondered about it as I turned my attention to the old building.

Goodness, I thought. *It is in real need of paint on the north and west sides of the building.*

The building itself was made of some brick, lots of glass, and lots of wood. The whole place had been painted white, and when we took it over, Daddy had repainted the south and east sides of the building, which were the most visible from the road. On the north side of the building, bushes and vines had grown up, and there was a grove of great shade trees that now hid much of the north wall from view up on the road. However, just about wherever there was some wood or wood-trim, the paint was peeling off and chipping away. To my amazement, someone–evidently years ago–had originally painted a beautiful advertisement across the entire north side of our station. The picture, almost completely faded now, showed a uniformed, smiling man wearing a hat and wiping down the windshield of a classic, convertible car with a beautiful, smiling girl sitting at the wheel of the car. The girl was wearing sunglasses, and she had a scarf around her neck. At the top, off to the right, I could just make out the advertising caption, which said: "Use our Hi-Test; It's the Best." Down below, almost completely covered by the growth of wild bushes, the sign was completed by the faded letters, Valvoline, and the picture of a can of oil, under which the sign read, "The Pennsylvania Oil."

Over the years, the station's concrete driveway had cracked and broken in a number of places. Patches of green grass were growing up between the cracks in the pavement. Initially, we tried to keep all that grass pulled up, but it was almost a losing battle–like the junkyard out back. To me, it seemed like the more dead batteries, old car parts, and worn-out tires that Daddy hauled off, the more ended up out there. One day, a few months back, I told Mama, "We need a work crew to come down here and he'p us move all our junk from the back of the station onto one of them freight cars that's sittin' back there idle."

"Well, son," she said, "I believe we got enough back there to fill three or four of them empty cars."

"Yes, ma'am," I replied.

Enjoying my free time, the warm weather, and a morning lacking in interruptions, I sat on that pail for almost another hour. Then Mama appeared at the station, and she had a load of vegetables, fruits, and eggs to set out on her table, so I helped her take it out of the old pickup truck and set it all up in its place on the table and in fancy-looking, wicker baskets. While I was helping Mama set up the fruit stand, the railroad men stopped at the Y and walked over to the tracks. They waited a few minutes, and way down the line, the locomotive horn signaled a couple of times, and then the freight cars on the south suddenly lurched backward toward the north–closing the gap at our road. In another moment, the railroad men coupled up the freight cars together into one complete train. In the next moment, the train's horn sounded two or three short blasts, and then all the freight cars suddenly heaved in the opposite direction. Before long, the train was moving slowly, but it began to pick up speed quickly toward the south.

"Mama, you just made it down here at the right time," I said.

"I sure did. I'm glad I didn't have to wait on the other side fer fifteen or twenty minutes. It's a pain waitin' on them long trains."

"Yes ma'am. I agree."

"Boy, it's gonna be a hot day, today," Mama said. She wiped the sweat off her face with her apron, and then she looked up at me. "What you grinnin' at, boy?"

"I dunno, Mama. I jist...well...I really love you, Mama!"

"Why, boy! Whatever's got into you?" she asked.

"Nuthin. I just been thinkin' this morning, that even though the times ain't real easy, we sure got it good. I mean, we got a good family, and a good place to live; we got clean clothes, and we eat good, too. Some of them kids what Starla...actually, I mean...what Brother Sutherland brung to the Bible school was some of the downright poorest kids I think I ever seen, Mama."

"Well, it's good you notice things like that, son. Makes you count yer blessin's, and you're right. The Lord has truly blessed us! And I just want you to know that I'm so proud of you fer yer honesty and what-not. You're growin' up, boy, and a whole lot faster than I want, too."

"Do you want me to watch the table, today, since Granddaddy's goin' over to Bentonville?" I asked.

"That'd be great. I'll set in the station and watch the cash box, and you sit at the fruit stand. If we get a customer, you can pump the gas, but if we get two at a time, we'll have to play it by ear," she said.

"Okay," I said.

Just about then, Mr. Crawford came with Granddaddy out of the station. They both walked over to Mr. Crawford's car.

"Arliss, you take care, now, you hear?" said Mr. Crawford.

"I will," Granddaddy replied. "I got to drive over to Bentonville today."

"We'll see you again tomorrow, then," Mr. Crawford said to Granddaddy. Then he turned to Mama, and he said, "Ma'am." And to me, he said, "You take care of your granddaddy, boy."

"Yassir," I responded.

Just before Mr. Crawford got into his car, he spat a big, nasty, brownish-green blob of tobacco juice on the ground again–almost in the same spot that I had just washed an hour or so ago. He got in his car, and then he looked at me with that same arrogant look, and he drove off toward the south. I went back over and got my steel water pail, and filled it with warm water. I walked back over and threw the water on that mess, and I thought to myself, *Why does he have to be so dang filthy?*

After awhile, Granddaddy announced that he was ready to drive over to Bentonville.

"I'm gonna communicate to Sheriff Parker what we know about that bank robbery," he said.

"Granddaddy, you be careful now, you hear?" said Mama.

"I, will. I'll be back in a couple of hours."

"Okay."

Mama took over the station, and I sat outside in the shade up by her fruit and vegetable stand. The railroad tracks had been vacant now for quite some time, and there was almost no traffic on the road in either direction. Whenever Mama worked the inside of the station, she always stayed busy by cleaning the floor, dusting all the fixtures, washing all the windows, and setting things in as good order as possible. It seems like she never rested even a minute. On the other hand, I was out sitting in the shade and daydreaming under a large oak tree. Now that I had figured out what it was, I couldn't help but see Miss Audrey Jane's face whenever I looked at that faded picture on the north end of our station. She was the one driving the convertible, and I was the one washing her windshield.

"Miss Audrey Jane, does your car use Hi-Test?" I'd ask her.

"Why, yes, it does, Mr. Stafford. Please make sure my tank is filled with Hi-Test," she'd say.

"Oh, yes ma'am. I'm at your service, completely, Miss Audrey Jane, and our Hi-Test–well, my goodness, it's the best."

"Thank you, kindly, Mr. Stafford. I know it's the best, because my car won't accept the rest," she said.

"You're welcome, Miss Audrey Jane."

"Mr. Stafford, please forgive me, if it ain't too much fer me to ask, but where did you get such beautiful green eyes?"

"I reckon I got them from my daddy," I replied.

"Well, they are the loveliest green eyes I've ever seen," Miss Audrey Jane said.

"Well, Miss Audrey Jane, I better check yer water, yer oil, and yer air!" I said.

"Yes," she said. "Please make sure it's all correct."

All of a sudden, I was frightfully awakened from my daydream by a loud, speeding car heading south down Highway 59. Coming from the north side of our station, the car sped right past me, and from its sound and its speed, I knew instinctively from previous experience that the car was moving headlong toward disaster. Whatever the cause, somehow I was familiar with this same set of strange circumstances, and it didn't matter whether it was the condition of the road, the weather, the sounds and smells, the birds and the insects, driver curiosity or inability, or a combination of all the foregoing, I knew instinctively that another tragic collision was about to happen in the next few seconds, and there was nothing I could do to prevent it. Immediately, I became aware of a tremendous increase in the pounding of my heart; my breathing became heavy and compressed; my mouth suddenly went dry, and my palms became sweaty. I jumped up from my bucket, turned, and quickly began to move down our driveway just as the southbound car went into the curve. The car was dark blue, and it looked like a late model Buick or a Pontiac. As it flew into the curve, it was well over the center of the road, and it crashed full-speed and head-on into a car moving at a high rate of speed and coming up from the south.

"Oh, my goodness!" I said. "Not again!"

The impact was awful. Fortunately, there was no fire, although the air smelled of burning rubber and oil. Pieces of junk and debris littered the road. The remains of two cars–now great hulks of scrap metal–were spread out across the whole road as well as up and down both lanes of the highway.

I ran quickly into the station.

"Mama! There's been a crash out at the 'Y'!" I screamed. "Did you hear it? I seen it! I need a nickel so I can call the police!"

She jumped up immediately and said, "Yes, son, I heard it." At the same time, she reached into her apron pocket and pulled out a handful of coins and dumped them into my hand. I ran back outside to the pay telephone booth that the phone company had installed on the south side of our station. I put a nickel into the coin slot, and I dialed the telephone operator.

"Operator…" she said.

"Yes, ma'am," I said. "There's been a terrible car crash here at the 'Y.'"

"A car crash? Where? What Y? Ain't no Y.M.C.A. in these parts, sonny. Where are you? You'd best be tellin' me the truth young man!" the operator warned.

"No ma'am. I mean, yes ma'am. I mean...not at any Y.M.C.A., but here at Y- City Station. It's on Arkansas Highway 59 between Gentry and Decatur...about half-way between."

"Oh...I see," the operator said. "Y-City Station? What kind of a station is that?"

"It's a gas station, ma'am! Please hurry. I think they're all dead!"

"Oh, okay, then. Yes...well, I'll call the Gentry police and get them out to you right away."

"Thank you, ma'am," I replied.

After I finished talking to the operator on the telephone, I turned my full attention back to the crash. By now, a short line of northbound cars was forming on the road south of the accident site. As yet, no traffic had appeared from Decatur, but I was concerned that any cars coming down from there would be traveling fast so I ran back inside the station.

"Mama, I called the telephone operator, and she said she'd call the Gentry police fer us. I don't believe anyone in them cars is alive, Mama. I got to make an emergency flag right away fer any cars comin' down from the north so as to prevent anything further from happenin' out there."

I found a long stick that we used as a prop to keep some of the station windows open, and I grabbed a red shop towel, and then I fixed them tightly together. As fast as I could, I ran up yonder past our fruit and vegetable stand and maybe another hundred yards farther. In the distance up the road, a car was coming our way. I crossed over the highway and stood directly in the middle of the northbound lane, and I waved my red flag wildly. The car began to slow down when it came near me, and then it stopped by my side. The driver rolled his window down.

"What's goin' on, sonny?" the driver asked.

"Sir," I said, "there's been a awful accident about three, maybe four-hundred yards down yonder at the curve. I just wanted to give you fair warnin,' that's all."

"Oh?" the driver said. "How bad was it?"

"Well, sir, both cars are wrecked, and I believe they's all killed. Don't see how anyone could have lived through it."

"Will there be a long delay?" the driver's wife asked.

"I dunno, ma'am. I've called the police, and they ought to be here any moment now. Where are y'all comin' from?"

"We're comin' down from Ft. Scott, Kansas," the driver explained. "We're on our way to Hot Springs."

"I see. Well, sir, I'm sure sorry about yer hold-up here."

In another minute or two, a second and then a third car came down and stopped in the line-up. I ran back and told the drivers about the accident, and I asked the last driver to explain the problem if any drivers came up behind him. Then I ran back to our station to be with Mama. As I was running, I could hear the faint sound of a police siren that wailed ever louder as it came nearer.

The Gentry police car arrived just about the time I got back to our station. Mama and I stayed at our station, but we could see what was going on down at the curve. I could tell that the policeman was frustrated by the wreck and all the mess and the junk. He looked inside both cars, and he tried to determine if there was anything he could do. After a few moments, he walked back to his car.

"Mama, I'd guess he'll be callin' fer another policeman or maybe even an ambulance or two," I told Mama.

Mama looked down at the two cars.

"Son, I believe yer right. I don't see how anyone could have lived through that."

A few moments later, another Gentry police car came, and then two ambulances arrived. One was from Gentry; the other came all the way up from Siloam Springs. In another moment, a tow-truck arrived. The ambulance drivers pulled a couple of bodies out from the wreckage, and then they found another body in the field east of the road.

After much work down at the crash site, one of the Gentry policemen came into our station.

"Howdy, ma'am. Son. I'm Officer Willard Thackston from the Gentry police. Did either of you see what happened?"

"I seen it," I said.

"That's correct," Mama said. "He seen it, but I only heard the noise out there."

"Well, ma'am," Officer Thackston said, "we're gonna need to sit down with yer boy and get his statement…that is,…an accurate description of what he seen."

"Well, sir," I said, "I only heard this one car–looked like maybe a Pontiac or a Buick–and it was screamin' by me headin' down yonder…." I pointed toward the south. "Before it got to that curve, it crossed over the center of the road and simply hit that other car that was a comin' up this way. Hit him hard and head-on, too. Sir," I said, "it was awful."

I told Officer Thackston everything. He wrote it all down in his little book, and then he wrote down all of our names and other personal information.

"Well, son," said Officer Thackston, "I appreciate all you seen and reported and also what you done to keep any more cars from hittin' each other."

"Thank you, sir, but I just did what anyone should have done."

"Well, ma'am," before I leave," said Officer Thackston, "would it be all right if we park them heaps out yonder in yer junk yard fer a couple a days? We need to look all through them fer any evidence or items and such fer the next of kin. The City of Gentry'll pay you storage for a couple of days, and then they'll remove them cars in a day or two."

"Well, yassir," Mama said. "I'm sure that'd be fine. If you don't mind, please put them toward the south end and as far back as you can so the customers cain't see them."

Officer Thackston walked back over to the crash site, and he instructed the tow-truck drivers to move the wrecked cars temporarily to the southwest end of our junkyard so that the highway could be cleared quickly and all the traffic–which was now backed up maybe a half mile or so in both directions–could move on.

Twenty-six

They found a total of three dead bodies. There was a woman's body behind the wheel of the northbound car, which was a black, four-door Chevrolet, model 1950. The crash impact had almost completely pinned her back against her seat and both the car's engine and its steering wheel assembly were pushed back into her body so that the woman was crushed to death. The officer told us that her driver's license showed her to be Lizzy Rutherford from Pea Ridge. And then, after a brief search, they also found a child's body out in the field east of the road. Evidently the child was Mrs. Rutherford's daughter, a young girl, perhaps a little older than Tawna Rae. It appeared that the little girl had been thrown completely out of the car, and she was instantly killed by the impact of the crash. This news literally made Mama and me sick, and I actually felt nauseous from it. I had to sit down when Officer Thackston told us about the little girl.

The third body was that of an older man. He was carrying no identification papers and no driver's license—nothing in his pockets. Officer Thackston said, "I have no idea who this man was. His face was all cut up with windshield glass, and I can tell y'all this—the man was about as drunk as one can be and still be conscious enough to operate a motor vehicle. We recovered several glass bottles of liquor that he had in the car with him, and he had a little suitcase–all locked up tight, of course–apparently on the seat next to him. We're gonna impound it all and do a investigation, and we'll know a lot more 'bout it in the mornin'.'"

Then Officer Thackston left the station and went back to the crash site until it was all cleared away. The backed-up traffic now began to move quickly through the area again. A couple of cars stopped in at our station, presumably for service, but mostly for information about the accident. We did sell a little gas, and one lady bought some of Mama's vegetables. This accident was clearly the worst I had ever seen, and it reminded me of the others that had also happened here. Again, I wondered why it had to happen.

Just because of that blasted curve near our station, I thought to myself.

I wondered if our gas station wasn't somehow gaining a local reputation of being the place in Northwest Arkansas that was closer to death than anywhere else. The thought disturbed me. At times like this, it seemed to me that death had become some kind of hideous but realistic personality who expressly decided to mark off his own territory, and, with the deposit of these two new junk cars, it almost appeared that he was now taking up residence somewhere out in our junkyard so that he could further lurk invisibly all around our station. Over and over again, I found myself asking, "Why here? Why?" And I reckon what actually disturbed me the most was the idea that some poor, unwitting, adult soul, who–for no more than a drink–was willing to exchange his reason and his self-control for the momentary exhilaration of irrational speed and merciless power that led to the tragic loss of an innocent mother and child.

It could have been my mama out there…and Tawna Rae with her, I thought.

After a short while, things around the station fell quiet again, and about three-thirty p.m., Granddaddy reappeared in his old pick-up truck.

"Did you talk to the sheriff, Granddaddy?" I asked.

"Yassir," he said. "I told Sheriff Parker, 'Now Sheriff, I've got certain information that pertains to that Gentry bank robbery case, and I feel obligated to share it with you, in confidence, of course, and whether you believe it or not. It may sound just a little far fetched to you, but I've got it on good reputation. Once I share it with you, it's up to you what you do with it.' And then I told him the whole thing," said Granddaddy.

Mama said, "Well, that's good. At least Sheriff Parker is aware of it, now, and like you say–what he does with it is up to him. I'm glad o' that, but Granddaddy, you missed all the excitement round here…I mean…it wasn't really excitin' so much as it was just noisy and a very sad event."

"Yeah, Granddaddy, after you went over to Bentonville, there was a terrible car crash earlier today out in front o' the station. It was awful. It was two cars, and in one of them it was a Mama and her little girl, and in the other it was an old man, and Granddaddy, he was drunk. I think they was all killed instantly. At least, that's what Officer Thackston thought. The little girl was thrown completely out of the car."

"Oh my goodness! That is indeed a sad thing to hear! And, son, you say the old man was drivin' drunk?"

"Yassir. Officer Thackston said he was near about dead-drunk."

"Well, now he is dead. I just wonder where he got his liquor from? He must have got it up on the state line or in Anderson somewhere. But, my! That is certainly heartbreaking to hear about that woman and her little girl. What an awful shame. I just hate to hear about that," said Granddaddy.

Mama said, "Yeah, it was truly awful. Officer Thackston said they was from Pea Ridge."

"Well, I sure am glad to be back all safe and sound from Bentonville," Granddaddy declared. "And by the way," he said, "while I was a visitin' Sheriff Parker, he told me–in confidence, of course–that they moved that old colored fellow outta the Gentry jailhouse and over to the county jail in Bentonville. I reckon it must have been last night after midnight when they moved him. Sheriff Parker said it was fer his own safety, 'cause he didn't think too many folks from Gentry would drive all the way over to Bentonville and try to bust him out of that jail. It's a stronger jail, anyway. Most of them folks in Gentry's got no ideal that he's been removed now anyhow. Sheriff Parker told me that most of the information that colored man gave about his background turned out to be bona fide–at least the part about bein' outta work and a comin' up from Loosiana and what-not. I'm a startin' to believe in my heart that he never done it; they're fer sure holdin' the wrong man, I think. I just cain't figure out why he would confess to it, unless they just beat it out of him."

"Well, Granddaddy," I said, "I hope they will truly find the ones that done it, and set this colored fellow free. I'd hate to see them send the wrong man to prison or hang him."

"Son, all we can do fer that colored man is pray."

"Yassir."

"It's a gettin' late, I believe," said Granddaddy. "Norma Jean? You about ready to go?"

"Just about, Granddaddy. Give me another minute or two so I can put all this stuff away, and then I'll be ready."

"All right," Granddaddy replied. "Is there a baseball game on the radio tonight boy?"

"Not tonight, Granddaddy. "Up in St. Louis, the Cardinals took all four games from Cincinnati. Before that, they beat the Cubs in Chicago–two out of three. Tonight they're takin' a break fer the All-Star game tomorrow, and it's gonna be right there at Sportsman's Park in St. Louis. Don't you jist wish somehow that Daddy could be there and get a seat?"

"Well, boy," he said. "Ever'one wishes he could get a seat at that game! But I don't believe yer daddy'll have much of a chance even to get near that ballpark–let alone get a seat. The whole house'll be packed."

"I reckon yer right," I answered.

In another minute, Mama came in from the garage where she had stored her fruits and vegetables for the night, and then we locked up the station and went home.

Twenty-seven

B efore I climbed into bed that night, I got down on my knees and prayed for that colored man. Granddaddy said it was about the only thing we could do for him, and, as I was quite certain that he didn't rob the Gentry bank, I thought it best to pray for him. I was sure that He couldn't have even known how to do it anyway. The local Gentry newspaper, *The Gentry Guardian*, was running a story that actually indicated that "the hobo now in custody was, in fact, the bank robber," and although "none of the money has been recovered yet, authorities were currently devising a plan so that it soon would be."

The story went on to claim that one, "Mr. Festus Williams, of Transmania, Louisiana, was a professional thief and hobo who frequently rode the freight trains north and south so that he might spy out an unsuspecting business or bank to rob at a time when the townspeople least expected it–when they were sleeping, relaxing, or simply unaware of what might happen." However, the paper stated that "in spite of all the systematic preparations this robber made, nevertheless, the people of Gentry had assembled in the park for a civic event on a national holiday–demonstrating, in fact, that they were actually alert and as ready as ever for any contingency." Williams merely caught the folks of Gentry "off guard," and he "cleverly took advantage of their patriotism; he robbed them while they were all watching the fireworks display in the park on the Fourth of July–a time when no decent American citizen would ever intentionally dare to be so unpatriotic as to avoid the celebration–even to keep an eye on the bank." The writer of the article went on to say that, "Besides, any individual who might willingly choose to guard a bank instead of celebrating the Fourth of July with all the rest of his fellow townspeople must certainly be in collusion with the bank robber."

According to the writer, it was evident that Williams was the robber "because he made a regular practice of jumping from freight trains in little towns just like Gentry to study the daily behaviors of the people, determine his best course of action, and know exactly when to rob the most vulnerable bank or business." The writer of the story further suggested that Williams had been in Gentry "many times before–choosing always to wander around after midnight when the police officers were tired and their watch was most likely to be interrupted by sleep," although the writer insisted that "the Gentry police officers were "at all times vigilant." The article said that, in this way, "the robber could also carefully examine the comings and goings of the people and predict their patterns of movement. Williams knew when every business in Gentry was open or closed, and he knew the names and the places of all the residents, the businesses, and even the city officials. Because many of the downtown businesses in Gentry had posted in their windows announcements of the big event, Williams was able to determine that all the people would be in the park on the evening of the Fourth of July."

Moreover, the article went on to state that "Williams had learned from all his previous stops in Gentry that a frontal entry into the bank after hours was dangerous because of its visibility and its alarm, and that the easiest way to the money was up the fire escape at the rear of the building and through a large window that could be broken without a sound or alarm. The vault, which contained most of the bank's assets, was downstairs, but a large cashbox was kept under lock and key and hidden in a desk drawer by one of the bank's officers in his second floor office."

Resulting from "his observations from his many visits to the town, Williams was able to analyze the bank's business dealings thoroughly and to deduce that the cash box would contain a large amount of the town's money over the Fourth of July."

Of course, I never saw Mr. Festus Williams in person, but according to

Granddaddy's description, the man was simply too old, too ignorant, and too unfamiliar with Northwest Arkansas in general and with Gentry in particular to have planned out anything like that reported in the newspaper. It seemed to me that the newspaper, which simply reflected no more than the thoughts and beliefs of most local people, had now fully established what the town hoped for–that Mr. Williams was guilty. All I could do was pray, and I did what I could. After my prayers, I climbed into bed and dreamed that night of playing baseball one day for the Cardinals in Sportsman's Park.

The next morning, we ate breakfast, and then we went back down to open the station. Throughout the day, I would be thinking and dreaming about the All-Star game going on up in St. Louis. Even then, as I thought about it, I recalled with great disappointment that the game would be played that afternoon rather than in the evening, and for that reason we would not even be able to pick it up with our radio. I mentioned this to Granddaddy, and he said, "Well, son, tonight we'll listen to KMOX anyway, and maybe they'll explain how the game went and tell us what the final score was."

"Well," I said, "I just want the National League to win; I cain't stand that American League."

When we arrived that morning at the station, I noticed that the two, new junk cars were sitting there now. To me, they were a fresh and visible reminder of yesterday's deaths. I went out there and sat down on the fender of an old Ford. I looked around, and I wondered how many of those other junk heaps were the end-product of death slipping in unawares to steal someone's life away. It sure made me think about some of the things that Brother Sutherland had preached one Sunday morning in church.

"Y'all jist don't know when death's a comin' to take you away! And Brother…and you, too, Sister…he's a comin' fer you, indeed. Y'all cain't just tell him to wait awhile. He listens to nobody. When he knocks at yer door, you simply go with him, and there ain't no argument with him. Folks…the Bible says that it is 'fully appointed for ever' one once to die, and then comes the judgment!' Oh brother and sister…cain't y'all see it? It is appointed…and death is out there today keepin' all his appointments! We don't know when they are, but he knows! Y'all need to get yourselves right with God, so y'all can be ready!"

As I thought about it all, I sure was glad that I was ready. I just couldn't stand the fact that death knew all his appointment times, but that I didn't know mine. It didn't take much intelligence to look around and see the truth in that.

Goodness! I thought. *Some of these folk who think they're so smart. If they was as smart as they say they are, and as smart as they think they are…why, they'd be able to figure out a way–if not to conquer and destroy death completely–at the very least to determine what their own appointment times with him are!*

And I was really thankful for Christianity, too, because it was all by faith. It was Daddy who always told us that, "most folk want to know the truth first so as they can believe it, but it ain't that way. God made us to be creatures of faith, which means we got to believe first, and then God reveals the knowledge that stands behind the truth."

And I thought, *Well, it also don't take too much intelligence to see the truth in that either, because people everywhere are surely moved to take action and make their final decisions more by what they believe than by what they know. And how much information and knowledge is out there that we just don't know…and might could never know?*

I suddenly heard Granddaddy's voice calling me; "Hey, where are you, boy?"

"I'm out here in the junkyard, Granddaddy," I shouted back. "I'll be right there."

When I came into the station from the junkyard, Granddaddy was sitting in his chair, eating a doughnut, and reading the *Tulsa World*. Mr. Crawford had arrived, and he was sitting on the other stool. As usual, he had a large chaw of Red Man in his mouth, and he was holding an empty, one-pound Maxwell House coffee can in his hand for a makeshift spittoon. I figured that Granddaddy probably found that for him and was making him use it.

At least he ain't spittin' his slop all over our floor! I thought to myself. Then I said, "Here I am, Granddaddy. Can I he'p you?" And then, "Howdy, Mr. Crawford."

"No, son. I just wanted to let you know that there was some doughnuts here now," he replied. "Here, get you one; they're mighty good today."

"Yeah, he'p yourself to some of them doughnuts, boy," Mr. Crawford repeated.

"Thank you, sir. Hope I don't spill the jelly all over my shirt, like I did the other day."

I reached in and got a doughnut, and I practically swallowed it up whole. Then I got some coffee, and after two or three short sips, the station bell rang, and I went outside to pump some gas. It was a red and white DeSoto model 1952 in good condition.

"Can I he'p you, ma'am?" I asked. It was a lady driver. She looked like she might be about sixty years old. She had gray hair, and she was well-dressed and groomed. She was also wearing some nice perfume, and it appeared that she had a dog–perhaps a poodle–riding silently on the passenger side of her front seat.

"Why, yes, young man. I'd like you to fill up my tank with Hi-Test, please."

"Yes ma'am," I responded. An' I'll be happy to check the water in your radiator, the oil in your engine, and the air in your tires."

"Thank you, young man. That'd be just wonderful. Thank you."

While I was servicing the DeSoto, Officer Thackston pulled into the station driveway and parked away from the pump in case another customer came. I waved to him, and he waved back at me. He disappeared into the station.

The DeSoto had a Missouri license tag on it. I always tried to check so we might have an idea where our customers came from.

"That'll be seven dollars and forty cents, ma'am," I stated.

The lady gave me eight dollars and said, "you keep the change, young man."

"Thank you so much, ma'am."

"Very kind of you," the lady said. Then she started her engine, and she drove out.

I went inside the station and gave Granddaddy the money. He gave me the change, which I put into my pocket. I heard Officer Thackston talking to Granddaddy and Mr. Crawford; apparently, their discussion was quite important so I didn't want to interrupt them. Officer Thackston was eating a jelly doughnut and drinking coffee as he talked. I went outside and sat in the shade for a while. Mama had arrived earlier, and she was arranging her table with items for sale.

About ten-thirty that morning, Mr. Riggins came down the road in his pickup truck and pulled into the station. Fishbait was riding with him in the truck.

"Howdy, Mr. Riggins. Hey, Fishbait, how you doin'? What'd you think of that picnic?" I asked her. "Would you like me to pump you some gas, Mr. Riggins?"

"Yeah, sonny. Fill'er up fer me," he said.

"I had fun out there. Y'all sure have lots of young people in yer church," Fishbait said.

Mr. Riggins got out of the truck and went inside the station. I began to pump some gas into the tank, and Fishbait got out and walked around to the side to talk with me.

"They ain't all from our church," I said. "A whole lot of them was Presbyterians and Methodists. There was a few from the Church of Christ, too. We just all got together after the picnic food fer the softball game and then the fireworks. But I thought it was fun, too."

"Well, I had fun there, and I might come back fer church sometime, too," Fishbait said.

"Yer always welcome, you know. Where do y'all go to church?"

"We don't go to no church."

"Well, y'all can come to ours then. Did you hear about the accident what happened out here yesterday?"

"Yeah! Wadn't that somethin'? That poor Mama and her little girl snuffed out just like that! It ain't fair…it just ain't fair," Fishbait said.

"Well," I said. "I seen it, and it was just awful…I'll never forget it. I seen it, and somehow, it got burned right into the eye o' my mind. I just cain't forget it."

"Why, that's awful, J.D.! Are you gonna be all right?"

"Well, yeah, I think so. It's just that when you see it, it's a little disturbin,' you know what I mean? And I just been a thinkin' about that All-Star game they're playin' up there in St. Louis this afternoon."

"I reckon so. Anyway, when y'all leave the station, try to look back there at our junkyard, and y'all'll see a couple of new ones…you'll see what I mean about awful."

"All right," Fishbait replied.

"What do y'all hear from Sky?" I asked, trying to change the subject.

"Nuthin,'" she said. "He don't ever write us at all, and it makes Mama angry."

"Have you seen Big Johnny B?" I asked.

"Yeah. He come around a couple of times, but he idn't what I'd call a gentleman. That boy's got a lot of wickedness in his heart, and last time he come to our farm, he didn't treat me right. Daddy told him never to come back. Besides, how do you know about him?"

"I don't know. I reckon Tex or Lloyd talked about him, and I wondered if you liked him or not–that's all."

"I don't like him at all. He cain't keep his hands to hisself, he's rough, and I had enough of that boy. He's got a dirty mouth, too. He ain't come around since Daddy told him to stay away. I wouldn't be the least bit surprised to learn if he's in jail."

"Well, fer your sake, I'm glad he ain't comin' around." I wanted to change directions with Fishbait. "When are y'all gettin' yer café?"

"Daddy says we're gonna sign all them papers and what-not directly, and we'll get it in another three or four weeks or so."

"Are y'all excited about that, Fishbait?"

"Oh yeah! I cain't wait until I can start servin' up food. Mama's been a he'pin' me practice at home and makin' me serve Daddy his dinners. Of course, we're gonna need to clean up the place, fix it all up, and paint it to make it a nicer place than how Sleepy has it."

"Well, when y'all get that café, I sure hope y'all'll invite me down to test yer hamburgers and French-fries."

Fishbait said they'd be happy to have me come down and try out their food. I finished pumping the gas, and I checked all the other necessities of their truck. Fishbait got back into the truck. Mr. Riggins was still in the station, so I went in to tell him what his gas cost.

"Mr. Riggins," I told him, "your gas was six dollars even, sir. You can just give it to Granddaddy, if you want to."

"Thank you, boy. Here's a dime fer you."

"Thank you, sir. I appreciate it."

"Why, that's all right, boy. I appreciate your hard work."

As he was walking out the station door, Mr. Riggins told Granddaddy about his café, and he invited our family to come down and eat after they got it and cleaned it all up. Granddaddy said that it would be nice to have a good family restaurant around, and Officer Thackston said that the police needed a good restaurant where they could stop and get lunch or supper and take a good coffee break now and then. Everyone seemed to be excited about the new place except Mr. Crawford; he just sat there cynically and spat tobacco juice in his can.

"Well, I got to get back out there on that road," Officer Thackston said.

"Yeah, and I got to move on, too," said Mr. Crawford. He put the Maxwell House can down on the floor just behind the station door.

They both got up and walked toward the doorway. In another moment, both gentlemen were gone. And, of course, just before he drove off, Mr. Crawford, true to his natural form, spit a sloppy and nasty wad of chewing tobacco just about in the same place he did yesterday. I anticipated this, so instinctively, I went out to find my steel pail, and I filled it with hot water.

I thought to myself, *I don't know if these daily jelly doughnuts are worth cleanin' up after all his slop.*

I washed off that part of the driveway, and then I thought, *It's so hot and dusty today, I might as well wash the whole driveway off.* I got the hose and sprayed the whole area around the station. When the cold water hit the hot concrete, little jets of steam rose up into the air, and the dust either flew off in different directions or turned to little patches of mud that eventually washed away. Somehow, the water made the whole station smell cleaner, and for awhile, the air seemed just a little easier to breathe. Since the driveway wasn't completely level, a few little puddles formed here and there, and, it seemed as if the cold water had given new life to the grass and the dandelions growing up between the cracks in the concrete. After an hour, most of the water had evaporated, and the concrete was just about dry again, but all the dust was gone.

Granddaddy, Mama, and I ate ham sandwiches for lunch. Mama also sliced a couple of her big tomatoes and cucumbers, and we had some Dr. Pepper pop to drink. I was thinking that the All-Star game would be starting shortly, and I was dreaming of what it might be like to sit there in Sportsman's Park–especially when they announced the four Cardinal all stars–Larry Jackson, Hal Smith, my favorite–Stan Musial, and Arkansas' favorite–

Wally Moon. In my mind, I could imagine all those hometown fans going crazy.

While we were eating our lunch, Granddaddy said, "I had a long talk with Officer Thackston."

"What was that all about?" Mama asked.

"Well, first of all, he told me that the unidentified man who was involved in that accident yesterday was also the person who actually caused the crash, and second, that he has now been identified."

"Who was he, Granddaddy?" I asked.

"It was Deacon Ellis," Granddaddy said.

"No!" said Mama. "No! It wadn't really…was it?" Mama sat there in disbelief.

"It was Deacon Ellis," Granddaddy repeated. "The county coroner has confirmed it. And, according to Officer Thackston, he had over two thousand dollars in that little locked-up valise that he had with him in that car."

"Well, how awful fer his family!" said Mama.

"I agree. But how ashamed are they gonna feel when they find out that he was drivin' drunk?" said Granddaddy.

"Well, I wonder how they're gonna explain all that money in his satchel, Granddaddy? Now, I'm thinkin' that this money maybe could have been his share of that robbery, and maybe he was makin' his getaway or somethin' like that," I said.

"Officer Thackston also wondered where all the money in his satchel came from, and he told me that right now the Gentry police are tryin' to determine independently from the sheriff's office if there's a possible connection between that colored hobo and Brother Ellis." Granddaddy said. "In any case, now the police are workin' on it, and you know what, son? Maybe their views on the robbery'll challenge the sheriff's ideals about it. I didn't tell Officer Thackston what I told Sheriff Parker–about us knowin' that those three men were out there plannin' that bank robbery. We'll just have to see how it all plays out in th' end."

At least for the sake of the deacon's family, we were all sorry about his death. However, in my view, our sentiments were premature. Mama and Granddaddy were both especially shocked to learn about his drunkenness at the wheel of a car, and we all knew that this matter would be a great embarrassment to his wife and children–as well as to the church. And, if it were later proven that somehow he had been involved in the Gentry bank robbery–as we all believed–things would only get worse, and his reputation would surely be ruined. Most importantly, however, we were all especially saddened regarding the deaths of Mrs. Rutherford and her little girl, not only because they were now instantly removed from all their loved ones, but also because they were totally innocent in this whole affair.

Twenty-eight

By the time we got home that afternoon, I knew that the All-Star game was already over. It was still too early in the evening, however, to pick up KMOX on our radio, but we heard about it just as soon as they started to broadcast the news on KUOA. The National League team made a valiant effort in the bottom of the ninth inning, but nevertheless, the American League won the game by the final score of six to five. From KMOX later that evening, we learned that Musial had doubled in the fourth inning. Moon batted in the sixth inning, but he grounded out. From the radio broadcasters' analysis, I got the impression that Billy Pierce may have intentionally walked Musial in the bottom of the ninth inning.

"I guess, Granddaddy, they was afraid to pitch to him," I said.

"Of course they was. But at least he led their big scorin' drive, son, and in that case, his walk was just as good as a home-run. He never gave up," Granddaddy said.

"And, at least Moon didn't strike out," I said later. "I reckon it'd be perty embarrassin' to strike out in the All-Star game."

"Son, the worst embarrassment in that batter's box is to strike out lookin'," said Granddaddy. "There ain't no tryin' in lookin', and you cain't win without tryin'."

We switched off the radio before the analysis of the game was over, and then Granddaddy and I talked about the game. Both of us were pretty disappointed in the outcome, but we were still very proud of those Cardinal all-stars and their contribution to the National League team's overall efforts. Later, we just sat there on the back porch, and we didn't say anything more. Granddaddy sat and rocked in his chair; I sat on my chair and looked up at the stars. Quietly, the crickets and locusts were chirping and buzzing. Every so often, they would become totally hushed–making no sound at all. We were both thinking about the world in which we lived.

After a long silence, Granddaddy said softly, "I'm sorry to say it, son, but we're sure presentin' your generation with a twisted and troubled world."

One of our cats slipped out of the barn, tiptoed silently up the stairs, and sat on the porch at the other end. The cat was staring off somewhere into the yard, probably looking for mice. The day's heat had now dissipated, and a light breeze moved the air around. In the northwest, heat lightning flashed periodically across the sky. I heard that ever-retreating, train horn way off in the distance, and it reminded me once again of the colored hobo. Thoughts of the All-Star game had completely replaced him in my mind. When I had the opportunity to sit out on the back porch in the evening, it was easy for me to forget about almost everything in the world.

To me, the world out yonder seemed to be larger than my ability even to dream, let alone comprehend. However, my little world–the Ozarks, Y-City Station, our family, our neighbors, our church, our school, and our lives–all of that was manageable; in fact, nothing else really mattered to me. The rest of Arkansas lay to the east, and, in truth, all I could say about it with any certainty at all was that I knew nothing about whatever lay between us and the Mississippi River. Up north, it was Missouri, and though, I rode two or three times under those bluffs at Noel, wound through those hills and curves at Ginger Blue to visit some of our relatives up at Anderson, and returned again by way of Jane, what could I really know from those experiences? What could I say? Toward the south lay our great city of Ft. Smith and almost as much of Arkansas yonder to the south as to the east. I had never seen Ft. Smith or a city anything like it; I could only imagine it. And what could I say about life in the deeper south? I knew nothing about plantations, cotton, rice, or colored people; they were all completely foreign to an exclusively Ozark existence. And then, there was Oklahoma and the Indians directly to our west–what could I say–having never been there? When Granddaddy claimed that the world was 'twisted and troubled,' I had no reason to doubt it. I believed him implicitly and without any mental reservations whatsoever. But I could only measure this through my personal experiences and then know it for myself through my own personal assessment of the way that life was lived in our tiny corner of the world. And despite all the good people of Northwest Arkansas and their many positive intentions, nevertheless any neutral observer could see that the worst sort of twists and troubles of the world definitely existed here, and, if here, then how much greater in the larger, external world beyond? Not only did I believe that Granddaddy was right, but also I knew it. There was evidence all over the place.

After a long silence, Granddaddy broke up my thoughts when he said, "Boy, I believe I'll turn in to bed now. It's gonna rain tomorrow. Good night."

"I'm ready fer bed, too," I said. "See you in the mornin', Granddaddy."

Granddaddy was right. When I awoke the next morning, it was raining steadily. The sky was gray and heavy with thick clouds that hung low. The fields were soaked from the rain, and in various sections of our back yard where no grass grew, sloppy mud was beginning to form around the larger puddles of water that had settled. Later during the day, J-Earl and Tawna Rae would enjoy going out to play in the mud, if they could get away with it. On the trees, the leaves glistened from all the rainwater that clung magnetically to them and pulled them downward like a good crop of ripe fruit.

Whenever it rained, we all moved much slower than usual. With rainfall, neither Granddaddy nor I were in a big hurry to open the station, for we knew that business in the rain was always slow. Mama would take advantage of these weather conditions to sleep in a little longer than usual, too. It was good sleeping weather.

"Ever'one knows that we all sleep better when it rains," Mama would say.

Although Grandma would be up and about, she would also move a little slower today than she regularly did because she always "felt the rain comin' on in her bones," and if she didn't intentionally make the effort to slow down, "Why, that rain would just rust my joints!"

Granddaddy and I finally got down to the station that morning about ten o'clock. Our road was all shiny and wet from the rain, and when we crossed the empty railroad tracks, we saw that they were silver and slick. Highway 59 to the north was so clean and black that it reflected the low clouds off in the distance. Puddles of water stood here and there across the station driveway, and the rain made all the grass and the dandelions stand up straight and tall between the cracks in the concrete.

We got the station opened up just in time for Mr. Crawford's visit. Under the rainfall, I didn't care so much if he unloaded a tobacco spit-ball on our driveway, because the rainwater would carry it away in just a few minutes. Still, I thought it was a nasty, filthy habit–even if they did practice it in the major leagues. As usual, Mr. Crawford brought the *Tulsa World* and a sack of doughnuts, but having heard the All-Star news on the radio the night before, I wasn't very interested in reading about it all over again. We drank coffee and ate doughnuts, and when the rainfall slacked off, I went outside to pull grass and dandelions. They were a lot easier to pull up when the ground was wet.

About eleven o'clock that morning, the rain had stopped and I was pulling up some of the weeds when I heard the sound of a car turning left onto our road and then right into our station. I stood up and moved out of the way. It was Reverend Sutherland in his Packard.

"Mornin' young man," he said.

"Mornin', sir," I replied. "How are you today?"

"I'm fine, although I'm greatly saddened by the sudden and accidental death of our beloved deacon."

"Yassir. I saw the whole thing." When I said that, I couldn't help but think about Mr. Martel's Sunday school comment to us regarding the 'whole whale.' As I was thinking about it, I concluded that there probably was a great deal of difference between seeing "the whole thing" compared to seeing only a part of something–especially if it were a car crash.

"It was awful, Reverend," I said.

"I understand," Pastor Sutherland said. "Son, are you all right with it, or do we need to talk about it?"

"I'm all right, sir. But it all brought back to my mind what you said about bein' ready because death keeps his appointments, and we don't know when our time is up."

"That's right, son. We all need to be ready."

"Well, sir," I said, "do you need some gas?"

"Yes. Please fill up that tank with Hi-Test. I need to go inside and talk with your Granddaddy."

"Yassir."

I filled up his Packard with gas, but it only took about four and a half gallons. Reverend Sutherland went inside. He didn't ask me, but I checked the air in his tires and washed all his windows. I opened the hood to his car and checked the engine oil and the water in his radiator, too. Everything about that car was tip-top and first-rate. I went inside to tell the reverend that the cost of his fill-up equaled all of ninety-seven cents, for which he gave me a dollar and a dime. I was inside the station for no more than a minute when the rain began to come down in heavy sheets again.

Granddaddy, Mr. Crawford, and Pastor Sutherland were all talking about the car crash and the deacon's death.

"The funeral will be held tomorrow out at the Grange House," said Reverend Sutherland. "Are you plannin' to attend, Brother Arliss?"

"Why, yes, of course," Granddaddy said. "I've known Deacon Ellis fer many years."

"We weren't the closest of friends, but I knew him well enough," Mr. Crawford said. "We had some common bidness associates." In Reverend Sutherland's presence, Mr. Crawford had removed the tobacco chaw from his mouth, and he hid his spitting can somewhere so that it was no longer in view. I figured that he was probably trying to show some kind of respect to Reverend Sutherland.

"He was a deacon in our church for the past eight years, just as he was at Bethel Baptist in Gentry for seven…maybe eight years before that," Pastor Sutherland explained. "On the deacon board, he was probably my closest associate and supporter. I know it is deeply distressin' fer his family–and to me, of course–that he died under the influence of alcohol. In all my years of his acquaintance, I hadn't known him to be a public drinker, leastwise not a heavy one, anyway. It just goes to show you how little we actually know about each other, and how much of ourselves we're able to hide even from our friends. In any case, tomorrow I'm gonna focus my funeral message on his service to our church. I want to spare his family as much embarrassment as I can, you know."

181

"Tell me, Reverend," said Mr. Crawford. "What do you make of all that money they found in the deacon's satchel?"

"Well sir," replied Reverend Sutherland, "I suppose your guess is as good as mine. It was certainly an awful lot of money to be totin' around in a satchel. That money could have come from any of a thousand sources, and, at this time, I don't want to speculate about whose money it was or where it came from."

"What time have you set the funeral fer, Reverend?" asked Granddaddy.

"We're gonna start the service promptly at ten-thirty tomorrow mornin'," Reverend Sutherland responded.

"Well, I'll be there," said Granddaddy.

"Buford, yer always welcome to stop back by and visit our church up at the Grange House," Pastor Sutherland stated. "And, of course, we always appreciate yer donations. By the way, we're gonna have that ol' clock repaired before too long."

"Well, thank you, Reverend. Deep down inside, which I'm sure you know, I'm still a Baptist at heart–even in the Methodist church–and I'll always be a Baptist. Born a Baptist, an' die a Baptist."

"Buford, I really appreciate hearin' that. You jist keep on a testifyin' over there as our silent representative there before all our Methodist brethren at Shining Light then."

"You can count on me," Mr. Crawford said.

Once again, the rain began to let up, and Reverend Sutherland left our station. He got in his car and drove over across the tracks up our road toward the Grange House. Mr. Crawford also took advantage of the break in the rain, and he drove south in the direction of Gentry.

"Granddaddy, I expect it'll be a difficult funeral service tomorrow fer Reverend Sutherland, the deacon's family, and fer all the church folk, especially those that know more about the deacon than he wanted them to find out," I said.

"Well, son, it's really sad, I reckon. I knew him since many years ago. That man exerted most of his life and efforts attemptin' to convince other folks of his religious piousity. And I can tell you fer sure; I am truly shocked to learn about his part in that robbery, his secret drunkenness, and what-not. But, boy, I tell you this–the Scripture says 'your sins will find you out,' and they sure did his. Here's a classic case of that principle. The man basically hoodwinked us all–even the reverend–right up until Monday morning, when he came unawares to the abrupt and sudden end of his long life. In no more than a brief flash of light, the sovereign Lord revealed to our whole community what He knew all along; this old deacon–that we all thought was so good– he turned out to be a scoundrel. I know one thing–I'd sure hate to be preachin' his funeral tomorrow."

Mama didn't come to the station that day because of the rain. In the afternoon, the rainfall slowed up, and by two-thirty or so, it stopped falling completely, although there was still a heavy cloud cover. I was able to pluck up almost all of the grass and dandelions from all the cracks in the driveway. I also went completely around the station building and pulled up all the weeds growing in the cracks along its edge. Later in the afternoon, however, the air became humid and uncomfortable, so I decided to go back into the station office.

Just before we were ready to close the station, Officer Thackston drove his police car into our driveway and rang the station bell. He was followed by a tow-truck that pulled alongside of the gas pumps on their outer sides.

"Howdy, Mr. Stafford," Officer Thackston said. "We're gonna pick up them two junkers that was in the crash out here the other day and haul them off yer property. I told Mrs. Stafford the other day that the city of Gentry would pay y'all fer storage, and they pay ten dollars per car per day. I got sixty dollars cash fer you right here. All you need to do is sign this official receipt."

Granddaddy signed the form, and Officer Thackston instructed the tow-truck driver which cars to hook up.

"Of course, it'll take two trips," said Officer Thackston. We all knew that, but I got the impression that the policeman was simply trying to be extra friendly and informative. The tow-truck driver went out and backed his truck around to our junkyard. We could hear him clanging his chains and hooks– metal to metal–as he worked.

"Officer Thackston," Granddaddy asked. "Did y'all determine if there was any connection between the crash driver with the satchel of money and that colored man they're a holdin' as the main suspect of the Gentry bank robbery?"

"Well," said Thackston, "our office in Gentry talked to the sheriff's office up in Bentonville. We didn't tell anyone about the money we found in the suitcase, and the sheriff's office just said they didn't believe there was any relation between the hobo and the driver of that car. We also asked the sheriff's office if we might could interview their prisoner, and they said, 'Yeah, come on up.' So we sent a 'vestigator up to their jailhouse to talk to that colored boy last night. You want my honest 'pinion?"

"Well, of course!" said Granddaddy.

"That old colored boy don't know nuthin' about nuthin'. He never robbed no bank. Here in Gentry, we're bein' real careful about it all, and I'm gonna let y'all in on a little secret. We're a whole lot closer to solvin' that mystery than they are up in Bentonville, and I don't care what they say up there! They might have a confession and even a confessor, but they ain't got the robber— I can assure y'all of that!"

He didn't have to exert a lot of energy or effort to convince us. We sensed that the Gentry police department might be inching down the right trail toward a proper solution, and we didn't want to muddy up their investigations at this point with claims of what we knew. We had already told everything to Sheriff Parker anyway, so it was up to these two different law agencies to work it all out correctly.

Twenty-nine

At the supper table that evening, Granddaddy suggested that he attend the funeral, and Mama and I work at the gas station the next day. We also discussed how personal and close to home these recent events were. Until this summer, they were the kind of activities that happened to other people only in far-away places, and we would maybe read about them now and then in the *Tulsa World*.

"It sure didn't take long fer the outside world to come to Y-City Station," Mama said.

"Well," Grandma said. "It shows you that you cain't just isolate yerself and yer little ones from the world out there, no matter how hard you try. When it comes to raisin' them kids right, we all got to work together."

As this was the last day of the All-Star break, there would be no ballgame on the radio again tonight. Granddaddy got a book, and he went out on the back porch to read while he rocked in his chair. Tawna Rae, J-Earl, and I helped with the dishes, and then Grandma and Mama had a big basket of peas and beans that needed shelling out on the porch. Mama told Tawna Rae to bring her little box of toys out to the porch where she could play under their care and close supervision. Since there was no baseball game, J-Earl and I decided to go out and play some catch together for awhile. We were determined to throw the ball back and forth, but the grass was still soaked from all the rain, and there was a slushy mire all around the barn area. In less than half an hour, the ball was turning heavy with water, our gloves were saturated, our clothes were dripping wet, and we looked like two Arkansas mud-crawlers.

Mama happened to look up from her work and saw us. Shocked by our appearances, she said, "You, boys–I say right now–that's enough of that! We're gonna have to hose y'all down out there before y'all can step one foot in this house. Jefferson Davis Stafford! You get yourself over to that hose right now and start squirtin' all that slop off a yer little brother–but quick, young man!"

"Yes ma'am!" I knew that Mama meant business. Whenever Mama called me by my full name, it was my signal that she was angry enough to skin me alive. J-Earl also knew this. As a result, he hopped over toward that hose like an electrically charged little bunny. I got the hose, turned it on, and immediately began to wash all the mud off my own clothing first, and then I directed the water toward J-Earl.

"Hey! That water's ice cold!" J-Earl screamed.

"After all that mud is washed away, y'all get them wet overalls and shirts off–and them socks and shoes, too! Come on! Get 'em all off!" Mama said.

"You mean down to our underpants, Mama?" asked J-Earl.

"Yassir. An' I'm gonna tell you what–if them underpants is muddy, too– y'all are gonna strip them off, as well!"

J-Earl knew that Mama's threat–to suffer the indignity of standing there stark naked in front of Tawna Rae and Grandma while being hosed off–was frighteningly real. J-Earl had observed the two or three times in the past when I had gotten so muddy for one reason or another that Mama came out, grabbed the hose, and washed my overalls, after which she pulled off all of my clothes and then hosed me down before I was allowed back into the house. Compared to me, J-Earl was merely an amateur at being hosed down. As far as I knew, this was the first time that he ever got so muddy as to risk this level of Mama's wrath. Naturally, the water coming out of that hose was ice-cold, but it didn't take long to wash all the mud off our clothing and to rinse ourselves clean. Of course, from my past experiences, I knew that the hose-down began with Mama's genuine anger, but by the time we were fully rinsed off with the hose, we would all be laughing, and we would all end up wet–

including Mama. So it was again tonight, and the best part of it was that we didn't have to take a bath before we went to bed.

When I got up the next morning, Granddaddy was already up and drinking his black coffee out on the back porch. I got some coffee and joined him. Except to say "Good mornin'," we both usually sat there together for a good while before either of us said another word. I knew that he usually read a short portion of Scripture after he got up, and he liked to think about it and meditate on it while he sat there and drank his coffee. I could tell that Granddaddy appreciated me respecting his unspoken request for quiet and honoring his commitment to private meditation. When he was finished with his reflections, he would begin the conversation.

As I sat there, I considered that today was Thursday, July the eleventh. The summer was almost half over. Every day was a new day, and each passing day carried with it incredible significance, at least for someone, I thought. All over the world, today would be a meaningful day for some people. People would be born, get married, buy new cars and homes, be sentenced to jail–and get out of jail–discover heretofore unknown knowledge, and celebrate a thousand other reasons for remembering this very day, including mourning the dead. Under ordinary circumstances, it probably wouldn't have meant anything to me at all, but on this day, Deacon Ellis was going to be buried, and for whatever reason, that was meaningful. He was a man whom I hardly knew, yet, a man whose life had affected my own, regardless of his good or bad intentions. It amazed me now to understand how a funeral makes a person view things differently, even if only temporarily. The deacon's end in this life had already come–and gone, for that matter–but somehow, his funeral–an unplanned event, scheduled by someone else for today–would officially mark that end for everyone who attended the funeral or whoever knew him. It was the world's way of granting recognition to his passing and saying its final good-bye, although, in fact, he had already passed on without any acknowledgment from the world at all. He didn't bother to stop and say "good-bye" to anyone, to cancel his appointments for next week, or to take even a little time in advance to get his affairs in order.

So, what does it all mean? I thought to myself.

The more I thought about it, the more meaning I saw in it. It didn't matter if I liked it or not, or if I agreed with it or not. That simply wasn't the issue here. Was it meaningful that Deacon Ellis was gone? It was to somebody. A wife no longer had a husband. A church lost a deacon. An employer lost a worker. Children lost a father, and employees in a funeral home would get paid this week. This one little speck on the time line of history carried more meaning than I could ever imagine. Daddy would have summarized it all something like this:

"It's jist a little bit like the bark of a dawg. We don't think much about it at all, except when the dawg's a puppy and he ain't barked yet or even opened his eyes. When he don't bark, we want to hear that little dawg bark, and it means somethin' to us when we first hear him bark. And when he finally does bark, we cain't understand a word that he barked; we're just glad that he did it. After a while, we get used to the dawg barkin', and we don't pay him any attention about it anymore–unless, of course he gets on our nerves with all that barkin'. And even so, if he barks a lot, he might have a real good reason fer it, whether we know it or not and whether we like it or not. But here's the real meanin' in the bark of that dawg. God designed them dawgs to bark, to wag their tails, and what-not, and when they bark–they're just doin' what they was designed to do–and that means a whole lot to the One that designed them. Ever'time they bark, they're a bringin' glory to God."

"Boy, I can tell that you been a ruminatin' this mornin', too," Granddaddy said.

"Yassir. I been a thinkin' on this funeral today, Granddaddy. I'm sure glad that you're goin' rather than me."

"Well, son, less go get another cup of coffee and see if they got any breakfast fer us in the kitchen."

After we finished our breakfast, Mama and I went down to open the station. Granddaddy said that he would come down after the funeral was over. Somehow, it seemed to me that, after all the rains yesterday, the front of our station looked sparkling clean and pure white–even beautiful–this morning, as the brilliant sunlight radiated out across the field in the east. Our driveway was pristine and spotless–not a weed in sight. The rain had washed all the tiles on the roof, and each one reflected the fluorescent orange glow of the sun. On this morning, there wasn't a cloud in the sky, and against the backdrop of the deep green leaves on the surrounding trees, our station looked to me a little like it belonged in a museum painting. The painter was obviously an accomplished impressionist who insisted on the use of intense colors that he brushed abundantly across his broad canvas.

"Mama," I said. "Isn't it just beautiful?"

"Well, son, I reckon it is…sort of…yes, of course it is; in its own way."

"Somehow, it just seems so much cleaner and pertier after the rain. I think it even smells cleaner."

"The rain does seem to clean ever'thing up a lot," Mama said.

We opened up the station, and while Mama worked the station office, I set up her fruit and vegetable stand. As usual, business was slow, so we had lots of time to think and to observe things all around the station. That morning, I noticed that there was an unusual amount of truck traffic on Highway 59. Quite a few poultry trucks passed in both directions by our station. Some of the trucks were full of chickens, but others were empty. A few cars passed, and about nine-forty-five, a southbound, KCS freight train rolled through. I always enjoyed watching the trains. I liked to count the freight cars, but I usually thought about counting them only after ten or fifteen cars had already passed. By then, it was too late to start.

As soon as the freight train had passed through Y-City Station, an old farm tractor chugged over the tracks and turned into our station. Mr. Blanton was driving it, and he was pulling a wagon that carried two empty oil drums. He steered his rig around to the west side of our driveway between the station and the pumps and drove the tractor forward enough so that the wagon was beside the gas pump. When I saw him pull in, I ran down from the fruit stand to the pump and greeted him.

"Howdy, Mr. Blanton. How're you doin' today? I ain't seen you in a long time, sir," I said.

"That's right, son. It's been awhile," he replied. "How's yer daddy and mama?"

"They're doin' well. Daddy's on the road, but Mama's inside."

"That's good. Son, I'd appreciate it if you'd fill up them two drums with gasoline. I practically run out today, and I like to keep about two hundert or so gallons on hand up at the farm," Mr. Blanton said. He slid out of his tractor seat and started to walk toward the station.

"Sir," I said. "Did you want me to fill up both drums…full?"

"Yeah, that'd be fine son." Mr. Blanton said. "Normally, I get all my gas down in Gentry where I have an account at the Apco station. But it don't make much sense to drive all the way into Gentry when I can get gas right here at the Y. "

"Yassir," I said. "I agree."

"While yer fillin' up them drums, I'm goin' inside and chat with yer mama fer a spell."

Suddenly, I was overjoyed at this sale. Sometimes, whole days might go by, and our total sales were only ninety or a hundred gallons. I was really surprised and very thankful to get an order from just one customer for over a hundred gallons of gasoline. It took a good while for me to pump over a hundred gallons of gas. While Mr. Blanton was inside and I was filling his drums, Mr. Crawford also stopped in at the station for his daily visit.

"Mornin' Mr. Crawford," I said.

"Mornin', boy. Got the *World* and some doughnuts this morning. Yer Granddaddy inside?"

"No sir. He's gone to that funeral. Mama's workin' the office this mornin'," I said.

"Oh, yeah. I forgot. Well, when you get done up there, come in and get a doughnut," he said.

"Yassir," I responded.

After I filled the drums with gasoline, I got down out of the wagon and put the nozzle back on the pump. I went inside and told Mr. Blanton and Mama the price of the sale.

Mama said, "Well, son, Mr. Blanton's opened an account here with us, and he'll be gettin' all his gas with us from now on. He's also gonna send his foreman over sometime next week and get another hundert gallons or so."

"Well, that's good news," I said.

"But I'm gonna start that account by payin' fer my order today, and chargin' the other half when my foreman comes next week…if that's okay with you, ma'am," Mr. Blanton said.

"That'll be fine, sir," Mama said.

"Hey there, boy!" Mr. Crawford said. "Come get you a doughnut."

"Yassir," I replied.

I reached into the white paper sack and grabbed a thick doughnut that was oozing peach jelly all over my fingers and over all the other doughnuts in there. I pulled out the doughnut, and the jelly dripped down on the floor.

"Sorry, Mama," I said. I set my doughnut down on a piece of old newspaper and went back into the garage to get a shop towel. I found a fairly clean one and went back into the station office and cleaned up the mess I'd made.

Everyone was eating a doughnut and drinking coffee. Mr. Crawford hadn't started chewing and spitting yet, and I was hoping that maybe today, in the presence of my mama, he might show her a little respect and just forget about it.

"Mrs. Stafford, do you run this place all by yerself…ever' day?" Mr. Blanton asked.

"No, no, Mr. Blanton," Mama answered, and she giggled at the idea. "Normally, my father-in-law–the boy's granddaddy–keeps things goin' around here. I usually just run that fruit stand out there. That's about all I can handle."

"Granddaddy's gone to a funeral, today," I said.

"I see," Mr. Blanton said. "Whose funeral is it?"

Anxious to join in the conversation, Mr. Crawford said, "It's fer that deacon out there at West Bethel Baptist. He died in a car accident right out there at that curve," and he pointed to the spot where it happened.

"Oh yeah," Mr. Blanton said. "I guess I heard about that from my foreman. He asked me last night if he could have a couple of hours off to go to the funeral, too. I reckon the deacon was a friend of his."

After a few more minutes, he said, "Well, I need to be gettin' back to the farm and get to work. I got more'n I can handle out there, and I cain't leave it all to the help, cause you cain't trust them to do their jobs any further than you can see them."

"How's that herd of yer cattle doin'? Idn't it kind of a unusual breed fer these parts?" asked Mr. Crawford.

"Yeah, it is, as a matter of fact. Them cattle are not native to the United States anywhere, and you might say, actually, that they're a rare breed. A little more than a hundert years ago, someone brought some of their stock over here from Holland where they was bred for the king. They call them Lakenvelder in Holland, but here we just call 'em Dutch Belted cattle. I think they're sure perty to look at, and they produce real good milk, cheese, and what-not, but you gotta give 'em an awful lot o' care."

"Well then, you take care of 'em," Mr. Crawford said, with a little sarcasm in his tone.

"Thank you, Mr. Blanton," Mama said.

"Yeah, thank you, sir," I echoed.

"I'm glad to be doin' bidness with y'all," Mr. Blanton said. He paid for his gasoline order, and Mama made a little account book for him. Then he left the station, started his tractor, and drove back around and out on the highway to turn up our road again.

"I need to get goin', too," Mr. Crawford said. "Mrs. Stafford, you take care now."

"Thank you," Mama said. "We always appreciate the doughnuts and the paper."

"It's all right," he said, and then he departed, too. This time, he went away without leaving his typical trail of tobacco juice and slop all over our driveway, and I thought, *Maybe he is something of a gentleman, after all.* After he was gone, I looked over at Mama and I said, "I sure love you, Mama," and I grinned at her.

"Boy! I don't know about you!" she replied.

Things slowed down dramatically for the next several hours. Mama and I ate lunch together, after which, we sold some gas perhaps to no more than one or two other customers. Lacking customers, we knew that summer days could be long and especially hot. Mama had a fan in the station office, and she kept herself occupied with a variety of little tasks. I decided to find my steel pail and go sit on it out near the fruit and vegetable stand in the shade. There wasn't much traffic that afternoon, and I began to think about playing baseball for the Razorbacks and the Cardinals.

Perhaps about one-thirty that afternoon, a car from the sheriff's office came down from the north and parked at the south end of our station. Deputy Watkins got out of the car and walked over to the side of the highway, where he looked down in the opposite direction toward Gentry, and then he looked up in my direction. I waved at him, and he waved back at me, but I was too tired, too hot, and too comfortable sitting in the shade on my upside-down pail to get up, walk down, and greet him. He turned and looked up our road, and then he looked up and down the railroad tracks. I couldn't figure out what he was looking for. In another moment, he walked into our station office.

I reckon he's a lookin' fer Granddaddy, and he'll get all the information he needs well enough from Mama, I thought to myself. *If he needs to talk to me, let him come up here.* I leaned back on my pail, and I dreamed of standing on that mound in Sportsman's Park.

Thirty

For at least the next ten minutes, I was in St. Louis playing baseball at Sportsman's Park. I had only pitched one inning against the Milwaukee Braves. I struck out Johnny Logan and caught him looking at three straight fastballs. Eddie Matthews took two strikes, and then he hit a high fly ball–just behind the plate–a foul ball that Hal Smith caught. Then I faced Red Schoendienst, who came into the batter's box swinging. After hitting two or three foul balls, Red got hold of my next pitch; he popped it over three hundred feet away, and I held my breath as the wind carried it just inside the foul pole, where a fan in the upper deck reached out and made a spectacular, bare-handed catch.

"Get a hold of yerself, Stafford," I said to myself. "You cain't let him do that to you! You got to overpower him. Now, come on–bear down on him!"

I went into my wind-up and kicked up my right leg–turned into the breeze and twisted–and fired a ninety-mile-an-hour curve ball that Schoendienst swung at all over the air. It seemed that he was still swinging when Smith stood up, showed him the ball, and said, "Hey Red! You lookin' fer this?"

In our inning to bat, Wally Moon was up, facing Lew Burdette. On the first pitch, Moon swung and cracked a base hit out over the second-baseman's head. Moon took a nice lead at first, when Musial stepped into the batter's box. He stood there taking his swings, and then he wiggled his rear-end in that classic Musial pattern that had become his trademark. He swung and missed. On the next pitch, he repeated his swings and his wiggle, but this time, he would not be outdone by Burdette. He smacked the ball out to right field and ran to first base.

Then over the loudspeakers, the announcer said, "ladies and gentlemen, please welcome our next batter to the plate–J.D. Stafford, the Cardinal pitcher." I was up, and I wanted to make the most of it. I stepped into the batter's box with two men on base, and I took my practice swings…

I recalled Granddaddy saying, "Don't go in there lookin', boy; you step into that box and swing!"

I swung at the first pitch, and missed. Then we went through the same routine again…with the same result.

"Come on, Stafford! Get a hold of yerself," I said. "You cain't let him do that to you! You got to overpower him. Now, come on–bear down on him! Come on! Bear down on him!"

It seemed that the whole ballpark was saying, "Come on, Stafford! Bear down on him!"…after which I heard…the loud screech of burning tires. I suddenly awoke from my glorious daydream at Sportsman's and a horribly deafening commotion in our station office brought me back to my complete senses at Y-City Station. The tire noise was interrupted by ear-piercing, female screams of repeated calls of "Jefferson Davis Stafford! Where are you, boy?" Instinctively, I jumped up from my pail, and in the same second, I saw the sheriff's car disappearing in the distance as it headed down toward Gentry.

It was Mama. I pulled the screen door open and ran into the office where Mama, by now, half-exposed in her partially-shredded dress, was just pulling herself up from the floor. Her face and arms were bruised, and she had a black eye. She tried to cover her bare shoulder, but her blouse had been torn too much to do any good. I took off my shirt and draped it over her shoulders.

"Oh, Mama! I'm so sorry! What happened?" I asked.

Mama sat down on the chair behind the glass counter that separated the customer area from the proprietary area of the office. She was clearly embarrassed, and she was crying. I put my arms around her and held her tightly.

"It's all right, Mama. It'll be all right. Please tell me what happened."

In another minute or two, her crying turned to sobbing, and then she began to talk.

"Well," she said. "Deputy Watkins come in here, and…" she sobbed again, and then she continued, "he said somethin' like he knew what we knew about the robbery, and that none of it could be true, because they were a holdin' the colored hobo, and he already made his confession, and we don't need to be talkin' any more to the sheriff, about what we know. He said, if we don't keep quiet, they're gonna 'charge us with obstructin' justice' and 'deal with' us in such a way that we'll regret it the rest of our lives.'" She began to cry again.

After a moment, she stopped and continued, "Then he started getting sweet on me and sayin', 'Norma Jean, why'd you ever get hooked up with that ol' Stafford boy anyhow?' and then he put his hand on my shoulder, and he said to me, 'You know I always loved you more than Clayton ever could!' I just couldn't stand him touchin' me like that, nor insultin' yer daddy. I backed right away from him and tried to get his hands off me. I told him that it ain't got nuthin' to do with justice or anything. I tried to get away from him, but he grabbed me hard and said, 'Y'all are gonna regret this, Norma Jean,' and I kept on tryin' to back away from him all the more. He just kept on a comin' at me, and then he pulled on my arms, and he tried to pull me toward him. He was tryin' to kiss me, but I kept backin' on around that counter. I remember tellin' him to leave me alone, but he followed me around the backside of that counter, and started comin' at me again. He pulled me up against him again and said, 'Come on, Norma Jean,' and I screamed, 'Leave me alone,' and that's when I started callin' out fer you. But it was like he don't take 'no' fer an answer! He kept grabbin' me, and he hit me some more and started tearin' my clothes all off. I was screamin' fer you and trying to fight him off me at the same time. Then I grabbed that ol' oil filler spout from that back shelf, and I hit him with it. Next thing I remember is you comin' in that door and he'pin' me up off the floor. He was gone then."

"Mama," I said. "I am so sorry. I was a daydreamin' out there. Otherwise, I'd have been in here a lot quicker. Mama, what are we gonna do?"

"Oh, goodness," she said. "I don't know. I need some time to think, but I can tell you this right now—we Staffords are not going to back down or run away from the truth. I expect yer Granddaddy'll be along here directly, and we'll just get his ideals on it."

Mama settled down from her upset state, and she wasn't sobbing anymore. I knew she felt violated by Deputy Watkins. She must have conked him pretty good–there was some blood on the floor, as well as on the puncture part of the oil filler spout.

"Mama, where did you hit him at?"

"I don't know. It all happened so fast. I must have hit him…goodness! I guess–comin' around that counter–I must have grabbed that filler spout with my left hand, and I reckon I hit him with it, too. I think I hit him just over his left ear on his head."

"Well, then, Mama!" I joked. "Maybe we do have two southpaws in the family!"

Within the next half hour, Granddaddy arrived at the station. He had already changed from his funeral outfit to his work clothes, and he ate lunch at home before coming down to work.

"Why, Norma Jean! What has happened to you?" he asked.

"Well, Granddaddy," she began. She started to sob again, and I put my arm around her. Once again, she settled down, and she told Granddaddy the whole story.

"Oh, my goodness!" he said. "Oh my dear, Sweetheart, Norma Jean. I am so sorry about this. Maybe if I'd have been here, this wouldn't have happened. Honey, I've got an old work shirt out back. I don't believe it's too dirty, and I think it'll cover you up a little better. Let me go get it fer you."

"It's all right, Granddaddy," she said.

"No, no. Let me get it."

He went out and got the shirt. He brought it back in, and he helped her put it on. She buttoned the shirt, and then we continued.

After thinking the whole thing through, Granddaddy said, "Well, it is obvious to me that someone in the law offices–I don't know which, at this point–is tryin' to shut us up from talkin' about what we know. I cain't say exactly what Deputy Watkins' interest in all this is, but somewhere along the line, I suspect he's involved somehow, maybe coverin' things up or takin' money from someone. In any case, it ain't gonna do us any good to come right out and fight this until we know more about what he knows and what his involvement is. Without any real witnesses what seen him do this to you, Honey, it's basically your word against his. Less just keep it quiet fer a while until he shows us more of his hand. We'll also talk with Clayton about it when he comes home tomorrow or Saturday.

"That sounds good to me," Mama said.

"And to me, as well," I replied.

"Well, Granddaddy, how was the funeral?" Mama asked.

"It was real sad. I believe Reverend Sutherland did his best to try to keep the deacon's sordid past and his embarrassing activities quiet. They kept the deacon's coffin closed all during the service. As I understand it, his face got cut up so bad in the collision that none of the family wanted him to be seen like that."

"It sounds like it was perty sad, Granddaddy," I said.

"How was Reverend Sutherland's sermon?" Mama asked.

Well, I'm sure that the point of his message was to comfort the Widow Ellis and her family. He talked about the ideal that, fer the believer, death has no sting and no victory, and he called us all to live in that truth."

"He said, 'Y'all don't need to be fearin' death. Y'all need to be ready, but when it comes, don't be afraid of it.'"

"He also talked about the ideal that 'many Christians are back-slidin' into the sins of the old life. Come out from that,' he said. 'Sometimes, Christians are the biggest hypocrites in the world,' he said, 'and they're a bringin' a reproach on the Lord's name. Yank off that mask!' brother Sutherland said. 'That's right—it's a mask yer wearin,' fer that's the real meaning of the word hypocrite—one that's wearin' a mask so as to look like someone else.' It was a good sermon, but it was a sad service."

Book Four

Thirty-one

Friday was a slow day with little significant activity. Granddaddy and I opened the station in the morning, and Mr. Crawford came, as he usually did, about ten o'clock. Mama came down and opened her fruit stand later in the morning. We sold a little gas and some tomatoes, cucumbers, and peppers. About two-thirty that afternoon, an old man driving a well-dented and rusty Chevrolet pick-up truck pulled slowly into the station. The engine sounded like it was running on only five cylinders, and the back of his truck contained a chaotic mess of broken bricks and concrete blocks, a broken sack of animal feed that had scattered all over the pick-up bed, several lengths of rusted pipes, some old tools, and several pieces of useless wood. The driver was wearing faded blue overalls, and he had long, white hair and a white beard. Coming down the road from Decatur, He was heading south when one of his tires picked up a nail somewhere along the way. Slowly, he pulled his truck in past the pumps on the inside and got out.

"Can you fix it, sonny?" he asked.

"I think my granddaddy can," I said.

Granddaddy came out to look at it.

"Yeah," we can fix it," said Granddaddy.

"How much you charge me?" asked the old man.

Granddaddy said, "If all it needs is a patch, it'll be just one dollar."

I noticed that, on the passenger seat in the truck, the man had a tattered and scratched-up suitcase over-stuffed with clothing which was hanging out from three sides of the suitcase. A lazy, brown hound was sleeping on top of the suitcase, almost as if it were his job to keep the thing shut. Granddaddy told the old man to pull his truck around into the garage and over the lift-rack. After the old man got out of his truck, we ran the lift-rack up about three feet, and then I began to unscrew the lug-nuts on the wheel. When the truck began to rise, the hound also rose up and looked around, but then he lay back down on the suitcase again. We pulled the wheel off the truck, and then we separated the tire from the wheel and pulled out the inner tube. There was a roofing nail in the tire, which was already pretty well-worn, but we pulled out the nail and found the puncture in the tube, and we put a patch on it. Granddaddy wanted to let it set-up awhile, so we all went into the station office.

"Cup of coffee, mister?" Granddaddy asked the old-timer.

"Believe I will, yassir," he said.

"Where you from?" Granddaddy asked, while he poured the man his coffee.

"I'm originally from Boone's Landin' up in Missoura," the man said.

"Don't believe I rightly know where that is," said Granddaddy with a puzzled look on his face.

"It's a little village over on the Miss'sippi River just a ways above the Cape. Legend has it that old Dan'l Boone first come ashore there from Kaintucky when he was out lookin' fer Indians. I don't know if it's true or not, but I don't live there no more. Fact is, I ain't been back there in years, and fer all I know, the Landin' has probably slipped off into the river by now. Back in... when was it? Thirty-nine? No... in May of thirty-eight we left the Landin' and come down here and got us a little goat farm over there between Berryville and Eureka Springs. I cain't believe it's been that long ago. My son went off missin' in the war, and I ain't heard nothin' from him or about him since. My wife died in forty-seven, and in fifty-two, my daughter run off to California with some fast-pokin' sweet-talker what stole her away from me and the goats."

"I'm sorry to hear about all yer misfortunes, sir," Granddaddy said.

"Yassir," I said, trying to lend my support and agreement.

"Well, if you don't mind me askin', what are you doin' in these parts?" asked Granddaddy.

"No, I don't mind at all. I'm just a passin' through. I'm a headin' down to Ft. Smith. I still got kin. I got a sister what lives in Ft. Smith, and her and her husband done fairly well to equal out most of my bad luck on their side, if you know what I mean. Some years back, he got into the car bidness, and now they're the owners of the Porter Cadillac Store down there. Maybe y'all heard of 'em?"

"Don't believe so. We don't see many Cadillacs from Ft. Smith comin' up this way," said Granddaddy.

"Actually," I said, "we don't see many Cadillacs 'round here at all. The reverend's got a Packard, though."

"Well, they're doin' all right down there in Ft. Smith," the old man continued.

"Well, I suppose you got someone back there in Berryville lookin' after them goats?" asked Granddaddy.

"Yassir. Them goats'll be fine; they're all right."

We all finished drinking our coffee, and we went back into the garage to check the progress of the patch. The patch was ready, and after Granddaddy tested it, he put the tube back in the tire and re-inflated it. In another moment, the wheel was back on the truck, the lift-rack came down, the old man paid Granddaddy, and then he was backing his truck out of our garage.

"Thanks fer all your he'p," the old man said.

"Yer welcome," I said.

"I reckon you already know the best way to Ft. Smith," Granddaddy said.

"Yassir. I do. Been there a thousand times, so I don't need any he'p on that one," he said.

"Well, you take care, then," Granddaddy said. "And drive careful."

The man pulled his pick-up truck out to the edge of the road. The engine in his truck sputtered and hesitated; it sounded like it was laboring and missing. He had to wait for a couple of cars traveling in both directions, but then when the roadway was clear, he pushed down on the pedal. The truck instantly misfired, and there was a loud pop. His exhaust pipe flashed, and the truck jerked forward and then bucked back again several times. Eventually, the old man was able to pull the truck out on the highway, and he turned it to the left to head back up north on Highway 59.

"Why, Granddaddy, lookie there! He's headed up north!" I exclaimed.

"He don't know if he's comin' or goin', boy. That old dawg of his raised up his head one time, and he never once barked. I believe he probably lost a few up there at the Landin', too," Granddaddy said.

Granddaddy and I spent the better part of the next hour teasing each other and making fun of the old goat man for driving north.

"Granddaddy, you'd like to have that old boy's back-firin' pick-em-up truck to ride in on yer way down to the Cadillac store," I might say.

Then Granddaddy would give him a name and say, "and you'd like to wear ol' goat Joe's wardrobe of fine clothing down to the Cadillac store."

"An' you'd like to pawn that suitcase of his over to the Fayetteville Pawn Shop fer a hundert dollars, Granddaddy."

"No, two hundert!" Granddaddy would say. "An' you'd like to pawn his dawg."

We were just passing the time–teasing each other and laughing–when Mama came into the station office from over at her fruit stand.

"Sales ain't too great today. What are y'all laughin' at so much?" asked Mama.

"Mama, we was just teasin' each other about ol' goat Joe." I said.

"Who is that?" she asked.

"It was that old boy what was just in here gettin' his flat tire fixed," Granddaddy said.

"He don't know north from south, Mama!" I said.

"Well," said Mama, "I guess that's true of a whole lot of people. I get turned around a lot myself to where I cain't tell the difference."

"But you never meant to go down to Gentry by goin' up to Decatur," I said.

"Well, I guess I certainly know the difference between them two places."

Granddaddy said, "Well folks, we already done all the damage we could today, so less close up the station and go home."

"Yeah, I agree. It's time to go home. Yer Daddy's suppose to come in late tonight or early tomorrow mornin'," Mama said, "and I'm so much lookin' forward to him bein' with us."

Even though it was a little early that afternoon, we closed the station and went home. When we got to the tracks, we saw that a train was coming, but it was still a long way down the track, so we crossed over.

"What do you reckon that dawg's name was, boy?" Granddaddy asked me while we were on our way home.

"Gladiator," I said.

Thirty-two

At the supper table that evening, Granddaddy announced that he would play catch with J-Earl and me after supper. We were totally surprised and overjoyed, as he hadn't done that for a long time, and we were so eager about it that we all cleaned up the dishes and the kitchen. Mama and Grandma couldn't believe their ears.

"Catch?" they asked. "With J-Earl and Jefferson? You ain't played catch in thirty years! About all you're gonna catch is a throwed-out arm, a throwed-out back, and if you don't watch it, you'll catch one right on the nose because you won't see it comin'! We don't think you need any of that!"

"Well, I'll take it easy on them boys. We had so much fun today down there at the station with that old goat Joe. I just thought I'd keep the fun goin' on through this evenin', that's all," Granddaddy said.

After clean-up, we were all anxious to get outside. J-Earl and I couldn't get out of the house fast enough, and we went out and stood a few feet apart with our backs close to the barn. Granddaddy, who stood closer to the house, faced us. He was about sixty feet away. He located something that looked like an ancient baseball mitt, and he found an old baseball hat out in the barn. Wearing those overalls, he was just Granddaddy. But wearing that hat and that old mitt, the living silhouette of Granddaddy standing behind that house suddenly appeared as large as that of former Cardinal greats–Cy

Young, Grover Cleveland Alexander, and Dizzy Dean–all in one. After a few practice tosses, we got serious about playing catch.

First, Granddaddy threw the ball to J-Earl. I thought the throw to J-Earl was pretty hard. J-Earl threw the ball as hard as he could back to Granddaddy, but Granddaddy had to reach out for it; he pulled it into his glove like it was a little mosquito. Then he threw the ball to me. He fired that ball so hard and so fast that I had no time to see it. From the sound it made, I simply reacted–reaching out where I thought it should be. The ball hit my glove like an incoming mortar shell pounded out from an army tank. I caught the ball, but my glove provided absolutely nothing to pad my hand from the sting.

"Wow! Granddaddy, that was a mighty powerful throw!" I said.

"Well," Granddaddy said, "I'm just a tryin' to limber up my arm a little bit, that's all."

He threw another one to J-Earl, and of course, J-Earl sent it back to him. Then it was my turn again. In the same way, he fired another pitch at me that was so hard and so fast that I couldn't really see it. I could hear this sound of something coming toward me–or at me–and all I could do was reach out and stop it.

Whack! The ball hit my glove with a deafening sound, and I caught it right across my palm. The pitch came in so fast and so hard that I had no time to adjust the placement of my glove so the ball could land precisely in the pocket designed to receive the ball and its incoming impact. Already with Granddaddy's second throw, I could tell that my right hand was starting to bruise, but I couldn't stand the thought of whining about it or asking Granddaddy to slow down his pitches.

"Granddaddy," I said, "where'd you learn to throw like that?"

"Well," he said, "I done a little pitchin' in my day." He was breathing a little harder, and he was stretching his arms up and out.

"Boy!" I said. "I'll say you did!"

I threw the ball back to him, and then he threw another one over to J-Earl. J-Earl tried to catch this one with two hands, but the ball stung him on his right-hand fingers just as it came into the glove, and as a result, he dropped the ball.

"Ouch, Granddaddy!" J-Earl cried out.

"Did I get you, boy?" Granddaddy asked. "I'm sorry, son. I didn't mean to hit you that hard."

J-Earl threw the ball back.

"I'm all right, Granddaddy," he said. I just wasn't ready fer it, that's all."

"Now you boys tell me if I throw 'em too fast or too hard."

"Yassir…yassir," we replied, almost in unison.

Now it was my turn to receive the next one, and I had to steel myself to get ready for it. I started thinking, *That ain't really a seventy-year-old man standin' over there. That's a pitching machine what looks like my granddaddy pre-set to throw his pitches at two hundert and seventy-five mile an hour! And he ain't throwin' ordinary regulation baseballs. No! Thems baseball-sized, stainless-steel, ball bearings comin' at me—faster than bullets and hotter than fireballs!*

Whack!

I considered myself lucky just to catch the ball. I didn't drop any catches, but I knew my right hand would be sore and bruised tomorrow. After a few more minutes, J-Earl had played enough and dropped out. Dropping out didn't matter to J-Earl, as he had no one to impress. In my view, it was impressive enough that he had played. However, I didn't want to look like a quitter, so I played on, but I began to pray that Granddaddy would soon tire and want to stop for his age, his arm, his back, or some other silly reason.

A couple of times, I was able to let the pitch simply hit the barn and get away with it.

"That was a wild one, Granddaddy!" I said. But—if the truth be known—I had just stepped aside from the pathway of the incoming ball, which hit the barn so hard that it sounded like a workman had just hit it with a sledge-hammer.

"Well, boy, it looked perty good to me!"

"Startin' to get dark, Granddaddy!"

We played for a little while longer. I let another one go by, and it cracked the barn board.

"Goodness, Granddaddy! Where'd you get that curveball?"

"Thought it was a fastball, boy!"

I had to catch two or three more pitches before the Lord answered my prayer. The answer came by way of Grandma, who said, "Now, Arliss, that's just about enough for one night! You come on in here before you throw yer whole back out, too."

"Yes ma'am!" I answered.

Granddaddy looked at me with a puzzled expression on his face, and then, mimicking me, he said, "Yes ma'am!"

"Less see if there's a game on the radio tonight, huh Granddaddy?" I suggested.

"Well, there ought to be one tonight, I'd say, shouldn't there?"

We walked up to the back porch and sat down. Mama brought out some ice-cold lemonade, and Granddaddy tuned the radio in to Harry Carey on KMOX. The game was already in progress; the Cardinals were playing the Giants in New York. We sipped our lemonades and listened to the game as the evening sky went from amber to red to deep purple-black. The cold glass of lemonade felt so good to the palm of my right hand. All my fingers felt like they were tightening up and becoming thicker. Every now and then, there was a little static coming through over the radio speaker. The stars slowly became visible. Then the crickets began to chirp, and the locusts started to buzz. About nine-thirty, there was a fading train whistle somewhere out on our tracks, and then I thought, *I wish I could tell whether it was coming or going.* I thought about that strange goat man who turned left instead of right.

Now, don't you be doin' that to me, Jefferson Davis Stafford! my conscience said to me. *We got better things to do than to sit here and ponder about all them people out there that don't know left from right, right from wrong, or up from down. It's too good a night to waste on them! It ain't philosophizin' night–it's Friday baseball night!*

During the seventh inning commercial break, I thanked Granddaddy for playing catch with us.

"I'm glad you boys enjoyed it," he responded.

"Mama, we got any more ice in there?"

"There's more lemonade inside, and more ice, too. Just he'p yourself."

I kept my glass full of ice, and the Cardinals beat the Giants by a score of five to one.

Thirty-three

D addy arrived home in the middle of the night while everyone was asleep. He parked his truck out beside the barn and slipped quietly into the house without anyone's knowledge, except Mama's. I awoke fairly early the next morning, but Grandma and Granddaddy were already up. We had coffee together for awhile, and then Grandma began to make breakfast.

"What say we have a little breakfast, boy, and then we go down and open up the station?" Granddaddy asked.

"Probably be a slow day again today," I said. But I loved working at the station, and I was always ready to go down there. "Sounds fine to me, Granddaddy."

Grandma made biscuits and gravy, eggs, bacon, and grits for breakfast. She, Granddaddy, and I ate together, and then J-Earl got up and wanted some breakfast, too. Grandma began to fry some eggs for J-Earl, and then Tawna Rae came out in the kitchen, too.

"Baby, you want some eggs, too?" asked Grandma.

"Yes ma'am," she answered. She sat in one of the vacant chairs next to J-Earl at the table, and in another few moments, they were both stuffing their mouths with eggs and biscuits. Tawna Rae liked butter and jelly on her biscuits, but she didn't like gravy at all. J-Earl always wanted his gravy on the side, and he would dip his bacon in the gravy. He also liked to eat his eggs with jelly on them—a delicacy that I have never understood. Neither of them ever ate all their grits completely, and then I thought, *Mama lets both of them get away with so much more than she ever let me get away with.*

About nine o'clock, Granddaddy and I headed down to the station, but there was a long, southbound freight train passing slowly along the tracks, and we had to wait about twelve extra minutes for it before we could cross over the tracks to our station. I started counting railroad cars as soon as we got to the crossing, and I counted forty-four cars to the caboose.

Granddaddy parked his pick-up truck along the south wall of our station. After we opened everything up properly and set out all the signs and the fruit-stand, I decided to wash down the driveway again. I got the hose and turned the water on, and within a few minutes, everything seemed clean and fresh from the water. There was no business, so I found my steel pail and went over under the shade trees up near the fruit stand, and I sat down. Lots of cars passed by going in both directions, but none stopped. I figured it would be a long, dull day.

About eleven o'clock, the monotony was broken by the sound of the driveway bell ringing. It was a blue Ford station wagon—late model—perhaps 1954 or so, and it was occupied by a five member family. The car had a Missouri license tag on it, and on the back of the car, there was an advertising sticker that said "Neosho Ford—Neosho, Mo." I had never heard of Neosho, and I wondered where it was.

After I ran down to the pumps, I asked, "Can I fill her up fer you, sir?"

"Yes, boy. Fill her up with regular," the driver said.

I ran around and opened the flap and removed the gas cap. Then I cranked the pump and put the nozzle in the filler tube and squeezed. While I filled the tank, the mother and her three kids all got out of the car and walked toward the station. There were two boys and a girl. I figured they would all go to the rest rooms. I finished filling up the tank, and then I put the nozzle away. As I washed all the windows of the car, I thought, *These station wagons sure got a lot of windows to clean!* I also checked the air in the tires and all the fluids under the hood. Then the driver got out of the car.

"I see, sir, that your car has a sticker on the back that says 'Neosho, Missouri.' If you don't mind me askin', where is Neosho?" I asked.

"Why, it ain't but about forty-five or fifty miles just north of here," the man reported.

"Then it must be an Ozark city," I replied.

"That's right. It's in the Ozarks, boy."

"I see. Are y'all passin' through?"

"Yeah. We're goin' south to Texas, boy. We got kin in Oklahoma and in Texas, and we're stoppin' along the way," he said.

"I see. Well, it'll be four dollars and twenty cents, sir."

"Y'all got any cold drinks here?"

"Yassir. In that ice box over yonder. We got Co-Cola and Nehi—orange and grape. I think there's also some Seven-Up in there, too."

He opened the ice box and reached his arm down inside.

"Boy, them drinks ain't very cold!"

I followed him over and reached into the ice box, but almost all the ice was melted, and the water was barely cool.

"I'm sorry, sir. Ice man only comes out here on Mondays and Thursdays. Guess we'll have to get some more ice delivered, but it won't be until day after tomorrow."

"Well, why don't y'all get one of them new-fangled Coke machines that keeps drinks cold automatically by electricity? They count yer money fer you, and they keep yer drinks cold. Why they even give you change if you put too much money in 'em. Eh. . .what difference does it make anyway? You sure ain't gonna get one before we leave here today, and slightly cool drinks is better than no drinks at all. We'll take 'em with us. Here's five bucks, boy. You keep the change."

He paid me the money, and I said, "Y'all have a good trip, sir, and I apologize fer them drinks."

As I walked toward the station, his whole family started to come back from the rest rooms. The mother and the daughter were both wearing gaudy pairs of sunglasses. The two boys appeared to be about ten and eight years old or so. They were wearing overalls and tee shirts. The mother reminded me a little of Mrs. Morrison, a lady who went occasionally to our church, but the kids didn't remind me of anyone. The dad acted like he was in a hurry, but the rest of them just seemed to take their time getting back in the car. The man gave each child a bottled drink, and one to his wife.

"Oh, my drink is warm," the little girl whined.

"Yeah, mine, too," said the eight-year old. "It ain't just warm; it's hot!"

"Just shut up and drink it!" screamed the mother. "I've had just about enough of yer complainin' on this trip, Robert Dale Junior! Oh, I've got me a crackin' headache! Will you come on, Bobby Dale? It's hot! Less get on outta here!"

Immediately, the man got back in the car and started it, and in the next moment, he punched the accelerator pedal so hard with his right foot that his back tires began to smoke, and the car spun from side to side, as they all headed back down Highway 59. He didn't even look to see if any traffic was coming or going. Fortunately, there wasn't, or surely we would have had to place five more crosses out there at the Y.

If nothing else, it was always just a little amusing for me to watch some family or individual come in and put on a little circus display like that. It provided an animated break from our otherwise daily and generally dull routine here in Y-City Station I returned to my steel pail to enjoy some more peace and quiet.

Just before one o'clock that afternoon, Daddy and Mama came down to the station. As soon as I saw them, I got up and ran over to the station, and I yelled out, "Daddy!"

"Hey there, y'all," Daddy said. "How's bidness?"

"Well, howdy stranger!" said Granddaddy. "How you been doin'?"

"Hey, there, son!" he said to me, and then to Granddaddy, "Been doin' good up on that highway, Paw. Been doin' real good."

"Boy, yer Daddy's got somethin' here to show you. Lookie here, Granddaddy!" Mama said.

Daddy had a sack in his hand, and he reached inside. All our eyes were fixed on that sack, and he pulled out a brand-new, shiny-white baseball with bright red and gold stitching. The words "Rawlings, Official National League" were printed on it. Daddy handed the ball to me. In my hands, the ball felt completely different from any baseball I'd ever held before. It felt smooth and heavy; it was solid and graceful. It smelled genuine and new–sort of like the way brand new cars smell. It wasn't like any baseball that I had ever thrown or caught.

"Daddy!" I exclaimed. "I ain't ever felt a baseball like this one. Did you buy it fer me? Granddaddy! Feel of it!"

I handed it to Granddaddy. His big right hand seemed to cover the entire ball, and he gripped it respectfully–almost reverently–with all the skill of a surgeon. He turned the ball gently in his hand and fingered it. He rolled the ball with great precision across his palm, through his fingers, and back again. Then, Granddaddy grinned with a full smile that seemed to light up his whole countenance. He held the ball out to me, and he whispered in my ear, "Boy, read that imprint again."

I read it again, but I just couldn't believe it. I had played ball with lots of baseballs that said as much as Official National League, but I knew that they were all cheap imitations. Nevertheless, this was truly different. I wondered, *Could this really be a genuine baseball? And, if so, how could it be?*

"Daddy! Is it really real? Where did you get it? Please, tell me!"

Daddy looked at me, and then he looked at Granddaddy. Mama was beaming with joy, and she said, "Jefferson Davis, this is a genuine National League baseball!"

"Where did you get it? How did you get it? Did you buy it from someone?"

"Listen to this," Mama said.

"Believe it or not," said Daddy, "here's the story. I was in St. Louis this past Tuesday morning, and they was late to load my trailer. The traffic manager up there, Mr. Mason...he comes up to me and says, 'Hey, Clayton. They're goin' to be a while loadin' you up. I got some tickets to the All-Star game this afternoon and...'"

"No! Daddy, you're fibbin' me!" I interrupted him.

"No! I ain't," said Daddy. "And Mr. Mason says to me, 'You wanna go with me to the game?' And, of course, who wouldn't wanna go? So I said, 'Sure, Mr. Mason! I ain't ever been before,' and I was perty excited about goin'. So, we get in his car and drive down there to Sportsman's Park, and I ain't never seen nothin' like it before in my life. We parked the car a few blocks away on some colored fellow's front lawn, and he says, 'Two bucks fer the game, and I watch yer car right here.' I was a little suspicious about it, but Mr. Mason says, 'It's all right...I do it all the time–like everyone else,' and so we park. Cars was parked on all them front lawns. Then me and Mr. Mason walk on over to the ballpark, and I mean to tell you–they're a crowdin' in that ballpark just like bees on a jar of spilt summer honey. We get up there to the gate, and they take them tickets, and we go in. They got carnies all over the place sellin' peanuts, pop, pennants, and programs, and I mean it's a regular picnic. Well, first we walked up this ramp and then that one, and after while, we got to another entry where you can look down and see that field–the greenest grass I ever seen! We went in there and started to go down. Mr. Mason was leadin' us to our seats which was pretty good ones just up a ways behind the Cardinal dugout; the seats was perfect fer us."

"So then, you bought this ball right there in the ballpark?" I asked, impatiently.

"No, boy. Listen to this–the best is yet to come. We sat down and waited fer the game to start. And I mean it is all just a beautiful as it can be. After the game begun, I saw Stan the Man, Mickey Mantle, Mays, and Ted Williams; Aaron and Mathews; Burdette, Spahn, and Schoendienst, and Wally Moon, too. I mean…it was super, and until then, I ain't ever seen anything like it!

"Well, anyway, Musial done real good. About the sixth inning, they sent Moon up to bat, but he just grounded out. But in the eighth inning, the National League was batting, and after Cimoli struck out lookin,' Schoendienst come up to bat. Well, Red stepped into the batter's box, but he didn't do nuthin' except ground out. Before he done it though, he hit a couple of high foul balls, and one of 'em come right over my way, and Mr. Mason shouts out, 'Catch that ball, Clayton!' I reached out, and…well, here it is, boy! I caught it, and it's all yours to keep!"

I was absolutely awe-struck. Immediately, I wanted to show it to Donnie Joe, Lester, and J.R., and all my other friends. But then I knew that Bubby would probably want to chew on it for a while, and if I showed it to Tommy Green, he would try to grab it and play catch or keep-away with it. Of course, Billy Stevens would say something like, "Well, if Musial didn't hit it, then I wouldn't really want it. Besides, Schoendienst isn't even a Cardinal; he's a Milwaukee Brave!"

I was proud of it mostly because Daddy gave it to me. I didn't care that Schoendienst hit it, or that he was a Milwaukee Brave. And the more I thought about it, the better it got. After all, I knew that Schoendienst had at least started his career with the Cardinals. And, like Musial, he was an All-Star playing on the same team, so in the end, what difference did it make?

215

The fans in those stands certainly had no say about which batter would hit the next foul ball–or even if it would be foul and come over your way. Neither Billy Stevens nor anyone else I knew in all of Northwest Arkansas had a brand new, official National League baseball, and most certainly not one hit last week by Red Schoendienst at the All-Star game up in Sportsman's Park. That baseball represented a better treasure to me than if I had discovered a whole trunk full of gold coins in that cave up north of Gravette. Later on, when Schoendienst returned to the Cardinals in 1961, it was almost as if he had been a secret Cardinal all along and had finally come back home to his real team; for me, his return only increased the value of that baseball all the more.

Thirty-four

Granddaddy suggested that I ask Grandma about keeping the baseball in her display cabinet in the parlor of the house.

"It'll be safe in there because that cabinet locks, and you can always see it through the glass," he said.

I thought it was an excellent idea, and when I asked her about it, she said, "Of course you can put it in there, boy. It's fer our treasures, and I'm happy fer you to show it off there. Just let me go and get the key."

In her display cabinet, Grandma had some beautiful crystal glasses on display and a number of other small pieces of pottery, glass, and porcelain. She also displayed a few pieces of china, some silverware, and some very old, little family pictures in delicate frames. She had a couple of old dolls in fancy dresses, as well as some napkins and other handmade cloths. Certainly, most items in her display cabinet were irreplaceable and of great value to her.

Grandma came back with the key, and she opened the cabinet and put my baseball on the fourth shelf up and toward the back.

"What are these old pictures, Grandma?" I asked.

"Why, I haven't pulled those out in long time," she said. "Less just see…"

She pulled out two tiny photo albums. Each one had about twelve or fourteen brown and white photographs. We sat down together on the divan, and she held the album where we both could see. She opened the first one, and immediately she said, "Oo…oo…oh! My goodness! Look how young I was back then! Son, this is me before Granddaddy and I got married."

The picture, somewhat dim and fuzzy, seemed a little strange to me. It was the picture of a young, unrecognizable but pretty girl.

"That's you, Grandma?"

"Yes. That's me."

"Well, Grandma, you was really perty when you was young," I said.

"And lookie here…that's my daddy and this one is my mama. Goodness! These pictures sure are old!" said Grandma. She continued to turn the pages. "Why lookie there…there's your granddaddy when he was young. Boy, you sure got his eyes!" she said.

We looked at the pictures for almost an hour. Grandma tried to identify most of the people in the album, and she told me a little about what life was like when she was growing up, but she said that now she couldn't remember exactly who some of the people in those pictures were. When we finished, we got up and put the albums back in the cabinet, which Grandma carefully locked.

"Grandma, are you sure that baseball don't look funny in there beside all them cloths and china pieces?" I asked.

"No sir, it don't. You could say them dolls and crystal glasses look funny next to that baseball, maybe," Grandma said, "but all them little treasures just look good the way they are. Maybe they don't go together, but I didn't put them in there to go together. I put them in there to treasure!"

I decided only to tell my friends about my baseball rather than to show it to them. That way, Bubby couldn't get in to it and chew on it, and Billy Stevens couldn't play catch with it or lose it. I figured that, if they wanted to see it, they could always come by the house and see it in Grandma's display cabinet.

Mama also reported to Daddy what Deputy Watkins did to her earlier in the week. Daddy said, "We'll leave things be fer now. I'll be observin' and a watchin' him, and I'm just as likely to catch him off guard as not. When I do, I'll deal with him and square it up then."

The next day, we all went to church. All my friends and I were hoping that Mr. Martel would be our teacher again, but we were disappointed because

Brother Pickett was in attendance that morning. He forgot to begin our class with a prayer, and he just went right into the Sunday school lesson, which was a very unusual thing for him to do. Wayne Spillman raised his hand.

"What you got on yer mind, Wayne?" asked Brother Pickett.

"Well, didn't you mean to start our lesson with prayer?"

"Why, did we forget to pray?" Brother Pickett asked.

"Yessir. We ain't prayed yet, sir," J.R. said.

"Well, boys," Brother Pickett said. "I'm sorry that I forgot. I believe I'm just a little out of sorts today. Y'all know that I was away, well…uh…I was out sick last weekend, and I'm a feelin' just a little bad about our dear brother, Deacon Ellis, who got killed so suddenly and unexpectedly last week. Well, then, less pray…."

After his prayer, Brother Pickett asked, "now then, boys, who was yer teacher last week?"

"Sir," J.R. said, "our teacher was Mr. Martel."

"I see. Well, what did he talk about then?"

"He talked about the whole whale story in the Bible," Bubby reported.

"He did not!" Lester said. "He talked about livin' the Christian life out in front of the whole world, Bubby."

Brother Pickett made an attempt to teach a good Sunday school lesson, but unfortunately, his preoccupation with his own bad example before us, the robbery, and the death of Deacon Ellis–among other things–actually prevented him from communicating effectively with his students after that. Now, apparently disconnected from the Word of God, his teaching withered and his testimony wilted. At least in my heart and mind, his message– whatever it was–seemed completely devoid of the convicting power that commonly associates with genuine spiritual truth, and his manner failed to evidence the confirming proof that correlates actively with a living testimony to it. Even among the rest of the boys in our class, I sensed that Brother Pickett's teaching no longer held any serious meaning for them. Of course, each was there for his own reason, and some of those boys were still likely to be unbelievers who never appropriated any truth, regardless of the instrument through which it was transmitted. However, at this point in our relationship with him, most of us had–for many different reasons–given up on him as a Sunday school teacher who had any integrity. Because these were our formative years, I also felt, on behalf of my classmates, that this situation was terribly disappointing. As we all grew older, I knew that some of my friends in that class were becoming increasingly disillusioned with Sunday school, as well as with church, and they were not far away from making the final decision to forsake Sunday school and church attendance altogether. Having Brother Pickett for our Sunday school teacher could never motivate them to arrive at the right choice. We needed someone like Mr. Martel for our teacher.

After our Sunday school was over that morning, we walked up the stairs to the worship hall in the Grange House.

"Donnie Joe," I said, "I know it sounds strange, but believe it or not, my daddy went to the All-Star game last week."

"You're kiddin', Stafford," he replied.

"No. I ain't kiddin' you at all," I answered. "And at home, I've got the baseball to prove it; Daddy caught one of them foul balls that Red Schoendienst hit, and he brought it home and gave it to me. It's jist beautiful!"

"Really?" J.R. asked.

"Next time y'all come over to the house, I'll show it to you. It's in my grandma's treasure cabinet."

By the time we all got into the sanctuary, my whole Sunday school class knew about the baseball. Everyone was asking when it would be a good time to come over for a viewing.

"We'll have to ask Mama," I said. "She don't want the whole troop comin' all at once."

Bubby considered that answer to be a delaying tactic, whereupon he said, "Stafford, you ain't got any baseball that Red Schoendienst hit! That's all muck. If you did have one, you'd bring it out an' show it to us now! Nobody takes such a ball and hides it in a ol' lady's treasure box."

Wayne said, "Why would he lie? He ain't never lied to us before. I believe he's got it–just like he says!"

"I do have it, Wayne."

"Well," said Billy, "if it was mine, I'd been throwin' it all around and proud to show it off."

"Well, it's all the same to me," I said. "I got the ball, and you ain't."

Coming up the stairs, we made such a loud commotion that Mrs. Perkins and Mrs. Shelton heard us, and they both demanded that we show reverence to the assembly.

"Now here, here, you boys. Y'all don't need to be so loud comin' up into this here house o' prayer. Less all be mindful o' where we are and hold our voices down and be gettin' quiet now!"

"Yes ma'am," we said.

We took our places and got quiet. The service began. After the opening prayer and the announcements, we sang a few songs under the direction of Mr. King. Then Miss Audrey Jane played a special worship selection on the organ, followed by Reverend Sutherland, who came to the pulpit to make a special announcement.

"Now, folks, I want to unveil my plans for our new building program. We are growin'…in fact, we are growin' so much that we're a outgrowin' our space here at the Grange House, which means that real soon we're gonna need some more room. I don't want to build an overflow tent out there on the lawn. I want to challenge you all to consider contibutin' to our new building fund. And I know that some of you farmers and ranchers here at the church got some extra acreage out yonder behind the lower forty. I want to encourage y'all to pray about givin' what you got to the Lord's cause here at West Bethel Baptist Church. If you can give a dime, then you give your dime. If you can give a dollar, then you give your dollar. And if you can give an acre of land, then you just give it. Our deacon board has directed me to begin the first phase of our building program for our congregation. I'd like to reach our goal of breakin' ground one year from now. Folks, it ain't goin' to be easy. It ain't ever easy, but with God's he'p, we can do great things. So y'all be thinking about how y'all can each do your part."

After we sang another song and they collected the offering, Reverend Sutherland returned to the pulpit for his morning message. That morning, when he stepped up to preach, it seemed as if Reverend Sutherland suddenly became transfigured into a completely different person—one of intensely biblical proportions—somewhat like Moses or Elijah. I had never witnessed this before. Without doubt, it was clearly Pastor Sutherland, but that morning, he appeared to possess the special, heavy hand of God's anointing on his shoulder like never before. From his pulpit, he took a moment of silence to gaze out at every individual across his entire congregation, and in that singular instant before he ever opened his mouth to preach even one syllable of his sermon, his eyes began to penetrate the darkest shadows of our hearts so fiercely that we all felt like we had just been pierced asunder by the double-edged sword. In that moment, Brother Sutherland's countenance immediately assumed a dreadful but transcendent appearance like that of the judgment angel, and for no more than a brief second in the light of his examination, I experienced a personal sense of overwhelming disgrace and embarrassment. It was almost as if the pastor's scrutiny had now also proclaimed me guilty of being completely vile and contaminated, and by some strange determination, I had now been identified to receive his harshest spiritual cleansing; I simply wanted to run away and hide. Behind the pulpit, Reverend Sutherland slowly raised his right hand to that level where his index finger now extended out like a mystical shepherd's rod, he pointed it accusingly at each terrified member of the flock, and then he spoke.

"Church," he said with a loud voice. "The Sovereign God of the universe has consigned to me this day the serious responsibility to deliver to y'all the most stinging and burdensome prophecy I've ever been called upon to preach." He lifted his Bible in the air and shook it at the people. Then he thumped his cane on the wooden floor and his fist on the pulpit.

"Oh, beloved brethren!" he shouted. "May I never, ever shrink back from my task. But I speak today with the heaviest of hearts..." Reverend Sutherland became deeply passionate of heart, and his voice began to quiver. At this, some of the church members began to tremble, for they understood that they were about to receive a very serious sermon, and they came immediately under the conviction of sin. Frequently raising his voice and pointing his finger at the people, Pastor Sutherland continued.

"Before God today–as He lives and is my Witness–it is my grave duty to show y'all yer sin. In our church, there is a most putrid form of sin and corruption among us. We have violated the Lord's covenant, and we have stolen the sacred things. Like Joshua standing before the Lord after the battle at Ai, I can prophesy to you this morning that we are going to expose this iniquity and root it out." Brother Sutherland pounded his fist down on the pulpit several times, and each time he did, there was a loud report like that coming from a gun. Then he thumped his cane again.

"Brothers and sisters," he continued pounding and speaking, "we are not going to tolerate even the slightest retention of an Achan in our midst. Achan was that awful, despicable Judas of our beloved Old Testament, and today–even in this very hour–we have a Judas in our congregation! He is here now. Well, I can tell you…no!…I mean to promise you that by the power of the Holy Spirit of God that we are going to discover that scoundrel abiding among us, and we are going to punish him severely. We are going to identify him!" He thumped the podium.

"We shall extract his confession!" followed by another thump.

"We are going to purge him; we are going to obtain his repentance; and we are going to cast him out utterly from among our midst, even if we have to place every heart–young and old, man or woman, rich or poor–under the omniscient scrutiny and the cleansing blood of our Lord and Savior, Jesus Christ!"

Brother Sutherland paused for a moment. He was both angry and passionate. This was a deeply personal offense to him, and many church members now became simultaneously offended. Each looked around at the other, and there were whispers among the people.

"Who is this Judas?"

"Where is he?"

"Who among us could have 'violated the Lord's covenant?'"

"What does he mean by stealing 'the sacred things?'" People were checking their hymnbooks and looking around to see if anything had just gone missing.

"In my church, there is to be *no* violation of the Lord's covenant!" Pastor Sutherland shouted. He smacked the pulpit again. "I want to tell you, Mr. Achan, in our church, you know who you are. I want to announce to you Mr. Judas of West Bethel. You hear me out, and you listen to me good! When the Lord reveals you to me, I guarantee you–you are going to deal first with me. Then you will deal with the law. Finally, you will deal with the Lord God, and may our dear Lord have mercy on your soul!"

He continued to preach his message–screaming, pointing, thumping, and pounding. That sermon was probably the most effective one he ever preached. The pastor never stated that any money had been stolen from the plate. He never mentioned any names. He simply went on to present the sinful theft of Achan, to criticize the wicked betrayer of our blessed Lord Jesus

Christ, and to equate our nameless scoundrel and in-house thief with both of them. Most uncharacteristically, we did not have an invitation that Sunday. We didn't even sing a closing hymn. Pastor Sutherland simply ended his message by saying that "Today, no altar call is needed. We don't need a rush of minor sinners approaching our bench; we just need to be cleansed of this great sinner, and I say to you, great sinner, come forward!"

Like a fixture, Brother Sutherland did not move from the stage. He directed the people to stand and move quietly toward the Grange House door.

"And y'all can be sure," he said, "that in the days ahead, the Holy Spirit will surely reveal the truth to us, and then God's judgment will fall. So y'all quietly go on home and pray for forgiveness, and I pity the poor soul who did this."

Thirty-five

After we got home from church, and we were all sitting around the dining table, Granddaddy said, "That was certainly a powerful message that Brother Sutherland preached this morning."

"Probably the best one he ever preached," Daddy said.

"I believe he was perty angry about all this stealin' and what-not," Mama said.

"Well, do y'all suppose the Holy Spirit'll tell him who done it?" I asked.

Daddy said, "I think he already knows who done it, 'cause I told him about it first of all. I think he's jist a waitin' awhile fer that thief to come forward on his own. Brother Sutherland wants him to wait a spell so his guilt will get worse, and when he comes forward, the pastor'll slice him to ribbons. Please pass me that gravy, Norma Jean, would you, Honey?"

"Well," Grandma said. "I wouldn't want to be in that old Achan's shoes fer nuthin'. If the pastor gets a hold of him, there won't be much of him left to deliver over to the law; you can be sure of that."

"I never heard the pastor shout so much like what he done today," J-Earl said. "Tawna Rae, was you a-scared o' all that shoutin' and hollerin'?"

Tawna Rae just nodded her head and stayed real close to Mama.

"Now, J-Earl!" Mama said. "Don't you get her started and be upsettin' her again. She don't need to be riled up anymore. You know it makes her get all sick, and then she throws up all over the place! Why would you do that, child?"

"Well, Mama, I never…"

"J-Earl, I said enough!"

"Yes, ma'am."

After we finished dinner, we washed all the dishes and cleaned up the kitchen. I decided to go into the parlor to see how my baseball was doing. It was still on display there in Grandma's treasure cabinet. Somehow, that baseball seemed to look even better behind the glass. I could hardly believe it was mine. Looking at that ball inspired me to go outside and play some catch with J-Earl or Granddaddy, but I knew Mama wouldn't allow that because it was Sunday. Normally, after Sunday dinners at home, our whole family would take a long nap for most of the afternoon. I wasn't very tired, but I decided that, if I couldn't go out and play catch, there wasn't much else to do but to go to my room and lie down to rest for a while.

In my room, I had some good books, most of which I had read over and over again. At that moment, I remembered that, before school ended back in May, Mr. McLemore told us to read a lot of books over the summer and to try to keep track of them. He told us that, "Come August, y'all'll have a new English teacher, and she's gonna ask y'all 'How many books have y'all read over the summer?'"

Goodness, I thought. *Come August? Here it is already past the middle of July, and I ain't even read one book yet!* At first, I was feeling a little bored, but now I started feeling guilty. Then I thought, *Well, I'm sure glad that Starla Sutherland ain't in my class; otherwise, she'd be tellin' that new English teacher that she read a hundert books over the summer, and then they'd give her a certificate with a blue ribbon and a gold seal on it, and she'd be gloatin' about it and a wavin' that thing all over the place in front of ever'body.*

Of course, Starla Sutherland wasn't even in our school, but of those in my class, I knew that both Tommy Green and Wayne Spillman would read several books. You could be sure that Sue Linda Culpepper would probably read as many as Starla did, but at least Sue Linda would not wave her certificate all around. Donnie Joe wouldn't read much, and Bubby would only read whatever books he could chew on or maybe even eat. I decided that it was in my best interests to read something rather than nothing, so I selected one of my old favorites, *Treasure Island,* and I lay down on the bed to read. Within fifteen minutes, I was asleep.

I woke up from my nap about four-thirty that afternoon. My *Treasure Island* book had apparently fallen out of my hands, and while I was sleeping, I must have rolled over on it and bent about fifteen or twenty of the pages in half. Fortunately, none of the pages were torn, although the book's back cover was ripped at the spine down about one inch from the top. J-Earl and Tawna Rae were still sleeping. I rubbed my eyes and stretched, and then I got up quietly.

I heard voices speaking out on the front porch, so I went out there. I was startled to see the law parked on the grass out front. It was Deputy Watkins, and he was out leaning against the front of his patrol car. Granddaddy and Mama were sitting on the porch, but Daddy was sitting on the third step down from the porch floor. Evidently, Deputy Watkins had not been there for more than five or six minutes, but I got out on the porch just a little late in the overall conversation.

"All I know is that Sheriff Parker said he got a call from the Gentry police chief, and he said there was a whole lot o' money in that deacon's car when he died," Deputy Watkins said. "They got all that money down at the Gentry police station, and they're a holdin' it until they can determine what all's goin' on with it." Deputy Watkins had a long piece of yellow grass in his mouth, and he was chewing on it nervously.

"Of course, y'all would like to get all that money under your jurisdiction now, wouldn't you?" Daddy asked, with just a little sarcasm.

"I reckon it's best fer the sheriff hisself to answer that question, now, idn't it?"

"Well, Jimmy, I cain't say as I know anything about that. Are y'all trying to connect up the deacon an' say he was in cahoots with that colored hobo?" Daddy asked.

"I dunno. He might could have been, Clayton. Who knows? One thing's fer sure, idn't it?" asked Watkins.

"What's that?" Daddy asked him.

"Well, we cain't jist ask the old deacon to tell us the answer to that, now, can we?" Deputy Watkins replied. He was becoming visibly irritated.

"Well, you boys represent the law. What's that ol' colored man sayin' over there at the jail these days?"

"He ain't talkin' any more. Some quack, Yankee lawyer has heard about his case now an' come down here from Chicago or somewheres up north, and he's agreed to defend him. He is sayin' that this nigger's...what I mean is...he's claimin' that the boy was forced into a confession 'gainst his will, and he's tellin' that boy to extract his admission and shut up. On top o' that, this Yankee lawyer has told Sheriff Parker that the judge may have to set him free fer some blasted little loophole in the law, and he's threatenin' to have the sheriff's job over it all. Leastwise, that's the talk over there."

"Well," Daddy said. "We cain't he'p you no more. We done said our whole piece to Sheriff Parker–everything we know about that robbery," Daddy said. "Y'all are simply gonna to have to work with the Gentry police department and solve that problem about the money, but I'm gonna tell you one thing: I believe that, when the real truth comes out, y'all are gonna find that your colored hobo up there in the Benton County jail never done it–and he won't need the he'p of some northern lawyer to prove it."

"Well," said Deputy Watkins, "we'll see about that." Arrogantly, he began to walk around to the door on the side of his patrol car.

"And by the way, Jimmy Lee," Daddy said. Daddy stood up and walked down the rest of the steps and stood in front of the patrol car on the grass. "You consider yerself warned this time, Jimmy Lee. You stay far away from my wife. If I ever hear that you come 'round toward her again, I'm gonna set you in your grave, Jimmy Lee."

After Deputy Watkins was gone, Daddy came up the stairs again, and Mama got up and hugged him.

"Thank you," she said.

Granddaddy said, "He didn't come round here to tell us all the latest news about that case. He's keepin' an eye on us."

"I know it, Paw," Daddy said. "He may be watchin' us, but he knows that I meant what I said. Paw?"

"Yeah?" asked Granddaddy.

"Please stay real close to Norma Jean and the kids this week, would you?"

Thirty-six

Very early the next morning, I heard Daddy starting his truck, so I knew he was leaving for Joplin. Before getting up, I laid awake for a while there in bed. I was thinking about our lives together as a family. Daddy was starting to make a good wage, but he was always away. That wasn't good for Mama, and we didn't like it either. Of course, Granddaddy, Mama, and I were working the station, but I knew—we all knew—that the gas station wasn't really paying off, and we suspected that it never would. Even though we supplemented it with the fruit and vegetable stand, the ham sandwiches, the car accessory lines, and all the other things we tried, the station barely covered its own expenses, and in the end, there was almost no real profit from it at all. A few of our customers maintained accounts with us, but most of them went unpaid from month to month. The station, already old and unattractive, seemed to be deteriorating faster than we could restore any of its troubles; we simply could not afford to improve it in any major way. In another few weeks, school would be starting again for J-Earl and me, and during school hours, Granddaddy and Mama would have to pick up the slack and assume the tasks created by my absence from the station during my presence at school. As the fall season approached, supplies of fruit, vegetables, eggs, and other homemade products for sale would decrease in the same way the daylight hours would diminish and darkness would prevail; then, winter would set in, and the station's capacity to generate a living for anyone would practically disappear. Whether we liked it or not, we knew that our little station was doomed to such an end.

I also thought about Granddaddy and Grandma, both of whom enjoyed favorable health, but they were both getting older and slower. Their house was certainly big enough for all of us, but it was also old and in need of a whole variety of repairs as well. None of us had the time, the aptitude, or the resources to invest in these, as each passing day already seemed to require from all of us too much attention to other things. Even at my young age, I wasn't worried or alarmed about any of these matters, but I wondered where all these circumstances would lead. As time went on, how would each of the threads of our lives—the different people, the chain of events, and all the other variables that affected us daily—interlace themselves together? Thoughts of the future, how we would all arrive there, and what it might look like quickly became too burdensome for my mind, so I decided to get up and make my bed.

"Make your bed the moment your two feet hit the floor. That way, it is done, and you don't need to come back to it later," Mama would say. She had trained us well.

As usual, Granddaddy was on the back porch, and Grandma was already making breakfast. Mama came into the kitchen a few minutes later and said good morning. She began helping Grandma, and before much longer, we were all eating our breakfast.

Within the hour, Granddaddy and I were down at the station ready for a full day of work. I decided that it would be a good idea for me to bring some books to read. After all, sometimes a whole hour or more might go by between customers, and I figured that I could probably read ten or twenty books down at the station between now and the day school would start. With Sue Linda in my class, I didn't really expect that our new English teacher—whoever it might be—would be much impressed if I read only ten or twenty books over the summer. At this point, there was absolutely no hope of catching up with Sue Linda. I suspected that, by now, she had probably read eighty or ninety books already and would easily have a hundred done by the start of school. At times I was tempted to enjoy the rest of the summer without reading any books at all. To be sure, I could always tell the new English teacher, "it was because I had to work at our gas station all summer, and I didn't have any time to read." However, the more I thought about this, the more convicted to read I became. *Reading is enjoyable. How can you truly enjoy the summer without reading?* my conscience asked. This conviction led me to the certainty that if I read no books over the summer, the new English teacher would surely develop such a lasting, negative impression about me, that she would mark me as a total failure on the first day of school and maintain that view of me throughout the rest of the year.

Goodness! I thought. *I'd better bring ten more books with me tomorrow. I'll let Donnie Joe make that kind of impression on her.*

About nine-thirty that morning, Mr. Crawford arrived. After he got out of his car, he spat a big load of tobacco down onto the driveway, and then he went into the station.

Yuck! Look at that mess! I thought to myself.

"Mornin' there, boy," he said, on his way in. "Come in and get a doughnut."

"Mornin'," I said. "I'll be in directly. Just let me clean that up first."

"Yer always cleanin' up, boy!" he said.

"Yassir."

I knew that Granddaddy made Mr. Crawford use that Maxwell House can when he sat around inside the station so I decided to go out back to our junkyard and look for an old five gallon paint drum to make him an outside spittoon. I figured that, if he must chew and spit that nasty slop, surely he couldn't miss the opening of a five-gallon can anymore than he could miss my hint that, by providing him a can, he ought to use it. Out back in the junkyard, I found several old oil and paint drums. One of the paint drums had a lid on it, and it felt and sounded like it still had paint in it. Just after I lifted it, I spotted a large, copperhead snake curled up below in the space formed by the wooden pallet. Exposed by the light and startled by all the movement, the noise, and my body heat, the snake instantly began to coil around itself and moved its head threateningly upward, perhaps six inches above the pallet. The serpent's eyes met my own, and it propelled its forked tongue in and out nervously before it opened its mouth. Immediately, I froze all my movements and then gradually began to back up a step or two while I moved the paint drum slowly around between the snake and me. In the next moment, I saw the snake retreat back and then disappear under the pallet and move off into the little spaces between the pieces of junk in the opposite direction.

Back around in the front of the station, I pried the lid off the paint drum. I opened it and saw that it had a mixture of about a gallon and a half of very thin, now-yellowed, white paint and about two inches of scummy water on top. I walked up behind our fruit stand and dumped the mixture out in the tall grass behind the trees. Then I came back down to the garage and, using the hose, began to wash out the old paint. When most of it was gone, I retrieved a wire brush from the garage and began to brush off all the dried paint particles. After another good rinsing with water, Mr. Crawford's outside spittoon was done. I carried it down by his car and placed it on the driver's side just behind the door where he could spit in it and then just drive off. Then I went inside for a doughnut.

"Boy, where you been?" asked Granddaddy.

"I was out back in the junkyard, Granddaddy. I found a large old drum that Mr. Crawford can use for his outside spittoon, so I cleaned it up and put it out there behind his car. I also saw a copperhead out there…in the back."

"What's that you say, boy? You made me a spittin' can?" asked Mr. Crawford.

"Yassir. I think you'll find it a little more convenient than spittin' on our driveway, sir."

Granddaddy said, "There's probably a whole den of snakes out there, boy. You be sure to watch yerself when yer out there."

"Yes, sir," I responded. I grabbed a jelly doughnut–squeezing it just a little too much–and some of the red jelly squirted out the other end of the doughnut right on the backside of the upper left arm of Mr. Crawford's shirt. At that same moment, he was looking at Granddaddy, and neither of them saw it. I began to laugh out loud immediately.

"What you laughin' at, boy?" Mr. Crawford asked.

When that mess of jelly hit his shirt and he failed to notice, I initially thought to myself, *Well, don't that jist serve him right? Why, you betcha; fer all his tobacco slop that I've had to clean up, let him clean up a little of my jelly slop. Serves him right!* Of course, I couldn't tell him that to his face, so now I had to think fast.

"Well, sir…I…well, I was thinkin' about how funny it would

be…yes…to have…maybe to have one of them rubber snakes…and…put it in the ladies room…yeah…when one of them girls–like Fishbait–goes in there. That's what I was laughin' at."

"I don't find that so funny," Mr. Crawford said. "My wife could be the one what goes in there…or my daughter." Then he pulled out a big old wad of chaw from his Red Man packet and stuffed it directly into his mouth; now his right cheek looked like a blimp on the side of his face.

Granddaddy said, "Well, you ain't got much of a sense of humor, then, Buford. Them rubber snakes can be mighty comical. I've seen 'em over at the carnival, and I've used 'em now and then to play a practical joke or two."

"Well, I've had enough o' yer so-called comedy fer one day, and I've got to get on down the road now, Arliss."

"Well, thanks fer the doughnuts Mr. Crawford," I said.

"You don't need to go away mad, now Buford," Granddaddy told him, and then he looked at me and quietly moved his lips to say silently, "Just go away!"

We both started laughing, and then Mr. Crawford said, "Well, boys, I ain't mad. But sometimes I think y'all Staffords are a bunch of screwballs!"

Just about the time that Mr. Crawford began to walk toward the door, Mama came into the station.

"Good mornin', Buford," she said.

"Mornin', ma'am," he replied curtly, and then he was out the door.

"What's wrong with him?" she asked.

"He forgot his sense of humor this morning, Norma Jean." We laughed again.

"Well," said Mama, "he ain't really ever had much of one, anyway."

I said, "Well, don't tell him that, Mama. That's what we was tryin' to say to him sort o' indirectly, but he didn't like it."

"Granddaddy!" Mama teased. "You been puttin' this boy up to no good?"

Granddaddy looked over at me and winked. "Why, no, Norma Jean! Whatever give you that idea?" he said, chuckling.

"Why that old scoundrel!" I said.

"What?" Mama asked. "What happened?"

"Well, I was just lookin' out the window…watchin' to see if Mr.

Crawford would spit his mess in the new outside spittoon I made for him, and he…"

"Spit his tobacco juice all over the driveway again?" Granddaddy interjected.

"Yeah!"

"He ain't got any manners, either."

After Mr. Crawford left, we all took up our respective places in the station. Granddaddy was in the main office, Mama was working the fruit and vegetable stand, and, I, sitting on my pail, was waiting for some gasoline customers to come into the station. I decided to prepare for the new school year by reading books. A few cars and trucks passed by in both directions out on Highway 59, and a long freight train came through and disconnected for the railroad crossing there at the Y. The train sat there practically all afternoon. By the time a customer came, I had already finished more than half of *Treasure Island.*

The customer was coming from the north, and she pulled her car across our driveway up next to the gasoline pumps on the outside lane.

"Good afternoon," I said. "Do you need some gas?"

"Good afternoon, young man. Yes, I do need the tank filled up with regular, please."

"Yes, ma'am."

She had a pretty face and a lovely smile. She was driving a red and white, 1955 model Chevrolet Bel Air sedan. Her car, which had an Arkansas license plate, was full of clothes, boxes, and household effects. I went back to the pump and got the gasoline nozzle and began to put the gas in the tank. The lady got out of the car and looked back at me. I noticed that, as she stood there in the sunshine, for a brief minute she unwittingly struck a natural posture and a captivating attitude which lasted no more than an instant, but it awakened something in me that I had never quite known until that moment in my life, except maybe in church when I saw Miss Audrey Jane. This lady was beautiful, and before the light, she formed the silhouette of an attractive, youthful female figure through her light-colored clothing.

"Is there a ladies' rest room in this station?"

"Yes, ma'am. The key is in the office."

She went inside to the station office and got the key. I finished pumping her gas, and then I looked at her tires. They were all fine. I checked her oil and water, and then I washed all her windows. Her car was in tip-top shape, and it was a beauty. After I finished, I got my book and went into the office. The lady came out of the restroom with the key, and she came back into the office.

Before I could tell her the price of her gasoline, the customer asked, "Young man, when I pulled into the station, I saw you sitting up there reading a book. Do you like to read a lot?"

"Oh, yes ma'am." I couldn't honestly say that I really liked reading–or any school subject for that matter–as much as Sue Linda did–or as much as I liked fishing or playing baseball. But if she saw me there reading a book and I answered "No ma'am," she'd probably think I was an idiot, and then she wouldn't give me a tip. So I toned down the strength of my "Oh, yes ma'am" by adding, "I'm in the summer readin' program. I'm jist tryin' to read a whole bunch of books over the summer for my new English teacher when school starts." And then the thought occurred to me, *Now, what if she asks you, 'How many books have you read already?' You're really going to look stupid.* Fortunately, she didn't ask.

"Well, that's wonderful!" she exclaimed. "But don't just read them for your new English teacher. Read them for yourself, and here's a little advice that has been very helpful to me–read everything in print that you can get your hands on. How much do I owe you?"

"The gasoline was five dollars and sixty-five cents, ma'am."

She gave me six dollars and said that the rest was for me.

"What is your name, young man?"

"I'm Jefferson Davis Stafford, ma'am."

"Well, Mr. Stafford," she said. "My name is Miss Mary Kay Westbrook. You have a good day, and I'm sure we'll be seeing each other again."

"Yes, ma'am," I responded.

Miss Westbrook left the office.

"She sure was nice, Granddaddy."

"I talked to her for a moment, too. She's new here," he said.

"Her name is Miss Westbrook, and she said she'd be back to see us. Maybe she'll become a long-term customer–wouldn't that be great?"

"She'd be a great customer," Granddaddy said. "She's got a nice disposition, and she don't spit tobacco juice all over the driveway."

"And," I added, "I noticed that she's perty good lookin,' too."

"Well, boy! When did you start noticin' the girls that are good lookin'?" Granddaddy asked.

"I dunno, Granddaddy. A while back, I guess. The ones that are good lookin' just stand out on their own. They're a whole lot easier to look at than the ugly ones, that's all."

"Well, tell me boy…how many girlfriends you got now? Ten? Twenty?" Granddaddy asked. He was starting to tease me now, and, as I was committed to reading these books, I thought I'd better get back out to my pail before he started hooting, hollering, and calling the hogs.

I went outside and noticed that Miss Westbrook was still here. She was up at the fruit stand talking with Mama. I walked up that way and sat down on my pail, and I began to read my book again. A little later, Miss Westbrook finished talking with Mama, and she walked back toward me and on to her car.

"It was a pleasure meeting you, Mr. Stafford," she said to me as she walked by.

"You, too, ma'am."

About ten minutes after Miss Westbrook pulled out of our station, I heard an old farm tractor coming down from our road. The tractor made a sound that got louder and louder as it neared the railroad tracks. I kept on reading and didn't pay much attention to it until after it crossed over the tracks and moved in our direction. I recognized the tractor, which was pulling a wagon carrying some large oil drums, as Mr. Blanton's, but I could see clearly that the rig was being driven by someone else–most likely Mr. Blanton's foreman. He pulled the tractor forward so the drums were adjacent to the gasoline pumps, and then he shut the engine down. The driver dismounted from his seat on the tractor. He was tall–well over six feet–and a lanky man, perhaps between twenty-five and thirty years old. He was wearing Levi's blue jeans with a western belt and a big silver buckle, a black cowboy hat, a red western shirt with a bandana around his neck, and a pair of old, well-worn rattlesnake cowboy boots. He had a long hunting knife in a sheath attached to his belt on the right side, and he looked like he would have no trouble taking care of himself.

"Good afternoon, sir," I greeted him. "You Mr. Blanton's foreman?" I glanced away at the gasoline pumps for a second.

"That's right, boy," he said. "We got an account here, and I want you to fill up them drums with regular gas."

The man's first word rang true and echoed clear in my ears, and its sound instantly shot the worst fear of sudden death into my mind and heart. Abruptly, my eyes shot up at his face, and I froze absolutely dead in my tracks. He was the man! He was the third man whose voice, until now, I had heard only once in my life before–there in the outhouse on the evening of the church picnic–where I had overheard the plans of that evil trio of conspirators to rob one of our local banks. Right here and now, the self-revealed owner of that third but unknown voice stood over me in the flesh, and my entire being succumbed to the weakness of total disadvantage. The man caught me now completely off guard and by surprise, and I was not ready to meet him like this. Fear gripped me as it never had before, and I grew lightheaded, and then...the next thing I remember was that I was trying to get up on my feet.

"Hey, boy! Are you all right?" the foreman said. He asked me again, "Are you all right, son?" The foreman helped lift me up.

"What happened, sir?"

"Well, somehow you suddenly went pale and all white–like you seen a ghost or something, and then you fell over forward and hit the wagon."

My mind suddenly communicated a message to my heart: *Be calm, don't be afraid, and remember that your advantage over him is that he doesn't know that you were in the outhouse that evening.*

"I apologize, sir," I replied. "I think...uh...I believe...maybe I been in the sun too long."

From her fruit stand, Mama had seen me fall over, and she ran quickly down from there to help.

"Did he faint or somethin'?" she asked.

"Yes, ma'am, I believe he fainted...maybe from the heat," said the foreman.

"I'm all right now," I said. "I'll be all right."

"Are you sure, boy?" Mama asked.

"Yes, ma'am. What can I do fer you, sir?"

"Well, I need them drums filled up with gasoline, and you can put it on the Blanton account."

"Yassir."

I regained my composure and convinced myself that my advantage over him was greater than his over me. While I filled his drums, he talked to Mama for a minute or two, and then he went inside the station. It took a good while to pump about a hundred and ten gallons or so. The foreman came outside again, and I tried to get a better look at him. He walked over to the cold drink box and pulled out a bottle of Bubble-Up.

"Hey, boy," he shouted up at me. "You put that cold drink on Blanton's tab, too."

"Yassir."

Without any doubt, I knew this was the man. I tried to study him so I could understand and know what kind of person I was dealing with. Clearly, he was wiry, strong, and commanding. He had big hands and long arms. He maintained an arrogant, challenging attitude that seemed to suggest outright that people ought to stay out of his way or face the consequences.

I finished pumping his gas, and I put the nozzle up.

"It come to twenty-three dollars, in case you want to tell Mr. Blanton," I said.

"It's all the same to me."

"Well, we appreciate it, sir."

He never said another word. He just climbed up in the wagon and drove off.

Thirty-seven

U pon learning the identity of the third conspirator, I became so nervous and animated that I could hardly contain myself. As soon as Mr. Blanton's foreman had left our driveway, I ran immediately into the station office where Granddaddy was sitting on his stool.

"Granddaddy!" I screamed. My heart was still pounding, and I was breathing fast. "That was him! That was him, Granddaddy! That was the man! It's him; I know it's him!"

"Calm down, boy. Jist take a minute and catch yer breath. Now, what are you sayin'?" he asked.

"Well, remember when I told you about when we was at the church picnic, and I heard them three men conspirin' to rob the bank? Surely you remember! One of 'em was Brother Pickett. Another one of 'em was Deacon Ellis. The third one I couldn't place because I had met him, and I never heard his voice–I didn't know him then, but now I know, Granddaddy. When he come in here and started talkin' to me, I knew right away that I heard that voice somewheres. Oh, Granddaddy, it's him; I know it's him!"

"Well, good!" Granddaddy said. "Now, that's good; we've solved who that third person is. Good work, boy! Well done! This part we're goin' to have to keep to ourselves fer awhile though. We need to be watchin' how this fellow plans to meet up with Brother Pickett and so forth."

Granddaddy was right. We couldn't very well just go down to the Gentry police or the Benton County Sheriff and say, "well, we know who your third man is; go arrest him." Somehow, we'd have to have more evidence on him than just our accusation. His case, like that of Brother Pickett's, was still too loose. In fact, even all that money that was left in the deacon's satchel might not prove anything; it could all turn out somehow, to be his own money. I was merely a witness to a conspiracy that, until now, had never been corroborated. And, technically, I heard them say specifically they planned to rob the bank in Decatur, when in fact, it was the bank in Gentry that was robbed. Maybe it wasn't them at all. Maybe it was just coincidence that the Gentry bank was robbed on the same night that I heard all that, and in fact, maybe they are still waiting. Maybe the colored hobo…no…no, I just couldn't accept that. He couldn't have done it. Whoever robbed that bank knew something about Gentry and knew something about that bank.

Well, it's gonna be a long time before Deacon Ellis robs the Decatur bank, I thought to myself. *And what about Brother Pickett's strange behavior? And the strongest connection of all–I saw the deacon take money from the plate in church–and later, I heard them admit their part in it all when they said, 'It's not enough.' No, they're the ones all right, and in time, the truth will come out.*

Time. That was our problem. Who could know how much time it would take? If time, somehow, could reveal the truth sooner, the two scoundrels who were left would get their just rewards quicker, and maybe the colored hobo could be exonerated without sitting too much longer in jail. On the other hand, if time delayed too long in revealing the truth, the two rascals could go scot-free for the length of the delay, and it would eventually run out for the colored hobo, and he would go to prison–perhaps forever.

"Granddaddy, we need to pray that God will reveal the truth in all this sooner rather than later," I said.

"That's right, son. At this point, about all we can do is wait. We wait on Him."

Mama came down to the station office; she had already closed up the fruit stand.

"Do we need to have the doctor check you over, son?" she asked.

I explained to her what really happened, and she fully understood. There

240

was no more talk about the doctor after that, and we closed the station down and went home for the night.

That evening, KMOX helped us get caught up on our baseball. From New York, the Cardinals moved on to play a double-header against the Phillies yesterday at Shibe Park in Philadelphia, but they lost both games–six to two and eleven to four. Since their great winning streak at Cincinnati, they had done nothing but slump everywhere else on the road–not especially good for any first-place team. Harry Carey came on the air and announced that Vinegar Bend Mizell would be the starting pitcher for tonight's game. We sat out on the porch all evening and listened to the game. In spite of all our best hopes that he might turn things around, even Mizell was powerless to assist those Cardinals tonight, for the Phillies trounced them again, six to two. It was a disappointing game, after which we all went to bed. After getting in bed, I noticed once again a locomotive horn fading away into the night somewhere out there on our railroad tracks. Before falling asleep, however, I resolved from then on to read at least two or three chapters of a book every night.

The next day was just about like every other day had been that summer. We got up, had breakfast, went down and opened the station, and did what business we could as the day went on. Mr. Crawford came and brought doughnuts and the *Tulsa World*, and, as usual, he slopped his nasty tobacco spit all over the driveway instead of using his new outside spittoon. Mama came down to work her fruit stand, and we all had lunch together between whatever customers stopped for gas. That day, as I recall, we did have a few more customers than usual in the morning, as we were quite busy, and by noon, there were no doughnuts left.

That afternoon, Reverend Sutherland paid us another visit, which was quite unusual.

"Can I fill yer tank, sir?" I asked him when he pulled into the station.

"Well, son, it seems that my gas tank is still almost full, so I don't believe I'll be needin' any more gas right now. However, I do need to sit down with yer Mama, yer Granddaddy, and with you, son. We need to talk about somethin'."

Reverend Sutherland went inside the station. I ran up to the stand and told Mama that Reverend Sutherland wished to talk with all of us, and I told her that it sounded serious to me. She and I walked back down and went inside.

"Good afternoon, Norma Jean."

"Afternoon, Reverend."

"I got a call this morning from the Gentry police," Reverend Sutherland began. "They asked me to come in to the station there in town, because one of our church members–Brother Dwindle Pickett–I believe he was your Sunday school teacher, son…wadn't he?"

I nodded my head in affirmation.

"Was?" Mama asked with emphasis. "Reverend, what do you mean, was?"

"Yes," he said, "was. Brother Pickett was found dead yesterday morning in the back of his insurance office there on Main Street in Gentry. A customer came in and found it strange that his office was open fer bidness, but no one was around. Evidently, the customer called out for him several times, and when he got no answer, he began to look around and found Brother Pickett shot in the head. He was lying on the floor in a massive pool of his own blood. Apparently, it was a suicide, as there was a gun nearby with his fingerprints on it, and a suicide note in his own handwriting that he left on his desk. Officer Thackston of the Gentry police department is handling the case in cooperation with Sheriff Parker and the county coroner. They are investigating the whole thing, but it looks like a perty tight case. Officer Thackston asked me to come down there and read the note that he left behind. They kept the note fer evidence, but it went something like this:

This is to inform you–whoever should find me thus–that I could no longer live with myself after hearing Reverend Sutherland's sermon this past Sunday. I am one of two partners in our church that stole money out of the offering plate. The other was Deacon Ellis who died earlier in a car wreck.

We was stealing money for about a year not every week but whenever we could because of our awful high gambling debts. We might get thirty or forty or maybe fifty dollars or so a week, but out debt was more than two thousand dollars. We just couldn't stop drinking that wiskee and playing them cards and our debts to Elwood Slade and Jimmy Lee Watkins always growing bigger. They was partners against us, and they said if we didn't pay up, they would tell on us and then they was going to kill us.

We met with Elwood Slade and he agreed to help us rob the bank in Decatur, but later that night, we all changed our minds and decided to rob the bank in Gentry because Jimmy Lee Watkins said it was easier with all them fireworks that night and with him to be the guard on the streets for us in his patrol car. Jimmy said he would do a safety inspection for the bank, and he would leave a back window unlocked for us upstairs. The Gentry bank was not so hard to rob where we got almost $8,000.00. After they found a nigger in an old car by the railroad tracks, they made him drunk and Jimmy said he could beat him up to make him confess to our crime, but that nigger never robbed the Gentry bank; he is innocent. Deacon Ellis already got his share and was going to pay Elwood and Jimmy when he killed hisself in the car crash. I never paid out my share yet, so you will find the money in my safe what is unlocked. Jimmy and Elwood already got all the rest.

I know we was bad examples to our boys in the Sunday school class, and I pray now they won't ever do what we done, but would always do what the reverend says. I cannot live any longer with all this guiltiness. I am sorry that I let you all down.
Dwindle Pickett.

Needless to say, we were all shocked to hear this report, but I personally felt a sense of great relief and vindication by the truth which had now come out. We knew about Brother Pickett and Deacon Ellis. We also knew that a third man was involved, but only yesterday did we learn that it was Mr. Blanton's foreman. Today, we learned his name–Elwood Slade. We never knew about Deputy Watkins' involvement until now. Unless the law had already arrested them, those men were still free.

"Reverend Sutherland?" I asked.

"Yes, son," he replied.

"Do you know if the law has already arrested the other two men yet?"

"I don't know about that," he said.

"Well," I said. "I wonder if they have let that colored hobo go free?"

"I doubt it," Granddaddy said. "They won't let him go until they know fer sure he ain't done it or involved in it in any way. It'll be awhile yet before they turn him loose."

"Reverend," Mama said. "Jimmy Lee Watkins has…has…well, he has tried to hurt me in the past, and I don't mind tellin' you, the thought of him bein' out there on the loose scares me an awful lot."

"I understand, ma'am. Well, Sheriff Parker said that he knew Deputy Watkins could be a wild young man and what-not, but he also said that he was very surprised that the deputy would get involved in a robbery like this. He suspected the deputy of a handful of little pranks and misdemeanors and so forth, but not robbery. Of course, when Brother Pickett is about to kill hisself, he ain't got nothin' to lose in tellin' the whole truth. Sheriff Parker also told me this morning that he didn't expect Deputy Watkins to come in and pull his watch until later this afternoon, at which time he said, 'Our good deputy will find hisself under arrest.' Now the sheriff also said he had no idea who this fellow–Mr. Slade–was. He said that he'd be going out directly to track him down."

"Well, I know him!" I said. "He's Mr. Blanton's foreman!"

"I'm quite certain that Sheriff Parker'll be comin' after him," Reverend Sutherland said. Then he looked at me seriously, and he said, "Son…"

"Yessir?"

"You goin' to be all right? I'm a little bit concerned 'bout your Mama and you."

"I think I'll be all right, Reverend," Mama said.

I had tears in my eyes, and my heart hurt. This whole matter of death gripped me whenever it came around, and especially when it was someone like Brother Pickett, whom I once trusted and honored.

"Well, Reverend, I'm disappointed…in my Sunday school teacher and what he done." I began to cry harder, but I tried to hold it back. "But I think…I'll be all right…and…I believe I'll get over it directly."

"If you ever need me to sit down with you and talk about it, you just let me know" he said. "I'm here fer you son; you know that, don't you?"

"Yessir. I 'ppreciate it, sir."

"Reverend," Granddaddy said, "I just want to say that you preached a right powerful sermon this past Sunday."

"Well, Arliss," he said. "It's just a downright shame that Brother Dwindle didn't confess his sin and repent while there was time, but I guess the guilt in him was too much to live with. We cain't he'p him now."

After a few more minutes of conversation, Reverend Sutherland said good-bye to us, and he went outside and got into his car. He gave us a solemn wave as he drove through our driveway toward the south.

After he was gone, Granddaddy said, "Well boy, you was just about on target with that whole conspiracy."

"Yassir," I said. "But it don't make me feel any better that my Sunday school teacher went and killed hisself over it."

Mama said, "Boy, don't you ever believe fer one moment that you were the cause of it! Never! Not fer one second. Even though you was aware of it before any of this ever happened–it don't mean that you was responsible in any way fer it."

"I don't, Mama. It just hurts me so bad to see someone I looked up to even fer a while–like Brother Pickett...." I began to sob, and in the next moment, I couldn't stop crying. I felt like I was going to break apart. Mama put her arms around me and held me close to herself. I kept thinking that, just two days ago, he was alive with us in our Sunday school class, but now he is dead and gone. I cried for another moment, and then I resumed where I left off: "It just hurts, Mama, because I trusted Brother Pickett. You should always be able to trust yer Sunday school teacher, don't you think? He really let me down."

It was about four-thirty in the afternoon. We were all exhausted from this bad news, and our hearts were heavy and discouraged. Until the death of Deacon Ellis, I couldn't remember the last death among the people in our church. None of us ever thought that Brother Pickett could commit suicide, and yet, it was true. Now our church family had experienced two deaths in two weeks. Mama was also deeply disturbed that Deputy Watkins and Mr. Slade were running loose around the county. She saw them as two clever thugs; she feared that the deputy might try to hurt her again. It was about four-thirty in the afternoon when Granddaddy said, "less go on home."

While we were on our way home, I asked, "Now, Granddaddy, two of our church members have died in the last two weeks or so. Up until Deacon Ellis died, who was the last person in our church that died–can you remember?"

"Well," he said. "Let me think on that fer jist a minute. Less see now...I believe it was old Doc Gibson what died, or...no...was it Brother Weems? No, it wadn't Brother Weems. He died before Doc Gibson. Yes, it was, and...well, less see...it must have been almost four years ago, I'd say. Brother Weems died the year before. Doc Gibson was a very old man. I think he was about ninety-seven years old when he died. Yes, I think so. That was a good while ago. Boy! It's been a good while since the Death Angel's darkened our door, and I'll tell you what! If that ain't a blessing of the Lord, I don't know what is!"

Thirty-eight

Throughout the rest of the week, Brother Pickett's suicide provoked a lot of gossip all over Northwest Arkansas. The death of Deacon Ellis just about a week earlier had also aroused considerable talk, but it wasn't as sensational as Brother Pickett's. In fact, Deacon Ellis, who was a member of all the local civic organizations and a distant relative of the mayor of Gentry, actually enjoyed much greater recognition among the people than Brother Pickett did, but suicide, which was certainly more scandalous than an auto accident, had the effect of setting people's tongues to wagging much quicker and longer. Suicides were isolated events that occurred only to mysterious nonentities who materialized somewhere in the remote world and hopelessly vanished out yonder; they just didn't fit into our little world, particularly among Christians. For this reason, Brother Pickett's decision to end it all seemed to turn everything completely upside down throughout our whole county. After all, Brother Pickett was a Sunday school teacher, a member in good standing of a local Baptist church, and a professing Christian, but these allegations only served to increase the complexities of the problem. Like the deacon, Brother Pickett held a place of stature in Gentry and in the surrounding community; he was esteemed as a fine, upstanding business man. He was a member of the Chamber of Commerce and several civic clubs. He had a wife and three grown children, all of whom knew him to be a secret smoker, although none of them ever knew that he was a drinker and a gambler–let alone a thief, a conspirator, and a robber. It was practically impossible to withhold this information from the general public for the simple reason that, upon killing himself, Brother Pickett left the suicide note in which he made a public confession of his participation in each of these secret iniquities. Upon inquiry as to the nature of his death, local people would obviously want to know why, and they would be satisfied with nothing less than the truth.

As a result, most of the general public drew the conclusion that Brother Pickett's initial curiosity in his more surreptitious vices was merely diversionary, but as he persisted recurrently to practice them over time, they began progressively to possess him–and without his knowledge or permission. Ostensibly, the dangers of drinking himself to the point of frequent drunkenness and the risks of gambling away his wealth to ever greater debt–without getting caught–only heightened Brother Pickett's fascination for these vices, and they presented him with some kind of thrill that was clearly missing from the rest of his life.

According to Reverend Sutherland's eventual analysis, Brother Pickett lived two lives–one keenly visible and that generally untainted for all to see, and the other–deeply sinister and hidden entirely from view even by his closest family members. Later, in the pulpit, Pastor Sutherland would go on and refer often to this case as the one that typically represented the pattern that sin always follows to ruin an individual's life.

"Folks," he would say, "I've seen it so many times before, and it has even affected some of our own people. It starts with temptation–maybe to liquor and cards–or to some other worldly pleasure–like women. Temptation somehow weasels itself into your life, and before too long, temptation's gonna produce in you a powerful attraction. Ha! You think you can play around with it? You try dabblin' with it, and it ain't long after that, this attraction soon turns into your personal compulsion. And then, when you're under compulsion, you succumb to its addiction, and ultimately, brother, that addiction is gonna escalate far beyond your control. Then you're caught like a catfish hangin' on a tight, curly-q hook connected back to a cane pole! Church, let me tell y'all, now, don't mess with temptation."

Mrs. Pickett only saw and experienced her husband's visible life; she never knew his dark side. Based upon what she saw and what she knew, she had completely given him her undivided love, her unquestionable trust, and her complete support all these years. However, after the funeral, Mrs. Pickett would also testify that her husband's covert behavior now explained his long and frequent absences away from home in the late afternoon hours until the very early morning hours.

"I always thought he was a workin' down at the office, and of course, I might call him, and if he wadn't there, he would tell me he was out doin' an adjustment or making some sort of estimate and what-not," Mrs. Pickett said.

Moreover, she was as surprised as anyone to learn about his problem with liquor.

"I never knew nor suspected him to be a drinker," she explained. "He always lived such a moral life before me–I mean–I knew that he smoked them cigarettes and cigars, but I always required him to practice that repulsive habit out of sight–somewhere where people couldn't see him or smell it. But a drinker? Him? Where could he possibly get liquor around here? Benton County is dry! How did he get it?"

In addition, upon learning about Brother Pickett's gambling habit, Mrs. Pickett was fully shocked. When she learned of his enormous debt, she practically fainted.

"Oh, my goodness! My husband–and a gambler, too? How could I live with him these past thirty-three years and only just now find these things out about him? Did he leave any outstanding debt?"

Clearly heartbroken, Mrs. Pickett agreed to pay any and all debts that her husband left outstanding.

"If he still owes anything," she sobbed, "I'll do all I can to make it good. What else did he do? Is there any more?"

After learning that there was still more, Mrs. Pickett expressed her steeled commitment to stand strong and make every effort to survive even the exposure that Brother Pickett was also a petty thief who had been involved in conspiracy and had taken part in a bank robbery.

"This is all absolutely beyond belief!" she cried. "How, I ask you…how could all this be? Is this the dear, sweet Dwindle Pickett that I married, lived with, and knew?"

With most of Brother Pickett's dark side now uncovered, Mrs. Pickett could still express out of her heart her many years of love, trust, and support for him. But there was one more thing. The worst news of all for Mrs. Pickett to accept was the reality of Brother Pickett's suicide.

"Oh! Please…no, don't tell me this!" she grieved. "This is killing me! Committed suicide? No! How could he do this to me?"

This news devastated Mrs. Pickett, and it shook her to the very foundation of her Christian faith. She could believe the drinking and forgive it. She could live with the gambling and excuse that. She could even bring herself to accept that her husband was a scoundrel who stole, conspired, and robbed–and pardon all of those acts. But she simply could not abide that he would kill himself. She believed that every sin–except the unpardonable sin, of course–was forgivable, but she also believed in her heart that no true Christian could ever really commit suicide; God's grace was sufficient enough even to overcome the thought of it. Over these many years, Mrs. Pickett had loved, supported, and trusted her husband to such an extent that she fully believed they maintained no secrets from each other, and consequently, she viewed him as a true southern gentleman, a Baptist, and an honorable Christian. As a result of this single action, however, Brother Pickett's deception of his life-long partner was complete. By his suicide, Dwindle Pickett had stung his wife so deeply that it raised nothing but doubts in her mind regarding the nature of salvation–not about hers–but his.

Thirty-nine

Early on Wednesday morning, Reverend Sutherland stopped by the station to inform us that Brother Pickett's funeral would take place tomorrow. Mama and Granddaddy decided that, this time, we would shut down the station on Thursday morning, go to the funeral, and then we would open back up again after it was over. Apparently Mrs. Sutherland and Starla were consoling and supporting Mrs. Pickett and the members of her family in this, their hour of grief. In addition to helping Mrs. Pickett make all the funeral arrangements, the pastor was also assisting the Gentry police department in putting together some of the more bewildering puzzle pieces of this case. Reverend Sutherland told us that the police had found two large quantities of money in Brother Pickett's safe. Almost two thousand eight hundred dollars in cash alone was in a large brown envelope. In another section of the safe, there was a zippered, cash pouch in which police found another seven hundred dollars in cash and receipts—obviously money received as payments for insurance and other services. As these were very busy days for him, Reverend Sutherland couldn't stay for a while and visit with us.

Shortly after the reverend left our station, Mr. Crawford pulled in. As soon as I saw him, I ran outside and grabbed the spittoon and ran over toward him.

"Mornin', Mr. Crawford," I said.

"Mornin', son," he said. And then he spit a big mass of juice and slop–not in the can–but all right along the top edge and in such a way that the whole mess ran down the outside of the can only to drip all over the driveway. I hated to admit it, but he was starting to get on my nerves. From our watermelon seed-spitting contests, I knew that any moron could spit more accurately than Mr. Crawford did. Even Bubby, who preferred to eat the seeds, could precisely spit a bad-flavored one up to twenty feet.

"Son," he said. "If you cain't catch my t'backy better'n that, we're gonna have to send you down to the minors where you can get a whole lot more practice."

"Well, sir," I said. "I believe we're makin' a little progress." I lied about that.

He had the *Tulsa World* under his arm and a sack full of doughnuts in his hand.

"Your Granddaddy inside?"

"Yassir."

He went inside while I cleaned off the driveway again. As soon as I finished, I went back inside and grabbed a doughnut from the sack. Mr. Crawford, Granddaddy, and Mama were all discussing the suicide and the contents of the note.

"Way I understand it," said Mr. Crawford, "Deputy Watkins went into the sheriff's office over at Bentonville, and he reported late for work yesterday afternoon. Evidently, Sheriff Parker said somethin' like, 'Well, I been a lookin' fer you, Jimmy Lee, an' I b'lieve you know why.' Then he said, 'Now, Jimmy, don't you make it hard on any of us,' and the sheriff stood up and told him he's under arrest. Deputy Watkins acted just like he was gonna give hisself up, but then he tricked ol' Sheriff Parker, and he got the upper hand on him. Y'all know that Jimmy's a big, tall ol' boy. Jimmy Lee Watkins grabbed ol' Sheriff Parker's gun and his handcuffs, and he dragged ol' Parker to the jail behind the sheriff's office where he cuffed the sheriff to the jailbars."

"Oh, my goodness!" Mama exclaimed. "That ain't no good at all!"

About that time, someone pulled into the station and parked up away from the pumps over close by the trees. It was a pick-up truck. We heard the door slam shut, and in another moment, Mr. Whittaker came into the station office.

"Mornin', Cecil," Granddaddy said.

"Mornin," Mr. Crawford echoed, joined by Mama and me.

Mr. Whittaker said, "Good mornin' to y'all."

Right away, I asked him, "Is Caesar with you today?"

"You betcha, boy. He's out there in the truck. Ain't nowhere I go but that dog don't follow 'long."

Granddaddy said, "Well, Cecil, we ain't seen you around here fer a couple of weeks. What you been up to?"

"I been workin' my farm. Lots of brush to clear and scrub trees all over the place. I bought me some new hogs a week or so ago, and I noticed the other day that one of them sows got a big ol' ruptured belly muscle. She look like she tried to jump over a chain-link fence or somethin' like that. She's all tore up, an' half her stomach's hangin' out. I'm gonna have to get that vet to come out and look at her."

Mr. Whittaker got a cup and poured himself some black coffee. He saw the sack of doughnuts, and he helped himself to three doughnuts. One was a jelly doughnut that was dripping all over with cherry jelly. He tried to wipe the jelly off the doughnut with his finger, but the jelly just dripped on the floor. Then he licked the jelly, and he squeezed that doughnut just a little too tightly, and a big old mess of red jelly squirted out on his shirt.

"Well, Cecil, you do it up right, now," Mr. Crawford said.

"I am," he said. "I'm a gettin' it all over the place. But you better watch yer step, now Buford, 'fore I point the next one over yonder in your direction. Say, did y'all hear about all these strange things been goin' on lately?"

"You mean about Dwindle Pickett's killin' hisself, and the sheriff bein' handcuffed to his own jail by one of his own deputies?"

"Yeah. That's it fer sure. What in tarnation's goin' on around here?"

"Cecil, it's gettin' to be where it just ain't safe to live in Northwest Arkansas any more," Granddaddy stated. "The sheriff cain't even trust his own deputies these days. Today people'll go in the room and turn on their own mother–and fer nuthin', too!"

"Have you heard anything new on the situation, Cecil?" Mr. Crawford asked.

"Well, I seen Deputy Watkins drivin' his patrol car up our road out there by the Blanton place. I believe he stopped out that way fer a spell. He had his uniform on, and I presume his gun was at his side. I actually thought he's still on duty, and I didn't know he was a wanted man until I stopped in at Miss Hatfield's place on my way, and she set me straight about him. She's got a telephone out there, and I believe she stays connected on that phone all day!"

Mama said, "Yeah, she does. She gets all her news and information and such from her party lines. One of 'em lives in Gentry, but I don't know where the other one lives."

"Fer all we know," Granddaddy said, "her third party line is right in the Gentry police department! That woman knows things almost before they happen! Some of them holy rollers out there at that Pentecostal church…what's it called out there? Spring…uh, Spring Creek? Uh…y'all know…they meet in a big tent, or at least, they did last time I knew about it."

"Spring Falls Holiness Tabernacle," Mr. Whittaker said.

"Yeah," Granddaddy said, "that's it. Out there, they all think she's a prophetess what can see right into the future."

Mr. Crawford asked, "Do they put that tent up ever' Sunday?"

"No," Mr. Whittaker said, "they don't. It stays up all the time. They never take it down. But some of those folk out that way actually do go in to her fer readin's, fortune tellin', and prophesyin' and what-not."

After a while, we had just about worn out all interest in the conversation, and I excused myself to go out and sit in the shade and read some more books. I tried to avoid the temptation of spending any time near Caesar because I knew that I'd get no reading done, and all that time would go to waste. I went over to look at him, but he was asleep in the truck. A few minutes later, Mama also came out and went up to work her fruit stand. I knew that she was worried about the deputy and Mr. Slade being out on the loose. I also knew that Sheriff Parker would do all he could to bring those two men in custody as quickly as possible when we could do little, if anything, at all. Still, she said she wouldn't feel completely safe until Daddy was home, too.

Mr. Whittaker came out of the office, soon followed by Mr. Crawford. They both got in their vehicles and drove away. Just before noon, we sold gas to two customers. Product sales always provided a little encouragement. The weather was real nice that day, and we decided to eat lunch outside up by the fruit stand. I heard a train blow its horn way off in the distance, and shortly afterward, I walked over to the tracks and looked down the line. I could see a small rise of diesel smoke. The train was headed north and coming up our way. Maybe half a mile down from our road, the train blew another warning series and then a warning signal as the locomotive approached the crossing. The locomotive was long, black, and shiny with the white words Kansas City Southern there on the side. The engine was putting out a heavy plume of black smoke and pulling the train at a good pace.

"One...two...three...," I began to count all the cars with the determination to know exactly how many cars were attached to this train. As I counted, I noticed several G.M. & O. box cars were in the row, lots of M.K.T. tank cars, some Southern Pacific cars, as well as some Santa Fe coal cars. About car number thirty-three or thirty-four, the train began to slow down. I could see the caboose coming, so I knew it wasn't a real long train. This train had forty-two cars behind the locomotive, and after the caboose had passed our crossing, the train slowed down even further, although it continued along toward Decatur.

I decided to find my pail and a book. I moved over into the shade, and I sat down and began to read. A few customers came in the rest of the afternoon–three, perhaps four. One customer wasn't interested in buying anything; he just wanted directions to Fayetteville. It was always a little frustrating when they didn't want to buy anything, but I couldn't show my true feelings about it; I had to be friendly and courteous whether they were paying customers or not. That's how gentlemen act.

About four o'clock, a large tanker truck pulled into our station and parked at the south end of our driveway. Along the side of the tank on the truck it said, Meador Bros. Oil & Gas Co., Ft. Smith. The driver climbed down from his cab and went inside the station office. A few minutes later, he and Granddaddy came out and walked up toward Mama at the fruit stand. I sat there on my pail and just watched the office door.

"Norma Jean," Granddaddy said loudly. "Do we need any gasoline?"
Mama left the fruit stand and came down to talk.

"It's been a long while since we bought any, and I'd guess that our tank is runnin' low. Did Clayton ever show you how to read it?"

"Yeah, he did. Want me to run out yonder real quick and see?" Granddaddy asked.

"Would you mind, Granddaddy? It's awful hard fer me to climb up there and take a reading, and it's so slick and dirty."

"No, no, Norma Jean. I'll be happy to take care of it. You don't need to be doin' that kind o' work, too."

"Well, Granddaddy, you be careful."

Granddaddy shuffled quickly around to the back of the station. We had three gasoline tanks out there. One tank held a thousand gallons of Hi-Test, and the other two tanks held regular gas. Of those two, the first was a thousand gallon tank, and the second was a reserve tank of five hundred gallons. The tanks sat up on concrete piers about twenty feet behind the station building. At the end of each tank, there was a ladder, and Granddaddy would have to climb to the top, open the tank, and read the quantity by dipping a measuring stick down into the tank. It was an easy job, but it was dirty and greasy up there–and slippery.

"Sir, would you mind goin' out there to make sure he don't fall off them tanks?" Mama asked the tank truck driver.

"No, ma'am. I don't mind at all. In fact, I could have done all that myself to he'p y'all out, if I'd a known…" the driver said.

He ran out back to assist Granddaddy. I was just a little worried, too, that Granddaddy might slip or hurt his hand or something, but I wasn't going to leave Mama standing alone out in front of our station.

A few minutes later, both Granddaddy and the driver came back out front.

"Norma Jean, it looks like we have about five hundred gallons of Hi-Test left in the tank. But our big regular tank is empty, and the reserve is sittin' on a little more than a hundert gallons," Granddaddy reported. His overalls were now completely black and greasy from lying on the top of those tanks. His hands and face were black stained, as well, and he had black oil in his white hair. He smelled strongly of gasoline.

Mama asked the driver, "Do you have a thousand gallons there in your truck?"

"I got close to two," he said.

"Less fill up our regular reserve tank, and put about six hundert gallons in the regular main tank. That'd be about a thousand gallons or so," said Mama. "And I'd appreciate it if y'all would invoice me within thirty days."

"Yes, ma'am. That's no problem," the driver said.

The driver backed his truck around the south side of our station and just as close as he could get to those tanks. He had a reel of hose on the back end of his truck, and he unwound it and ran it back to the tanks. This time, he had to climb up on those tanks; he filled our reserve tank first, and then he added about six hundred gallons to our main tank. When he was finished, he got down and began to reel his hose back in. He was as filthy as Granddaddy. The driver had a clipboard with papers on it, and he wrote out a bill of sale and asked Mama to sign it. He gave her a copy, and then he said, "I 'ppreciate your bidness, folks. The invoice comes within thirty days. Y'all take care now." He climbed back up in his truck, started it, and drove on down the road.

That would be the last transaction for this day. We were all tired, dirty, smelly, and ready to go home.

Mama said, "Well, we got some gas now, and it ought to last us fer awhile."

With a more serious tone in his voice, Granddaddy said, "Honey, we're gonna be needin' to do somethin' about them tanks back there before too much longer. The tank seams are beginnin' to rust away, and that gasoline is startin' to fume up round them seams; I can smell it out there."

"What can we do about it, Granddaddy?" she asked.

"I don't know, Sweetheart," he said. "That ain't an easy decision to make because it's expensive and it could be dangerous."

Mama knew that when Granddaddy called her 'Honey' or 'Sweetheart,' that he was being serious with her. It was his special way of showing the most heartfelt concern and love to his daughter-in-law. I knew it, too, because he also did that with Tawna Rae. Next to Grandma, Tawna Rae and Mama were his dearest girls.

Just before we closed the station to go home, Granddaddy put a sign in the window that said, "Closed for Funeral." Then he said, "Now if we just didn't have to attend that dern funeral tomorrow, we wouldn't have to go home and take baths, would we?"

Forty

Grandma did her best to keep the supper warm while we all took baths. Granddaddy was first; then Mama took hers, and I was last. Actually, I didn't think I was all that dirty, but Mama insisted. However, that evening, it seemed to me that, somehow, our warm food actually tasted better to me after I had taken a bath and cleaned up. I wondered if it was because I was simply hungry, or did cleaning up have any effect on how supper tasted? I was really too tired to think about it, so I put it in the back of my mind to recall later–when maybe the science teacher at school would ask us all for our ideas about science projects. I knew, however, that my problem with shoving projects to the back of my mind for later recall was not a good thing to do because, later on, I always had trouble trying to pull them back out to the front.

For whatever reason, I didn't feel like listening to the Cardinal game that evening. Granddaddy had it on the radio, but I felt like I needed to keep reading books. At the same time, I was also tired, and I wasn't much looking forward to a funeral the next day. I went to bed and started to read a little, but I fell asleep with the light on and with my book, which fell out of my hand when I fell asleep. I woke up about eleven-thirty, and I tried to read a little longer, but I finally just gave in to my weariness and went to sleep.

The next morning, I woke up thinking about the forthcoming funeral for

Brother Pickett. I didn't know anyone who really liked funerals, except maybe the undertakers, and that was a guess on my part. We didn't know any undertakers, at least, not personally. No undertakers ever came around our house, and I wasn't aware that any ever attended our church.

Since we were not opening the station that morning, but going to a funeral, we were not in a great hurry. Granddaddy told me that I missed a good game last night; the Cardinals beat the Dodgers in Brooklyn by a score of seven to three. Why is it that they always seem to win when I'm too tired to listen to the game?

It was a slow morning, but we were out the door by nine-thirty and at the Grange House before ten o'clock. People were already gathering in the worship hall. Brother Pickett's casket was at the front, and there were flowers all around it. The casket was closed. Reverend Sutherland, who would be preaching the memorial service, had already arranged for Brother Pickett's Sunday school boys to sit together with Mr. Martel in a special section at the front of the hall as a matter of honor. Before we went into the hall, we talked about Brother Pickett:

"Can you believe that he's dead and gone now?" Donnie Joe asked.

J. R. said, "It's hard to believe. He was just with us this past Sunday."

Billy Stevens said, "Well, even though we poked a lot of fun at him, I know that I'll miss him. Now I'm really feelin' a little bad about all that teasin' and cuttin' up."

"Well, in spite of all that he done wrong there at the end, and how he let me down personally, I…" I started sobbing. After a moment, I said, "I…really did love him because…well…because he was my teacher, and…I…" I just couldn't finish expressing my thought.

"Well," Bubby said, "he wadn't always right, but he sure cared about us. I know that much." Bubby had some chocolate stuck to his teeth, and he had a bag of broken cookies in his hip pocket.

"Yeah, that's right," Donnie Joe said. "He did care about us."

"And now he's gone," said Wayne.

"Gentlemen," Mr. Martel said, "Let's move on in to our places."

We went in and sat down. The worship hall was practically filled with people. Miss Audrey Jane was playing the organ softly. Mrs. Pickett was weeping. as were some of the members of her group–presumably family members both distant and close.

Reverend Sutherland stood up and approached the podium. "Let us pray," he said. After his invocation, Reverend Sutherland began to eulogize Brother Pickett. He began by prompting the congregation to recall his decades of service to the community and to the church. He talked about all the years that he taught the young boys' class in Sunday school, and he reminded the younger fathers who were present that some of them also sat in Brother Pickett's classes during their youth. Focusing on the natural and human side of life, Reverend Sutherland talked about how Brother Pickett got saved when he was an older teen-ager, but it was only later in his life that he fell in with the wrong crowd and made a lot of mistakes.

"I know that he later repented of his gettin' in with the wrong crowd," the pastor said. "But he was an ordinary man, and who among us hadn't succumbed to the Devil's many and grievous temptations?" the reverend asked.

At this question, there were several "amens" among the congregation.

"An', believe me–I ain't tellin' y'all somethin' that Brother Dwindle wouldn't a wanted said, because he told me long ago what he wanted said at his funeral. He told me practically ever' wicked thing he ever done–ever'thing, and he told me he was sorry about it all." Reverend Sutherland avoided making any reference to his suicide, however.

"…and, brothers and sisters…I can assure you that if our dearly departed brother Dwindle were standin' right here before us today, why, his own personal message to each of us would ring out loud, clear, and true in these words–'I ain't proud o' what I done, but at least I'm proud of what I knew in my head. Therefore, from my heart, I say unto you–don't do what I done, but do what I said.'"

Reverend Sutherland paused for a moment and attempted to smile somewhat weakly at all the funeral congregants. His objective was to inspire a little hope and joy into what otherwise was an extremely gloomy service. "Folks, I am quite confident that our dear brother Dwindle has confessed his shortcomings before the eternal Throne of grace, and he has made his peace with the King of Glory."

I wasn't quite sure how the pastor could honestly say all these things. I wondered if he was really convinced about them, or if he merely said them to conciliate the grieving family? In any case, it wasn't for me to question. Reverend Sutherland now found it convenient to shift his message from eulogy to homily, which, under these circumstances, would be extremely difficult for any preacher. How does one talk truthfully about a formerly upstanding Sunday school teacher who turned to theft, drink, gambling, and robbing, not to mention suicide? Who could ever be adequately equipped for such a task?

In his sermon, Brother Sutherland talked generally about the brevity of life and how important it was that we all learn early in our lives to make the right choices and stick with them until the Lord calls us home. Without specifically criticizing or belittling the character of the deceased, he was alluding to the fact that Brother Pickett began well but finished poorly. The reverend pointed out that good people–even believers–can sometimes go bad and come under external, negative influences that can turn them around and act negatively on them beyond their control. At the end of his sermon, Reverend Sutherland asked all the current members of Brother Pickett's Sunday school class to stand up in honor of their beloved teacher, and then he challenged the audience to learn from the life of Brother Pickett. After closing in prayer, Reverend Sutherland called for the pall-bearers to carry out the casket and set it into the hearse for its removal to the grave.

Indeed, the funeral service was a sad affair, when in fact, it might have been–indeed should have been–a joyous occasion–except for all the misery of the untold truth. In spite of my genuine love for him, the truth was that, in the end, Brother Pickett was a man who made bad decisions, and he never considered the doubtful, hurtful, and damaging effects that his choices might impose on others, particularly his loved ones. The collective sadness that hung over the entire congregation was produced primarily by a truth never stated, yet it was universally recognized–Brother Pickett's life came to its end in a most awkward manner; indeed, by his own hand, which in itself was a clumsy embarrassment for a man considered by all to be a southern gentleman, a Baptist, and a Christian. According to the Christian faith and the unwritten creed of the south, any individual blessed with all those unique advantages alone ought to experience a long and happy tenure that terminates naturally and proclaims boldly the glorious hope of the eternal resurrection confirmed by the supernatural joy that accompanies a life of increasing righteousness according to the pattern of our Lord and certified as blameless by the witness of external testimony. Instead, the unstated truth of this case revealed only the backwardness of a life gone sour–a life lived worse at its end than at its beginning. Brother Pickett might have hidden his flirtation with suicide forever, and no one would have ever known. But his actual and ultimate act of self-destruction brought his dark mind–not to mention the blackness of his deed–out to the light, and it succeeded in creating thousands of everlasting doubts about him in the minds of all others who knew him. Clear to the marrow in my bones, I shuddered to think that Mrs. Pickett and her family could live out the rest of their lives faced thenceforward with an infinite number of unanswerable questions accompanied by ceaseless doubts and disbelief regarding the secrecies of their beloved Dwindle. Just his one act led to this. They would never truly know about him what he should never have really denied them.

The funeral procession moved on from the Grange House to the Fair Meadows Cemetery in Gentry. The sadness continued at the graveside; all the Pickett relatives were weeping in despair. The widow Pickett was wailing loudly, and occasionally, she could be heard crying out, "Oh! Dwindle! Why? Oh! Why, Dwindle?" A few times, she had to be taken aside and consoled by family members.

"Ashes to ashes, dust to dust…" Reverend Sutherland said. And then he tried to conclude the service with prayer.

At the end of his prayer, he said, "…and we commend the soul of our dearly departed brother, Dwindle Pickett, unto Thee, Oh Lord."

At that point, Mrs. Pickett again screamed out loudly. She couldn't bring herself to accept that her beloved Dwindle was gone. Moaning and crying, she squirmed and wiggled toward the casket, but a small crowd of relatives tried to hold her back. Intent, she began fighting them and crying out at the same time. She continued almost violently, and eventually, she broke away from the people, rushed forward, and threw herself headlong onto the casket and cried out, "Oh, no! Oh, my Dwindle, no!" With her fall, the flowers on top of the casket slid off the casket and right into the grave cavity, and then the casket slipped perilously close to the edge of the frame that held it over the opening. I thought she might fall into the grave, too, but some of the family members grabbed her immediately and pulled her to her feet. She continued to moan and sob, and making every effort to console her, they pulled her away from the casket. She was still resistant, but they finally got her into a funeral car and drove away.

After the funeral, we went home and ate lunch. Around the table, we all discussed the morning's activities. Later, in the afternoon, we re-opened the station. I anticipated only a few customers and an afternoon of heavy reading, so I brought several books with me. Mama brought several new baskets full of tomatoes, peppers, lettuce, cucumbers, beans, and some squash to replenish her diminishing supplies up at the fruit stand. Granddaddy just brought himself, but he was wearing a clean, fresh pair of overalls.

I was wrong about expecting an afternoon of heavy reading. About a half hour after we opened the station, Sheriff Parker stopped by.

"Afternoon, Sheriff Parker," I greeted him. "You need any gas?"

"Well, let's see," he said. He looked at his gauge, and then he said, "Yeah. Why don't you fill it up fer me?"

He went inside while I pumped his gas. I cleaned the windows of his patrol car and checked the air in his tires. I also checked the water and oil; everything was fine. Then I went in and told him that his bill was four dollars, which he paid to Granddaddy. They were talking together.

"We're lookin' fer Jimmy Lee Watkins. He ain't one of my deputies any more, and we notified all the police and state troopers in the four-states about our one-time deputy gone crooked. Evidently, he's been takin' bribes from folk all around the county fer a long time now, and he was takin' money fer speedin' tickets, too. It's all comin' out now. We're also investigatin' a recent report that Jimmy's got some secret ties to the Klan, and with all this information from the Pickett note, we know now that he's been involved in a lot more. In fact, there are a couple of young girls–one up there at Gravette and the other over near Centerton–claimin' that he tried to seduce 'em, too. When we get him, he's gonna have a lot to pay fer."

"Well, Sheriff," Granddaddy said, "where do you suppose he's holed up at?"

"I dunno, Arliss," said Sheriff Parker. "We found his patrol car parked up in a deserted area just off of Flint Creek over there before you get to Maysville. It looked to me like they were keepin' a little picnic area way back in there right next to the creek. It is so shady back in there that you cain't see the sunlight under those trees. You could never tell what was in there because the brush is so thick and it's all covered over with trees. Arliss, I tell you, there are places in this county where a man could hide for a lifetime, and people would never know they was there."

"Have y'all located this fellow named Slade?"

"We went over and talked with Mr. Blanton, and we was at least able to verify that Mr. Elwood Slade was his foreman, but he's gone now. As I understand it, Jimmy Lee Watkins come around to the Blanton place late that same afternoon when he handcuffed me to the jail bars–that no-good, dirty scoundrel. We believe that's when Slade took off. He gathered up all his things and, believe it or not, he stole Blanton's old half-ton stake truck and followed Jimmy up to Flint Creek. Mr. Blanton said he ain't seen Slade or his truck since."

"How'd Jimmy handcuff you, Sheriff?" asked Granddaddy.

"I don't rightly know." The sheriff was embarrassed by this question, but he went on: "Arliss, I got up to arrest him, and I thought he'd go easy–sort of as a favor to me. I come over toward him, and he acted like he was a goin' easy, and then he jumped me, overpowered me, grabbed my gun and got my cuffs, and–next thing I know, I'm a locked up at them jail bars. You know, that boy's bigger and younger and stronger than me, Arliss, an' I'm a lucky he didn't shoot me," the sheriff said, apologetically.

"I ain't faultin' you, Sheriff. I know he is," Granddaddy said. "What about that colored boy over at the jail? What they gonna do with him?"

"Aw, he's all right. We've checked out his story, and he's tellin' the truth, mostly, as far as we can tell. Now that we know fer sure that he ain't the one who robbed that bank, we're gonna let him go directly–probably in another few days now. We gotta do it right, ya know. We don't need any trouble around here with him. You know, they're a havin' all that trouble down there in Little Rock right now, an' we don't need the likes of it up here. Once we get all the paperwork done, he'll be free to go. Besides, the last thing we need is fer his yankee lawyer who come down here to be stickin' his nose in the whole mess any further, and then make a bigger to-do about it all."

"Well, Sheriff," said Granddaddy, "what do you hear from the Gentry police department…anything?"

"Well, I can tell you, their Officer Thackston over there has been a mighty big he'p to me. We're staying in close touch with them." Then the sheriff said, "I need to be goin' directly. If you hear anything, Arliss, please give me a call, will you?"

Granddaddy said he would, and he thanked the sheriff for coming around and sharing the news. Shortly after the sheriff drove off, Officer Thackston rolled into the driveway.

"Good afternoon, Officer Thackston," I said. "Do you want some gas?"

"No, son. Still got a full tank, but thank you, anyway."

"Yer welcome," I said. "You just missed Sheriff Parker."

"Was he here? I wadn't really lookin' fer him. I thought I'd come by and talk with yer grandfather, son."

"Sure," I said. "He's inside."

We both went in, and Officer Thackston greeted Granddaddy.

"How are you doin', Officer Thackston?" Granddaddy asked.

"I'm doin' fine; how about y'all?"

Granddaddy responded, "We're doin' all right."

"I just wanted to let y'all know that we're doin' our best to locate these two remaining thieves. We found Mr. Pickett's share of the robbery money in his safe, just as he said we would. We're hopin' to recover the rest of it when we catch up with them two crooks—if they hadn't already spent it all."

"You got any leads on 'em, Officer?" asked Granddaddy.

"There ain't nothin' definite on them yet, but I got a hunch they're a hidin' out somewhere down around Lake Francis. Of course, on the other hand, them two no-goods could both be long gone to Texas by now."

"Well, Norma Jean, the boy's mother, is worried that they're out runnin' loose," Granddaddy said. "Jimmy Lee Watkins tried to assault her once, and she's afraid he'll try it again."

"I just hope we get him before he does any more damage," Officer Thackston said. "Y'all take as many precautions as you can, and we'll do all we can to get 'em."

"Thank you," Granddaddy said.

Officer Thackston got back in his patrol car and drove off toward Gentry. I was able to read for more than an hour that afternoon, but we didn't sell much gasoline. About five o'clock that evening, we decided to shut the station down, and we went home. Later that evening, I decided to listen to the baseball game with Granddaddy out on the back porch. It was a very exciting game with lots of hits and runs on both sides, but in the end, the Dodgers prevailed over the Cardinals, ten to nine. Wouldn't you know it?

Book Five

Forty-one

Friday was our favorite day. We always looked forward to Fridays because that was the day when Daddy came home from his week up on the road. Sometimes he made it home by early afternoon, and other times he didn't come in until after midnight. We knew that his exact arrival time in Y-City Station always depended completely upon his driving schedule, but if the day was Friday, Daddy was usually due home.

On this particular Friday, Daddy arrived home at Y-City Station early—about two thirty in the afternoon. Because it was still early in the afternoon, he didn't drive his truck all the way up to our house. Instead, he pulled into the station driveway and parked along the westernmost edge where the concrete met the grass just to the south of the station. Daddy's truck was huge; it was clean, bright, and majestic, and it just seemed so perfect sitting there in front of our station.

"Now it looks like a regular truck stop," Granddaddy said.

"If only more trucks would actually stop here," said Mama.

"Where would we put them?" Daddy asked. "Our driveway couldn't hold more than three or four of those trucks at the most, and four of them would probably block the gas pumps."

"We'd have to expand," I said. "Y-City Station Truck Stop."

"There you go, boy!" Daddy said. "Those are the kind of dreams I like to hear about!"

It was really good to have him home after such a long and tough week. Mama explained to Daddy about all the events and activities that had taken place during his absence.

"Goodness!" Daddy said. "Seems like I been gone a whole month instead of just a week! It's hard to believe that so many things have happened since last Sunday."

By Friday, after driving up and down Route 66 all week, Daddy was always tired and anxious to get home and relax. Before we shut down the station that afternoon, Officer Thackston stopped in.

"Good afternoon, folks," he said.

"Good afternoon, Officer," Granddaddy spoke, and then Mama and I greeted him in unison.

"Officer Thackston," Granddaddy said, "I'd like to introduce you to my son, Clayton Stafford. Clayton, this is Officer Thackston with the Gentry Police department. He's been a workin' on that bank robbery case and more recently the Pickett case."

Daddy and Officer Thackston shook hands.

"Pleased to meet you, sir," Daddy said.

"It's my pleasure," Thackston said.

"That your truck?"

"Yessir, sort of. It actually belongs to the Interstate 66 truck line," Daddy said. "I just drive it."

"She sure is a beauty."

"Thank you," Daddy replied. "She does real good up there on that highway."

"Well," Officer Thackston said, "I just stopped by to let y'all know that we got a message from the Siloam Springs Police department, and they said that they spotted a vehicle similar to Mr. Blanton's stolen stake truck, and it had two men in it. They were unable to give a description of the two men, but they said the truck was last seen headin' south down on Arkansas Highway 59. As I said yesterday, I believe they may be hidin' out down there somewhere near Lake Francis which is somewhere down along that way. We got back in touch with the Siloam Springs police and asked 'em if they could run down that way and have a look-see fer us, and they said they would. As soon as we hear back from them, we'll let y'all know about our progress."

"Officer Thackston," Daddy said, "I just wanted to thank you fer keepin' us informed about all this. My wife is real nervous about that Jimmy Lee Watkins runnin' around free; he has hurt her before, and she don't feel real safe–and won't–until Jimmy Lee's behind bars."

"You're welcome," he said. "We're just doin' our jobs, but we do want to protect all the innocent. Evidently, ol' Jimmy Lee's been doin' an awful lot of bad things fer a perty long time now–even before he worked fer the sheriff. But we're gonna get him. I can assure y'all of that."

"Well, we appreciate it a lot. Thank you." Upon receiving this appreciation, Officer Thackston grinned just like a little boy who had been praised and honored by his mother for doing something right.

When we got home, Grandma was surprised that Daddy, who moved his truck up to the house, was already home. She hadn't started cooking yet, so Daddy said, "What say we do somethin' we ain't ever done before? Less all pile into them pick-em-up-trucks and head down to Sleepy's Café fer a chicken dinner–what do y'all say?"

"Surely you ain't serious?" Mama asked.

"Well, I'm all fer it," Grandma said.

"Daddy?" I said. "Did you know the Riggins are takin' over Sleepy's in just a few more weeks?"

"No, son. I guess I didn't know that. Where'd you hear that from?"

"Fishbait told me."

"Well, then. We'd better get on down to Sleepy's and get some chicken before it ain't Sleepy's any more then, hadn't we?" And with that statement, Daddy grabbed Mama and began to twirl her around–dancing and singing out the following made-up tune:

"Yeah…we're goin'…we're goin'…goin' on down to Sleepy's…to get us some chicken…."

Now Granddaddy, who would never be outdone, also began to sing, and in the same way, he grabbed Grandma, and, together, they began to twirl around and then two-step back and forth. Grandma was smiling and keeping her movements in perfect step and timing with him, and then she began to sing in harmony with the others.

Finally, J-Earl joined in the singing, and he grabbed Tawna Rae and spun her around a few times, too. Tawna Rae wasn't quite sure what was going on, but since everyone was singing and laughing rather than crying, she assisted everyone else by dancing, giggling, jumping up and down, and making noise, too.

After a moment, Daddy and Mama, exhausted, fell together into a kitchen chair together with Daddy on the chair and Mama on his lap, while Granddaddy and Grandma continued to put on a great demonstration for a few more moments. We were all amazed at their performance. When they finally stopped, Daddy and Mama gave them an energetic round of applause. With all the hand-clapping, J-Earl and Tawna Rae also stopped and then clapped their hands as well.

"Why, we never knew that y'all were such lovely and charming dancers!" they said. "That was absolutely beautiful!"

Granddaddy said, "Well, back in our day, when we was young and first in love, we used to do perty well among some of those crowds down at the local, Saturday evening barn dances."

"Do perty well?" Grandma exclaimed. "Why, Granddaddy was the lightest man on two feet in 'em days, and had I not come along to claim him jist in the very nick of time, there were at least a dozen other girls at them barn dances that would've rustled him away fer his dancin' ability alone! But I got him fer love!"

"And I got her fer love and fer cookin'!" Granddaddy said. "But just you wait a minute there, Darlin'…you cain't say you wasn't light on yer feet, too, you know. Ever'body knows that we was really a pair together. I couldn't have done it without you, Sweetheart." Granddaddy hugged Grandma and gave her a big kiss, which, for its indiscriminate length embarrassed Grandma a little, and the rest of us as well.

"Granddaddy, weren't you a little afraid of gettin' caught by the pastor, or maybe someone turnin' y'all in to him fer dancin'?" I asked.

"Well son, back then, we was Methodists, and it wasn't a sin fer Methodists to dance–leastwise if only jist a little. But I'm gonna let you in on a little secret, boy…it really ain't a sin fer Baptists to dance either…they jist don't know it yet! But I predict there's a day comin' when some of 'em will come around, too."

Daddy, Mama, and Grandma all enjoyed a hearty laugh at that, but I was a little puzzled by it. My face must have shown it, so Granddaddy continued:

"Boy, you can rest assured that with as much joy as we're gonna be havin' up there in heaven, that there's gonna be a little dancin' goin' on. The Bible talks about David dancin,' the Jews dancin' in the streets, and Jesus talked about them dancin' at their weddin's, too. It's just a part of human life, and where there's any joy and happiness and freedom among men and women in life, there's dancin'. It's like ever'thing else…yer dance can either honor the Lord or dishonor him, that's all."

After we all got cleaned up, we all piled into our pick-up trucks and headed out toward the highway. We crossed the tracks just before a freight train came rolling through. It was almost six-thirty when we arrived at Sleepy's Café. We almost never ate out in a café or a restaurant, so for J-Earl, Tawna Rae, and me, this was a very special treat. For that reason, Mama warned us privately to be on our 'extremely' best behavior, or we would suffer the most serious consequences. J-Earl didn't quite understand what she meant by 'extremely' best, but after she said that it meant 'better than church behavior,' he recognized immediately what she expected of us.

Sleepy's Café was down almost at the intersection of Arkansas Highways 59 and 68. The restaurant was a fading, white-painted, long and low concrete block structure with a gable roof and a low overhang in front and back. Across the front of the roof, there was a neon sign with a red line across the bottom and a green line across the top, and between the lines, there was a neon strip that said "Sleepy's Café" in script. At night, when it was dark, the sign was just the most beautiful thing, except that the 'l' in "Sleepy's" would flash erratically or maybe not even light up at all–so that it sometimes looked like it said "S eepy's Café."

There was plenty of parking space for cars and trucks to park on a white stone driveway. Several cars were already parked there when we arrived. Whenever cars pulled in or out of the driveway, the tires moving across the stone threw up a fine white dust that got caught up in the wind and blew all around until it dissipated. At the entrance of the café there was a slab of concrete on the ground which was covered at the roof by the overhang. On the slab immediately in front of the door there was a dusty red floor mat that said, "Arkansas Razorbacks," both words being separated by the familiar illustration of the university's mascot. The door was all glass, and it was heavy. Inside the café, the walls were paneled with cheap pine wood paneling that had become yellowish-colored with age. Old, black and white, framed pictures lined all the walls. Some of the pictures were of people; others were of cars; still others showed old farms and chicken houses. Three of the walls were lined with booths, each of which had a central table that separated two little couches that faced each other. In the middle of the room, there were different sized tables all around. Some people were sitting at tables, and some sat at the booths. Off to the right side, there was a long counter with some swivel-stools in front, but no one was sitting at the counter. At the end of the counter, there was a short glass display case that revealed several different kinds of cakes, pies, cookies, and other delicious treats that were all for sale. Behind the counter, there was an open window through which you could see back into the kitchen, and to the left of it, there was a door that swung in both directions. I am quite certain that, at that time in my life, everything all seemed so much fancier, so much larger, and so much grander than it actually was.

The café smelled good–like home-cooked food. Granddaddy arranged for us to get one of the longer tables at the back of the café. The table had a blue and white checkered tablecloth on it, and it was already set with plates, glasses, and silverware. Granddaddy seated Grandma, and then Mama told us where we were supposed to sit, but we weren't allowed to sit down until Mama sat down. Daddy seated Mama, and then we all sat down in our respective places. In a moment, the waitress came out of the kitchen door.

"Good evenin'," she said. "What'll y'all have tonight?"

"I'll have lemonade," Daddy said. "What do you want to drink, Sweetheart?"

"I'll have a glass of iced tea, without sugar," Mama said. "Each of the children will have a glass of milk."

Granddaddy and Grandma each ordered an iced tea.

"Our special dish tonight is the fried chicken dinner or the fried catfish dinner. The chicken comes with mashed potatoes, yer choice of two vegetables from corn, fried okra, baked squash, or black-eyed peas with hot rolls or cornbread, butter, 'n' honey. The catfish special is similar but it comes with French fried potatoes instead of mashed. Dessert is included in the price, and tonight we have apple pie, peach cobbler, or chocolate cake. Fer parties of four or more, we serve family style here at Sleepy's," the waitress said.

The waitress was big and heavy, an unattractive woman who wore a black dress covered by a white apron on which there were two grease stains. Her arms looked like solid tree branches, and her hands were especially big and muscular for a woman. She had black eyes and gray, stringy hair, and in a certain light, it appeared that she had a slight moustache. Her face was big and round, and it reminded me of pictures I had seen of the moon with a man's face in it. In her hair, she wore a dark hairnet that pulled her hair and scalp in tight, and it made her look very uncomfortable.

Daddy said, "We'll just have the family style chicken dinner with mashed potatoes, fried okra and corn, please. We'd also like a combination of hot rolls and cornbread, please."

"Yessir," the waitress replied, and then she disappeared. She reappeared again momentarily with a huge tray of drinks and napkins which she quickly served before returning to the kitchen. Maybe five minutes later, she brought us a basket of hot rolls and cornbread with butter and honey. This prompted Daddy to say grace, after which we all began to eat the rolls and the cornbread. We were all hungry. In no time, our bread was gone, as were our drinks.

"My, goodness!" the lady said. "Y'all were sure hungry!"

"Yes ma'am," Granddaddy said. "Could you please bring us each another round of the same?"

"Yessir," she said.

While we were waiting on her to return, the door opened and Mr. and Mrs. Blanton came in. I recognized him right away, but I had never seen his wife before. At first they didn't notice us, and Mr. Blanton seated his wife at a vacant booth over on the front side of the café. After he sat down, Granddaddy waved at him, and Mr. Blanton got up and came over to our table for a moment.

"Why, good evenin', y'all," he said. "I never knew that y'all ate here."

"We never did. This is our first time," Mama said.

"Well, the chicken here is good," Mr. Blanton said. "You'll enjoy it. I guess y'all have heard about that lousy foreman of mine—stealin' my stake truck and runnin''round loose with that crooked deputy?"

"In fact, we did," said Granddaddy. "That was really rotten of him to do that to you."

"It just goes to show you that you cain't trust anyone these days anymore—regardless of his references," Mr. Blanton said. "You cain't even trust the law!"

"No, you cain't, and that's perty sad," Granddaddy replied. "Ya know, Jess, sometimes their references were former bosses an' employers who jist wanted to get rid of 'em as quick as possible, an' they turn 'em loose an' give 'em a good reference fer no other reason than to be freed from 'em."

"Well, that's exactly what I mean. You cain't trust anyone these days."

"Well, tell me," Granddaddy said. "Have you heard anything about it…any news about your truck or those two thugs who stole it?"

"No. We'll just have to wait a spell and see what turns up."

"Well, let us know if there's anything we can do."

"I will. Y'all enjoy yer dinners."

"Thank you."

After Mr. Blanton rejoined his wife at their booth, the waitress brought out our food on a big round tray. She served all our food in large bowls, and the fried chicken came piled high on a big platter. Mama dished out our food from each of the large bowls onto plates, and she passed the plates around to each person at the table.

"Well, this sure tastes good," said Daddy, a few minutes later. "There jist ain't nuthin' like Arkansas fried chicken!"

Granddaddy looked over at Tawna Rae and J-Earl. Already, they both had gravy all over their faces and their hands.

"Now, how'd y'all get that gravy all over you-selves so quickly?" Mama asked.

With a mouthful of food, J-Earl tried to answer her question, but his response was an incomprehensible mumble, and Mama immediately interrupted him:

"Not with yer mouth full, J-Earl," she said, and she put her index finger up to her mouth to indicate that he shouldn't talk like that.

"Gentlemen don't talk with their mouths full."

"Hey, y'all, is that good fried chicken, or what?" Granddaddy asked, looking at J-Earl and Tawna Rae.

They couldn't talk, so they both just nodded their heads and grinned. J-Earl was chewing on a chicken thigh, and it looked like Tawna Rae had a whole drumstick in her mouth.

"It is goo – ooo – ood!" I said, musically. I was spilling gravy all over, too, so my manners weren't all that commendable either. As long as I live, I don't think anyone will ever really know how hard I try everyday to keep from making little messes. No matter how hard I tried–whether it was jelly from a doughnut, gravy on biscuits, the soft yoke from a fried egg, or motor oil out of a can–if it could be slopped, I could slop it, and it seemed that I could do it more thoroughly than anyone. Mama always told me that it was the curse of being left-handed in a right-handed world. I think she was right.

Mama said, "This chicken's perty good, Grandma, but it ain't near as good as yours."

"I don't know about that, Honey," she said. "It tastes awful good to me, an' I'd settle for ol' Sleepy to do our cookin'–and our cleanin' fer that matter–ever'day."

"That's fer sure," Mama replied.

We all enjoyed more than we could eat, and when the dessert came, we could hardly eat any. After supper, we just sat there for awhile. Tawna Rae, J-Earl, and I got a little bored, so we got up and walked around the restaurant a little, but Mama called us right back to our seats.

"What do y'all think yer doin'?" she said. "There ain't gonna be any of that roamin' around. Y'all just get right back in yer seats now."

The waitress came and brought the bill. Daddy paid it and gave her something extra. After the adults drank some coffee for a few minutes, we all got up to go home. We were all completely stuffed from eating fried chicken, and even though it was still fairly early, I was tired. However, riding home in the back of our pick-up truck, I felt like the wind in my face woke me up to a certain extent. When we arrived home, Mama said, "You children were generally well-behaved tonight. I just want y'all to know that I'm right proud of the way that y'all conducted yerselves." We knew that she was quietly overlooking the gravy slopping and the roaming around without permission.

"Thank you, Mama," we each replied.

Granddaddy, Daddy, and I, together with Grandma, all went out and sat on the back porch. Granddaddy turned on the radio and tuned in to KMOX. The game was already in progress, and the Cardinals were playing the Pirates at Pittsburgh. They were off to a terrible start; it was only the fifth inning, and the Pirates were ahead by a score of four to nothing. I was tempted to abandon that game and go into my room to read, but I stayed faithful to the end–to the bitter end–as the Pirates won it by a score of seven to nothing. What was happening to my team?

Forty-two

The next day was Saturday, and we were all up much earlier than usual. Grandma and Mama made breakfast, and while we were eating, Daddy told Granddaddy that he wanted to begin making some minor repairs to our station.

"It might be a good ideal," Daddy said, "if we would start fixin' some of those things that we been puttin' off fer awhile down at the station."

"What you got in mind, son?" Granddaddy asked.

"Well, Paw," he said, "seein' how this is the end of the third week in July, I got to drive up and down 66 again all next week, but durin' the next two weeks after that, I got National Guard summer camp. I done cleared it all with Mr. Waldrup. Our unit will be formin' up down at Camp Chaffee, and then we're gonna convoy out to Ft. Sill over at Lawton fer about ten days of drill duty. That means I wouldn't be able to do any work around the station until mid-August at the earliest, so I thought we might get a start on some of it today. What do you think, Paw?"

"I think that's a perty good ideal, son. Seems to me that there's a lot of little projects and jobs we need to get done, and it'd be better to get 'em started now anyway. When Jefferson starts up with school again in the fall, be just his Mama and me down at the station through most of the day; I'll be a hand short," said Granddaddy.

"We can begin today with some of the smaller jobs, and later on, when

I get more time, we can cover some of the more complicated ones," Daddy said.

"Sounds good to me," said Granddaddy.

We finished our breakfast and helped get things all cleaned up. Mama gathered up her baskets of vegetables, eggs, and fruit, and I got two books to read. I finished reading *Treasure Island*, so I chose *The Adventures of Huckleberry Finn* and *The Count of Monte Cristo*. We all got in the pick-up truck, and in a few minutes we were at the station. It didn't take us long to open the place for business, and when Daddy was with us, I felt like we were really a team–all working together toward a common goal. Somehow, on other days, when he wasn't there, things were different. I could offer no empirical explanation for this, but his presence with us today certainly confirmed that fact in my heart and mind. Whatever it was, we were all happier, and we all felt more secure in our work. We felt like we were really working for Daddy.

Granddaddy and Daddy got the office all opened up, and then Granddaddy made coffee. I got the garage door opened and the big fan turned on, and then I helped Mama get her things ready to carry up to the table under the shade trees. As we came out of the garage together, I noticed that there were three or four big, black crows fussing and fighting over a dead animal or something lying in the dirt up in front of Mama's work table. They were squawking terribly and making a great commotion; they were both frightening and abhorrent.

"Mama, look at those nasty crows up there," I said. "Looks like they're fightin' over somethin' dead–maybe it's a rabbit or a squirrel."

"Might be one of them station cats," Mama said.

I put down her things and grabbed a push broom from the station garage and unscrewed its long handle. I carried the handle up where the birds were; they were just insolent and arrogant–bantering about and hardly moving– even when I came within their range. I began to swing that broom handle. At the last moment, they flew up in the air and then off, maybe a hundred yards or so up the road where they came down again and landed audaciously in the middle of the road, as if to defy all the drivers on the road. Fortunately for them, no cars were coming, but they just sat there like obnoxious, disgusting beasts and making their disagreeable sounds.

In fact, the little carcass did belong to one of our station cats, but the birds had already picked it over and pecked at it that I could hardly recognize which cat it was. We probably had five or six cats that roamed around the station and lived in the junkyard our back. We never named any of them, although sometimes we would leave some scraps of food or a small bowl of milk out for them. I was able to capture what was left of the limp corpse on the end of the broom handle, and I carried it down toward the station. When I got there, I turned and saw that the crows had returned to the tiny shreds of cat fur that were left behind.

"Hey! Hey!" I called up there, and I waved my arms in the air. "Get outta here!"

I ran back up with the broom handle and chased them away again. Again, they flew up the highway, and after a few cars passed, they landed in the middle of the roadway again. In their absence, I used the broom handle to stir up the cat mess, cover it over with dirt, and spread it all over a much greater area. I went back to the station, and I found a shovel, with which I picked up the cat remains and took them out back to the junkyard and buried them carefully–recalling my earlier encounter with the copperhead.

I grabbed my steel pail and filled it with warm water. I returned once more to the place where the crows were, and I threw the whole pail of water onto the spot just to rinse it clean.

"Mama?" I called. She came out of the garage and looked up at me. "It's all right now fer you to bring yer things up here."

I went back down and helped her carry her things up until she was finished and all set up. The crows were still sitting in the middle of the highway. However, when a few more cars came, the birds eventually flew away and did not return. I walked back down to the station to get a cup of coffee and to get my books. I thought I would try to read during the quiet breaks between customers. Daddy had other ideas for me that day.

"Boy, you think you and Mama can watch the station while we run down to Gentry fer a while?" Daddy asked.

"Yessir. We done it once before, when Granddaddy went over to Bentonville. I think we can manage fer awhile. Will y'all be gone long?"

"Not too long; maybe an hour and a half to two hours or so. Need to get some paint, some plaster mix, some lumber, and some other items so we can start makin' some o' them small repairs around here, especially before winter sets in," said Daddy.

"I can watch the station office, and Mama can run her table up there. I know she'll come down if I need her."

"Well," Daddy said, "we're gonna run down to Gentry, then."

He and Granddaddy got in the pick-up truck and drove off toward Gentry. I started reading one of my books, but a short while later, the driveway bell rang, and there was a customer. I ran outside to serve.

"Please fill 'er up fer me, sonny," the driver said. "It takes Hi-Test."

The car was a late model Oldsmobile Eighty-eight. Painted white and aquamarine blue, it was a beautiful, two-tone convertible and the top was down. The driver was obviously proud of the car; it was all polished up and shined like new. The tank took almost eighteen gallons of gas. I washed his windshield, though it hardly needed it. I also asked the driver if he needed me to check the oil and the water under the hood, but he shook his head and said, "It's all fine. Checked it all myself earlier."

"That sure is a perty car, Mister," I said. "I'd bet she'll get up and go."

"I'll tell you, boy," he said., "she will definitely get you where you wanna go and do it right quick. I've got to hold her back."

"Yer cost, sir, is seven dollars," I said.

"Well, son. Here's seven-twenty-five, and you keep the change."

"Thank you, sir. That's mighty nice of you, and I appreciate it."

"Well, yer welcome, son."

The man drove off, and I put the money in the register. I picked up *Huckleberry Finn* again and continued reading where I had left off. I was able to get a lot of reading done that day, as we had only two or three more customers before lunch. Just about the time that I was ready to put my book down and go out to see if Mama was ready for lunch, I heard her scream as if she were in a terrible fright. I ran to the office door and looked outside up toward her table in the shade, and I saw someone beating her. By now she was screaming repeatedly and loudly, and it pierced my ears. Fearfully, my heart began to pound, but I resolved to come to her aid as quickly as I could. I turned around and lunged toward the glass counter, and I was so nervous that I tripped behind it. I caught myself without falling to the floor, and I could only think of Granddaddy's shotgun.

Get that shotgun! I told myself. *Where is it? Goodness! Where is it?*
I heard Mama still screaming while I looked around for the shotgun. It wasn't in the cabinet under the glass counter. I looked over in the corner, and I looked up on the top shelf, but it was in neither location. I finally found it lying across the inside of the lower cabinet attached to the back wall that was behind the glass counter, and I pulled it out. There was an open box of shotgun shells next to the gun. I grabbed a couple of shells, checked the gun, and inserted a shell into the chamber. I ran quickly back to the door, and, once outside, I could see the man trying to push Mama into his truck. The top of her dress was almost torn off completely, but Mama was fighting hard and resisting. As I drew nearer, I recognized the man; it was Jimmy Lee Watkins. I wanted to shoot him, but using the shotgun, I was afraid I'd hit Mama, too. I knew the shotgun was only a single shot, but I decided that the best course of action would be to hold it up in the air and pull the trigger. I figured that the sound of a twelve gauge warning shot might somehow bluff Jimmy Lee into thinking that I was holding a pump shotgun with a few more rounds in it. I hoped that I might have enough time to reload the gun, to get up there quickly where Mama was, and then shove that barrel of that gun flat in his face and take him down or give him the chance to run off. In either case, I was not about to let him beat my mama anymore.

After coming out of the station office, I held the gun up in the air and pointed it off toward the northwest where there was nothing but railroad tracks winding gently around to the northeast. I pulled the trigger and held on. The report was deafening, but I held on, and recomposing instantly, I pointed that shotgun up toward that truck.

"Leave her alone!" I shouted.

Jumping into the truck, Jimmy Lee was paying absolutely no attention to me. Mama suddenly backed away as Jimmy started the truck. He spun the tires a few seconds before they finally took hold in the gravel, and in the next instant, he was up the road without any delay. It was a good thing for him that no traffic was present. At last, I reached Mama's location.

"Are you all right, Mama?" I asked her.

Once again, Mama was hurt, embarrassed, and bruised in several places. She was crying. Jimmy Lee had struck her on her shoulders and had squeezed her arms; he also hit her in the face. Her face was bleeding, and her hair was tousled. As she pulled her torn dress back up over her shoulders, I tried to tie it a little so she wouldn't have to hold it so awkwardly.

"Knowing that Jimmy Lee was on the loose, I was afraid this would happen," she said. She was crying. "It all happened so quickly again. He…Jimmy Lee…it was Jimmy Lee Watkins, and he pulled up in Mr. Blanton's truck and jumped out right at me. He grabbed my arm and said something like, 'Yer goin' with me; less go,' but I tried to resist him. He started pullin' on me and draggin' me toward that truck–tryin' to make me get in it and go with him. And then he said, 'I done killed ol' Slade already and got his money, and if I got to, I'll kill you, too.' Then he pulled harder at me, and I tried to kick him in his private parts, and that's when…" Mama began crying again. After a moment, she settled down again and said, "…that's when…when he hit me here." She pointed to the cut on her face. "If you hadn't have shot that shotgun off, I don't know what I would have done."

I tried to comfort her. I placed my arms around her shoulders and hugged her. Then I turned her around and began to move her toward the station office.

"Mama, less get you down there to the station. Maybe you can go into the ladies restroom and get yourself cleaned up a little before Daddy and Granddaddy see you like this. Maybe you ought to stay in there…just lock yerself in there in case we get another customer. You don't want a customer seein' you like this. You'll be safe in there. Jimmy Lee Watkins don't know if we got any more ammo or not. I believe that my warning shot and maybe your kick probably scared him off fer a good while, and I'm bettin' he ain't comin' back–leastwise not today. But I also believe he's been a watchin' us…spyin' out our station and waitin' until Daddy and Granddaddy was gone. He's a low-down, dirty coward fer pickin' on women and children like that, Mama!"

"Well, from what he said, he ain't only a crooked cop gone bad. He's also a robber, an embezzler, and now apparently he's a murderer, too. He just now told me that he killed Slade fer his share o' the money, too."

"He killed Mr. Slade?" I asked, surprised.

"Well, he said he did," Mama answered.

"Wow! That's somethin,' Mama. An' did you say that he said he'd kill you, too?"

"Yes. He sure did."

We arrived back down at the station office, and Mama decided to go into the ladies restroom and clean herself up. She had some bad bruises, but she would be able to hide some of them. The cut on her face stopped bleeding, but it would sure be ugly for awhile. She took my advice and locked herself in. We had two more customers, and I served them both, but neither of them needed to use our ladies' restroom.

Daddy and Granddaddy returned shortly after the second customer pulled out of the station. I briefly explained to them what happened, and Daddy ran around to the ladies restroom and knocked on the door.

"Norma Jean, Darlin', are you in there? It's me–Clayton. Are you all right?"

Embarrassed, Mama opened the door and she began to cry again. Daddy saw her, and he was deeply struck by her wounds and bruises. He pulled her close to himself and hugged her.

"Oh, Darlin', I'm so sorry about this. We shouldn't'a left y'all alone like that. I just wasn't thinkin' straight. I'm so sorry." He continued to hold her closely, and she sobbed quietly.

"Aw, it ain't yer fault, Clayton," she said. "You cain't stop doin' what needs to be done fer the sake of that scoundrel, Jimmy Lee Watkins. We cain't live like that. God knows what he done, and God'll punish him sooner or later."

"Well, I know that, Sweetheart, but I'll be doggone if he don't stop beatin' up on my wife!"

"Darlin', you know I been puttin' up with him since he was pullin' my pig tails back in the third grade. He ain't never got over the fact that I married you, an' that's all there is to it. And I married you 'cause I love you, and I always will. Jimmy Lee Watkins'll never compare to you, Darlin'."

"Well," Daddy said, "we're gonna have to get you home, but before we go, I'm gonna call Sheriff Parker and let him know what happened."

"All right, Clayton. You go ahead and call Sheriff Parker, and unload the pick-up. I'll be all right, and then we'll go home," said Mama.

Daddy went down to the pay telephone directly outside our station, and

285

he called Sheriff Parker. The sheriff said he'd have to come out and file an official report, and he told Daddy to call the Gentry Police department, too. After a short while, Officer Thackston came out to the station. He was driving his patrol car, but as he was off duty, he was wearing his regular clothes. For whatever reason, he didn't look quite right to me when he was wearing ordinary clothing. I could only envision him properly in his uniform. Granddaddy gave Officer Thackston some coffee, and he agreed to wait until Sheriff Parker arrived so they both could conduct one interview together instead of making Mama and me repeat it all twice. After a little while, the sheriff arrived, and Daddy gave him some coffee, too.

He took a drink, and then he said, "when did y'all make this coffee?"

Granddaddy said, "Why, it's fresh-made this mornin'."

"Tastes like it's been sittin' there since yesterday," the sheriff said. "Sorry, Clayton, but it's too thick fer me."

"Well, I like it," Officer Thackston said. "Tastes mighty fine to me."

Daddy said, "Well Sheriff, our Hi-Test tastes even better'n that! You want some Hi-Test?"

"What's in it?" the sheriff asked.

"One-hundert octane," Daddy joked. "I'm sorry, Sheriff. We don't guarantee our coffee; jist our gasoline."

"Well, it's a good thing. If y'all run outta motor oil, y'all can use that coffee to sludge up yer engines, and then y'all can grow that junkyard out back."

Granddaddy was getting a little sore with all this. "All right, Sheriff. You made yer point. So we ain't coffee brewers like y'all are over there in the jailhouse. Less start all over again. Would you like a cold drink from the box outside?"

"I'll have a Co-Cola if y'all have it."

"We've got it. Hey, boy, run out there and grab the sheriff a Coke, and less get on with the interviews then."

"It might not be very cold, Granddaddy."

"Aw, Sheriff Parker won't care if it's hot or cold, boy."

I ran outside and got the sheriff a Coke.

"Thank you, son. Where's yer Mama?"

Daddy had given Mama a shirt. She came in, and both Sheriff Parker and Officer Thackston interviewed her and me about the events that had unfolded earlier. They were both very interested to learn the news that Jimmy Lee now claimed that he killed Mr. Slade and got his money. They were angry when she told them that he threatened to kill her, too. Of course, they wanted to know all the details about that, but Mama said that Jimmy Lee never gave her any details–only that he admitted to killing Mr. Slade and that he said he would kill Mama, too.

After our interviews, we had to sign our names to some forms, and then the sheriff and Officer Thackston both drove away in different directions. Daddy unloaded the pickup truck and placed the paint, the lumber, and the other supplies neatly at the back of the station garage. Then he decided to take Mama home so she could get a bath and rest up from this fresh attack at the hands of Jimmy Lee Watkins.

Granddaddy and I stayed until about five-o'clock. Business picked up late in the afternoon, and we sold quite a bit of gasoline. I kept both my eyes open for Mr. Blanton's stolen stake truck. Jimmy Lee was driving it now. I had already re-loaded a new shell into the chamber of Granddaddy's shotgun, and I was going to be ready for Jimmy Lee if he dared to show up. However, he never appeared. At the end of the day, we shut down the station and went home.

Grandma had supper ready for us by the time we arrived. It was good to come home to a hot meal, for we all enjoyed her good, home-cooking. Mama had enough trauma for one day, and she went to bed directly after supper. Later that evening, Granddaddy, Grandma, Daddy, and I sat out on the back porch to hear the game. The Cardinals were in Pittsburgh again, but this time, the outcome was quite different. The Cardinals were playing like our team once again, and they pounded the Pirates by a score of nine to four. It was about time that they emerged from their slump.

Forty-three

After the game, we all decided that it was time to go to bed. However, I wasn't particularly tired so I thought I might read a little before going to sleep. I read more of *Huckleberry Finn* until almost eleven-thirty, and then I shut out the light. I must have slept for an hour or so before I was awakened by a horrible tumult of noise going on somewhere in the house. I got up and found that everyone except the two younger children was awake and out of bed; all the adults were scurrying about. Quickly, I made my way to see what was going on in the kitchen where all the noise was coming from. There was a light on in the kitchen, and a policeman was there. Granddaddy and Daddy were getting dressed quickly.

"What's going on?" I asked.

"This officer has just informed us that our station's on fire!" Mama said.

Daddy shouted to me, "Jefferson, hurry it up. Go up and get dressed, because we're likely to need yer help. Hurry!"

"Get up there, boy, and get yerself dressed!" Grandma said. "Be quick about it!"

I ran upstairs and threw my shirt, my overalls, and my shoes on as fast as I could. Suddenly there was a great aching sensation in my heart, and it seemed to move out from there and to possess my entire body. It was paralyzing me and making it hard for me to move. Tears now began to flood my eyes, and I couldn't see to tie my shoes.

"Our station's on fire!" I kept hearing Mama say, over and over again. *How could it be?* I thought. *Why? What happened? What is going on down there?* I didn't have any time to think, and yet, my mind was racing with a thousand thoughts. "How? Why? Who?" All I could remember was that I had to get downstairs and help Daddy and Granddaddy right away.

"Less go, boy! We got to go!" Daddy shouted up, impatiently. "Come on!"

"I'm comin'!" I shouted back.

I flew down the stairs, and in another minute we were in the pick-up truck heading for the station. The policeman was already gone. It was somewhere between one-thirty and two o'clock in the morning, and most of the sky was about as black as it gets. A few stars were peeking through, but many of them were covered and then uncovered repeatedly by smoke billowing around in the sky. The smoke was coming from our station, and there was a foul, heavy smell of petroleum in the air. To the east, the whole sky was bathed in an awful red glow creating the false appearance of a hideous and untimely sunrise. Granddaddy was driving fast, and I was bouncing around in the back of the truck. At this hour, there would be no train coming through, although a long stretch of railroad cars might be parked there. We could see flames coming up from the station now as we neared the tracks. The flames caused my heart to sink and my eyes to well up with tears. Indeed, the crossing was clear and open, and there were freight cars lined up along the southern side of the tracks, but they were as silent and as dead as their black silhouette against the red glow.

We pulled into the station and slid to a stop some distance away from the burning building. How could I possibly describe the overall extent of my feelings, impressions, and observations? My heart was pounding violently, yes, even breaking, and my emotions were running wild and dripping all over me. I was shaking, I was crying, and I wished for just a moment that I could somehow set aside what it meant to be a Christian, a southern gentleman, and a Baptist. I admit that, for the first time in my young life, I experienced genuine hatred; I hated whoever did this, and I wanted to lash out at him. Of course, my number one suspect was that scoundrel and self-acknowledged murderer, Jimmy Lee Watkins. And for a brief moment, I had to confess that I was harboring murder in my own heart–even making me equal with the likes of that murderer, Jimmy Lee Watkins. I shuddered at the thought, and I struggled simultaneously with the reality that, although I might set these truths aside in my own life, God never would, and somehow, with His help, I desperately wanted to choose for the other extreme and reach out to the responsible individual and forgive him. Could I do that? I wasn't sure at that moment. Should I do that? Yes, and absolutely! I knew that, precisely because I was a Christian, a southern gentleman, and…well, sort of a Baptist. If nothing else, at the very least we had to fight personally against the kind of evil that was now bringing our station down to ruin.

Even though I was just a young boy, I felt like our station was as much my own station–my own life–as it was Granddaddy's and Daddy's. Now, everything was becoming a mess; everything was going away; everything being lost. Our entire lives were disappearing–up in smoke–before our very eyes, and there was little we could do to prevent it. They had a volunteer fire department down at Gentry–and one up in Decatur–but what could they accomplish way out here? We had no fire hydrants or water tanks in Y-City Station; outside of the official city limits of our neighbors, there were none anywhere along Arkansas Highway 59. We did have a hose, which Daddy used immediately to water down whatever he could. But it was hopeless; a little water hose against flames like these!

All the wood in the building was on fire; the desk and all the cabinets in the office were blazing away along with all the business paper work. The wooden filing cabinet with all the files–they were all burning away. The frame of the garage door was burning; the wooden ceiling under the roof tiles and the rafters were just about gone. Roof tiles had fallen in and broke everywhere into pieces of tile. There was almost nothing we could do about it. Granddaddy was very concerned that the gasoline tanks out behind the building might blow up from all the heat. Daddy went around to check them, and then he came back around.

"It's perty hot back there, but I believe they're still far enough away from the house that they should be all right. Most of the flames are on the front half of the roof, and we might be able to get back there and water down part of that area to kill the sparks and flyin' coals that might be fallin' back that way. It cain't hurt us to give it a try."

Daddy watered down as much of the station office as he could, and then he moved up to the garage. After watering down the inside of the garage, Daddy, with Granddaddy's help, pulled the hose around the north side of the building and started to water the backside of the building and all that area out there. At least we had good water pressure, and that little water hose actually helped to contain some of the fire by making things all wet. The plaster on the side of the building wouldn't really burn; it merely broke up into chips and fell off, and the concrete blocks wouldn't burn either. However, the heat caused them to expand and break apart, and when the flames began to die down, we could see that the whole structure was simply collapsing into ruins.

Upon my first witness of the overall situation, I was so focused on the fire, as well as its damage to our property and to our business, that I failed to notice the three patrol cars up at the north end of our station where Mama ran her fruit and vegetable stand. In addition, Mr. Blanton's stolen stake truck was there as well, and it was actually hemmed in by the three police vehicles. In fact, the Gentry police, the Decatur police, and the county sheriff's office all had cars here, and they had actually closed Highway 59 to all traffic. One of the policemen from the Decatur police department walked down toward the gas pumps, where I was standing, and he asked me where Daddy was.

"He's out there around back hosin' things down," I replied.

"Well, when he gets done out there, I'm sure he'll be interested to know that we got the man what done it, and he's a sittin' in custody up there in that deputy sheriff's patrol car," he said.

"Officer," I said, "is it that crooked sheriff's deputy–Jimmy Lee Watkins–that was wanted by the law all over the county?"

"Yes, it is, son. It's former deputy Jimmy Lee Watkins."

Tears came into my eyes, and I began to cry. The officer tried to console me.

"Are you all right, boy?" he asked.

"Yessir," I said. "I'll be all right. It's jist that…well,…before all this happened, I always thought the law was a little like yer Sunday school teacher, or at least, ought to be."

"What do you mean, son?"

"Well, sir, you don't expect yer Sunday school teacher, the deacon, the preacher, or the law to lie to you and to steal from you, or…to go wrong at all. They're all sort of…like…sacred, or they're supposed to be. They're supposed to be people who do the right thing. I used to think a lot of Jimmy Lee because he was the law, but he really went bad. Together with my Sunday school teacher and the church deacon, he robbed the bank; he hurt my mama twice; and then he murdered Mr. Slade. Now he's burned down our station. I don't look up to him anymore, because I cain't trust him to do the right thing."

"Well, son, you're right. If they don't do the right thing, how can we expect others to do it?" the officer said. He paused for a moment and just looked at me. Then he said, "Son, you're a perty smart young man. I hope that you'll always try to do the right thing–regardless of what others do."

"Thank you, Officer," I said. "I ain't always done it, but I'll sure try hard. And I'll tell my daddy that y'all are holdin' Jimmy Lee over there in that patrol car."

"Thank you, son."

Granddaddy came around to pull the hose back to the front of the station, and in another moment, Daddy followed him.

"Daddy…Granddaddy…it was Jimmy Lee Watkins what done it. They're a holdin' him in custody over there in that deputy's patrol car."

"Well, it don't surprise me at all," Daddy said. "But how'd they know he done it?"

"I dunno, Daddy. The officer told me to tell you, and he said that y'all might be interested in talkin' with them up there."

"Less go see what's goin' on," Granddaddy said. "And, Clayton,…I want you to control yerself up there. Don't you go gettin' all upset and angry to where the police have to take you in with him, too…you hear?"

"Yassir, Paw. Come on, boy. You can come along, too."

We walked up to Mama's fruit and vegetable stand. Daddy looked inside of the Decatur patrol car; Jimmy Lee Watkins was handcuffed, and he was sitting in the back seat.

"Why'd you do this to me, Jimmy Lee?" Daddy asked.

"It ain't none of yer dern bidness, Clayton!" Jimmy Lee screamed back.

"Well, it sure was my bidness, Jimmy Lee–even if it was a struggle to run!

An' now it's gone! Why'd you do it? I want to know why, Jimmy Lee?"

"I ain't tellin' you! You jist leave me alone!"

We could see that we were getting nowhere with Jimmy Lee. We backed away from the car, and turned our attention to the three officers.

Granddaddy asked the sheriff's deputy, "How'd y'all catch him?"

"Yeah, how do we know fer one-hundert percent sure it was Jimmy Lee that done it?" Daddy asked.

"You tell him," the deputy said, pointing to the officer from Gentry.

"All right. Well, gentlemen, a real strange passer-by comin' down this way from somewheres up north come straight into Gentry earlier tonight—must have been just a little after midnight or so. I never seen the likes of this fellow before in my entire life. The ol' boy was drivin' a beat up old Chevoley pick-em-up truck full of junk and what-not in the back. Truck sounded like it was a runnin' on five cylinders. He reminded me a little of one of them Mars men or space people from the moon or somebody like that what you see in the comic books. The man had long white hair and a white beard, and he was a wearin' faded overalls, and he had a big ol' brown houn' dawg sittin' there in the truck with him.

"I was out there in my patrol car sittin' there on my guard duty in the Gentry square. He pulled that ol' noisy Chevoley right up next to me, and I says, 'Can I he'p you, sir?' And then he says, 'Officer, I don't mean to trouble you none, but I jist now come through Y-City Station a little south of here. I always slow down when I come through there because of that dangerous curve down there. Anyway, I seen a ol' stake truck sittin' up there where no stake truck's rightly s'pposed to be, and I noticed somethin' awful strange a goin' on out there. It was a lookin' to me like there was a man out there sneakin' around with his flashlight and shinin' that light all over the place. And he was tryin' to bust down the front door of that station house. I'm thinkin,' 'Somehow, this ain't right,' so I says to myself, 'You got to tell the police.'

"Anyway, this white-bearded stranger come right up to me and he says, 'Officer, I don't mean to trouble you none, but you might ought to check that station out down there fer yerself.' At first, I thought he might be a drunkard, since he said that Y-City Station was south of Gentry, but then I started thinkin,' 'Maybe I ought to drive up yonder and check on it; it cain't hurt.' I have no ideal where that old man went—he probably went back to Mars or the moon, as far as I know–but I decided to come up here for a look-see. I parked my patrol car at the south end behind 'em bushes, and sure enough, by the time I walk up here behind them gas pumps there, this old crooked deputy's runnin' around here and there and a settin' the whole dang station on fire. He broke into the office and was a pourin' gasoline all over the desk, he was dumpin' gasoline on the back shelves, and then he was pourin' it all over the floor behind the garage door, too. He set the whole thing to blazes, and I caught him red-handed as he's a comin' out the front door. I told him to lay down flat out on the ground; I cuffed him but quick and put them leg shackles on his ankles and then chained him to the gas pump until he'p arrived. Gentlemen, I'm terribly sorry about your station–wadn't nuthin' I could do about that all by myself."

"That's all right," Daddy said. "Ain't none of us could do anything about that fire. I'm just glad them tanks out back didn't blow."

"Well, it's a miracle they didn't," the officer from Decatur said.

Granddaddy said, "Well, I guess y'all know that this crooked deputy, Mr. Jimmy Lee Watkins, has committed some major crimes here in the county."

"That's right," the deputy sheriff said. "Sheriff Parker has informed all of the staff over there at Bentonville to be on the lookout fer Jimmy Lee. I'm sure that y'all in Gentry and Decatur were aware of it, too?"

The officer from Decatur said, "Most of what we know has been fairly recent."

"Well," the Gentry policeman said, "he's got some complaints of assault against him from a couple of teenaged girls. He's also wanted for robbery and a few other things."

"Well," Daddy said, "he assaulted my wife twice, and the second time was earlier today. When that happened, he also told my wife that he had killed his own robbery partner for his share of the plunder-money, and further, he threatened to kill her, too."

"It sounds like he's gonna be goin' to jail fer a long, long time," the Decatur officer said.

"Well, boys," the deputy sheriff said, "I think we've done all we can do fer one night. I'm gonna take Jimmy Lee over to Bentonville right now and get him locked up. I'm sure that Sheriff Parker'll be gettin' in touch with y'all about all this–probably tomorrow afternoon."

"It looks to me like the biggest part of the fire has just about burned itself out," the Gentry officer said.

"Yeah, I reckon we can open up the highway again," the officer from Decatur said. "Again, we're real sorry about the fire." They both agreed, and we all shook their hands. The policemen got in their cars, and they drove toward their respective towns.

"Paw," Daddy said, "I'm gonna wet it all down one more time so it'll be too wet to re-start itself up again."

"That's a good ideal, son," Granddaddy replied. "You need a little he'p with it?"

"No, just rest yourself there for a while. I can do it."

Daddy grabbed his hose, and he sprayed down some of the hot timbers and the smoking coals. Then he watered down the whole area once again for a final rinse, and then he quit. We were all exhausted when we got into the pick-up truck to go home. Soon, it would be sunrise. As we drove home, somehow, I knew that our lives would never be the same.

Forty-four

We were as dirty, smoky, and sooty as we were tired, and for that reason, we all had to take baths before we could crawl back into bed. Being the youngest, of course, I was the last one in the tub. As soon as I could, I got cleaned up, and then I put on fresh underclothes. I was so tired that I could have fallen asleep right there in the warm bathwater in that tub. I collapsed into my bed, and although it was Sunday, I knew we wouldn't be attending church today.

When I woke up, it was well past ten o'clock. J-Earl and Tawna Rae were already up, as was Mama, Grandma, and Granddaddy. Grandma was keeping our breakfast warm and serving it as we got up. After eating some pancakes and some scrambled eggs, I drank some coffee and felt a lot better. As usual, Granddaddy was sitting out on the porch. I didn't want to disturb him, so I waited for my opportunity to sit down and visit with him. Eventually, he came inside for a cup of coffee, and that was my signal. I filled up my cup, and we went out on the back porch together.

"Well boy," he said, "what're we going to do now?"

"What can we do, Granddaddy? It's over."

"I don't know as we can do anything," he said.

"You suppose Daddy'll have any good ideals?"

"I dunno," he replied.

He and I just sat there for awhile, drinking coffee and waiting for Daddy to come out. A few minutes later, Granddaddy said, "I suspect we'll go down there again this morning and survey the damage, but I'm afraid we're gonna be outta the oil bidness here directly. Now, when your Daddy gets up, just let him alone fer awhile so he can eat and think a little bit before we talk with him."

"Yes sir," I said.

Granddaddy and I just sat there on the back porch. We were looking out at the land. We didn't know it yet, but Daddy was already up and having his breakfast in the kitchen.

"Granddaddy, how about some more coffee?" I asked.

"No, thank you, son. I've had enough fer now."

I got up and went back into the kitchen to refill my cup.

"Mornin', son," Daddy said.

"Good mornin', Daddy."

"Is Granddaddy out on the porch?"

"Yes sir."

"Tell him I'll be out there directly, son."

"Yes sir."

I went back out and relayed Daddy's message, but it wasn't even another minute before Daddy came out and joined us. He sat down, and we waited for a moment or two, and then he spoke.

"I believe we need to go down there this mornin', look at the station, and consider our damages," Daddy said.

"Are we outta bidness, Daddy?" I asked.

"Most likely, yes, but less go down and look, and then decide."

None of us was in a big hurry to leave. In our hearts, we were all fighting against what we already knew was true. Deep within our souls, we were certain that it was over, and we knew that the sooner we saw the condition of the station, the more compelling our certainty would be. So we were merely delaying the inevitable–having another cup of coffee; sitting down to discuss it; waiting for this or for that–doing whatever we could to put off going down across the tracks to see once again in broad daylight the evidence that would only confirm all our conclusions.

Finally, Daddy said, "Less get on down there and see what we're up against."

Our station looked like the scene of an incredible disaster. The entire front half of the building was destroyed, and the back half was thoroughly ruined. Everything had been blackened by the soot and the smoke. Most of the roof had either burned or collapsed. All the station glass was broken, and there were shards and pieces of broken glass everywhere. All the glass in the garage door was broken; most of the frame was either totally burned or missing, although a part of it was still hanging in the heat-malinged, overhead track. All of Daddy's new lumber had burned to ashes, and his newly purchased supplies were now reduced to rubbish. Broken roof tiles and blackened tile pieces were all over the place; pieces of discolored plaster were strewn about everywhere. In several places around the entire structure of the building, the concrete block walls had cracked from the heat and separated so badly that there were places in the building where I could see right through to the junkyard out back. There were numerous puddles of blackened water standing inside and outside the station. Everywhere on the property, there was burnt out debris–fragments of wood, pieces of glass, broken tiles, chips of plaster, chunks of concrete, oil cans, burnt paper, and ashes.

We stood there solemnly, and we knew.

"It's over, and we're outta this bidness," Daddy proclaimed.

"Cain't do nuthin' about it," Granddaddy said.

Suddenly, feelings of hurt and anguish sprung up from my heart once again. Tears came into my eyes again, and my heart ached beyond description. Although I couldn't possibly separate my own association with the station from Daddy's, my heartfelt concerns were primarily focused on him and his investment of personal care, time, and money in this work, as well as his hope that, one day, it might truly become a success and support his family and their future.

"Why would he do this to us?" I asked. "He took our lives away from us."

"No one really knows why, boy," Daddy said. "But I tell you, son. I don't want you to forfeit yer good character over this. In this life, we don't really know why bad things happen to good people, or why good people turn evil.

They just do, and this is one of the most important lessons that you can ever learn in this here world. It's like–they get out there on some road–like Highway 59, fer example–and they're drivin' up and down that road, and they're a mindin' their own bidness, and then, suddenly, they come to the "Y" in the road, and they don't know what to do. Some of 'em turns up one way, and some turns down the other, and they really cain't say why, because they never bothered to stop fer a moment before they made their decision and consider the consequences of their choice. They just did it without thinkin' about it, and before too long, they find themselves so far down the road that it's too late to come back."

"But God knows all about it, son," Granddaddy said. "God knows."

"That's right," Daddy affirmed.

"And one day, son, when we come into His presence, He's gonna reveal it all to us," Granddaddy said.

While we were standing there, a southbound car coming down from Decatur pulled into the station. Now, there was no point in my running over and saying, 'Can I he'p you?' The driver got out of the car and walked over to us.

"Why, conniptions and tarnations! Whatever happened here, y'all? Looks like y'all had a really bad fire!" the driver said. "How bad was it? Anyone hurt or killed in the fire? When did it happen? What are y'all gonna do now?" The driver continued to talk and ask questions faster than another person could think, and he became an instant annoyance for all three of us.

"Why this is jist terrible…a terrible thing!" the driver began talking to himself. "Why, y'all are going to need some he'p cleanin' all this up, and…" He continued to chatter away. We were not paying much attention to him, and we all began to walk away from him. But then he said, "well, y'all, I need some gasoline in my tank. Did you hear? I need some gas. Can you pump some in fer me?"

For Daddy, that was it. Daddy walked over a little ways and found a piece of charred, heavy wood, and then he walked over to the station building and found a chunk of broken plaster that hadn't been too badly blackened.

"Why, what's he doin'?" the man asked. "What's he doin'? Don't he understand that he could make a little money here by pumpin' me some gas?" The man continued to rattle on and on.

299

Granddaddy turned and began to move slowly toward the driver, who began to back up toward his car. With the charred piece of wood, Daddy was writing on the small white area of the building the big letters–"CLOSED."

"Thank you, sir, fer yer bidness," Granddaddy said. "But, as you can see, the sign says we're *closed.*"

The driver got back into his car, and he drove off.

We stayed at the station for a little while longer, and we sensed a great need to clean up the place, but our efforts were generally wasted. Essentially, the place was a total loss, and we all knew it. Earlier, none of us was in a hurry to get here; now, none of us was in a hurry to go home. Each one of us had grown so completely and personally attached to the station that it had almost taken on a personality of its own and become sort of an eighth member of our Stafford family. Once again, we were all three delaying the inevitable action that henceforth would detach us personally and forever from the genuine realities of life–with all its dreams and hopes and opportunities; its joys and sorrows; together with all its tears, laughter, and memories–that had once become ours here at Y-City Station. Nevertheless, we had to put it behind us.

"It's over," Daddy said. "Less go home."

We got back in the pick-up, and Granddaddy drove us home.

Grandma and Mama had prepared a fine Sunday dinner for us all. After we sat down and said grace, Grandma and Mama were particularly interested to know Daddy's thoughts regarding the station, now that he, Granddaddy, and I had looked it over.

"Clayton, what are we gonna do?" Mama asked.

"We're gonna give it up, Darlin'," he answered. "I know how much we all grew to love that station. And no one had higher hopes fer it than I did. I so much wanted it to be a success." Daddy's voice cracked, and he had tears in his eyes. "I wanted...." He paused a moment to wipe his eyes dry, and then he continued, "I wanted that station to become a strong financial source fer all of us so we wouldn't...so we...so we wouldn't always be poor." He struggled hard to get that out. "But...it just wasn't meant to be. We all know that the station was in a bad location, and no matter how hard we all tried, we just couldn't make folks buy their gas there. We just have to live with that fact, and that's all. So…we're gonna give up the oil bidness, hang onto the truckin' bidness, and we'll just keep on trustin' in the Lord to see how he leads us."

While we were eating and talking, someone knocked on our front door. Granddaddy excused himself to see who it was, and when he came back, he brought Reverend and Mrs. Sutherland in, together with Starla.

"Good afternoon, folks," Brother Sutherland said. "I'm mighty sorry to disturb y'all during the Sunday dinner hour, but we heard the news about the fire at y'alls' station, and we saw the ruins this mornin' as we come up fer church services. We wanted to come by and offer our condolences and our encouragement. We missed y'all this mornin' at church, but of course we knew that y'all had to tend to matters down at the station as the most important priority."

Mrs. Sutherland walked over to Mama, and then to Grandma, and she put her arms on their shoulders and said, "Oh Norma Jean…Mrs. Stafford…I'm so sorry about y'alls' loss. Please, if there's anything that Starla and I can do…just please let us know, won't y'all?"

"Thank you," Mama said. Grandma also expressed her thanks.

"Do y'all have any firm plans about what y'all are gonna do?" the reverend asked.

"Yessir," Daddy replied. "I'm gonna keep on drivin' up on Highway 66, Reverend, and I believe were gonna give up the oil bidness, eventually. Of course, we ain't gonna make any snap decisions about it all, but this unexpected fire has just about closed us completely outta the market. Even when we was in it, we couldn't collect half our accounts because most folk just don't have the money. And we ain't got the money to rebuild it, and anyway, it never was in the right location to turn a profit. Our insurance policy was held by old Brother Pickett, and now he's gone. Fer all I know, our insurance went with him to the grave. We're just fortunate that we made an honest go of it, and we're thankful that no one got hurt in last night's fire."

"And, Reverend," Granddaddy said, "with all that heat, it was truly a miracle that them gas tanks didn't blow."

"Well, we need to be gettin' on home," Reverend Sutherland said. "I just wanted to drop in fer a moment and let y'all know that y'all can count on us in the church fer any he'p y'all might be needin' in the days ahead. By the way, the church took up a special collection to he'p meet any immediate needs y'all might have, and I wanted to stop by to give it to y'all."

Reverend Sutherland reached into his outside right coat pocket and drew out a white envelope. He handed it to Daddy.

"Oh, Reverend!" Daddy said. "That was just not necessary! Y'all didn't have to do that! I don't believe we could possibly accept it, Brother Sutherland."

"Well, I know that we didn't have to do it any more than the Lord had to reach down and meet our needs. But He did, and so did we." Pastor Sutherland walked over to Daddy, and he placed his arm around Daddy's shoulder. He looked Daddy square in the eye, and he quietly whispered something in Daddy's ear. None of us could hear what he said, but afterward, Daddy reached out his right hand and shook the pastor's hand.

"Thank you, Reverend. And thank the church folk, too."

"You thank 'em next week, Clayton."

"Oh! I cain't come fer the next two Sundays! I'll be away with the National Guard unit," said Daddy.

"Then Arliss can thank 'em next Sunday, and you can thank 'em in three weeks! Mommy! Starla! Less go!"

After they were gone, we settled back down to our food, but it was cold, and our appetites practically well gone.

"Clayton," Mama said, "what did the pastor whisper in your ear that made you take that money?"

"He said, 'Clayton, I want you to accept this gift. God wants you to receive this gift. Don't you dare rob our church of the blessin' of sharin' with those what's in need now.'"

Daddy opened the envelope. It contained almost four-hundred dollars and a little note that said:

July 21, 1957

Dear Brothers and Sisters Stafford and Family,

We were so sorry to hear about the loss of your gas station due to fire. Please receive this gift as a token of our Christian love, and use it as you all see fit to meet your needs.

In Christian love,

Your Brothers and Sisters
at the West Bethel Baptist Church

Forty-five

After we helped to clean up the Sunday dinner dishes, Mama told J-Earl, Tawna Rae, and me to go upstairs and take our regular, Sunday afternoon nap. Since I wouldn't be working at the station any longer, I now figured that I had lots of time to complete the summer reading program before school started. Nevertheless, by reading lots of books, I was learning to enjoy reading even more; thus, I resolved to go up and read a little before taking my nap.

I lay down in my bed and opened up *Huckleberry Finn* just about the same time that Sheriff Parker pulled his patrol car into our property. Hoping not to disturb J-Earl or Tawna Rae, Mama came up to my room and asked me to come downstairs to meet together with the sheriff.

"Folks, first of all, allow me to say how sorry I am about the loss of yer gas station. I know that my apology don't make y'all feel any better, but it's sad when that sort of thing happens to anyone. And I can tell you, the Jimmy Lee Watkins that we've all seen lately is certainly a much different person than the one I hired to be my deputy. All I can say to you about that is, on behalf of the county, I'm deeply sorry fer his offenses."

"Thank you, Sheriff Parker. We appreciate your kindness," Mama said.

"Now folks, I needed to come over here this afternoon to get y'all to make some formal statements and to get y'all to sign some paperwork," the sheriff said. "As y'all know already, my former deputy, now known as one, Mr. Jimmy Lee Watkins, has been taken in custody fer a variety of crimes that he done, and fer which we're goin' to pursue his punishments to the very end and the full letter of the law. Our prosecutor over in Bentonville is known as one who requires hard justice and does not abdicate any of his responsibilities toward them that are convicted."

"Well, Sheriff," Mama asked, "what's going to happen to Jimmy Lee?"

"Well, Mrs. Stafford," the sheriff said, "officially, Jimmy Lee's in a peck of trouble fer all he done, and we're learnin' more about his misdeeds ever' day. And unofficially, I hope they hang that scoundrel by his ears fer lockin' me up to the jailhouse in front of all them prisoners."

"What about that colored hobo?" I asked.

"Well, when he saw Jimmy comin' in as a prisoner to that jailhouse, I believe he turned white as a sheet and then just about as red as a beet, before his face returned back to its original shade of black. I guess he thought ol' Jimmy Lee was goin' to lay into him again, but when his face turned white, we knew he was a tellin' the truth about Jimmy Lee beatin' him up. We got his Yankee lawyer in there, and we took down his statement, and the boy identified Jimmy Lee as the perpetrator of that beatin'. Once that hobo identified Jimmy, he realized he needed to come clean about it. And then, when the hobo seen them cuffs on Jimmy's wrists and them shackles on his ankles, he started shoutin' out, 'le' me at him... just give me five minutes alone with him.' But I told him, 'If we do that, ain't nuthin' your Yankee lawyer can possibly do, and you and he both be goin' down to the Cummins Unit,' and I said, 'They're so stupid down there, that they'd confuse you fer him and send you up to death row at Tucker.' Then I tol' him—I said, 'You jist sit down and wait; you're about to get set free so you can go back down to yer family in Loosiana. You don't want to lose that, do you?' Then he settled down right quick because he knew it ain't worth it. He'll be released and goin' home in another day or two."

"Well," Mama said, "it is one big relief to me that y'all got Jimmy Lee Watkins behind bars. I've had enough of his pawin' all over me and tearin' my clothes off me."

"I'm sorry he done that, ma'am. Ain't no call fer it," the sheriff said.

Sheriff Parker asked all of us to explain clearly and exactly our perspectives about what happened yesterday. He was taking rapid and profuse notes. Every now and then, he would stop and ask us to repeat something, or he would say, "Let me make sure I got that right. You say that it happened like this?" And he would restate it. "Is that correct?"

"Yes sir," we would reply, or "no, it wasn't quite like that. It was like this...."

"Well, at this point," the sheriff said. "As we put the whole thing together, here's where we are. Originally, we had a total of four men involved in the bank robbery, which actually started a long time before as a repetitious church robbery. We understand that Mr. Dwindle Pickett and Deacon Sherman Ellis conspired to rob the West Bethel Baptist Church offering plate a little at a time to help them pay fer their drinkin' and fer their gamblin' debts, which they owed to deputy Jimmy Lee Watkins and Mr. Elwood Slade. Later, both Mr. Watkins and Mr. Slade became co-conspirators and partners in the robbery of the Gentry branch of the Farmer's State Bank of Gentry. Of course, Deacon Ellis died in his own car crash, but we was able to recover his share of the stolen money from the bank, although at the time, knowledge of his participation in these criminal activities was, as yet, unknown. However, with the suicide of one, Mr. Dwindle Pickett, and his revealing suicide note, we learned of the deacon's involvement in the crime, as well as the note's forthright indictment of the other two, previously named scoundrels who participated in the same crime. Moreover, upon the death of Mr. Pickett, we were also able to recover almost half of the stolen bank money which he had deposited in his own personal vault."

Sheriff Parker continued. "When we learned of former deputy Watkins' role in this crime, as his superior officer, I confronted him and made an attempt to arrest him, whereupon...." The sheriff was embarrassed for a moment, and his face turned red.

"Uh...whereupon...well, that no-good deputy overpowered me, locked me to the jail bars, and fled—utilizing official county property to perpetrate further criminal activity. After finding his abandoned patrol car, we learned that he hooked up with Mr. Elwood Slade, and we know that, after stealing a stake truck belonging to Mr. Jess Blanton, these two crooks moved about all over the whole county. And by the way, after interrogating Jimmy Lee, we now know that he did, in fact, kill Mr. Slade, though he claims it was in self-defense. He said that Slade tried to overpower him at gunpoint for Jimmy Lee's share of the money, and then the two men struggled. According to Jimmy Lee, Slade's gun somehow got pointed in his own direction, it went off, and, evidently, Slade was killed. We are still talking with Jimmy Lee to determine where he left the body of Elwood Slade. Jimmy Lee is facing charges of assault, auto theft, conspiracy, robbery–maybe even murder–not to mention his crimes with them two young girls and his associations with the Klan. With all these complaints and charges stacked against him, Jimmy Lee's gonna have a very difficult time proving that he killed Slade in self-defense–especially since we found Slade's share of the money together with Jimmy Lee's in Blanton's truck. And, as it happens, now we have recovered just about all of the money–give or take a few dollars–that had been robbed from the Gentry bank. Mrs. Stafford, I don't believe you're gonna be needin' to worry about Jimmy Lee Watkins ever again."

Once again, we reviewed and re-checked all the information that the sheriff was requesting, and then Sheriff Parker got up to leave.

"Folks, thank you fer all the information. I really appreciate it, and once again, I sure do apologize fer what Jimmy Lee done to y'all. Remember that if there's anything we can do to he'p, please let us know," Sheriff Parker said.

"Well, Sheriff," Granddaddy replied, "thank you so much fer all you've done fer us now. We appreciate it more than we can say."

"Thank you. If there ain't anythin' else, then I'll be on my way back to Bentonville."

The sheriff shook hands with everyone, and then he went out the front door. He had been there for much of the afternoon, and I was tired of interviews and questions. I decided to sneak back upstairs and try to take a little nap. I was overwhelmed with all the activity and the excitement. *Goodness!* I thought. *Y-City Station is really nothing and nowhere, but there's been more excitement here these past few weeks than in Times Square New York City–wherever that place was!* Then I thought to myself, *I'll sure be glad when things get back to dull, old normal again!*

When I woke up from my nap, it was almost five o'clock. I joined Daddy and Granddaddy, who were out on the back porch. They were listening to the local news because it was too early to pick up KMOX. Nothing was happening in the news, but the sports announcer said that the Cardinals had already taken the first game of a Sunday afternoon double-header in Pittsburgh by a score of seven to three. The announcer also said that the Cardinals were ahead in the second game, too. Finally, after they dropped out of first place into second, they were starting to turn things around, even if they were going in the wrong direction.

Forty-six

Late that evening, Daddy said his usual good-byes, and then he started up his truck and departed for Joplin. For a few days, none of us went down to the gas station at all. We were all making an effort to understand what it meant to live without a station any longer. During that week, Sheriff Parker returned to our house for signatures to our typed statements. The sheriff said that Jimmy had finally revealed where Elwood Slade's body was. The night he burned down our station–when he was flashing his light wildly all around–he had placed Slade's body in the one junk car that was located the closest to the railroad tracks out behind our station. It was also one of the newer ones out there. Evidently, as some sort of sick joke, Jimmy sat the body upright in the driver's seat, put a hat on his head, fixed a pair of sunglasses to his face, and he leaned his right hand over the steering wheel. Then he propped the body up on its right side so it couldn't fall over, and finally he took Slade's left hand and rolled it up tight in the window to make it appear from a distance that there was a driver in the car who was waving at all the trains that passed by. And he did all that before he burned down our gas station.

"Jimmy Lee was a perverted reprobate," the sheriff said. "By the way, I thought y'all would be interested to know that yer colored hobo was released early this morning. He said he was goin' back home to Loosiana to get back together with his wife and kids. I feel really bad when it turns out that we was holdin' the wrong man, especially when the right man who went wrong–that rotten Jimmy Lee–was sittin' right under our noses all the time."

Toward the end of the week, Granddaddy and I went down to the station once or twice more. We decided that it wasn't worth the effort of trying to clean up the mess. In a year or so, all the effects from the summer heat, the wind, the rain, the hail, the winter snow and ice, and each of the other elements that we simply take for granted throughout the year would eventually bring it down, cover it up, and bury it all completely in time. All in its season; everything in its time.

The Riggins farm got put on quarantine again, but somehow, by the end of August, 1957, they managed to come up with all the money they needed to buy out Sleepy's Café. I believe they borrowed the money, but no one can say for sure. Thereafter, the Riggins attempted to renovate the whole restaurant under the direction of the one-time, Queen of the Ozarks herself. Unfortunately, her sense of interior decoration never quite equaled her certified claim to hillbilly fame, and most of Sleepy's former patrons entered into the Queen's new domain–either in silent admiration or merely in silence–upon viewing the odd mixture of eclectic ornaments and implements that Mrs. Riggins somehow brought together in that old dining room. Among some of the local women, Mrs. Riggins' unconventional creativity was soon adopted informally as a style that later became officially known more or less as the 'Ozark Style.'

After their remodeling job, the Riggins renamed the place The Ozark Queen. Fishbait's dream of serving there as a waitress became a reality, and indeed, she was able to arrange an invitation for us to come out and try their food for free. In general, the food was pretty good; the coffee was real good, the hamburgers were typically greasy, but if you were lucky enough to order the catfish right after they changed the oil in the deep fat fryer–umm! It was scrumptious and down-home good! Unfortunately, the Riggins had only owned the café for three weeks when word came back from Kansas that Sky had lost his life out there while cutting hay on a farm with his cousins. It was a serious and hard blow to the whole Riggins family, and they had to close the café for several days until after the funeral. When they returned, they took down the Queen's enshrined photographs on the wall next to the door and

310

replaced them with an old photograph of Sky when he was just five or six years old. All around the photograph, they regularly attached real flowers, and they hung a metal cross below the picture. On a 3 by 5 card, Dudley Dan wrote, "Gone, but not forgotten" in blue ink, and he pinned the card to the wall below the cross.

After Brother Pickett's funeral, Mrs. Pickett, in what was commonly considered her final moments of sanity, ordered a huge granite gravestone–perhaps the largest in the entire cemetery–for her dearly departed husband. On the smooth face of the stone, the masons had carved only two words–Why, Dwindle?–in letters that were at least three feet high. Mrs. Pickett visited the gravesite everyday and brought flowers, but within six months, her grief became a heavier burden than she was able to bear, and eventually she was committed to the state mental hospital where she was never heard from again.

Not long after our fire, Sheriff Parker got in touch with Mr. Blanton who was able to retrieve his stolen stake truck. He claimed that he always had difficulty hiring foremen. "They never stay very long," he said. "And you cain't trust 'em worth a hoot!"

The sheriff also stopped by our place to visit and to see how we were doing. He seemed happy to know that we were surviving and adjusting to life without a gas station.

"Sheriff," Mama asked, "what have they done with Jimmy Lee Watkins?" After Jimmy Lee's two attacks on her, she was forever concerned about his activities and his whereabouts.

"Well, Norma Jean, right now, he's in jail, awaiting trial fer bribery, theft, car theft, assault, use of official county property to commit a felony, robbery, violation of liquor laws, and murder, as well as a number of other things. He'll be comin' up to his trial directly."

"Sheriff, could you let us know when it happens?"

"Yes ma'am."

A few months later, Sheriff Parker kept his word. He came by our house on a Saturday afternoon, the day after Jimmy Lee's trial ended.

"Thought y'all would like to know that Jimmy Lee Watkins' trial concluded yesterday," Sheriff Parker stated. "The jury didn't buy his self-defense claim against Slade. They found him guilty on ever' count against him, and fer Slade's murder, he got the death penalty. He's gonna by-pass the Cummins Unit, and he'll be transferred directly to Tucker next week. Norma Jean, I think you can rest easy now; he's outta yer life."

To all of us, this news was bittersweet. It was sweet to know that he'd never come around to hurt Mama again. But it was bitter, too. He had once been a man of the law–presumably–a man on the side of honor and everything good, but a man gone rotten to the core. Why? No one knew.

Without a gas station, we no longer had regulars to visit with us everyday. A few short weeks later, school started again for me, and I was amazed to discover that I had actually read thirty books from the moment I set my mind to it up until the first day of school. Moreover, I was doubly surprised to learn that Miss Westbrook–that young, attractive lady customer who pulled her car into our gas station that day and caught me reading a book–was our new English teacher. I sure started the year off right with her, but Donnie Joe? He hadn't read a book all summer, and she gave him nothing but grief and trouble all year long.

Right after the All-Star break, the Cardinals fell from first place, and they never recovered; they finished the year in second place. Nevertheless, Wally Moon–the pride of Arkansas and the St. Louis Cardinals–received a great honor when he was named the National League's Rookie of the Year. Of course, my greatest treasure was that souvenir baseball that Daddy brought home for me from the All-Star game. A number of years later, during a trip to St. Louis, I had the personal opportunity to see a Cardinal game at Busch Stadium. By then, I knew that Red Schoendienst was managing the team, so I brought that special baseball with me to the game. Somehow, before the game started, I was able to get down to the dugout and meet him.

"Mr. Schoendienst, sir," I called from a short distance away. He heard me, and being the true gentleman that he was, he came over to me.

"Yes?" he asked.

"Sir, in the 1957 All-Star game, when you played for the Milwaukee Braves, you hit this ball–a foul–out into the stands. My Daddy caught the ball, and brought it back to me in Northwest Arkansas, and it has been a special souvenir treasure of mine ever since. Would you mind signing it for me, please?" A true gentleman, he signed the ball–"For J.D. Stafford...Red Schoendienst."

Grandma turned up sick around Christmas time that year, and she died in January 1958. Before the end of that year, Granddaddy followed her; we were certain that he died of a broken heart for loss of Grandma. Daddy and Mama inherited their property, but things didn't change too much or too quickly. One day, while driving up on Route 66, what came to be known as 'The Main Street of America,' Daddy met another truck driver who drove for Coast to Coast Truck Lines out of their Springdale terminal. He told Daddy that Coast to Coast was always looking for experienced drivers, and he encouraged Daddy to check it out. If nothing else, at least his main operating terminal was closer to home. He checked it out, and they offered him an even better driving opportunity which also provided numerous benefits.

It turned out that we did have an insurance policy that covered the loss of our gas station due to fire. It took a long time for the insurance company to settle because of Brother Pickett's business shenanigans and misdealings. Eventually, however, the parent company settled with Daddy, who finally received a check in the amount of eighteen thousand dollars for all the damage caused by the fire. Daddy was able to pay off the mortgage, as well as his creditors, and he still came out ahead. Not long after, the State of Arkansas came through and offered Daddy seven thousand dollars for his little triangle of land that created the original "Y" between the railroad tracks and Arkansas State Highway 59. The state wanted to purchase the property and use it to straighten out the dangerous curve in the road to reduce the number of auto accidents that had occurred at that location. When construction began, the state came in and removed everything associated with our gas station–the building ruins, the rubble, the gas pumps, the tanks, the signs, and all the junk back in the junkyard. Today, everything is gone. The state left nothing behind–not one shred of evidence to prove that Y-City Station ever existed. When the construction people appeared, they straightened Highway 59, they paved our road, and then they gave our road an official name–today, the sign at our old road reads "Y-City Road"– although no city was ever built at that location. No one knows why they forgot the "Station."